	DATE DUE	
12-14-95		
1/6/96		
7-2-97		
JUL 26 1997		

Mazel

REBECCA GOLDSTEIN

Mazel

VIKING

VIKING
Published by the Penguin Group
Penguin Books USA Inc., 375 Hudson Street,
New York, New York 10014, U.S.A.
Penguin Books Ltd, 27 Wrights Lane, London W8 5TZ, England
Penguin Books Australia Ltd, Ringwood, Victoria, Australia
Penguin Books Canada Ltd, 10 Alcorn Avenue,
Toronto, Ontario, Canada M4V 3B2
Penguin Books (N.Z.) Ltd, 182–190 Wairau Road,
Auckland 10, New Zealand

Penguin Books Ltd, Registered Offices:
Harmondsworth, Middlesex, England

First published in 1995 by Viking Penguin,
a division of Penguin Books USA Inc.

1   3   5   7   9   10   8   6   4   2

PUBLISHER'S NOTE
This is a work of fiction. Names, characters, places, and incidents either are the product
of the author's imagination or are used fictitiously, and any resemblance to actual
persons, living or dead, events, or locales is entirely coincidental.

LIBRARY OF CONGRESS CATALOGING-IN-PUBLICATION DATA
Goldstein, Rebecca, [date]
Mazel / Rebecca Goldstein.
p.   cm.
ISBN 0-670-85648-7
I. Title.
PS3557.O398M39   1995
813'.54—dc20   94-31271

This book is printed on acid-free paper.
∞

Printed in the United States of America
Set in Garamond No. 3
Designed by Francesca Belanger

For Sarah

CHILDHOOD ROOMMATE AND
LIFELONG COMRADE
REMEMBER WHEN

Acknowledgments

There are several people whose readings of this book, in its various stages of incompleteness, were critical to me. Modest people all, they will cringe at being publicly thanked, but too bad. So, thank you, Danielle Goldstein (wise beyond all years), Sheldon Goldstein (a very tough critic), Yael Goldstein (even tougher), Ruth Katz (from whom I continue to learn), Georgie London (what's the female equivalent for a real mensh?), and Harriet Wasserman (literary agent nonpareil).

Contents

PART IV

Vilna, Poland; Vilna, Lithuania

PART V

Again, New Jersey

PART I

Lipton, New Jersey

Mazel, which is luck in Yiddish, encountered Saychel, or brains, on the road one day, and the two fell into a conversation. Before too long they began to bicker about which of them was the more important.

Saychel claimed that with brains anything is possible, but Mazel argued that without luck all the intelligence in the world will come to nothing.

Soon Saychel and Mazel had reached the point in an argument where there's no going forward without going backward, and at this moment a baby boy was born. Both Saychel and Mazel agreed that one of them should enter the boy, and they would see what would come of it. It was Saychel who slipped himself in, while Mazel settled back and watched.

—To be continued

CHAPTER 1

THIS PLACE

Sasha's not a strong believer in the principle of causality. Sure, if you look back, with all the unfazability of retrospection, you can say that, because this had happened, so then, that had happened. But that doesn't mean such a "this" will ever again be followed by such a "that," not in the whole history of the world. Maybe it will, maybe it won't. You can never be certain, and that's because there's such a thing as mazel.

Mazel, as Sasha expounds it, is the great confounder of closed systems and their pretenders. Mazel is the imp of metaphysics.

"I once knew a certain couple," Sasha's telling her granddaughter, Phoebe.

The two of them are stretched out on lawn chairs under a flower-laden apple tree in Phoebe's backyard in Lipton, New Jersey. This backyard—like the split-level house to which it's attached, so indistinguishable from its neighbors that Sasha always has to count from the corner to know which one is Phoebe's—comes equipped with all the clichés of suburbia, including a redwood deck with a gas barbecue.

Some thirty minutes by car is the altogether different world, the genteel, the posh, the Waspy world, of Princeton. Princeton is where Phoebe works, a recently tenured professor of mathematics, with an unlikely specialty in the geometry of soap bubbles (unlikely only if you hadn't known Phoebe as a child, solemnly blowing her bubbles for hours on end, contemplating the restless clusters of shimmering fragility), commuting every day from the ungenteel, un-Waspy world of Lipton.

There are quite a few other academics who make this commute in the opposite direction, teaching at Rutgers University and living in Princeton, which has a certain logic to it. Princeton, so magnificently transcending the limitations of New Jersey, is an enviable place in which to live. But not according to Phoebe.

No, God bless her, Phoebe thinks that Lipton is enviable.

One of the many bludgeoning remarks Sasha had let fall on first visiting Lipton, the weekend before Phoebe's wedding to Jason Kantor, *also* of Lipton, was that the place manages to combine all the banality of suburbia with a few flourishes on the hideous all its own.

She had made this remark to her daughter, Chloe, Phoebe's mother, who had smiled wanly in response, frankly growing a little weary of Sasha's eloquent hostility to everyone and everything she chanced to encounter that weekend.

"A few flourishes on the hideous all its own," Chloe had repeated with her pale ghost of a smile. "Colorful choice of words. And just what might these hideous flourishes be?"

"Are you pulling my *leg?*" Sasha had retorted, giving almost full throttle to the vast vehemence at her command. "Do I have to spell it out for you? How can a place like this not drive you crazy? Maybe you'd better check your pulse and see if you're dead?"

Sasha herself lives in Manhattan, in a rambling apartment with views of the Hudson in a prewar building on Riverside Drive, a few blocks above the boat basin on 79th Street. She had first moved in when Felix Zakauer—whom she had known since way back when, since Warsaw yet—had bought the building. He comes, a penniless refugee, a survivor of three different labor camps, and a few years later he's buying an apartment building, on Riverside Drive yet. The rent that Felix—may he be reaping his reward among the saints of Paradise—had asked from her was like a joke with a history that gets better with each telling, like maybe they were all still sitting in the

Café Pripetshok, where night after night Felix used to pick up the tab for the whole lot of them. This had always been his way of excusing his capitalist presence among all those ardent artistes and other assorted paupers. To her he had been an old man even way back then, so old she'd been incredulous when her beautiful friend Rosalie had taken up with him. He had had a face that had made her think (may God forgive her) of one of those caricatures, in their own time very popular, of "the Jewish capitalist," drawn by a very talented anti-Semite.

Sasha's lived in Manhattan ever since she first came to this country from Warsaw, by way of Tel Aviv. New York City had been love at first sight. She'd fallen for it as she'd always fallen for what was larger than life. It was funny, but she had hardly felt herself to be an immigrant— not like the others. Even as a newcomer she'd had no patience to listen to the self-described exiles, the Yiddish writers and actors who used to gather in those days at the Café Royale on Fourteenth Street in order to *kvetch,* one more sour than the next.

This was exile? From what? From *Poland?*

Sasha had decided, from the very start, that somehow or other she was a born New Yorker.

Her daughter, Chloe, a professor of classics at Columbia University—as Sasha will let you know early on in the conversation, if by any chance you haven't yet heard—has an apartment on Claremont Avenue, right around the corner from Barnard College. Just like her mother, Chloe has always had the sense to show little inclination to live anywhere but in Manhattan. Of course, Chloe, just like Sasha, is an enthusiastic traveler, and always spends any leaves of absence she manages to get abroad, usually in Italy or England or Greece. Her last sabbatical she spent wandering like a mendicant through India.

"That's the Gypsy in you," her mother says. "You know, we have a little Gypsy in us, too."

Phoebe, on the other hand, hates to travel. Almost every invitation to attend a conference abroad—and she tends to think of anything outside of a few closely demarcated neighborhoods as "abroad"—is conscientiously considered and then declined. She grew up in Manhattan, but you'd never know it. Even there she had always clung to a few chosen trajectories, as if determined to discern the tidy village submerged in the chaos.

In fact, if you can believe this, Lipton, New Jersey, seems to be the very first place in which Phoebe feels quite entirely at home. No more the shy-eyed little waif with the bundle of academic achievements slung carelessly over her shoulder, shrinking back before the grown-ups, Phoebe has finally stepped over the threshold into womanhood. And it looks good on her. It looks terrific.

Even Sasha, stretched out today beneath the tree's perfumed shade, has to admit to herself that the sight of the blue sky, of an intensely vivid shade, glimpsed through the thick embroidery of the apple blossoms, is something exquisite. And the fact that Phoebe, too, appears to have taken permanently to bloom here, has softened the harsh tone in which Sasha had initially pronounced her judgment upon the place.

"My God, you're being severe," Chloe, speaking in her quiet, even tones, had finally felt forced to declare.

Severe. A *horrible* word. Sasha had found the attribution intolerable, as Chloe, with all the intimate cunning of a daughter, had known she would.

Intolerable—and intolerably apt. Sasha could feel her very lips pursed into incredulous disapproval, as if a drawstring had been pulled through them. It was an expression unbecoming for all types of faces and unusual for Sasha's. "Live and let live" is the benediction she more characteristically lavishes upon the world at large.

But not, somehow, upon this particular community of Lipton, New Jersey.

Jason Kantor had grown up in its bosom and had returned, after Harvard, to live with his parents, Beatrice and Nat, and work down the road, at Bellcore, in Piscataway.

Do you *hear* this? With his parents! What kind of boy comes back from graduate school and lives with his parents?

"I lived with you for a while after graduate school," Chloe, serene as a goddamned saint, had answered her mother.

"There's no comparison!" Sasha had yelled back.

❀

Funny, how a mother should sometimes still have to wrestle the urge to slap her daughter. Slap? Strangle!

After the wedding, Jason and Phoebe would be living on Creekfall Road, virtually *around the corner* from Beatrice and Nat. And it was easy money that, sooner or later, Jason's younger sister, Debby, would be pitching her permanent tent in this paradise by the turnpike. How warm and cozy it was all going to be, just exactly as that Beatrice person had always planned it. The woman had the towering audacity to decree by fiat her children's lives, and then—such a mazel!—hadn't been forced into the rude realization of what *utter folly this is!* Phoebe had been caught like a little dazed fish in the cruel nets of Beatrice's vast, overreaching plans.

Beatrice had insisted that Phoebe's mother and grandmother be her guests for the entire weekend of the prenuptial celebrations, even though Chloe had feebly tried to insist on a motel—feebleness being the effect that Beatrice invariably makes on Chloe. There's something in Beatrice's habit of being absolutely certain about absolutely everything that Chloe experiences as absolutely debilitating—especially since the things about which Beatrice waxes endlessly knowing tend to be matters to which Chloe has never given a moment's thought (though in Beatrice's presence she can't help feeling that she ought to have).

So a weekend spent with the Kantors of Stellar Road had not meant a weekend of Dionysian delight for Chloe. Still, she had been entirely unprepared for what it had meant to Sasha.

Actually, what precisely it *did* mean to Sasha had at first eluded Chloe. All Chloe knew was that her mother, who could, when she so wanted, charm a whole roomful of disparate strangers with unfailing technique, was instead going out of her way to project this withering incredulity; and Chloe couldn't understand it, at least not at first. She couldn't understand how the patent fact of Phoebe's happiness didn't dissolve away all other considerations.

Of course, the future in-laws *were* somewhat trying, especially Beatrice. But what did that matter—what did any of them matter—when placed alongside the fact of Phoebe, happy? Phoebe herself managed to take Beatrice and all the rest of them in her stride. Couldn't Sasha—world-seasoned, live-and-let-live Sasha? But Sasha had been indiscriminately rude to *everyone* that weekend.

A friend of Beatrice's, an otherwise perfectly inoffensive woman, had cooed something in Sasha's direction about "the future Mrs. Jason Kantor," and Sasha had almost bitten her head off.

"My granddaughter's name is Dr. Phoebe Saunders. So far as I've been informed, matrimony will cancel out neither her education nor her identity."

"How proud you must be, Mrs. Saunders," the persevering woman had cooed in turn to Chloe.

"And my daughter, *too,* is *Dr.* Saunders!" Sasha had snapped. This time the woman had wisely retreated.

Chloe, consistently declining Sasha's invitation to disdain, had drawn some of Sasha's fire to herself.

"You're so open-minded, my dear daughter, that I think your brains must have fallen out!"

None too certain herself amidst the strangeness of Beatrice and her circle, Chloe had been both dismayed and alarmed by her mother's punchiness. Chloe, a reticent person, was used to letting her mother take over in any social setting that included them both. Now Chloe was uncomfortably aware of the need to assert herself in order to head off an ugly confrontation. To Chloe, any confrontation was ugly.

What if Sasha let loose something unforgivably blunt at the Kantors, especially at Beatrice, who was, emphatically, *not* the sort of woman who would laugh it off? This was a woman who could be counted on to provide abundantly throughout the years for any slights done her, so that she might take them with her to the grave.

Beatrice had obviously gone to enormous pains over every minute detail of this weekend. The flower arrangements adorning each room of her house must alone have cost enough to feed a small nation. All that she asked was that everyone present be stupefied into admiration and submission. Was that so much?

The two titans, Sasha and Beatrice, had come dangerously close to clashing on the issue of Sasha's clothes. If Beatrice could keep changing her outfits according to some rigorous schedule she had worked out with the obsessiveness she had lavished all around, well, then, Sasha could go upstairs and slip into something a little more comfortable, too.

"Pants, Sasha?" Beatrice had queried with heavy incredulity, intercepting the trouble before the others had yet caught sight of her. "And black leather, no less?"

"So *stone* me, Beatrice." Sasha's tone had been so grim that even Beatrice had faltered, and Sasha had proceeded on downstairs, bristling with indignation, while at the same time, Sasha being Sasha, kvelling in the drama.

Sasha had stood with Chloe, off to the side of the festive yard, surveying all that met her gaze with ill-concealed contempt, until finally Chloe had suggested that they go for a little walk.

"Is it just the Kantors getting to you?" Chloe had asked her mother, even though direct questions were hardly Chloe's style.

"No," Sasha had answered, staccato, her lips again pulled by the unflattering drawstrings. "It's not *just* the Kantors."

The two were walking down Stonystream Avenue, a wide street lined on either side with the regulation split-levels. There was an island running the length of the avenue, planted with magnolias, the blooms just beginning to turn brown and drop to the ground.

This hadn't been the first meeting between the future gang of in-laws. They had joined together in a celebratory dinner in a restaurant on the Upper West Side of Manhattan when Phoebe and Jason had first gotten engaged, three months before, in the middle of January.

Sasha's hackles had been far more relaxed on that occasion. In fact, she'd been perfectly charming, trying to coax the odd comment out of Nat Kantor, Jason's father, an orthodontist, and a rather sweet, if awkward, sort—certainly more than ready to concede the ladies, beginning with his wife, anything they might possibly demand.

Outside, wild winds, howling like demons, had taken possession of Broadway, making the atmosphere inside the softly lit restaurant—

"pseudo-Yuppie" though Sasha had pronounced it to be—all the more intimate and convivial. ("Pseudo-Yuppie?" Chloe had queried. "Don't two negatives add up to a positive?")

Afterward, back in the living room overlooking the Hudson (the Kantors had driven in from Lipton and, incredulous that lone women would even consider walking the streets after dark, had insisted on driving Chloe and Sasha the two blocks back to Sasha's apartment), Sasha had dissected the Kantors' marriage with gruesome analogies borrowed from the insect world.

It was *her* experience, she had told Chloe, that praying-mantis females like Beatrice always manage to get themselves appropriately attached to men like Nat, just made for having their heads chewed off in the very act itself.

Chloe, still stunned by her daughter's sudden engagement (at least it had been sudden to Chloe), had spoken in terms of another metaphor:

"It's January," she had remarked, "the month that looks both ways."

"Meaning?" Sasha had demanded.

"I don't know. Maybe the past and the future."

"Meaning?"

"I'm not quite sure. You probably understand what I mean better than I do."

"Well, if I do, I'm not telling myself."

Still, though it was predictable that Sasha wouldn't find the new in-laws, especially Beatrice, exactly her "cup of tea," the lavish scale of the contempt she had assembled in honor of that prenuptial weekend had seemed, to say the least, excessive.

It was true that here, in Lipton, Beatrice was in her own element, which wasn't a pretty sight. Actually, there was nothing so much wrong with the sight of her. A tall, dark, and rather handsome woman, in a heavy-featured sort of way, she'd been strenuously dieting for the wedding, and she'd looked positively svelte. She'd also dressed in quite daunting high style, changing designer outfits at a Reagan-era rate.

They had just left her entertaining her guests in a black silk

Armani suit, as she'd informed Chloe, to whom the name had meant nothing at all, but who had still been sufficiently impressed to wonder what Beatrice could possibly be planning to wear tomorrow, to the wedding itself.

Beatrice's blue-black hair, shining like satin and cut blunt to her chin line, matched the elegance of her suit, and she had pointedly asked Chloe where she was going to get *her* hair done for the wedding, which had suddenly made Chloe feel awfully self-conscious about the two bobby pins at her temples, holding back her fair, limp tresses.

No, the problem had certainly not been with the sight of Beatrice, done up with great expertise. The problem had been with the *sound* of her, which was *everywhere.*

"What a voice," Sasha had muttered to Chloe. "A fishmonger in an Armani suit."

"She's just excited," Chloe had tried to placate her bristling mother.

"Doesn't she remind you of those old Leona Helmsley advertisements? You know, the Queen herself standing guard."

And Chloe, in spite of herself, had had to flash her mother an appreciative smile.

Beatrice and her chosen circle had certainly been having an inspiring effect on Sasha's powers of association. She had been making unkind comparisons almost since first walking in the Stellar Road door. Beatrice, the Star of Stellar Road. Earlier that morning, Sasha, watching Beatrice amidst her admiring throngs, had spoken of "Mrs. Vanderbilt and her Four Hundred."

"It's like an Edith Wharton novel, in its own perverse way," she had said, not quite sufficiently *sotto voce.* "Wharton's descriptions of *her* tribe keep popping into my head."

"Well, then, enjoy it," Chloe had whispered back. "You love Edith Wharton."

"I *love* Edith Wharton because she *hates* this sort of thing. Oh, what Edith Wharton could have done with Lipton!"

And again Chloe silently had to concede that, in the midst of her mother's wild exaggeration, there resided a small and quiet truth.

There had been an elaborately catered "luncheon" at the Stellar Road home, spilling out into the yard, for all the multitudes of Beatrice's friends and relations—with only Sasha and Chloe representing Phoebe's side, because that's all that there are, in all the world, except for Sasha's sister-in-law, Harriet, who for years had taught piano lessons in New Rochelle. But Harriet, though just a few years older than Sasha, hasn't been wearing so well as she, and had moved down to a nursing home in Miami.

Beatrice had taken an obsessive interest in the wedding (though, of course, Jason and Phoebe, technically grown-ups, were paying for it), until, by the end, Phoebe had been only too happy to let Beatrice make all the decisions, right down to the flowers Phoebe would hold in the hands that would be manicured in an appointment Beatrice would make. If this foretaste was any indication, an embarrassingly overdone occasion this wedding was going to be, again with a few flourishes on the hideous all its own.

But if gentle Phoebe could bear it all with such good grace and self-possession, well, then, so, too, could Chloe—and *definitely* (or so one would think) Sasha, whose experience of the world could certainly be matched against anyone's, whether in Lipton, New Jersey, or beyond.

Lunch had been concluded at least four hours before, and still the house and yard on Stellar Road had been thronged with people, toward whom indefatigable Beatrice—the *grande dame,* the doyenne—had continued to hold forth, and Sasha, equally indefatigably, to bristle; until at last poor Chloe, uncomfortable herself amidst the very concrete conversation of Beatrice and her friends, to which she hadn't a word to contribute, had decided to take her mother out for a walk and air her out a bit.

"Is it just my imagination," Sasha had asked as they walked down wide Stonystream Avenue, "or is there some sort of putrid smell in the air?"

"I don't think it's your imagination," Chloe had answered. "I think it's that little brook that wanders so prettily through the neighborhood."

"That, too," Sasha had muttered darkly, and then had stared threateningly at the magnolias.

"What *senseless* trees. They flower for all of two minutes, then they rot. What's the *point?*"

She had turned back to Chloe, patiently keeping pace beside her, and had repeated, even more fiercely:

"It's not *just* the Kantors, though if I went about *designing* an insufferable mother-in-law I couldn't have improved on that model. But it's not just her. It's . . . *this place!*"

"This place," Chloe had echoed thoughtfully. And then light had come into her clear gray eyes, and she had looked, for a moment, quite absurdly happy—for Chloe always derives a certain degree of pleasure simply in figuring something out.

"Oh, I see what this place reminds you of! Of course!"

"Of course," Sasha had repeated in the same furious tone of voice. "Of course. Only it's not *of course. It's completely off course!*"

"Well, you know, darling," Chloe had said, ever so softly, slipping her arm through her mother's and giving her one of her truly beautiful smiles, brushed over with a delicate gloss of irony, "there's such a thing as mazel."

In response, Sasha had kept an emphatically stony silence, though Chloe, glancing over at her as they made their way back to Stellar Road, had been able to see the thoughts dramatically traversing her mother's face.

And just before re-entering the Kantors' front door, Sasha had given Chloe's hand one of those bone-crushing squeezes to which she resorted on the rare occasion when words failed her.

Sasha's belligerence had been blunted just enough so that she rode out the rest of the stay on Stellar Road, as well as the wedding itself, without the major confrontation with Beatrice toward which she had seemed inevitably to be heading. If Sasha hadn't been able to bring herself to exude exultation at the thought of her granddaughter's union with the Kantors, at the very least she had stopped throwing her misgivings about the match into everybody's face.

And yet the fact—abundantly clear after this year of her

marriage—is that Phoebe is happy living in *this place:* unprecedentedly, if unintelligibly, *happy.*

And Sasha, irrepressible champion of chance and disorder, has never been one for refusing to recognize a fact's right to exist on the flimsy grounds of its making no conceivable sense.

To be let in on a secret to which Sasha herself is not yet quite privy: Sasha has gone a long way toward making her peace with Lipton, New Jersey.

It isn't, of course, that Phoebe had been *un*happy before, not so anyone would ever have noticed, least of all Phoebe herself.

Still, much as it had sometimes seemed that Phoebe's entire being had been absorbed in the geometry of soap bubbles—Sasha has always gleefully told everyone that her granddaughter's field is the mathematics of froth—there had been indications that such was not the case.

There had been the lights that would sometimes, mysteriously, appear in Phoebe's large, dark eyes; the times when her entire being seemed heartbreakingly—at least it had broken Chloe's heart—luminous with these hidden lights, and every gesture she'd make, every expression, had seemed charged with an elusive shimmery quality. And Chloe and Sasha had been able only to wonder.

And then the glow would vanish, and Phoebe would look—maybe it was only in contrast, but so it had seemed to them that she had looked—dull and lusterless. And something would also have seemed to have gone out of her voice, and left it liltless. And, again, Chloe and Sasha had been able only to wonder.

So Phoebe, too—how could one have hoped she would escape it?—had had her dark side, a submerged, inarticulate . . . what? One couldn't have called it a *life,* since there hadn't been enough of anything down there to constitute a life.

In any case, Phoebe's now somehow less a poignant figure, more reassuringly prosaic, or as prosaic as a young woman passionately devoted to the precise mathematical description of soap bubbles can be. The hidden lights are gone, but so, too, are the disquieting shadows.

Chloe unambivalently welcomes this loss of poignancy in her daughter. One doesn't want poignancy in one's daughter. It had always struck terror in Chloe's heart. Her heart would suddenly open on a pit of icy terror.

Sasha, too, unambivalently welcomes this loss of poignancy in Phoebe, which had terrified her no less than it had Chloe. More than once she had found herself wishing that she could put her granddaughter under glass—to keep the world away, away.

A soul without a skin, without a skin. How can I keep the world from flaying her raw?

So it's not *all* bad, this Lipton, New Jersey. And the sight of the blue sky through the apple blossoms *is* dazzling; and the township has apparently done something about cleaning up the smelly brook.

Phoebe's busy marking her Princeton students' final exams, and she's huge with child. Though she turned thirty last month, she still looks, even pregnant, like a girl of fifteen, her dark hair curling around her shoulders.

. Sasha had told Chloe that her pregnant daughter looks like a wayward child. But it's of Fraydel that Sasha thinks, stealing glances at Phoebe, intent on her bluebooks, her long eyelashes seeming to rest on her ivory cheek.

"She looks so much like Fraydel right now."

And it's true. Something about these last days of Phoebe's pregnancy has made her little heart-shaped face even more childlike, so that the old haunting resemblance—striking when Phoebe had been younger—is reasserting itself.

There had been times when a certain look on Pheobe's face—or something she'd said, at odds with the world—would make Sasha fleetingly think that the child really *was* Fraydel. Fraydel returned, given a second chance at life. *Why not?* she'd think with a sudden rush of longing that verged dangerously on belief. *Of all who die before their time, why shouldn't my sister Fraydel be granted a second chance?* Then she'd chide herself for thinking the kind of superstitious nonsense she'd heard all too much of, growing up in the miserable shtetl.

"Big fool," she'd make fun of herself. "In the end, nothing but a big fool with a foot still stuck in Shluftchev."

Still, the resemblance is really remarkable, especially since nobody else in the family had looked like them, at least not to Sasha's knowledge. In a family that had produced strong, hale women, taller than average, with fair hair and light eyes and high coloring, Phoebe is, just as Fraydel had been, small and finely boned, her hair dark and her skin pale and her face brought to a type beyond pretty by the nightsky eyes. You rarely got an inkling as to what exactly was going on behind those eyes, neither Fraydel's nor Phoebe's—only that it was somehow different from what goes on for everybody else. No matter how much you studied them, no matter how much you *loved* them, you couldn't project yourself inside either girl's head and say how it was the world looked from in there.

To Sasha, Phoebe is—just as Fraydel had been—truly and literally wonderful: sometimes all you can do is to wonder. Since Phoebe was a little girl, solemnly blowing her soap bubbles for hours on end, Sasha's been wondering. Even now, as a certified grown-up, Phoebe's capable of stunning her grandmother into silence with statements that seem to come of an unplumbable innocence. Or maybe it's not innocence at all. Sasha can't judge. It still happens sometimes that Phoebe says something so that Sasha goes around thinking about it for days and days.

Phoebe is now more than a blessed decade older than Fraydel had been when her life had ended. She's crossed safely over into womanhood, even finding a place where she can feel at home in the world, putting down her delicate system of roots and blossoming. Okay, it happens to be in Lipton, an irony that clunks Sasha in the head with such a force that the world starts spinning like a top, shrilling a long high note of dismay.

Phoebe doesn't sound at all like Fraydel, though. She doesn't have that strange whispery voice that, together with her other oddities, had set Fraydel apart from everyone else, especially everyone else *there,* in that little nothing place of a shtetl, floating in the brackish backwaters of Galicia, where the girls were all supposed to be pressed out from the same cookie cutter, anything extra trimmed away. A pack of little boys, Fraydel's pitiless tormentors, used to make fun of her voice, imitating the way it would quiver and break, making their eyes fill up with a crazy look meant to frighten people away. Sasha could hear it until this very day—

—*a voice like no other, like a reflection on unstill water—*

—even though, come this June, it will have been sixty-six years. Sixty-six years.

Sasha's not what you would call a tradition-bound woman. Raised as a child in an atmosphere made unbreathable by piety and ritual, she had taken no small pleasure in breaking the tiresome taboos with as much noise and commotion as she could muster. The soul of discretion she wasn't. And her spirit of rebellion hasn't given an inch over the years. Even before there were entire departments at famous universities created for the purpose of demonstrating the point, she'd known that most of those ancient "do's and don't's" had been fashioned by men to keep things their way. And why not? She'd have done the same thing if she could have gotten away with it.

Listen, she could imagine one of the Talmudic sages confiding to another on a slow day in Babylonia. Just between you and me, my wife's cleanliness leaves a little something to be desired. Do you think we can write in a law about women having to bathe at least once a month?

Done! answers his friend. And maybe you can do a little something for me in return, my friend? Don't let this go any further, but my wife keeps the house like a pigsty. She says, What's the use cleaning? It'll only get dirty again. Who can argue with such a woman? Let's write in a law that every spring the women have to give the house such a cleaning that not a crumb of bread lurks in any corner.

Done!

Listen, says a third, who's been eavesdropping on the conversation. If you're smart, then, before you do another thing, you'll make a law that the women can't make any laws.

Can't even study the laws!

Can't even read the language in which the laws are written!

Done, done, and, again, done!

So much, according to Sasha, an unreclaimed iconoclast, for tradition.

And yet, for as long as Chloe can remember, her mother has lit a little memorial candle on the eve of the eighteenth of June. Of all the abandoned old ways, this remains the only one to which Sasha devoutly clings: a little wax-filled glass, purchased yearly at Waldbaum's, wrapped around with paper printed in Hebrew script. The candle, placed on the sideboard among the plants, burns all through the night and into the evening of the next day, throwing its dancing patterns of light and shadow around a magically transformed dining room.

Chloe, who had been a wildly imaginative little girl, with even more than the typical child's receptiveness toward ritual, had always been fascinated by this unexplained ceremony falling every year in unripened summer. "For the dead," is all that her mother had given as answer to her questions, a response only deepening the thrilling spookiness of the whole thing—the quivering shadows like the shades of night themselves, so that Chloe could succeed in convincing herself that all their dead, the large and vanished families of both her mother and her father, were silently gathered there in their dining room over-looking the Hudson, a wordless family reunion every year on the eve of the eighteenth of June.

Never once has Fraydel's name been mentioned in connection with this date that Sasha, for all her irreverence, has made significant. As a matter of fact, Sasha very rarely mentions Fraydel's name at all. Sixty-six years, and still such a thick haze of pain surrounding the memory of the girl—

—never, in all the years, another voice like it—

The stories Sasha tells about her own vivid past all take place later, years after Fraydel's death. Chloe and Phoebe have always assumed that Fraydel had died as the rest of Sasha's family had, as victims of the Nazis, and that Sasha has chosen, for whatever reason, the eighteenth of June as the date of their collective unrecorded deaths.

Though Phoebe's official due date is still another two weeks off, Sasha has assured Phoebe, just by looking at her, that this baby has definite ideas of its own, and she's given Phoebe another twenty-four hours at the most.

"Do you hear that?" Phoebe queries the bulge on her lap. "That's Sasha talking. Nobody, not even you, can dare to ignore Sasha."

Though she might caution her unborn child, Phoebe's more than accustomed to Sasha's apodictic utterances, delivered in the husky voice that had once intoxicated the audiences of Warsaw's Yiddish art theater.

Now, *there's* a story.

This isn't just any old grandmother, some *alta bubba,* sunning herself in the cliché-strewn landscape with her very expectant granddaughter. This grandmother had been, once upon a time, a member of a wildly avant-garde theatrical troupe. The Bilbul Art Theater, this troupe had been called, though, among themselves, the members had always referred to it as the *mishpocheh,* the family. And for one brief moment in time, the *mishpocheh* had held the spotlight, had been written about and spoken about as *inspired.*

Sasha is, *emphatically,* not the sort of person whose head is swiveled on backward, fixated on the past. Still, that brief moment in time is not the sort of thing a person ever forgets. She had come of age in that spotlight, and to this day she continues to live within the lighted nimbus of a *dramatic presence.*

The *mishpocheh* had believed in a radically cooperative form of theater. There weren't any stars in the troupe, at least not in theory. But if any one of them, in that brief moment of time, could have been called a star, it would have been Sasha. The Café Pripetshok had even created a dish in her honor: Blintzes Sasha, high in calories and appropriately flambé.

The strangely moving quality of her voice had once sent several otherwise sober men off on flights of far-fetched metaphors, in search of the right comparison.

"Were one to bottle that voice and drink it, it would go down smooth as an old cognac—and only later would one discover it had burnt a hole in the gullet!"

"And one thing for sure: no rabbi would authorize that bottle as kosher!"

The strangely moving quality is still there, carrying with it an authority that Sasha's not above exploiting. Still, Phoebe doesn't feel any particular need to rush through the grading of her Princeton students' exams on the odd chance that Sasha is as certain as she sounds. Everything Sasha *says,* everything Sasha *does,* is with emphasis.

While Phoebe marks her exams, Sasha's been reading, on and off again, from *The New York Times.* She's in the middle of the obituary page when she looks up and says to Phoebe:

"I once knew a certain couple."

There can be no doubt that there's a story coming, one of Sasha's *mysahs.* Phoebe, in no way resenting the interruption, obediently puts down the bluebook and turns her face to her grandmother.

"They lived not far from me on East Fourteenth Street.

"One day the woman was sitting out on her steps with her baby on her lap while the potatoes for dinner were boiling in a pot on her stove. She had just gotten up, and was going in the front door to check on the potatoes, when one of the other neighbor women happened to pass by on her way home from the pictures."

Sasha's voice, which she can ritzify to the upper reaches of Princeton or beyond, is basking in a folksiness just this side of a Yiddish intonation, no doubt entirely suitable to her story. This, after all, is her profession.

"The woman with the baby—Etty, I think her name was—anyway, she had a passion for the pictures. And of course now, with the baby, she couldn't go so often. So she turns back from the door and asks her friend if the picture had been any good.

"I think the name of the picture had been *Reap the Wild Wind.* Look at that, how I still remember. With Paulette Goddard, whose name, by the way, was in the beginning Levy.

"Anyway, the friend begins to describe the movie, reel for reel, and before they can get to the denouement there's a very distinctive odor.

"The woman goes rushing into her apartment, and not only are the potatoes no longer identifiable as potatoes, the apartment, which was all of one room, in the basement yet, is black with smoke.

"This poor Etty is beside herself, because her husband was something of a little tyrant. I remember I used to call him the tenor tyrant. When he yelled at her—and of course you could hear it as loudly as if you, God forbid, were the wretched wife yourself, Lincoln Center should only have the acoustics of that tenement—his voice would go sliding up the scale. He had a high G that would have been the envy of Mr. Pavarotti.

"Anyway, sure enough, when the tenor tyrant gets home, he goes into his full-blown operatics, complete with gasps for breath in the smoke-fouled air. And even though poor Etty had boiled up some more potatoes, the angry little man goes stomping out to a restaurant, leaving the wife, who had only loved the pictures over the potatoes, sobbing together with her baby.

"Now, in this restaurant there sits another man, whom all of us in the neighborhood already know as an up-and-coming *macher*, a mover and a shaker.

"Mr. Macher is sitting there impatiently waiting for yet another man, who's supposed to come in on some kind of real-estate deal with him, a piece of land about which Mr. Macher may or may not know something, all the way up past Harlem.

"Mr. Macher is getting very hot around the fancy collar, he doesn't like to be kept waiting, he takes it as a personal affront, a slap in the face. He says to himself: The next man who walks in that door, whether it's Mr. He Has Some Nerve Keeping Me Waiting or not, I'm going to talk to him, and tell him what I may or may not know.

"So who walks in but the tenor tyrant, and before you can say *s'iz taka a goldeneh medyna*—it's after all a golden country—the two of them are shaking hands, they're business partners.

"And the very next year, this land above Harlem is sold for a *fabulous* sum."

Sasha leans back and briefly closes her eyes, a long hand elegantly pressed to one temple, as if she's momentarily blinded by the memory of the sum.

Phoebe knows that, if she were to ask her grandmother what the exact figure was, Sasha would more than likely answer with an even more emphatic *"fabulous."*

"This piece of land, it turns out, is a necessity to the states of both New York and New Jersey. They both must have it because they're building a bridge across the Hudson River exactly there. That's where the bridge has to be, that's the piece of land that must be had, and this man," Sasha says, pointing to a boldface headline on the obituary page, reading SAMUEL KARLINSKY: DEVELOPER AND PHILANTHROPIST, *"this man was the tenor tyrant!*

"Now, how could anybody ever have predicted that, because in 1942 Hollywood produced a certain picture with the former Miss Levy, Samuel Karlinsky would get so much space in *The New York Times* when he died?"

And how is it, Phoebe's wondering, not for the first time, that all the people who have ever passed through Sasha's life come trailing the most unlikely of stories?

Perhaps the answer partly lies in the way in which Sasha tells a story. Sasha seems to have a lot at stake in making the case for life's abiding chanciness. For all Phoebe knows, when Sasha tells people about the relatively recent changes in Phoebe's own life—which to Phoebe have unfolded with a necessity approaching a mathematical proof—it might all come out sounding as improbable as anything else Sasha has to say.

"Look at that," Sasha's saying, *"The New York Times* says he leaves behind the widow Etta Karlinsky, as well as two sons, Sheldon and Myron. Sheldon must have been the baby on her lap."

"So Etty and the tenor tyrant stuck it out all those years."

"Well, why not? He owed everything to Etty's culinary skills. And anyway, I suppose, after the bridge across the Hudson, they could afford to hire a cook. What a thing mazel is!"

What a thing indeed.

Mazel, as Sasha expounds it, is the fundamental principle of cosmic abandon—and *this* is a principle that Sasha *does* wholeheartedly embrace.

Mazel exists only to wreak havoc on the natural order, into which it weaves its way like smoke, coupling and uncoupling events for no reason that goes beyond itself, the *causa sui* of chance and disorder.

Long ago, when Chloe had been a freshman at Barnard College, she had taken her first course in philosophy with a Professor Potts, an animal lover and a Wittgensteinian, who used to bring her pit bull along to class with her.

Whether it was the presence of the animal or Professor Potts's own fierce reputation that kept the class size down to a rather intimidated ten, Chloe didn't know. Chloe herself had become infatuated, both with the twinkling and gruff Potts, whose eyes might suddenly, heart-meltingly, crinkle up in laughter at an unlikely joke, and with her subject matter. The dog Chloe could have done without. And yet even in this there was that to melt Chloe's heart, watching the philosopher and the pit bull exchanging their intelligent glances. At some point during the semester, Professor Potts had been evicted from her Lower Manhattan apartment, and she, the pit bull, and a few sulking cats had set up home in Professor Potts's office in Milbank Hall.

Chloe had been, as a sixteen-year-old freshman, the same quiet, studious person she always would be, more comfortable remarking life than fully engaging herself in it.

But even back then, the air of almost formidable scholarship had been lightened by a very deep sense of humor—and a deep understanding, too, of something else. Perhaps her preference for books over people had always had something in the way of self-protection about it.

Occasionally, even when Chloe was in high school, an answer she'd give in English class, discussing a poem or story, would make a teacher shoot her a quizzical look, and wonder, in either prurience or distress, about the sort of experience that informed such an answer.

It must have been her own internal contradictions that gave Chloe her particular weakness for robust eccentricity. Her philosophy professor's combination of the austerity of pure reason with hints of a cultivated degeneracy completely won Chloe over, and Chloe had spent a good part of her undergraduate career silently in love—hopelessly, hopelessly—with Potts.

Only once during the course of the semester had Chloe found herself at odds with her mentor's point of view, and that had been when Potts had lectured on David Hume.

Potts had made a great deal of fuss over Hume.

According to Potts, Hume's devastating critique of empirical reasoning had sent epistemology forever reeling, exploding the foremost dictum of rationality: that all our beliefs be justified.

"How shall we proceed?" Potts had queried her class, now down to six, in a poignantly urgent tone.

"How shall we proceed after Hume has gotten through analyzing causality?

"He has devised the most rigorous of arguments to undermine our faith in reason . . . *and how shall we proceed?*

"Shall we all, from this day forward, believe, willy-nilly, whatever strikes our sweet fancy? Shall I dismiss you now from philosophy class to go off to study your horoscopes or to pay a visit to the woman on 104th Street who advertises her skill with Tarot cards?

"And why not . . . after Hume?

"Where's the difference . . . after Hume?

"I ask again: how shall we, as philosophers and devotees of reason, proceed . . . *after Hume?*"

Professor Potts had seemed so genuinely distraught, after Hume, that Chloe had felt she must really try to respond in kind. But how could she, when her overriding thought, while reading the assigned chapters of *An Enquiry Concerning Human Understanding*, had been that David Hume sounded *just like Sasha?*

All events seem entirely loose and separate. One event follows another, but we never can observe any tie between them. They seem *conjoined,* but never *connected.*

Hadn't Chloe been hearing something very much like this her entire life, *right down to the italics?*

The contrary of every matter of fact is still possible, because it can never imply a contradiction, and is conceived by the mind with the same facility and distinctness as if ever so conformable to reality. *That the sun will not rise tomorrow* is no less intelligible a proposition and implies no more contradiction than the affirmation *that it will rise.*

Was this the stuff that had exploded epistemology?

Was Hume's scathingly rigorous analysis of causality nothing more than Sasha and her insistence that there's *such a thing as mazel?*

CHAPTER 2

A SUBTLE BUSINESS

*F*rom inside the house comes the sound of the telephone ringing. Phoebe puts down the bluebook she's marking and begins to slip her legs over the side of the lounge chair but is halted by Sasha's emphatic *"Sit!"*

Phoebe smiles to herself as she watches Sasha stride toward the deck and disappear inside the sliding glass doors to the kitchen.

Here is Sasha, about to become a great-grandmother—*in the next twenty-four hours,* if she can be believed—and she's still a glamorous, fascinating, and *sexy* woman.

Phoebe, feeling about as remote from such qualities as one tends to feel at the end of one's ninth month, can only gaze and admire.

Sasha still carries herself with the sort of loping stride she had first perfected within the spotlight. A little stiffened now with age perhaps, but she's still loping. There's always something theatrical in her presentation of herself. She's never oblivious of the impression she's creating, not even in an empty room. As Maurice used to say, always with undiminished admiration: You can take the woman off of the stage, but you'll never get the stage out from the woman.

Sasha, yielding nothing to age, has kept her hair the deep honey blond that it had naturally been in her youth, and has also preserved, to a really astonishing degree, her graceful slimness.

In the world of the Yiddish art theater, she had been known, affectionately, in her day—or, rather, in *its* day, since it's still very much *Sasha's* day—as the "shiksa," the Gentile girl, because of the honey-blond hair, and the pale-gray eyes, and the long legs that started much farther up on her body than was expected of a Jewish girl. They were legs that splendidly gave themselves to that enchanting lope.

Perhaps her features were too assertive for her to have been considered beautiful, pure and simple, when she was a younger woman. She's never been photogenic. A still picture can't quite capture her quality. But whatever it is that eludes the camera, it's managed quite remarkably to elude time as well. The pronounced structure of her face has served her well. Going on seventy-five, she's still going strong, still beaming forth that sense of urgent vibrancy that makes a passerby, even in New York, notice and wonder.

And Sasha certainly dresses like no other grandmother Phoebe has ever known—Chloe has all her life made similar observations *mutatis mutandis*—her choice in clothes reflecting her love of high drama.

She's enamored of capes and scarves, anything that flows and swirls and *moves,* but almost always worn over pants. Sasha's devotion to trousers isn't only a matter of her nostalgia for the sense of blissful rebellion that wearing them had once given her. (What a *sensation* she used to create, walking down Leszno Street in her trousers.) The truth is that the one imperfection of Sasha's very fine figure is her thickish ankles, of which, even now, she's not about to have the world catch a glimpse.

Sasha had arrived early this morning at the train station in New Brunswick, where Phoebe, the suburban matron, had sat waiting in her little blue Toyota, the first Saunders woman ever to own a car. Phoebe had watched her grandmother descending the decrepit stairs, down to the semi-seedy street, enfolded in her latent sense of drama and an exquisite white cashmere shawl.

"Is it new?" Phoebe had asked, as, hugging her grandmother, she had registered the luscious feel of the thing.

"Slightly new," Sasha had conceded, smiling slightly, and then gave a little shrug of her cashmere-pampered shoulders in a characteristic gesture of both owning and dismissing her own excesses.

There's a good deal of self-love that's gone into Sasha's giving age

such a run for its money. Self-love and damn good genes. Phoebe and
Chloe, who are themselves women without any detectable vanity, almost admire Sasha hers. Or perhaps what they admire is something
larger, of which her vanity is only an aspect.

But Phoebe seems to have something of the age-defiant genes,
though otherwise she's not at all, at least in physical type, like
Sasha—or, for that matter, like her mother, Chloe. Both Sasha and
Chloe have a physical presence that Phoebe now, and forevermore, will
lack. On the first day of her classes, her Princeton undergraduates, taking for granted that she's one of them, never fall into a respectful hush
as she enters.

Phoebe's always assumed that her father, whom she's never known,
is a small man. (He isn't; rather tall and lanky, in fact.)

It was only relatively recently that she'd really found out who he
was, the man who had fathered her, more beyond his name, Oliver
Crittendon, and the fact that he had been a logician from Cambridge
University, visiting for a year at Columbia. That much she had always
known. But precious little more. It had always been obvious to Phoebe
that her mother didn't like it when Phoebe asked questions about him,
and so Phoebe hadn't.

Once, when she was about six, she had asked her mother whether
Oliver Crittendon, too, had liked chess, of which Phoebe was then extremely fond, and her mother, going white, had answered that she
didn't know. Phoebe never wanted to risk seeing that look on her
mother's face again.

*Lo, I am come to this land of Thebes, Dionysus, the son of Zeus, born of my
mother, Semele, by a flash of lightning.*

This is the first line of Euripides' *Bacchae.* When Phoebe was a little
girl, her mother would sometimes, quite wonderfully, act out scenes
from Greek tragedies using Barbie and Ken dolls. A great favorite of
Phoebe's—not least because of its macabre climax—had been Chloe's
very free adaptation of the *Bacchae.* Chloe, simulating a Bacchic frenzy
that was part Greek mystery religion, part Charlie Manson, would rip
the head and limbs from the sacrificial Pentheus/Ken and fling them all

about Phoebe's room, half chanting, half howling in an ancient Greek gone wild.

But it wasn't just a matter of the lurid special effects, courtesy of Mattel, Chloe provided that made Phoebe, at least for a while, beg nightly for the *Bacchae*. It was a matter, too, of the opening lines, with their intimation of a mysterious paternity, that always sounded some secret chord deep in Phoebe.

"Lo," she would sometimes say to herself, "I am Phoebe, daughter of Oliver Crittendon, born of my mother, Chloe, by a flash of lightning."

It was right around the time that Phoebe, already an assistant professor at Princeton, had met her future husband, Jason Kantor, that she risked introducing the subject of Oliver Crittendon to her mother.

"Was Oliver Crittendon Jewish?" she asked.

"Was Oliver Crittendon *Jewish?*" Chloe was too astonished even to panic.

This was the first question Phoebe had put about the man who was her father since the day, long ago, when she had been a little chess prodigy, and had wondered, having surveyed the limits of Chloe's own game, whether her *father* had liked chess.

Chloe honestly hadn't been able to answer. It was horrible to have so few answers available on the subject of Oliver Crittendon. She had thought she had been so thorough, but really, who, as her own mother was so fond of pointing out, could presume to anticipate?

Now, over two decades later, Phoebe was once again asking something quite extraordinary about her father. The question flew straight out of the blue, striking Chloe in the dark.

Why would Phoebe be asking this, of all things? Surely, it's an appeal, and more than justified, for me to come forth with the facts of her existence. Surely, it's time.

And so Chloe (sending up a silent little prayer to the goddesses Hera, Hestia, and Demeter, mothers all) had come forth, telling her daughter (though leaving margins at least as wide as the text itself) how it was that she had chosen to become a single mother in 1964.

(Who had ever even heard the expression "single mother" in 1964? Chloe had opted for an option that was so tenuous at the time as to be virtually nameless. Well, of course, there *was* a name for it, but not one that a young woman like Chloe would happily embrace.)

Chloe had been twenty-three. (Incredible, really. She had felt so ancient, already on the other side of passion, whereas here was Phoebe, a few years older, still trembling on the threshold of womanhood.)

A graduate student, she had had a disastrous love affair with a professor.

His name had been Timothy Wisdom. Yes. Wisdom. Chloe still regarded his translation of Aeschylus' *Oresteia* as the most beautiful one extant.

Of course, the *Oresteia*, Chloe conceded, was neither here nor there.

More to the point was the fact that the affair, the first Chloe had ever engaged in outside the precinct of her overactive mind, had been a crucible.

(She left the details in the thick margins.)

Very much to the point was her having come to the conclusion, at the age of twenty-three, that she hadn't the stamina for this sort of thing.

"Passion wasn't for me. I wanted to study the tragedies, not live them."

Phoebe remained silent at this, but she wondered at her mother's equation of passion and tragedy.

Must it be like that? *And for me?*

"Then, very soon after, I discovered that I had this enormous desire in me for a child."

Phoebe smiled.

"You make it sound like finding a tumor."

Chloe smiled back.

"Well, that may not be an altogether misleading comparison. Benign, as it turned out. It was very odd, but so . . . so insistent. I used to go trailing after young mothers pushing strollers down Broadway, feeling all sweetly weepy inside. It's a wonder nobody ever reported me, the dotty stroller-chasing woman of Morningside Heights.

"Men come and men go, I remember thinking, but a child is for keeps. Those words kept playing over and over again in my head, as I traipsed after those strollers, like a demented lullaby I was singing the babies. Or maybe the mothers."

Chloe (who never once had caught a glimpse of Phoebe's own impossible loves) didn't know, of course, that Phoebe had just recently met a young computer scientist named Jason Kantor, and that Chloe's demented little lullaby couldn't have sounded any more dismal a note for her daughter.

"So I set about," Chloe continued, "in my thorough way, reviewing which of the men I knew were likely to yield desirable genes. Oliver Crittendon won the jackpot. There was absolutely nothing, nothing between us. But you see, darling, not only did he have just about all of the attributes I value, but he was also English, he had this *breeding,* so I assumed that the good genes went back for generations.

"He was incredibly decent about the whole thing, as of course he would be, since a well-developed sense of decency was one of my criteria. I made him promise never to get in touch with you or me. I got from him exactly what it was I wanted: you."

So Phoebe—like the little boy who, only wanting to know if he, like his friend, had come from Philadelphia, stumbles upon the facts of life—had stumbled upon the true meaning of Oliver Crittendon, a.k.a. the flash of lightning.

But Oliver Crittendon hadn't been the incendiary event of Chloe's life. That role belonged to this new unknown, designated "Timothy Wisdom."

Listening to her mother, Phoebe had had the disquieting impression of glimpsing (it wasn't exactly the first time) another woman entirely. It was as if she'd caught sight of Chloe, at some ungodly hour, stepping out of her Reeboks and irony, to dance about Morningside Heights naked under the moon, like the pagans she adored.

Of course, Chloe *was* a pagan at heart. Phoebe knew this. The secret of Chloe's inspired scholarship was that she loved those pre-Christian Greeks of hers so well that their passions were her passions, their gods and goddesses her own. Phoebe herself had grown up half believing the ancient myths, frequently appealing to Apollo, her favorite god, preferring to call him by his name of Phoebus.

"It means 'shining,' " Chloe had told her, "just like you."

It had truly never occurred to Phoebe, who was certainly no stranger herself to the phenomenology of impossible love, that her mother might be capable of feeling passionately about anything other than motherhood and the ancient Greeks.

Timothy Wisdom, huh.

Men come and men go. But perhaps only because they're not the right one, the destined one, the *basheert.* This word had long been part of Phoebe's private vocabulary, though she would no sooner have uttered it aloud than she would have spoken any hint of the dense and hopeless crushes that so often consumed her inner life, the impossible loves to which she had been subject from about the age of seven onward.

To Phoebe, battered by her obsessions, it was always a sweet thought that Heaven Itself might meddle in the affairs of the heart, that somewhere in the middle of the muddle lay a preordained solution. A sweet, sweet thought, even though probably, in the end, to be taken with about as much seriousness as her mother's constant little prayers and paeans to the gods and goddesses of Mount Olympus.

Phoebe must, of course, have learned the word *basheert* from her grandmother, although Sasha would only have uttered it toward the most sarcastic of ends. The word, in Sasha's nostrils, carries the stink of fatalism, which to her smells exactly like that little place, Shluftchev on the Puddle, where she had been born Sorel Sonnenberg.

Sasha has less than little patience for the bedtime-story teleology of *basheert.* Against it, she summons forth her knowledge of—what else?—mazel: sly saboteur of cosmic coziness, subversive as the unholy laughter that was said to come from Shluftchev's studyhouse in the dead of night, when the demons took to arguing the Law.

In any case, Oliver Crittendon, entwined in their histories though he might be, had been nothing like Chloe's *basheert.* He had been a man whom Chloe had made promise to disappear from their lives.

Atop the mix of Phoebe's feelings, there floated a distinct thin thrill in knowing the answer at last. Phoebe has always had a great fondness for answers, the more final the better. She loves the click of a conclusion locking firmly into place.

Speaking of which: *was* Oliver Crittendon, the man who had been asked to provide Chloe, already the most devoted of mothers, with a good set of genes, Jewish?

"Well, no, as a matter of fact, he's not. Anglican, I suppose, though I didn't get the feeling that it figured all too prominently in his life, at least for the year that I knew him. He was quite leftist, though I don't suppose it's really the same. Does it matter, darling?"

In response, Phoebe had reproduced an almost exact replica of one of her mother's truly extraordinary smiles, brushed over with a delicate gloss of irony.

For a mother and a daughter, sealed together and yet worlds apart, questions and answers are always a subtle business.

The May day has warmed, and Sasha, returning through the sliding kitchen doors, is peeled down to a pair of cream linen pants and a linen shirt. She looks, as always, casually elegant, and Phoebe, in her denim maternity jumper, can only gaze and admire.

Though the youngest member of the family is waiting in the wings, the bulk of its things have yet to be purchased. Beatrice holds firm superstitions on this subject, and these have managed to infect even such women as Phoebe, Chloe, and Sasha. "Time enough to get everything once the baby is here," Beatrice says, and no one argues. There's nothing like issues of birth—or death, for that matter—for bringing out a person's weakness to magical thinking.

But Aunt Harriet, down in Miami, far away from Beatrice, has already sent some baby gifts, lovingly and exquisitely crocheted by her own arthritically knobby hands: a snowy-white blanket, a matching sweater and bonnet and tiny booties. They're laid out on the hand-painted white rocking chair in the corner of the otherwise empty room that will soon be the baby's; and it's amazing how their presence there has entirely shifted the feel of the house, as if something wonderful has already entered.

As Sasha lopes back across the lawn toward Phoebe, she's still talking on the phone, one of the several up-to-the-minute varieties that Jason and Phoebe own.

Jason is a computer wunderkind, whose talents have found a very happy home at Bellcore, which is the sort of place in which the normal work outfit is a shirt and jeans. That is to say, it's not the typical corporate environment, in which someone like Jason would probably manage to survive about thirty minutes, tops.

But Jason's surviving exceedingly well at Bellcore, thank you very much, where his official title is Distinguished Member of Staff, or D.M.S., and all he has to do is sit with his feet up on his desk and think. It's as good as being at a university—better, considering the salary and the absence of students.

In any case, one of the practical consequences of Jason's connection to Bell is that Phoebe and Jason own all sorts of state-of-the-art telephone gadgetry: mind-boggling toys that both Jason and Phoebe delight in and even *understand.*

When Sasha tells her friends that Jason is a wunderkind, she always adds that the emphasis is on the last syllable. Phoebe might look like a child of fifteen, but Jason, though almost twenty-nine, really *is* a child of fifteen. A very nice child, an absolutely *charming* and remarkably unspoiled child, but someone who is, in his very essence, ungrown-up—all of which is perfectly okay so long as he makes Phoebe happy.

The truth is, Sasha has grown enormously fond of Jason. How could one help it? He's *adorable*—with big, brown, long-lashed puppy-dog eyes, just begging for some affectionate gesture—and altogether lacking those sexist traits that Sasha had initially presumed he *must* have. Without making any big deal about it, Jason and Phoebe manage to live on the most perfectly egalitarian terms that Sasha's ever witnessed, since the black day—September 8, 1960—on which her own darling Maurice had passed—too young!—away. But, then, nobody has ever had a marriage such as theirs had been.

"Then again, Maurice," Sasha points out, having still the habit of speaking to her absent husband, a habit she had been forced to develop early on in the marriage, "in all sincerity, how many would have *wanted* it?"

All and all, Jason really is—especially if one takes into account whence he has sprung—Beatrice!—a wunderkind, this time with the emphasis on the *first* syllables.

Listening in on the conversation of those two, Jason and Phoebe, even a rational person might come to the conclusion that they, too, had been destined for one another; that an angel might have announced it, when Jason was still a twinkle in Beatrice's eyes: "Jason the son of Nat the orthodontist, to Phoebe the daughter of Chloe the classicist."

Who could have thought that there could be two such beings in the whole world as Jason and Phoebe? One such is unlikely enough.

When these two talk their impenetrable language of symbols and equations, deducing one thing from another with the fleetness of the six-winged seraphim, then, my God, you feel like a complete child next to them. Not just a child. A *stupid* child. Not only are they, these two, as happy as two socialists on strike in this brave new world of hardware and software and whatware, of which Sasha, personally, wants no part. It is people like them—people whose imaginations don't travel the normal story lines, don't crave the human element—who are writing the cold bright future encoded on electronic disks (the words themselves make Sasha shudder), who are creating this awesome systematic Something-or-Other that is as elaborate and remote and—frankly, to Sasha's taste, though Maurice had disagreed—as little appealing as Spinoza's *Deus sive Natura*.

But when these two wunderkinder talk about anything that remotely touches upon the murky doings of the world, when they are called upon to show a little insight into human motivation, into what Sasha's director, Hershel Blau—by the way, a *genius*—used to call the *ta'am*, which is the taste, of the plot, then, my God, you feel that it is *they* who are the children. The fairy tales, the happily-ever-after *shtuss*, which is nonsense, that these two believe!

An angel must have announced it: "Jason, the D.M.S. with the eager puppy-dog eyes, to Phoebe, the Princeton mathematician of froth."

Nevertheless, as fond as Sasha has come to feel of Jason, she does sometimes find herself wishing that Phoebe, so unhardened herself, might have found a more toughened-up soulmate, somebody who would be capable of offering some knowledge of, and protection from, the world, on the day its chaos decides to turn nasty.

Of course, there would *always* be Jason's parents, Nat and Beatrice, *especially* Beatrice, ready to step in and take over, an omnipresence which is both a blessing and a curse.

Well, Sasha supposes there must be a blessing buried in there somewhere.

Sasha has grown very fond of Jason, but she can never bring herself to think of Nat and Beatrice, *especially* Beatrice, as anything but a drag to the nth degree.

"Don't get me started on that woman," Sasha tells her friends. "Don't get me started on the inexhaustible subject of that woman's chutzpa!"

What a maven of pettiness that Beatrice is, rushing in where angels fear to tread.

Beatrice is a micro-manager, who has only her two children's lives—and now Phoebe's—to manage. She's always on the lookout for some deviation from her pathetically narrow definition of the norm.

"Of course, the major deviation Beatrice has suffered to date is that her own Jason is married to a girl who has Chloe as a mother and me as a grandmother!"

The questions the woman would put to Phoebe! *Unbelievably* nervy. Questions that Chloe herself, Phoebe's *own mother*, would never think to ask.

Hadn't Sasha seen how scrupulous Chloe had always been on the matter of Phoebe's privacy? Even when Phoebe was a child?

It's a subtle business, mothers and daughters. And Chloe, God bless her, Chloe was *born* with subtlety.

"And don't I know it?" Sasha would ask, with her wonderfully rich laugh. (Don't even *ask* what that laugh had been capable of doing back in Warsaw.)

But what does Beatrice Kantor know of these subtleties? About as much as she cares to know.

For her part, Sasha would love to set off a bomb under that woman's *Weltanschauung.*

Where *has* she been living?

Well, yes, in Lipton.

But how, even *there,* could she have managed to take in so little of *the world at large?*

"Yes, she's quite a character," Beatrice tells *her* legions of friends, with her little "public" laugh, putting a brave face on it.

Only her most intimate friends, sworn to secrecy, know anything of the lingering bitterness with which Beatrice has swallowed the hard pill of Sasha. And not even these intimates know anything about what Beatrice regards as Sasha's Past (of which Beatrice actually knows very little of what there is to know).

"Yes, of course, I've had a *Past,*" Sasha would have retorted, were she made privy to Beatrice's panting suspicions. "Of course I've had a *Past! I've had a Life!*"

"Those children were offered *no choices* in life," Sasha, for her part scandalized, says to *her* friends, referring to Jason and his sister, Debby, who is "still unmarried," though only Beatrice, again to quote Sasha, would describe a girl of twenty-two as "still unmarried." (Beatrice is "sick with worry" that Debby graduated college without an engagement ring. Every new wedding invitation arriving from one of Debby's friends, who are all "falling like flies," deepens Beatrice's despair.)

"Those children absolutely *had* to duplicate Nat and Beatrice's lives. No questions asked. No choices offered. Here is the plan, step by step, from cradle to grave. Take it or take it."

Chloe is very noncommittal on the subject of Phoebe's in-laws, though she laughs quite willingly at Sasha's endlessly sarcastic remarks about them.

In her shoe-box New York kitchen, Sasha, stir-frying some baby shrimp and cellophane noodles as Chloe looks on, will suddenly switch into Beatrice commenting on Sasha's cooking:

"Oh, do you do it like that?" asks Sasha-*cum*-Beatrice.

Sasha's ear is professionally acute, and she captures Beatrice's heavy, slightly nasal intonation exactly, so that there can be no doubt of whom she's impersonating.

"Well, of course, I suppose you *could* do it that way. But don't you think using chopsticks is going just a little bit too far? I suppose that's your *theatrical background*."

Sasha-*cum*-Beatrice has managed to make *"theatrical background"* sound like maybe it was *"venereal disease."*

Chloe laughs at Sasha's little improvisation, and yet she seems remarkably willing to take the Kantors, even Beatrice, as they are. She still consistently declines the invitation to disdain, even though Beatrice, for her part, patronizes Chloe *outrageously.*

But Chloe, or so Sasha explains to *her* friends, is on such a higher *level* of *existence,* that she doesn't even *notice.* (Actually, here Sasha is wrong.)

And, as noncommittal as Chloe is, Phoebe's even more so. Sasha knows that, if she, *God forbid,* had had a mother-in-law like Beatrice Kantor, they would either have lived on opposite sides of the universe, or have poisoned each other's existence, continuously and beyond endurance.

But here is Phoebe, living in this same small little town—not even a town: a village, a *hamlet*—with this overbearing mother-in-law, and taking it all in her stride.

Where, Sasha had wondered aloud to Chloe (who had smiled), had Phoebe learned to accept with such equanimity the intrusive attentions of such a *domineering woman?*

The amazing thing, as Sasha herself acknowledges, is that Phoebe, raised in a context of so much freedom, and Jason, raised with virtually *no freedom at all,* have ended up together, sharing one life and worldview, in this warped little region of space and time called Lipton, New Jersey.

Snuggled up together here, Phoebe and Jason—*and* Beatrice and Nat and all the rest of them, in spite of delusions of glamour and pretensions to worldliness—can convince themselves, in these closing years of the twentieth century, that it's the outside world that's warped and unreal. Together, they've taken the stuff of chaos and tried to give it the texture of coziness. Did they really imagine that they had managed to insulate themselves, in those indistinguishable split-levels, from the slings and arrows of outrageous mazel?

Dream on! Sasha inwardly hoots, and it's as if she could hear the soft, mocking laughter, almost too faint to catch, that used to waft out from the vacated studyhouse into Shluftchev's dark night.

This is, for her, an old fight, a very old fight. And it has everything—*everything*—to do with Fraydel. So how can Sasha ever give it a rest?

But there are days—increasingly frequent—when Sasha does give it a rest. The irony of the situation isn't lost on her, and she can't help bestowing on it a certain begrudging admiration: from one artist to another.

And today—beneath the blossom-heavy apple tree, beside the blooming Phoebe, who's balancing a Princeton bluebook on her ripened belly—today, of all days, Sasha gives it a rest.

Beatrice, however, doesn't. Beatrice has already called *several* times this morning:

Beatrice was going to "the avenue" and wanted to know if Phoebe needed anything.

(Are you cooking tonight?" Phoebe asks Sasha.

Sometimes when Sasha visits, she cooks. The fact is, those regulation split-levels come equipped with a very nice kitchen, very sensibly laid out, and Sasha often gives in to the impulse to cook up a storm.

"I don't think I'm cooking tonight, darling," Sasha answers, thinking to herself that this is *not a time to be thinking about food.*)

Beatrice has just tried to get in touch with Jason at his office, and he doesn't answer. Does Phoebe, by any chance, know where he is?

Beatrice has now been able to track Jason down at Hau Wong's office, and is just calling, this time, to inform Phoebe should the need arise.

"How do you manage to get anything *done* with that woman constantly pestering you?" Sasha demands. "Does she think you're as unoccupied as she is? Doesn't she realize that you have to *get your marking done?*"

"She's worse than usual today," Phoebe answers, smiling up at Sasha. "Maybe she also has a feeling that the baby's going to be early."

"A *feeling?* Since when, my darling rationalist granddaughter, do you consider knowledge to be a mere *feeling?*"

Sasha's smile gives away the precise degree to which her statement is self-parody: not high enough for you even to consider dismissing the content of what she says.

Sasha's prescience doesn't extend to the gender of Phoebe's baby, at least not so Sasha's telling.

Beatrice on the other hand, has gone down on record, repeatedly.

"It's a boy," she declared triumphantly, as soon as Phoebe began to show.

"The way you're carrying, it's definitely a boy."

Hearing her complacent declaration, Sasha always smiles mysteriously, so that Phoebe wonders what exactly her grandmother knows, or at any rate thinks that she knows.

So far as Beatrice's pronouncement is concerned, it's too interested to be of any predictive value. Beatrice, who has her mystical side, has long been offering Phoebe the end slices of bread loaves, having somewhere along the way acquired the belief that the consumption of such by a woman of childbearing possibilities produces males.

Beatrice tries to manage everything. Or perhaps (interesting thought) there's an element of self-parody in Beatrice as well?

In any case, when the phone rings, yet again, Sasha commands Phoebe to sit and goes off to deal with Beatrice Kantor for herself. On no account will Sasha tell Beatrice what she knows, or Beatrice will be over here, together with the Lipton First Aid Squad, before you can say *mazel tov.*

But Phoebe knows, by the way Sasha, loping back across the lawn, is animatedly talking to the person on the other end, that that person isn't Beatrice. Rather, in all likelihood, it's Chloe, who's also busy marking final exams. She has three unusually large classes this semes-

ter, and the bluebooks, piled up in the midst of all of her other preoc-
cupations this spring, have taken on the aura of a penance.

Every once in a while, Chloe allows herself a little break from her
marking and goes out for a walk on Broadway. More often than not, she
ends up browsing in a wonderful baby store on Broadway at 77th; First
Treasures, very Yuppie and pricey. These little outings invigorate her,
so that she returns to the apartment ready to tackle her students' garbled Greek once again.

"Some more dead languages for our family," Sasha had whooped
with laughter, when Chloe, then a junior at Barnard, had first announced her decision to major in the classics.

It's probably no accident that Sasha, a woman born to hold center
stage, should have a daughter who makes such a wonderful audience,
unstintingly giving of the gift of her attention, but rarely feeling the
need to step out of the shadows and over the footlights.

In the heady spring of '68, when the Columbia University campus
had blossomed into a colorful riot of rebellion, Sasha in a bandana had
been a presence at the barricades, while Chloe, although of the right
generation, had entirely sat out the revolution, grateful that the canceled classes gave her more time to read and be with her daughter. So
unlike her mother, whose drama is always *out there* for everyone to see—
constantly—Chloe's drama, no less intense, is kept quietly to herself.

What a thing, then, that Chloe should have recently found herself
the astonished cynosure of a minor academic event she's unwittingly
created around herself.

A little scholarly article she published—taking off from Medea's
act of infanticide to examine the images of mothers and motherhood in
Greek drama—has, for reasons still obscure to Chloe herself, been seen
by some as implying the next wave of feminist criticism, and as pernicious retrogression by others.

Chloe, who had naïvely thought herself only to have been reading
the texts as closely as she could, doesn't quite know how to react to the
little drama in which she's reluctantly starring, and, in fact, has only
the dimmest grasp of the political issues involved.

"How's the tempest in the teapot?" Sasha's asking her. "Or should I say the inquest in the inkpot? Any death-threats in the mail today?"

Yes: it's definitely Chloe.

"You don't say? What a thing. You wouldn't think it could be so dangerous to write about the fifth century B.C.

"But listen, darling, listen to me. We have some news that's a little more current. Hold on a minute."

Sasha hands Phoebe the receiver.

"*You* tell her. Tell her to get herself down to Penn Station immediately if not sooner.

"Tell her: *twenty-four hours at the most!*"

PART II

Shluftchev, Galicia

The 1920s

he boy with the brains but no luck was born to a very poor woman who couldn't afford to give her child any education, and he grew up hungry and in rags. But a goldsmith in the village noticed the intelligent gleam in the boy's eyes and made the boy his apprentice. Before long, the apprentice had far surpassed his master. Since there was nothing more for him to learn from his master, he decided to seek his opportunity in a larger city. The goldsmith regretted losing his skillful apprentice, but the boy was eager to make his way in the world.

He wandered about until he came to the capital city, where the King of the land lived. This seemed the right place for a young man with expectations. Soon enough, he met an expert tailor who sewed the clothes for the royal family itself. The boy asked to be made apprentice to this tailor, and the tailor, seeing the intelligent gleam in the boy's eyes, agreed.

Before too long, the boy was inventing such wonderful new designs that the King himself called the tailor before him.

"Who is making these exquisite new clothes for the royal family?" asked the King.

"It is I, your most humble servant, your Highness," said the tailor, bowing low. "Every night, I lie awake in my bed and dream up new ideas to fashion in the morning."

The King was delighted and rewarded the tailor richly.

—To be continued

CHAPTER 3

SHADES OF NIGHT

*L*eiba's husband was a scholar, so Leiba supported the family through various enterprises. This was the way it was amongst the Jews. It was an honor for a woman to assume the financial burdens of the family, so that her husband might "sit and learn." Leiba was a very capable woman, with a good sense for business—with good sense, period.

All the women of Shluftchev, and even quite a few of the men, sought her advice. One of the wonderful things about Leiba was that, if she didn't know, she didn't pretend that she knew, which made her a rare person from whom to seek out opinions. But, between her home, her six children, and her various business interests, Leiba rarely had a moment to spare during the day for idle chatter.

Perhaps this is the reason why Sorel, who was Leiba's second-to-youngest child, got into the habit, starting when she was maybe two or three years old, of getting up in the dead of night to speak with her mother.

Sorel would go to sleep with the others. But then, sometime later, in the black stillness while the others slept, she would open her eyes, instantly becoming wide awake.

Carefully she'd climb out of the bed that she shared with her two sisters. Chana was a sound sleeper, but Fraydel often murmured in her dreams.

49

Suddenly wide awake, Sorel would creep out from under the eiderdown, and go off on bare feet to where her mother was preparing the next morning's bread.

Sorel knew that her mother enjoyed the solitude of her midnight house, the hush that fell like soft snow around her while the others slept, and for this reason Sorel was careful not to break the solitude. She only wanted to slip herself quietly into it, to slip herself in and have her mother all to herself.

Outside, the night was inky black, perilous with the unclean creatures Fraydel told her about in whispered stories, stories that took off with a wild life of their own, until even Fraydel herself was struck dumb with terror, the tears streaming down her pale cheeks, and her big, dark eyes gaping at whatever sight it was she saw. In her sleep she murmured, words that Sorel could never understand.

There was a ladder that led down from the loft where the three girls slept, a rickety wooden ladder, full of splinters, with six narrow slats for steps.

During the day, Sorel, who was always in a rush, would often get splinters, and have to submit to the probing point of a sewing needle that had been held in a sterilizing flame. Almost any sewing needle one might happen to pick up in the Sonnenberg house had an iridescent green-black sheen to it, having been used, at one time or another, to remove the splinters from Sorel's hands or feet.

It wasn't unusual either for her to slip on those narrow slats. The wind would get knocked out of her, and she wouldn't be able to find her voice for several terrifying seconds, not even to cry.

But in the darkness Sorel always made her way down with caution, tentatively feeling first with her toes before she'd shift her weight, and always in her bare feet, because stockings made the descent too treacherous.

It was icy cold in the winter, the dark, long winter of Galicia. Sorel's mother would gather her up and lift her high onto her own special nighttime place: the top of the clay oven.

There Sorel would sit, the fragrant warmth wafting upward from the logs burning within, her feet tucked under her long nightgown, and her mother all to herself.

Sorel's sisters and brothers knew nothing at all of this secret time that Sorel had discovered for herself in the middle of the night. They didn't know how different the house was then, the smell from the small kerosene lamp mingling with the sweet scent of Leiba's bread.

Sorel loved the taste of the raw dough, though her mother would allow her a piece no bigger than her tiniest finger, for fear it would give her a bellyache.

Often Sorel found her mother, sleeves rolled up over her muscular arms as she pummeled the dough, softly singing to herself.

Leiba had a beautiful singing voice. But during the day, Leiba would never have dared to sing, lest she be heard by some male outside of the family, which is forbidden by modesty.

Kol eesha: the voice of a woman. *Assur:* forbidden.

So it was only in the middle of the night, while all the rest of Shluftchev slept, that Leiba would sing. Their mother's singing was one of the nighttime secrets that Sorel jealously kept to herself.

All of Leiba's melodies wandered about in sad places, though you would think, to look at her, that Leiba knew nothing at all about such places. It was strange, the sad music that would come out of Leiba, as she pounded the dough in the night with her powerful fists.

Leiba looked up from the floury board to see Sorel silently peeking through the curtain. Who knew how long the child had been standing there?

When Leiba would look up and see her youngest daughter, wide awake in the middle of the night, sometimes she would break off her melody, and sometimes she wouldn't. But always she would dust off her floury hands on her apron and lift the child high onto the top of the warm clay oven.

For a few moments, it would be very quiet in the room.

"Sing, Mamma. Sing to me," Sorel would say, for fear that the quiet might tempt in something from the outside.

Sometimes Leiba would break the silence with a story. When Leiba wanted, she, too, could tell a good story, though, unlike Fraydel's stories, which took off with a wild life of their own, Leiba's stories all were true.

Some were the family stories, derived from both her side and her husband's. She herself came from a large and lively family—she had been one of eight children—so there were certainly plenty of good *mysah*s from which to choose.

It's important that a child know from where she's come, that a golden link of stories fix a child to her past. For this reason, all children, in their wisdom, love such stories.

Others of Leiba's stories came not from yesterday but from today. Her business interests took her out into the world, from which she brought back stories she would sometimes share with Sorel. Often she traveled all the way to Lemberg.

Unlike her husband, Nachum, and her two older sons, Asher and Dovid, who were, like their father, scholars, Leiba was fluent in Polish and Ukrainian, as well as Russian, and could converse with ease with the Gentiles.

Did she like doing business with the world? Who can say? But she understood the world very well and was never cheated in all her various enterprises.

All day long she was kept busy, running here, running there, buying up what could be had cheaply in one place, so that she could sell it at a small profit somewhere else. She bought up cosmetics in Lemberg, vials of lotions for the skin, and sold them to the women of Shluftchev and other *shtetlach*. Her husband was a scholar, the crown on Leiba's head, a beautiful man for whom the line separating the holy day of the Sabbath from the working weekday was blurred. It was she, Leiba, who inhabited the impure weekday, who knew the ways of buying and of selling, of scraping and of scurrying, of putting food on the table.

Sometimes, standing in the middle of the night pounding her dough, Leiba would think with a certain degree of amazement on her dealings with the world. How had she come to be buying here and selling there?

Six children sat at her table, like palm trees growing round a pool of water. Two infants, one a boy and one a girl, she had buried, and had locked her grief away in an airless box.

Sometimes Sorel imagined, while she sat in the midnight house with her mother, that she and her mother were alone on a boat, sailing across an ocean.

Sorel knew about the ocean from Fraydel, who had read in a book about the fantastic life that swarms down in its depths:

The leviathan, a giant sea serpent that lies coiled on the ocean's floor, holding in its vast body the spirit of rebellion, and on whom the righteous will feast in the days of our redemption.

Also creatures that are half woman and half fish, who sit on high rocks in the middle of the sea and sing strange songs that bewitch the sailors, so that they crash against the rocks and drown.

"Why are they so cruel?" Sorel had asked Fraydel.

Fraydel had shrugged her thin shoulders.

Though Fraydel was sixteen, she still had the body of a child, not of a woman. Even Chana, eighteen months younger, was already beginning to look like a girl of marriageable age, a *kalleh maydel*. Before one knew it, the marriage brokers would be approaching her parents. Other girls, only a little bit older than she, already had husbands of their own and sat together with one another on Sabbath mornings in the women's little section of the prayerhouse. They spoke behind their cupped hands, their heads, important in their marriage wigs, close to one another.

Before their betrothals, these girls had sat quietly beside their mothers and stared into their prayer books. But from the moment they got engaged, they were filled with conversation.

Every Sabbath morning, Chana sat beside her mother and stared at the young married women, not so much older than she, whispering to one another. Why did they always have so much to say to one another? Chana pictured herself sitting amongst them, a marriage wig on her head, whispering behind her cupped hand.

"Why are they so cruel?" Sorel had asked her sister Fraydel. "Why should they wish for the death of the passing sailors?"

Fraydel had shrugged.

"How can you say if they're cruel or not?" Fraydel had answered her. "You'd have to first think like a mermaid."

When Fraydel said things of this sort to her, Sorel would think about them for days and days.

The night outside was a black ocean, alive with roaming demons, just as the ocean Fraydel described to her was swarming with unseen marvels.

On a corner of the wooden breadboard, her mother had placed her wedding band while she kneaded the dough. Sorel was afraid something evil would snatch it away.

"Sing, Mamma." Her mother's voice had powers of keeping the uninvited from venturing across their threshold. Still, Sorel kept her eyes away from the low dark window, for fear of what might be staring back in.

Sometimes, just the same, Sorel caught a glimpse of a face, wild-eyed and leering. And though Leiba always assured the child that it was only her imagination, Sorel saw how Leiba herself would cast a quick eye at the black night outside, and how she would say a few words beneath her breath.

"Such things are," Leiba thought, "though it's better not to think of them."

It was said that in the dead of the night the studyhouse was inhabited by unclean hosts, who sat around the book-piled tables arguing points of the Law.

They would take the sense of the written words and turn them inside and out and upside and down, so that ugly blasphemies would emerge. Prohibitions would be changed into commandments to commit all manner of filth.

Soft, mocking laughter would follow the twisted words. And woe be to any Jew who heard that unholy laughter!

Such an unfortunate would be carried off by wickedness, or madness, or both.

Such things are, though it's better not to think of them. What's the use of such thinking?

Leiba saw the child give a quick frightened glance at the window. She looked for herself and saw nothing. Nevertheless, she murmured some words quickly under her breath.

"What are you saying, Mamma?"

"I'm asking the Holy One, blessed be He, to remember us with mercy and with kindness."

"Sing, Mamma."

Sorel would go to bed with the others, but then, sometime later, in the heavy stillness while the others slept, she would open her eyes, wide awake.

She lay between her two older sisters. Chana breathed slowly and evenly in her sleep, but Fraydel often murmured in her dreams, words that Sorel could never understand.

Sorel slept in the middle. Chana, who would sometimes fold her two arms across her chest in stubbornness, refused to sleep next to Fraydel, who tossed and turned all night long. And during the day, too, Chana kept her distance from Fraydel.

Chana, who had never had a mood in her life, was frightened by Fraydel's. Shamed by her own disloyalty to her family, Chana secretly believed the neighbors who said that Fraydel was somehow not completely right in the head.

"Is it anger that makes you do these things?" Leiba had asked Fraydel only this morning. "And if you are angry, then, please, I am begging you to tell me: why are you so angry?"

Sorel alone was not frightened of Fraydel's moods. Sorel alone understood that Fraydel didn't like to be bothered by people, and it was for this reason that she often pretended to be strange.

Once Sorel and Fraydel had been walking home in the dusk, and there had come up behind them a little group of small boys, returning home for the night from the cheder, each swinging a little wooden lantern to light the evening's shadows.

In Fraydel's long dark hair a few stray pine needles were entangled, and there was mud clinging to the hem of her woolen skirt.

One of the little cheder boys, Fischel, the son of the *shoychet,* the ritual slaughterer, had called out to the others:

"Look, it's Fraydel, the crazy girl!"
And all the little boys took up the chant:

> Fraydel, Fraydel, the crazy girl!
> *Fraydel, Fraydel, da meshuggena maydel!*

Fraydel had whirled herself around, so that she was facing her tormentors.

She had growled at them like a wild dog.

She had made her eyes fill up with a crazy look in them so that the boys had become truly frightened and had scattered home along the darkening road.

Seeing the fright that had erupted like a rash on their faces, the bulging eyes with which they had backed away and fled, Fraydel had laughed. She had turned her face back to Sorel and had laughed.

The blood showed through the thin skin of her cheeks in two circles of deep crimson. But her dark eyes, full of laughter, were as normal as those of any of the girls of Shluftchev.

Still, Sorel had put her hand back into Fraydel's with a small feeling of strangeness.

"Aren't you afraid that if you make your eyes go crazy like that you might really become crazy?" Sorel had finally asked Fraydel.

"An interesting thought," Fraydel had answered. "From that interesting thought it would further follow"—Fraydel's voice mimicked the singsong intonation with which the men studied the Talmud aloud with one another—"that all one must do is smile in order to be happy."

When Fraydel said things like that to her, Sorel went around thinking about them for days and days.

Sorel understood that Fraydel didn't want to be bothered by people, and that this was the reason she sometimes frightened them away. And because she understood this, Sorel was not really frightened. Not really.

Fraydel allowed Sorel, and Sorel alone, to hold her hand. For the rest, Fraydel hated to be touched. So, during the day, Sorel restrained herself from kissing her sister. But sometimes in the night, while Fraydel slept, Sorel would stroke Fraydel's hair, or plant a small soft kiss on Fraydel's thin white arm—a very soft kiss, so as not to disturb Fraydel's fitful sleep.

Sorel's eyes opened into the darkness. Fraydel murmured something in her sleep.

Sorel slipped out from under the heavy eiderdown and climbed carefully over her sister Chana.

The cold immediately penetrated her nightgown. Like icy water, it soaked through her skin.

The house had only one big room below. At the back was the "kitchen," a curtain hung from the ceiling to separate it from the rest of the house, where the others slept.

Leiba stood, softly singing over her dough.

Leiba, having thoughts of her own to think on this night, gave the child some dough to shape into her own little loaf.

"This one will be like me, made for hard work," Leiba thought, watching the child's capable little hands at their task. "This one will, thank God, always be able to take care of herself."

Leiba, who worked night and day, had the strong person's pity for those who are weak, for those who sit idle from weakness.

Leiba prayed to the Only One that she would remain of use, all the days of her life. It was all that she asked for herself. For others, of course, she asked more.

"Teach me the song you were singing, Mamma."

"That song? That's not a real song. It's just something I was singing."

"Then teach me a real song."

So Leiba called her thoughts back from the places you would never have thought she knew anything about and taught the child a song of the Breslover Chasidim.

Know that a person walks in life on a very high and narrow
     bridge.
The most important rule is not to be afraid.

"This one is like me," Leiba thought, listening to the child sweetly singing the melody she'd just been taught. "This one will, thank God, always be able to take care of herself."

"I don't understand you, Fraydel."

Leiba had said this, even though, with the good sense that made others seek out her opinion, she knew that it would do no good.

"Is it anger that makes you do these things? And if you are angry, then, please, I am begging you to tell me: why are you so angry?"

And Fraydel had stared unblinking at her mother for several moments and then had shrugged her thin shoulders and looked away.

Leiba's two strong arms had almost gone out from her with a will of their own.

She would have liked to take hold of those two thin shoulders, and pull the child close to herself, to gather her up and hold her near.

She would also have liked to take hold of those two thin shoulders and give them a good hard shake.

But Leiba's two capable hands had stayed down at her sides, of no use to her or her child.

"Sing, Mamma," Sorel said, afraid of what the quiet would invite inside.

Leiba would let Sorel sit there until she'd see the child's eyelids begin to flutter downward. Then Leiba would gather the child up and return her to her bed.

Leiba had also all her life needed less sleep than others. It was a trait that ran deep in her family.

Leiba's own father, Rav Dovid, may he intercede on High in our behalf, had been famous in his lifetime for his ability to go without sleep.

In the papers that were left after his death, he revealed that, as some of his students had suspected, he had used these nights for the study of the Cabala, delving into the utmost mystery of things.

Rav Dovid had been afraid for his students to know what it was he studied through his sleepless nights, lest any had wanted, God forbid, to follow his example.

Long ago, in the days of Rav Dovid's youth, a brilliant young yeshiva student had lost hold of his senses—may it never happen here—through the study of the Cabala.

He had appeared one morning with a chamber pot on his head, proclaiming it to be his long-lost skullcap. Laughing, he had taken the words of the Law and turned them inside and out, so that what was good was made bad, and bad was good.

Such things are, Rav Dovid knew. Such things can happen to a mind not yet ready to delve into the utmost mysteries of things.

Nonetheless, it was the custom of Rav Dovid, on certain weekday nights, to stay up in the study of the Cabala, while his wife, Terza, and their eight children slept.

It helps, of course, to have a wife, Terza, together with eight children, sleeping in the next room. But even so one must know that one walks on a very high and narrow bridge.

God forbid, then, that Rav Dovid's example should encourage any of his students to venture out over such treacherous, dark waters.

God forbid, for the young yeshiva student who had gone mad had been Rav Dovid's own beloved brother, Asher.

Nobody knew better than Rav Dovid what a high and narrow bridge he walked through his sleepless nights.

In the papers Rav Dovid left after his death, he had recounted the following story:

One night, sitting before his study table, he had heard a sharp rap at the window just behind him.

It was an hour deep in the night, in the bitter-cold month of Shvat.

Rav Dovid turned around and saw staring in at him the face of a man he himself had buried some years before.

Rav Dovid bent to pick up from the floor the holy volume he had dropped and softly kissed it. Only then did he go to the front door.

He opened it, and there stood the shade, may it never happen here, barefoot on the frozen ground and dressed in his shroud.

"I knew you would be up on this night, Rav Dovid," the dead man said. "And so I have come forth from my grave to speak to you."

"Speak," answered Rav Dovid. "But do so in a quiet voice. If you were to awaken my wife and she, God forbid, were to see you, then she would die from the fright."

"Rav Dovid," said the man. "Do you remember where it was that I was buried?"

"I remember. You were buried in the donkey's grave."

And at this the dead man began soundlessly to weep, as he must have been weeping all the years in the earth.

"Because I am a member of the priestly caste, and I nevertheless took, for my second wife, a divorced woman, Brayna Schneck."

"Assur," said Rav Dovid. "Forbidden. A *kohen* must not marry a divorced woman!"

"But I was lonely after my first wife died. And I was frightened, because I could feel in my body that my final sickness had entered. So I married the divorcée Brayna Schneck, even though I knew it was forbidden. And because of this marriage I am not allowed to keep my final rest within the walls!"

"That is right," said Rav Dovid, nodding. "That is as it must be. A defiled man cannot be put into consecrated ground."

"But I can find no repose in my donkey's grave!" the dead man had moaned, his head slowly going from side to side. "Rebbe! The dead, too, need the comfort of their own kind. The dead above all!"

Rav Dovid had stared for several minutes into the hollow eyes of his nighttime visitor.

In the early morning, when the men arrived at the studyhouse, there was no Rav Dovid. The others immediately became alarmed, knowing that only some misfortune could have delayed him past the hour for prayer.

The sexton was just about to run over to the rabbi's house when another spotted Rav Dovid hurrying from the hilltop that lay outside the town, a shovel over his shoulder.

Rav Dovid said nothing about his nighttime visitor, only asking that a glass of water be brought to him so that he might wash his hands of death's uncleanliness.

While Rav Dovid had lived, he had never explained to anyone why he had been seen coming before the morning prayers from the direction of the cemetery, with a shovel on his arm. But in the papers that he had left, there had been an account of the dead man's visit.

Such things are, though it's better not to think about them. Such things have also been made in accordance with His holy word, the veil of modesty placed so as to conceal with kindness all that is unclean in spirit.

So where's the wisdom in thinking of such things?

Sorel stood waiting before the curtain for her mother, softly singing over her dough, to look up and see her. Leiba dusted the flour off from her hands and gathered the child up into her two strong arms.

Sorel knew that her mother enjoyed the solitude of her midnight house, the hush that fell like soft snow around her while the others slept.

Against the low window the night pressed in with pitchy blackness, opaque as the night that had once fallen on Egypt.

Leiba called her thoughts back from the places you would never have believed she knew anything about and smiled at her youngest daughter, wide awake with her in the middle of the night.

This girl was no *fershlofeneh,* no drowsy soul. Of all her children, Leiba thought, this child was the one most like herself.

Leiba dusted off the flour from her hands so that she could gather the child for a few moments to her. She breathed deeply, inhaling the sweet scent of her childhood.

She would tell Sorel one of the stories the child loved, perhaps a story from yesterday, perhaps from today.

Sorel met her mother's smile with solemn eyes.

"What is it?" Leiba asked Sorel, seeing the strange look on the child's face, as if she were straining to hear something outside in the night, almost too faint to catch.

Sorel stared at her mother for several seconds before speaking.

"I'm wondering, Mamma, what would it be like to think like a mermaid?"

CHAPTER 4

A SABBATH AFTERNOON
IN AV

*I*n the month of Av, the days are very long.

After the Sabbath meal has been eaten, the Sabbath songs have been sung, and the table has been cleared off, the afternoon can seem to stretch on to eternity. Sometimes it's hard to know what to do with one's self, especially if one's self is still a child.

Leiba was taking her Sabbath-afternoon nap. So far as the children knew, it was the only time of the week that Leiba ever slept. The children's father was sitting and learning with his two older sons, Asher and Dovid, at the cleared-off table. The soft singsong of their study floated out of the window to where Chana and Sorel sat on the front step, watching the baby, Bezalel.

And Fraydel? Who ever knew where Fraydel was?

Even though Fraydel was the oldest girl in the Sonnenberg family, it was Chana, a little mother by nature, who helped out in the house and largely took care of little Tzali. Only these days it was harder to watch Tzali. Chana was not a person who liked to run. And since the day when Bezalel had suddenly picked himself up and started to walk, watching him called for a lot of running. Bezalel was a handful, which is why Chana generally tried to enlist Sorel's hands, as well as her two fast legs, in the effort he presented.

"Catch him, Sorel," Chana called now after her little sister. "Catch him before he goes near the puddle."

In the middle of Shluftchev there was a puddle.

In the autumn rains the puddle swelled, in the winter it froze, and in the summer it dwindled. But always it was there, smelling bad, especially in the summer.

Fraydel had various theories as to why the puddle of Shluftchev smelled so bad.

Sometimes she told Sorel that all the memories of Shluftchev had sunk into its bottom, the overwhelming majority of which were of a sort to give off just such a smell.

Sometimes she told Sorel that it was the Evil Eye itself that sat staring up at them from its slimy face.

"It's the stink of Evil, Sorel. The stink of Evil, pure and simple. All over the world, Jews—and Moslems, too, I've read—pray that the Evil Eye be kept far away from them, while we in Shluftchev are keeping it safe for the world in a puddle."

The people of Shluftchev walked around the puddle, as they went about their business. The children also learned to suck in their breath at just the right moment of passing it in order to avoid the worst of its smell. Only Bezalel had not yet learned that the puddle was a thing to be avoided. To Bezalel the puddle was the source of endless fascination.

"Maybe he can see the Evil Eye staring up at him," Fraydel had speculated to Sorel. "Maybe that's what draws him."

It was another of Fraydel's beliefs—though who knew if she really believed it?—that Tzali, who could not yet talk, had the power of seeing the unseen forms impressed into the ordinary, a power he would lose the moment he uttered his first word.

"The same thing happened to you, Sorel. The rest of them looked at me like I was crazy when I cried because you had begun to talk."

None of the assorted yelps, grunts, and chortles that Bezalel emitted—expressive as they were—qualified as a word, and whether this accounted for his fascination with the puddle, who can say? Chana had just now turned her back on him for only a moment, and he, the little bandit, had taken off on his surprisingly fast legs.

Sorel raced down the road and managed to grab him by the back of his short fancy Sabbath pants, just inches away from his desire. But then, in a move that no one—not even Bezalel himself—could have anticipated, he gave a lusty shriek and a desperate lurch, so that Sorel was left, astonished, holding the fancy short Sabbath pants by their suspenders, and Bezalel was sprawled up to his waist in the puddle.

This was, even for Tzali, too much of a good thing, and he began to howl.

"*Gevalt!*" Chana screamed, and herself came running. She was a stocky girl and very unaccustomed to running, so that she was red-faced and panting by the time she reached the puddle, even though it was only the length of six or seven houses away.

The one thing good that could be said for the situation was that Tzali's Sabbath short pants were still safely in Sorel's hands, perfectly clean.

"Drop them!" Chana had the presence of mind to order her sister, who was profaning the Sabbath by carrying.

Chana didn't hesitate, however, to lift Tzali out of the puddle— God forbid, he could drown!—keeping her two arms rigidly straight out from her gray taffeta Sabbath dress.

She deposited him on dry land, whereupon Bezalel looked down at himself and was so astonished that he immediately hiccuped into silence. He looked up at the two girls with utter incredulity in his blue eyes and then looked down again, pointing with his little muddy finger at his transfigured shoes, which had luckily stayed on his feet and not sunk to the bottom of the puddle, to sit with all of Shluftchev's memories.

He was, at least under better circumstances, a beautiful child. As was the custom, his hair had not yet been cut, and hung around his face, on better days, in long blond ringlets. None of the Sonnenberg sisters had hair quite so beautiful, so fine and so silky, as their little brother's.

When their two older brothers, Asher and Dovid, now swaying over their tracts of Talmud, had been Bezalel's age, they, too, had had such beautiful hair, until the day they had turned three, and all the curls except the earlocks had been cut off, in preparation for the beginning of their studies.

"*Gevalt,*" Chana murmured now, more calmly. She gave Sorel an exasperated look, but didn't rebuke her for failing to prevent Tzali's plunge.

Chana was the sort of person who was always much better after a crisis than before. Before, she only moaned and bellyached. After, she set about repairing the damage.

She took the handkerchief she wore around her wrist and wiped the mud away from the baby's mouth and eyes. Tzali, still stupefied, permitted Chana's attentions with an indifference completely out of his character.

He followed Chana docilely back down the road, still pointing in amazement, every now and then, down at his shoes, answering the squelching noise they made at every step with his own remarkably good impression.

"Wait right here for me," Chana told Sorel, indicating the step.

The moment Chana, followed by the squelching Tzali, disappeared inside the house, Fraydel appeared from behind a house across the road.

She was still laughing, holding one fist over her mouth. It was several moments before she could speak.

"Which was funnier?" she asked Sorel, and then again was halted by her laughter.

Fraydel laughed like a person who didn't know how, choking on it as if it were some foreign substance sticking in her throat, so that Sorel felt more sorry for Fraydel when she laughed than at any other time.

"Which was funnier," Fraydel finally managed to ask Sorel, "Tzali flying into the puddle, or Chana running with her fat behind down the road?"

Suddenly Fraydel began to pantomime the events, gliding out of one part and into another, like a Cabalistic soul slipping between bodies: Bezalel, a wicked gleam coming into his eye as he saw Chana's back turn, making his escape; Chana clapping her hands to her face and shouting "*Gevalt!*" Sorel left holding the fancy short pants; Chana running heavily down the road; Bezalel, dished up from the depths, pointing at his shoes like at the path back to Paradise. Sorel sat on the front step and applauded.

"Come," Fraydel suddenly said, holding out her hand for Sorel to take. Although Fraydel was small and underdeveloped for her age, she had a surprisingly elegant hand, with long slender fingers and perfectly oval nails. Her feet, too, were long and narrow.

Her mother had told her that she still had much growing to do. With such a hand and foot, Leiba had said, she was meant to be tall. Not, of course, like Leiba herself. Perhaps more like Grandma Terza.

Fraydel had seemed pleased to hear this.

She had held up her hand before her face and smiled at it, as if it had done her a favor.

It was a very warm Sabbath day in Av, and Fraydel had rolled her long brown hair into a knot on top of her head, which was becoming.

Fraydel had a habit of hiding behind her thick hair, pulling it over her face as if it were a veil. Now, with it knotted on top of her head, one could see how large and how beautiful her dark eyes were, and how graceful her neck was. She was wearing her summer Sabbath dress, pale-yellow taffeta with delicate lace scallops at the wrists and at the high neck.

Sorel, looking up at her now, thought how beautiful she was. Fraydel's fit of laughter had left behind a light flush on her cheeks, which softened her face, dissolving the harsh cast that sometimes settled over it and displaced what was sweet and girlish in it.

"Come," Fraydel said, offering Sorel her elegant hand. Only Sorel was allowed to take hold of Fraydel's hand. "Let's go for a walk in the woods. We need to cool down after so much excitement."

Shluftchev was a little place, a shtetl, or village, like many others, in the eastern part of Galicia. It had fewer than a hundred families, almost all of them Jewish, although there were plenty of Gentiles living in the surrounding countryside.

It had laborers, scholars, a ritual slaughterer, a cheder teacher.

It had a cemetery, a studyhouse, a prayerhouse, a post office with a telegraph.

It had a few better-off people, many paupers . . . and a puddle.

Its buildings were wooden, largely unwhitewashed, largely dilapidated. All of them stared out with blind empty eyes, so that, for a stranger, it would be hard to tell one from another. At least from the outside, the houses of the very poor didn't differ noticeably from the houses of those who were considered better off. Unlike their peasant neighbors, who were always whitewashing and hammering, sawing and planting, the Jews gave little thought to their houses and gardens.

The Jews had lived here for centuries. The cemetery on the hill was crowded with the bones of ancestors, the ancient headstones leaning together like old friends. Still, even the few in Shluftchev who enjoyed some means acquired only the kind of possessions that could be packed in a suitcase.

Shluftchev had just one road, and that one was unpaved, a river of mud in the autumn rains. If one followed this road out of Shluftchev for about a quarter of a kilometer and then turned off of it to the west, cutting across a peasant's field, one came to the pine forest. The road itself eventually ran near the pine forest, but one came to the forest much more quickly if one cut across the peasant's field.

There was no one else in Shluftchev, or in the neighboring village of Verchnikovitz, who knew the pine forest so well as Fraydel. She would go sometimes as far as the little clearing near the crossroads, where the Christian shrine stood.

Leiba had long ago given up as futile any effort to prevent Fraydel from wandering, just as she had given up forbidding Fraydel to read all sorts of *shtuss* in books.

It wasn't, of course, that Leiba herself had anything against books. There were books, secular books even, that touched a place so deep in the soul you would think that surely these books whispered a blessing on the Name. Leiba herself, when she was a girl living in the house of her father, Rav Dovid Broder, of blessed memory, would also often sleepwalk through her days, her eyes blank with dreams, and her head full of books.

During the summer months, she used to hide a borrowed book beneath some stones near the outhouse, the only place where she could snatch a few moments of freedom from the unceasing demands of the house and the eyes of her mother—

—*a door with a latch, a most precious strip of thin metal, bolt it quickly*

across the jamb and—freedom—sinking herself deep down into reading that
would close above her head like quiet water, breathing in the thick element of
another world, gulping it in, so deep and so sweet, time itself blotted out, the
world she knew reduced to a few faint noises from a faraway distance, having
nothing to do with her, no claim to make on her, until a knock on the outhouse
door would rudely jolt her to her senses—

Still, one must beware of books, even if they're beautiful—
especially if they're beautiful—resisting the pull of the pagan fascination. The idols of old lay smashed, their clay tongues dust. But the
luminous forms of the Greeks still hover near the ear, whispering,
whispering. Who can ever silence the Greeks?

And who in Shluftchev didn't know this? Who in Shluftchev
would deny that there are books that ought never to have been written,
dreams that you must banish like evil thoughts?

Only Fraydel, somehow, didn't seem to know this. Any book on
which she could get her hands had the power to absorb her entirely.
Give her a book on the constellations of the stars in the sky, or the
adventures of Marco Polo in China, a silly sentimental tale of love by
Shomer, or homilies on the modesty appropriate to Jewish girls: if it
was printed, Fraydel would devour it. The words she drank in from the
page seemed, more than the food at which she barely nibbled on her
plate, to give her the little nourishment sustaining her.

In her head there were so many stories, stories she had read, stories
she had invented, that it was a wonder she could keep them all straight.

"Is it true?" Sorel would sometimes ask her sister about some tale
or other that Fraydel had just related to her. *"S'iz an emesa mysah?"*

"True?" Fraydal would wrinkle her brow—whether in perplexity or
distaste, who can say?

Shraga the book-peddler came to Shluftchev once every other
month, walking beside his skinny nag, Beena, whom he treated with
such a tender consideration that many a woman wished in her heart
that her husband should only give a look.

Shraga was a God-fearing man whom Leiba trusted. She trusted
that no books of harmful intent would find their way into Fraydel's im-
patient hands and head.

Some others would disagree with Leiba, of course, though in Shluftchev itself it was hard to find anyone who voiced fault with Leiba.

Still, if a girl must have a book, there was the *Tz'enah Ur'enah*, especially written for women, to teach them a little Torah on Sabbath afternoons. Beyond that, what did a girl need from books? It was from freedom and idleness that all the problems sprang, may God preserve us.

But Leiba, having taken note of the fact that Fraydel's moods took a frightening turn for the worse when she was left with nothing to read, had long ago given up forbidding her to read what she would, just as she had given up forbidding her to wander.

"Come," Fraydel said now, holding out her elegant hand for Sorel to take.

Sorel immediately put her hand into Fraydel's and jumped up off the step.

"Wait for me just one little minute, Fraydel, I just have to run into the house, quick as a wink, and tell Chana that I'm going with you."

"Forget Chana," Fraydel said, making a dismissive wave with her hand.

Sorel hesitated. She didn't have Fraydel's freedom, to come and go as she pleased. Still, she hated to cross Fraydel.

"Mamma will want to know where I am," she said now, very softly.

"All right, all right," Fraydel answered. "Only be careful that Chana doesn't decide to come along with us."

Fraydel was clearly in a good mood. But even in the best of her moods, she could work up little patience for Chana.

Sorel walked into the Sabbath-hushed house. The shutters were closed against the harsh heat of Av. When you came in from the hot outdoors, it felt cool and fuzzy inside, like the bottom of a mushroom.

Chana was just laying a cleaned-up Tzali into the little crib that hung by four ropes from a hook in the ceiling. She placed a warning finger over her lips, leaned down, and gave the baby boy his sucking rag soaked in milk and sugar, and a little motherly kiss. She softly whispered, "Sleep well, little bandit," and then tiptoed out with Sorel.

"That was easy," said Chana. "He was so exhausted that he lay down almost by his own will."

"Maybe we should throw him in the puddle more often," Sorel said.

Chana looked at her as if she were, God forbid, crazy.

Fraydel had once told Sorel that, when Chana had been a little baby, their mother had once asked Fraydel to watch her on the table, and Fraydel hadn't paid close enough attention and had let Chana roll off of the table and onto the floor.

"Often I've thought to myself that maybe that fall is what did it. She must have hit her head right on the part of the brain that understands a joke.

"So I suppose, since it's my fault, I ought to feel sorry for her. Only somehow I don't.

"Maybe," she added after a few more seconds of thought, cocking her head to the right side as she often did, "maybe someone once dropped me on the head, and I hit the part of my brain that's supposed to feel sorry for Chana."

"I just came in to tell you that I'm going for a walk with Fraydel," Sorel now said to Chana.

"No," Chana said, crossing her arms over her chest. "You can't."

"Why not?"

"Because Fraydel loses track of the time."

"I'll keep track of the time."

"No."

"Why not?"

"Because I trust you to keep track of the time as much as I trust Fraydel."

"As soon as I see the sky beginning to turn dark, I'll bring Fraydel home. I promise."

"First of all, it's a sin to make a promise. Second of all, how can I believe your promise if you don't even know enough not to make a promise?"

"Sorel," Fraydel called from outside.

"Come with me," Chana said, taking Sorel's hand and marching her out the front door.

Fraydel was standing in the road, one elegant foot placed delicately before the other. Chana, who was deeply flushed either from the exertions of the last hour or a newly rising anger, walked over to her.

"Sorel can't go with you."

"Mmmmmm," said Fraydel, cocking her head to the right and staring at Chana.

"Oh, go away, Chana!" Sorel thought to herself. "Why do you have to ruin everything?"

Fraydel pointed to Chana's Sabbath dress.

"You have mud on your dress, Chana."

Chana looked down at her dress.

"Gevalt!" she shrieked, slapping her flushed cheeks with the open palms of her hands. But she turned back, one hand on the door, the other on her newly curving hip.

"You two are going to run off, aren't you, while I'm in the house? You'll go running off without me."

Fraydel shrugged her thin shoulders.

It seemed, for just a second, that Chana's pouting bottom lip trembled. Sorel, whose eyes were on Fraydel, didn't catch the telltale quiver, but it's possible that Fraydel did.

In any case, Fraydel, who was more than capable, for whatever reasons, of such sudden reversals, sat down on the step and said to Chana: "Go change your dress. We won't run off."

Sorel sat down beside her.

The whole look of the world shifted when Fraydel came near. An excitement swept after her, like the long swirling train of a noblewoman's dress, and it rearranged the world.

Fraydel had moods. This was Schluftchev's word for all that made Fraydel like no one else. She was as different from all others as the moon is from the sun. And though it was true that sometimes Fraydel's moods were such that she would refuse to talk or even to catch your eye, and a harsh cast settled over her face so that she lost all the softness of a girl, it was also true that there were good moods, just as inexplicable as the bad, with laughter and silly songs and nonsense rhymes spilling forth.

> *Vu iz do a vasser on zamd?*
> *Vu is do a melech on a land?*
> *Dos vasser fun oyg iz on zamd.*
> *Der melech in kortn iz on land.*

> Where is there water without sand?
> Where is there a king without a land?
> Tears from the eyes are without sand.
> The king of cards has no land.

In good moods, Fraydel also liked to make up words, words that sounded just like Yiddish or Polish or Ukrainian, or even the holy Hebrew that Tatta and the boys spoke to one another only on the Sabbath. But these words of Fraydel's meant nothing at all. You could die from laughter when Fraydel began to speak in these meaningless languages, long ribbons of nonsense flowing from her lips.

You never knew what would come next from Fraydel, only that it would be exciting, that it would be different from anything you heard from anyone else. She was as wonderful as some character stepping out of one of the many stories that ran around her head, like a dog chasing its own tail.

Sorel was never frightened of Fraydel, not really, not even when she knew it was wise to keep her distance.

She looked up now at her older sister, but all that Fraydel said was, "What heat," and fanned her face with her hand.

"It's like Gehenna," said Sorel, who had once heard Fraydel say exactly this.

Fraydel laughed.

"Right," she said. "Exactly like the long tongues of fire licking the poor sinners, until they are as crisp as fried poppy seeds!"

The terrible image Fraydel's description painted prompted Sorel to ask, "Are you sorry for them, Fraydel?"

"Who? The sinners?"

Sorel nodded her head.

Again Fraydel tilted her head to the right and thought for a few moments.

"It depends on their sins," she finally said.

Chana came back out. She had changed into the Sabbath dress of last summer, and her new curves pressed insistently outward against the seams of the bodice.

Chana sat down beside Sorel on the stoop. This also was a very tight squeeze, especially since Sorel was careful not to lean up too close to Fraydel.

A walk to the forest was now out of the question. Chana had to stay near the house to be at hand when Bezalel woke up. His naps tended to be far too short for everybody concerned. He wrestled with sleep like our father Yaakov wrestled the angel.

"Do you want to play 'Into the Circle' with us?" Chana asked Fraydel.

Fraydel shrugged.

It was a game that Sorel and Chana often played together, especially on long Sabbath afternoons of summer, when time moved so slowly as to seem almost to be moving backward.

One girl would begin a story and then stop somewhere, saying "into the circle," and the other would take up from there, until she, too, chose to issue the invitation into the circle.

The problem about playing this game with Chana was that she wanted all of the stories to follow a predestined line: A man has, through some misfortune, lost all his faith and has even uttered a curse against the Name. But then, through the good deed of an innocent child, the man's faith is restored to him once again, and he repents just in time for Yom Kippur.

This is the way one of Sorel and Chana's stories had gone once, and, ever since then, this is the way Chana had wanted all the stories to go.

The only details she allowed to vary were the nature of the man's fall and of the child's good deed. All else she wanted fixed. If Sorel pulled the story off into some unknown direction, Chana would tap her sharply on the shoulder and announce that she wanted "into the circle."

"Okay, we'll play," said Fraydel. "Only Sorel has to begin the story. Sorel, then me, and then you, Chana."

"I don't like that order," said Chana.

Fraydel shrugged.

"Shall I begin it in Chicago?" Sorel asked Fraydel.

"You begin it where you begin it."

Fraydel had read in a book about a city of this name, a fantastic city right in the middle of fantastic America. Chicago. Fraydel had become intoxicated with the name that sounded so drolly, so wildly improbably, like the Yiddish word for "drunken," *shikker.* Chicago. Chicago. She had repeated it to herself over and over again, experimenting with the sound of it, sliding the accent to first one, then another, syllable. Chicago. Right in the middle of the mythical land, a city whose name seemed as intimate in the mouth, as familiar and as close as one's own secret odors. Chicago.

Many of Fraydel's own stories were set in a strange shimmering place she called Chicago, the scene of wondrous events that could at any moment be blotted out with doom. Life in Fraydel's Chicago had a way of lurching into a bizarre dance, grinning with a grotesque face, spinning itself out of control. A drunkard's dance.

With the first crow of the rooster, the sun springs high into the sky over Chicago. Night falls just as quickly. No dawn, no twilight to soften the passing from the one to the other. Young girls wake up in their beds one morning to find they've become wrinkled. The whitened hair on their pillows spills down from memoryless heads, years not forgotten but unlived.

In one of Fraydel's tales, a girl, wandering in the forest of Chicago, finds a mirror that looks as if it's growing like a living thing amongst the roots of the trees. When she looks into its polished face, she sees the reflection of herself as an older woman staring back, a costly coral necklace round her throat and a fine lace holiday kerchief perched on her marriage wig. The older woman smiles back at the younger one with a look of calm complacency, one hand gently fingering the necklace. The next day, the girl brings along her friend, who sees nothing at all in the mirror. "It's not a mirror," the friend says, looking right through the glass to the roots on the other side. "It's a plain sheet of glass. Why did you make up such a tale of nonsense?"

From story to story, Fraydel had coated her Chicago, applying thickly pearling layers around the grain of a name she had found in a book about America; so that for Sorel, too, it conjured up a place she knew. She had only to say the name for herself, alternating the accent as Fraydel did, to see the supernatural city emerging from between the vowel-dipped syllables. Its wooden houses are painted in crazy zigzag patterns of colors, and the ripe onion-domed roofs are inlaid with strips of copper and zinc, so that the captive light, sullen on overcast days, on clear days is thrown, shrieking, from rooftop to rooftop.

Girls with dreamy eyes sit in the windows or lean over balustrades, combing their rippling hair. But when these girls with dreamy eyes open their mouths to speak, their voices come out rasping like a crone's, or barking like a dog's, jumbled words mixing with lost laughter.

The streets seem to be laid out perfectly straight, but once you begin to walk down one you encounter winding curves, hills embedded with stairways, alleys that keep going—going nowhere. You try to turn back and retrace your steps and find that everything has altered. It is in the nature of the streets to make a mockery of your memory.

Chicago. The sound of the word transported Sorel, so that she was walking deep inside of Fraydel's thoughts, behind the face worn sewn up tight.

"This story takes place in Chicago," Sorel said.

"In Chicago there lived a beautiful girl." Sorel always liked the girls in a story to be beautiful.

"Was she good?" asked Chana.

"How do I know if she's good yet? We don't have the story."

"You said already that she was beautiful. Why can't you say whether she's good?"

"If you can't see the difference, you're even a bigger dumbhead than I had thought," said Fraydel. "Go on, Sorel."

"Wait, wait," said Chana. "Did you say what the girl's name was?"

"You say, Fraydel." Names were always hard, and Fraydel knew such wonderful ones from all the books that she read.

"Oh, I've had enough of you two!" Fraydel's voice was high and harsh, and Sorel knew she was about to run off—who knew where? But then her scowl vanished, and she simply said. "What about Fredericka Bodayda?"

"Fredericka Bodayda," Sorel continued hurriedly, "was the only daughter of a very rich man named . . . Mayer Laybish. Mayer Laybish was the wealthiest landowner in all of Chicago. His vineyards covered the southern hills, and the wine that was made from his grapes was the sweetest ever tasted.

"Into the circle."

"Mayer Laybish and his wife, Pesha Sima," continued Fraydel, "had only this one child, and they lived every day to see her happy. Because they were so wealthy, and because they had no sons, they could afford to educate their daughter. They hired private tutors to teach her many subjects, many languages. Also music lessons on the mandolin. But when they saw that these studies gave Fredericka Bodayda no pleasure, they got rid of all the private tutors and instead arranged different sorts of amusements for her: picnics in the fields and hikes into the hills, also nights of music-making.

"But the truth is that Fredericka Bodayda was never particularly happy. On the other hand, she was never particularly sad either. Every moment, she had the feeling that she had lived that exact moment once before. 'Only that other time,' she would think, 'I was happy.' Or else she'd think, 'That other time I was sad.'

"As a child, she had been small. But then, when she was almost a woman, and the other girls of her age stopped growing, she continued to grow, until she was as tall and as graceful as a date tree in the desert. Her eyes were shaped like almonds, and her skin was like the Queen of Persia's.

"Into the circle."

"It was time for Fredericka Bodayda to find a husband," Chana continued. "But for such a daughter, Mayer Laybish found it very difficult to accept anyone as suitable.

" 'And why is this one good enough for my Fredericka Bodayda?' he'd think each time a young man was suggested. 'I don't see what's so oy-oy-oy about that one either.'

"Pesha Sima had taken to wringing her hands and moaning that her daughter, as beautiful as she was, would die an old maid, may it never happen here. 'Why did I have to have a daughter so beautiful?' she'd moan night and day. 'Or why a husband so stubborn?' And she made up her mind to hound Mayer Laybish night and day, day and night, until a bridegroom was found for her daughter.

"Into the circle."

"Finally, the head of a distant and very famous yeshiva wrote to Mayer Laybish," continued Sorel. "The head of the yeshiva described a young man, named Elazar, who would be a wonderful match for any girl, even one so beautiful and so rich as Fredericka Bodayda.

"At this famous yeshiva, they were known to study things very quickly. Tracts that it took others years and years to get through, they would finish in a matter of months. But Elazar could cover the same tract in days and know it perfectly by heart.

" 'Though he is not yet eighteen,' wrote the rebbe in his letter, 'the number of pages that he has committed to memory fill many volumes. And the interpretations that he gives these pages are in no volume yet written. All who have studied with him have come away with one word: *illui.*'

"Now, of course, when Mayer Laybish heard this word, he became very excited and wrote back immediately, inviting the head of the yeshiva himself to bring the boy with him to Chicago.

"Into the circle."

"At first," continued Fraydel, "when Mayer Laybish saw the boy, he was disappointed. More than disappointed: he was offended. The boy was almost eighteen, but when first you looked at him he looked barely twelve. Then you looked at him a second time and he seemed an old man, already rotting on years. But no matter how many times you looked at him, he never looked the right age for a bridegroom.

"He stood so crooked that at first Mayer Laybish thought with a shudder that it was a dwarf that had been brought as a prospective husband for his daughter.

"Mayer Laybish himself was a big strong man, blessed with the strength of two oxen, and with a full and lustrous chestnut-colored beard in which there wasn't yet a strand of gray. And here they offered a bridegroom who didn't stand straight and with a beardless chin and a face like a paste made of flour and water.

" 'No,' thought Reb Mayer Laybish in his heart. 'This is not my daughter's destined one.'

"The boy's rebbe could read in the eyes of the father what thoughts were in his head.

" 'Wait,' he told Mayer Laybish, and his own eyes twinkled as if with a good joke that he would soon be able to share with another.

"The rebbe asked the boy to explain the tract of Talmud he'd been studying on the wagon coming over. In a beautiful voice, not at all in the singing through the nose in which most boys learn, Elazar began to expound.

"And it was then that Mayer Laybish saw that Elazar's words were on fire. The moment they left the boy's mouth, they sprouted wings of flame and flew upward. The boy's moving lips, his beardless face, his crooked body—everything vanished behind a wall of fire leaping toward the sky.

"When Pesha Sima came in with a silver tray on which were arranged the heavy silver teapot and the fine pastries, Mayer Laybish found himself amazed to discover that it had grown completely dark outside. An entire day had passed, none of the affairs of business had been seen to, while the boy had been speaking the words that sprouted fire."

"What kind of pastries?" asked Chana.

Fraydel and Sorel burst out laughing.

"That's only for you to say, Chana. Into the circle."

"There were rugelach filled with almonds and raisins, just hot from the oven. And a great tall babka with a thick dusting of sugar and cinnamon. Also a sponge cake, made with fourteen, no, with fifteen eggs, so high and light as to melt in one's mouth."

Sorel and Fraydel were again laughing, this time from the look on Chana's face.

"Are you finished?" Sorel asked. "Or are we going to be here until next Shabbes, while you *fress* on Pesha Sima's goodies?"

"Okay, okay," Chana said, and even she gave a little smile. "It's true. I'm making myself hungry."

"Well, save some room." Fraydel laughed. "We still have the wedding feast to get through."

"Into the circle."

"Mayer Laybish," continued Sorel, "agreed on the spot to the betrothal of Fredericka Bodayda and Elazar. Elazar's parents, too, were more than satisfied with the girl and her family."

"Into the circle."

Sorel found that she didn't have the patience to try to make out for herself the direction in which the story was heading. She was anxious to deliver the story over to Fraydel, to let Fraydel take it where she would.

"One change," Fraydel said. "Elazar is an orphan. Agreed?"

Both girls nodded their assent.

"For weeks and weeks, all of the Jews of Chicago could talk of nothing but the approaching wedding.

"It was said that the seven rabbis who would pronounce the seven blessings over the pair would come all the way to Chicago from the holy city of Jerusalem.

"It was said that every species of fowl permissible to eat would be prepared, stuffed with spices from the four corners of the earth. Tastes never before imagined would be served up before rich man and beggar alike.

"It was said that there would be a vast and elaborate wedding cake, shaped like the Holy Temple that stood in Jerusalem in the days of its glory.

"And the strangest thing is that all of these rumors turned out to be true. Mayer Laybish had spared nothing for the wedding of his only daughter.

"And still, as Fredericka Bodayda sat in the midst of the other women, waiting behind the curtain for her bridegroom to be brought in for the veiling ceremony, she looked exactly as she had always looked, neither happy nor sad, only dazed by the memory of having lived exactly this moment before."

Fraydel's thin voice quivered in that strange way it had whenever one of her stories began to take off with a wild life of its own. Always a soft and whispery voice, a strange voice that little children liked tauntingly to imitate, it now sounded like a voice being carried by a wind.

"And now there was a loud commotion as the men, singing and dancing, led in the bridegroom, who was pale and trembling from his fasting, and also from the fear of seeing his bride for the first time.

"Elazar looked down at the young woman, sitting so calmly beside her mother, and he became lost. All of the pages of his learning flew out from him, like startled white doves.

"Fredericka Bodayda looked up at her betrothed, at the moment before the foaming veil was dropped before her face, and all that she could think was, 'Only the last time, I was happy. Or perhaps it was that I was sad.'

"At the first blessing of the wine, when her veil was briefly lifted so that she could sip the wine from the silver cup, Elazar caught a second glimpse of his bride's face. Now even the power of speech flowed away from him, like water running down a hill.

" 'What will happen to me if I look at her a third time?" he wondered to himself.

"At the wedding feast after the *chuppa*, Elazar sat pale and trembling, unable to speak, while all around him the Jews of Chicago celebrated the marriage of Mayer Laybish's only daughter with thunderous dancing and singing.

"The men jump up on the carved silver tables, stomping with their feet, so that all of the delicate dishes spill over with a crash to the floor.

The melody of the musicians picks up the crash, playing it back and forth so that the music itself laughs at the joke. The women, who on other days would sob aloud at the sinful waste of food, are pointing across the room and laughing, holding their sides so that they won't split wide apart from the violence of the laughter forcing its way through them.

"The women weave around in dancing circles, one circle within the other within the other, like ripples in the water. They feel the floor beneath them heaving with the weight of the men's great thuds, and this sets the women laughing again, so that the tears run down their faces, mixing in their open mouths with the taste of Mayer Laybish's sweet red wine.

"Today all of the women of Chicago have forgotten how to weep. They know only to laugh. Even Pesha Sima, whose face is usually creased between the eyes with the many worries of her household, sits smooth-skinned and blushing beside her daughter. Only the bride is silent, and also the bridegroom, who carefully keeps his eyes turned away from his bride, afraid to find out of what power of mind a third look will deprive him.

"Around the couple the dancers swirl. A circle of three men link arms about each other's shoulders and spin around. First one man lifts his legs straight out behind him as if he's flying, then a second, and finally a third, so that they are all three suspended in midair, whirling about like the circle of fire placed before the lost entrance to the Garden.

"It's the dead of winter, and outside the ground is frozen hard. The snow shines a soft blue beneath the moon. Nobody walks the streets. Everybody—even Shmulik the town lunatic—is inside, celebrating the wedding of Mayer Laybish's only daughter.

"The men who have the most honored seats at the eastern wall of the prayerhouse link their arms with the beggars and the lame. Women dance with their own servant girls, kissing them on both cheeks. Tonight even Reb Mayer Laybish forgets the dignity of all his gold. 'Drink!' he says, passing from guest to guest. 'Drink up tonight for tomorrow's thirst!' he says, giving Shmulik the lunatic a thump on the shoulder.

"In the room it grows hotter by the minute, from all the dancing and from Mayer Laybish's sweet red wine. The breath of the guests fogs the windows, so that nobody can see out.

"And now it is that a grinning man enters, tall and thin, and so pale and handsome that three girls immediately lose their hearts forever with the first glance that falls on him. All three girls will die old maids, mourning the lives they lost in that one glance."

Chana sighed deeply, and then asked, "How is this stranger dressed?"

"In a frock coat of black silk and velvet, a brocaded vest embroidered with scarlet thread, and a tall satin top hat."

Again Chana sighed.

"His eyes are very large and very dark. They're circled in black with greasepaint, like an actor's on the stage, so that they seem even bigger and darker, as deep and as filled with feeling as the ocean is with water.

" 'The badchen,' whispers one of Mayer Laybish's guests. And this whisper is repeated from one mouth to another, like the wind through the trees, until all the guests know that it is so. Even Shmulik the lunatic has heard the great news and is already clapping his hands in anticipation and laughing with his high laugh, like the whinny of a frightened horse, at the badchen's wit.

"Here, too, Mayer Laybish has outdone himself, for the badchen is like no other that has ever been seen or heard in Chicago.

"The wedding guests grow very quiet, a little ashamed of themselves before an important outsider.

"Again the news is whispered, and carried from mouth to mouth, that this badchen is a famous actor. He performs on the stage of a famous theater in a city far, far away. The wedding guests look closely and see that the frock coat of black silk and velvet is finer than their own, almost finer than that of Reb Mayer Laybish himself.

" 'What a prince is our Reb Mayer Laybish, to have given his daughter such a bridegroom and such a wedding, with such a badchen for the entertainment!' the guests whisper one to another.

"The badchen raises his tall hat to the head table, where the bride and the groom sit together with the bride's parents and the seven rabbis from Jerusalem. And then, with a few long strides, he goes to the very center of the room, holds up a long thin finger for silence in the soundlessness, and begins to recite his wedding verses.

"These verses are like his clothes, of a different era, of a finer stuff than has ever been known of, even in so wonderful a place as Chicago. He speaks an old Yiddish that one never hears spoken, as pure as the Hebrew that the learned speak to one another on the Sabbath.

"The badchen goes from table to table. At each table he picks out a person and weaves a verse around him.

"All of Reb Mayer Laybish's guests marvel. It's as if this badchen, from a strange city far away, has known them for all of their lives. It's as if he's lived with them in their own city of Chicago, has shared their every *simcha* and every sorrow with them.

"But as the badchen makes his way from table to table, the people slowly become uneasy. At each table the verse becomes a little less friendly, a little too knowing. Secrets better left unspoken are set forth in rhyming couplets for all to hear. Each person silently prays to himself, as he watches the badchen approaching his table, 'I beg of Thee, God of my fathers, let it not be me he chooses!'

"They glance at the head table, wondering why it is that Reb Mayer Laybish, or the seven rabbis from Jerusalem, don't order the badchen to stop his versifying, for now they are all trembling. Everybody's head has begun to ache at the temples, with a dull steady pounding that can almost be heard.

"Now the badchen walks with his long, long strides right up to the head table, and with the grin that has never once left his face he looks to Mayer Laybish and recites:

> A model Jew, Reb Mayer Laybish,
> With no secret that money can't hide
> Tonight he gets his greatest wish:
> His daughter is a bride!

" 'A toast!' cries out the badchen, snatching the untouched wine-glass of the bridegroom and holding it up before him.

"And all the Jews of Chicago find that they, too, have lifted their crystal goblets high into the air.

> The drunken lift their cups to Life
> To strange powers of unseeing and forgetting
> But even Night must take a wife—
> And Death will dance at the wedding!

"There's something so terrible in the smiling badchen's voice, something so unforgiving and so cold, that all the wedding guests shudder as one man.

"But nobody makes a move to silence the badchen. Even the seven rabbis from Jerusalem sit with their tongues cleaving to the roofs of their mouths. Elazar, the bridegroom, sits rocking back and forth, back and forth—whether in prayer or in terror, who knows.

"Now the smiling badchen turns to the bride herself. He speaks a verse that describes her beauty, so that all the women there remember again how to cry. Their eyes spill over with their shame for Fredericka Bodayda. Only she, of all the women there, doesn't cry. She lifts her almond eyes up, and they are smiling. Her face glows as if a lamp has been lit up behind the Persian skin.

> I've walked beside you, every step,
> And filled your dreams while you have slept,
> And whispered in your ear: No choice!
> You knew at once your husband's voice,
> That whispered in your ear: No chance!
> Come dance with me your bridal dance.

"Slowly Fredericka Bodayda rises up from the bridal table. The badchen produces a scarf from beneath his ruffled sleeve—a scarf so white it aches the eye—and presents a corner of it to Fredericka Bodayda. She sighs, only once and very softly, as her fingers take hold of the corner of the scarf. The sound of this sigh stirs the guests, so that they can once again partake of the powers of moving and of speaking.

" 'Unclean!' the seven rabbis shout out with one voice.

" 'Unclean!' Mayer Laybish and Pesha Sima and all of their guests respond with a terrible cry. For only now, when it is too late, it is clear with whom Fredericka dances the bridal dance. The bridegroom, alone, says nothing and makes sure to keep his eyes turned away.

"But Mayer Laybish and Pesha Sima and the seven rabbis from Jerusalem pull out their hair and cry out their hearts, as Fredericka and the badchen slowly circle the room in silence, each holding a corner of the softly gleaming scarf.

"The two dancers make no noise, but all around them the groans are piling up, the room is thick with them, as the Jews of Chicago see the girl taking on the face of the famous badchen from the city far, far away. Her eyes are dissolving into shadows of black, and her bloodless lips are giving way to the grin that rises up from behind them.

"Only Elazar, the bridegroom, never looks up, but sits rocking on his seat, back and forth, back and forth, muttering meaningless words and laughing like a boy of three at a spot of sun that dances on a wall."

Fraydel's voice, which had sunk to the faintest whisper, now faded off into silence. The three girls sat unmoving, still watching the bride and badchen's silent kerchief dance.

"So sad," Chana at last murmured, and the dancers vanished from before Sorel's eyes.

Sorel looked up at Fraydel's face. Fraydel still stared straight before her. It was hard to see in the gathering shadows, but Sorel thought that Fraydel's cheeks were wet. Fraydel often finished her stories with her cheeks bathed in tears, her eyes opened wide at the visions she saw.

Sorel, too, felt like crying. There was a great weight on her chest that would have liked to dissolve itself into tears. Perhaps tonight, while her two sisters slept, then Sorel would give way to the sadness of Fredericka Bodayda.

The sky had darkened, the glow in the west finally drained away to the last golden drop, but the heat of the day still sat heavily on the earth.

"What is the name of the story?" Sorel now whispered up at Fraydel.

Fraydel said nothing, staring ahead.

For several moments more, she continued to stare. Then she gave her thin shoulders a little shake, and looked down at Sorel.

"Did you say something?" she asked.

"The name of the story. Does it have a name, Fraydel?"

"A name?" And Fraydel wrinkled her brow—whether in perplexity or distaste, who can say?

"It's called 'The Bridegroom,' " she said after a few moments.

" 'The Bridegroom'?" Chana said. "I don't understand. He wasn't important."

"Now you've said something true, Chana," Fraydel said, with the coldness that could overtake her soft voice. "You don't understand."

Chana shrugged her shoulders and got up from the stoop to go inside. But she turned back, with her hand on the door.

"It was a good story, Fraydel. It will give me a nightmare tonight, it was so good! It will give me nightmares for a week."

And then she went inside.

Sorel carefully nestled herself a little closer to her sister, smelling the scent of the pine forest Fraydel always seemed to carry on her skin and in her hair. The night music of the crickets suddenly pressed in from every side, as if the insects, too, had been holding off until the story came to an end.

Fraydel didn't pull away from her, and Sorel shifted a little closer. She took Fraydel's slim, elegant hand into her own, and they sat silently together in the falling darkness, until they heard Mamma's voice calling them in for the prayer of Havdala, separating the Sabbath day from the rest of the week. The long Sabbath afternoon in Av had finally drawn to a close.

CHAPTER 5

THE TWO FRAYDELS

*A*lthough Nachum Sonnenberg had been born a motherless child, yanked into the world by the midwife seconds after Fraydel Sonnenberg, poor child, had shuddered her last, events had come to him all his life through the intervention of women.

Even his mother had spoken her will concerning him from beyond the grave.

Bezalel Sonnenberg, the widower, had greatly loved his young wife, and he named his son after the Hebrew word for "consolation."

Bezalel continued to grieve for his wife beyond the prescribed period of mourning. Nevertheless, not long after the year was up, he remarried.

The second Mrs. Sonnenberg, who, by chance, also happened to have been named Fraydel, was ten years older than Bezalel, who had himself been ten years older than his first wife.

The new wife was a pious and kindhearted widow, given to wishing those whose paths she crossed a silent blessing, her head bent down and her lips moving, so that if you didn't know better you might think, God forbid, that she was either drunk or crazy or both.

The second Fraydel Sonnenberg married Bezalel already having four sons from her first marriage, two of them long married and living on their own. The two that remained at home, Simcha and Henoch, were pale, lethargic boys, weak-chested like the poor man who had fathered them.

Little Nachum, in contrast, bloomed like the blossoms of spring, his silky fine hair falling in long golden curls and his lively eyes turning from their infant's blue to a deeper gray.

The second Fraydel Sonnenberg would not let herself form words in recognition of the child's beauty, not even in the silence of her own heart. From the moment she had entered the house, a red bit of string, a bendel, blessed by a Chasidic rebbe, had been tied about the child's ankle, a precaution taken against the Evil Eye, as is the custom with children of unusual charm.

At night, Fraydel, singing beside the little bed, could feel the menacing presence of bad-wishing spirits crowding in close, drawn toward the golden child as are moths to the flame.

> Sleep, sleep, my son,
> I will buy little boots for you.
>
> *Shluf, shluf, meyn zun,*
> *Ch'vel dir koyfn shtivelech.*

Every time the child whimpered or tossed in his sleep, Fraydel's heart would squeeze itself into a tight fist from fear, and she would hoarsely call out to an angel to cover the baby with its wing until the bright clear morning.

Even in the daylight, the child's beauty bore down on Fraydel's heart. She would press the heels of her palms hard into her eyes, trying to stem the flow of her tears. How it grieved her that the first Fraydel Sonnenberg had not lived to behold the sight of her son, that she had died, poor child, at the age of sixteen, a mere nine months after she had stood a beautiful bride under the wedding canopy and only moments before her firstborn was pulled, cold and blue, into this world.

"The face of an angel, and as pure as the night-fallen snow," the second Fraydel Sonnenberg would sigh, pressing her palms into her flowing eyes. "May she rest in tranquillity, singing the psalms with the angels."

For the sake of the first Fraydel Sonnenberg, the second Fraydel Sonnenberg bestowed on the motherless boy any favor it was hers to give. If something especially tasty came out of the pot—if, for example, Fraydel should open a hen and happen to find nestled inside a cluster of its unhatched eggs—it would be little Nachum who would find the delicacy floating in his evening bowl of soup.

And so Nachum bloomed, a beautiful infant growing into a beautiful child, watered by the love of his kindhearted stepmother.

Bezalel and Fraydel Sonnenberg were simple, God-fearing Jews. They were by no means, either of them, scholars. Fraydel herself, pious woman though she was, had never been taught to read the Hebrew prayers from her tattered prayer book, every page of which was stained yellow with tears. Here and there she knew how to say a few of the words and would mumble them with the women who sat with her in the balcony of the prayerhouse: just a few words, here and there, that stood like dry rocks rising in the sea of tears that were her prayers.

> *Shtivelech vel ich koyfn.*
> *In cheder vestu loyfn.*

> Little boots I'll buy you.
> To cheder you will run.

At the age of three, Nachum had been wrapped in his father's prayer shawl and borne on the proud shoulders of Fraydel to the cheder teacher, who had celebrated his arrival with presents of nutmeats and sweets supplied for the class by the parents. The teacher had pointed with his stick to a shape on a page. "Aleph," he said. And when the little golden-haired boy had obediently repeated this sound in a shy whispering voice, the teacher had smiled at the beaming Fraydel, pronounced the child a natural scholar, and dipped his finger into a pot of honey that stood waiting nearby, to offer the child a lick so that he might always know that knowledge is sweet.

So it had proved sweet for Nachum. Unlike his own father, Bezalel, who had lumbered ungracefully through the toil of his studies, Nachum had flown through the books as if with wings strapped to his little boots.

> *Loyfn vestu in cheder*
> *Lernen vestu k'seder.*

> To cheder you will run
> And study regularly.

On Sabbath afternoons, when the teacher made the rounds of the homes of his students in order to render a report on the week's progress, he always gave a glowing account to Bezalel and Fraydel, who bent their heads even lower than usual beneath the praises that came showering down on them. Then the whole family—even the two stepbrothers, Simcha and Henoch, as overcome as the parents with the strangeness of success—would celebrate together with the teacher over glasses of scalding tea and a small plate filled with almonds and raisins.

> *Gute b'sures un gute meylas,*
> *Tsu achtsn yor vestu paskenen sheylas.*

> A good reputation and fine virtues,
> At eighteen you'll solve rabbinical problems.

Bezalel, slouched heavily down in his chair in the evening, his limbs slack with the exhaustion seeped into him from his day's labor, would slowly shake his head in wordless wonder at Nachum, flesh of his own flesh, who sat swaying tirelessly over the letter-crowded columns of the holy tracts, singing beneath his breath the repetitious chant by which he studied, like the drone of honeybees.

So Nachum Sonnenberg bloomed, from a beautiful child into a beautiful young man.

At the age of thirteen, he was called up to the Torah as a bar mitzvah, and Fraydel sat in the women's balcony of the prayerhouse, pressing the heels of her palms hard into her streaming eyes.

Too soon it was time for Nachum to leave his beloved studyhouse and go out into the world to seek a livelihood, like his father before him. But whereas his father had closed the book he was studying with a shout of joy in his heart, feeling no regret at bidding a last farewell to the teacher who had always shouted at him that his head was like a sieve with holes as large as goose eggs, Nachum closed the book with a heavy sigh. He placed a little slip of paper between the pages, so that, at some later time, he might find the sentence at which he had stopped.

Bezalel and Fraydel were simple people, eking out a poor shtetl living, and, despite the lullaby foretelling a life of study that Fraydel had crooned nightly over the child's cradle, the idea of being worthy of the high honor, the *zchuss,* of having a scholar for a son had never occurred to either of them. Fraydel had sung the same lullaby to each of her five sons.

It was then that the first Fraydel Sonnenberg had spoken her will concerning her son from beyond the grave.

One night, only moments after Fraydel sank exhausted into her bed and closed her eyes, a woman appeared before her. The woman's face was turned away, so that it was only her slight, girlish back with which Fraydel was presented. Nonetheless, Fraydel knew immediately that it was the first Fraydel Sonnenberg who came to summon her from her bed.

The woman began immediately to walk, with swift soundless steps, and Fraydel followed silently behind her.

The two women walked quickly, one behind the other, through a strange tilting place, lit as at twilight. Fraydel didn't dare make out the dim shapes she passed, some motionless, some scurrying, but kept her eyes only on the first Fraydel Sonnenberg's back.

All at once, the first Fraydel halted. There was music coming from up ahead, the joyful notes of a wedding band playing. The first Fraydel hurriedly stepped to the side so that the second Fraydel could see.

A white wedding *chuppa* lay before them, held aloft by four elegantly dressed men bearing the canopy poles. Surrounding the canopy was a thick huddle of men, richly dressed in long black satin caftans and glossy sable-fur hats, crowding so close together that they made a solid wall about the canopy.

The second Fraydel drew a little closer, craning her neck and stretching up onto her tiptoes, so that she might see who it was who was getting married. The crowd of men parted for her so that she, a poor ignorant woman, might pass through with all honor.

In front of the canopy, seven rabbis stood waiting to pronounce the seven blessings of marriage. Each had a thick white beard that cascaded to his waist, luminous as the snow falling beneath the full moon. And this circle of men also opened so that the woman Fraydel could pass through.

And there, deep in prayer beneath the canopy, stood her own stepson Nachum, dressed in the simple shroudlike robe in which Jewish boys are married, in order both to remind them of the day of their earthly end and to trick the Angel of Death into staying away from the joy he's always anxious to spoil. At Nachum's side, on a beautifully carved throne of silver, rested the holy scroll of the Law, arrayed like a bride in gleaming white satin embroidered in gold, and engulfed in a bride's own aura of radiance.

So it was that the first Fraydel Sonnenberg had made known to the second Fraydel Sonnenberg her will concerning Nachum.

When the rest of the shtetl learned of what had happened in the night to Fraydel Sonnenberg, they all decided to contribute a certain amount yearly so that Nachum Sonnenberg might be able to go off and continue his studies. The first Fraydel Sonnenberg, having spoken her will concerning her son from beyond the grave, was never seen again, but slept in peace.

Sheyles vestu paskenen,
Droshes vestu darshenen.

Problems you'll solve,
Speeches you'll make.

Nachum Sonnenberg was sent off to Lemberg to study with the re-nowned Rav Dovid Broder, of blessed memory, in whose home the shy shtetl boy boarded, and who had an unmarried daughter, named Leiba.

Leiba was thirteen years old when Nachum first came to Lemberg to continue his studies. Her two older sisters, Shaindel and Tzippora, were already married, and her older brother, Yehuda, who studied in Vilna, was betrothed.

Leiba was a lovely girl to look at: tall and slender, with thickly plaited dark-blond hair that fell below her waist. Her parents had been brought several marriage propositions on Leiba's behalf, but Leiba was a very young thirteen-year-old, immature in her ways, her head in books.

The next-youngest daughter, Fruma, twelve years old, was also a girl whose head was filled with thoughts flitting from here to there like little birds in the forest. A hundred and one times during the course of a morning, a good intention would occur to Fruma. And just so many times in the course of a morning, another hundred and one obstacles would place themselves between the good intention and its execution. A hundred and one multiplied again by a hundred and one: it's a lot of obstacles in the course of one morning.

Though Leiba's parents were, of course, anxious to arrange a fortu-itous match for her, such as they had successfully brought to conclusion for her two older sisters, they thought that perhaps a long engagement period, of at least a year, if not even two, would be a good idea. That way, the girl would have a chance to grow up a little before being thrust into the full responsibilities of married life. These were the sorts of considerations that would never have occurred to their own parents, of blessed memory. But Rav Dovid and his wife, Terza, though they could never be accused, God forbid, of modern thinking, did not think in all matters exactly as their own parents had done either. Terza herself read newspapers, both Yiddish and Polish.

Rav Broder was a man who would rather go without food or drink for a week than suffer the presence of a fool for an hour. Everybody—his students, his children, even his fellow rabbis—chose his words care-fully in the presence of Rav Broder. His pale-gray eyes had a way of boring into your skull as you spoke, as if he were seeing straight into your mind and was disgusted at the confusion that he saw. Those who learned to think beneath the probing beam of this scrutiny emerged, no doubt, the better scholars for it. (Some, however, came to the conclusion that they weren't destined for a life of scholarship.) Years later, perhaps when arguing a shaky position, they would suddenly see the eyes of Rav Broder peering disdainfully into the muddle.

As strong a will as Rav Broder had, his wife, Terza, could be even stronger—when the situation demanded. There were certain matters in which Rav Dovid relied entirely on the opinions of his wife.

Nachum had been boarding with Rav Dovid for about four months when, all of a sudden, it seemed that Leiba might not, after all, require so long a period of engagement in which to grow up. As if overnight, her ways came to resemble less those of an awkward young foal, fighting the bridle, and more those of a gentle *kalleh maydel*. A new sweetness and patience settled down over her. She spent fewer and fewer hours hiding in the outhouse reading her books (she thought her mother didn't know) and instead willingly looked after the younger ones and offered her mother help at the stove, suddenly expressing an interest in the family recipes for potato kugel and carrot tsimmes.

It was certainly not for a modest young woman like Leiba, so refined and well reared, to pay too close attention to the young students who studied under the direction of her father and boarded in their home. It was certainly not for such a young woman as Leiba to give any thought to the question of who it was that she would marry.

Therefore, the admiration that Leiba felt for her father's newest student had nothing at all to do with any feelings of a personal nature.

In a purely impersonal manner, she simply took note of the air of abstraction that surrounded the young scholar, an air he wore like the royal robes of a young nobleman. At the table, he sat tasting indifferently from his plate, so that, in comparison, the others sitting with him and enjoying their food with such obvious relish appeared unseemly, almost coarse. Just from observing Nachum's abstracted manner of eating, Leiba derived a great amount of impersonal pleasure.

In a purely impersonal manner, she noticed the humility that sat like a crown on his head—a golden crown, encrusted with jewellike virtues, invisible only to the wearer.

In a purely impersonal manner, she came to the conclusion that there was no equal to young Nachum Sonnenberg in all the world. She didn't have to travel the world to know this. There was not another one like him, because there *could* not be. In a purely impersonal manner, but with so much sincerity that she felt her heart lurch like a drunkard, she wished Nachum Sonnenberg every blessing that she knew how to wish: a life full of good deeds and good mazel.

It was the custom of Rav Dovid, since youth, to fast on the second and fifth days of the week, which are the days on which the Torah portion is read during the morning prayers. Rav Dovid would stay up all the night before, studying from holy books, until it was time for the morning prayers. Then, returning home from the prayerhouse, he would take a short nap of a half-hour and awaken as refreshed as if he had spent a full eight hours asleep.

On one such night, as Rav Dovid sat swaying over his books, his wife, Terza, entered the room.

Rav Broder placed a finger on the word he had last read, and looked up at his wife.

"I've been giving some thought," said Terza, in the nonroundabout manner that was her custom, "to the question of Leiba's destined one, and the idea has come to me that perhaps he is one of the young men who are studying now with you."

There were three students presently boarding with Rav Broder.

"Have you been approached by a parent of one of these young men, that you have such an idea?"

"No, I haven't been approached, but nonetheless I have such an idea."

"Chayim Pomeranz?"

Terza smiled, for she had known that this would be the first name her husband would choose, and she hadn't needed the powers of a prophetess in order to know this. Chayim Pomeranz was indeed a jewel among young men, bringing with him a *yiches,* a prestige born of breeding, that had done honor to Rav Dovid. A cousin of Chayim's father had written one book on the laws of marriage and another on the laws of Passover. And on Chayim's mother's side, there were several family members of substantial wealth. His mother's own brother had gone to Germany several years previously, and tales of a great fortune in the making had gradually filtered back.

But no. Chayim Pomeranz, may he find his intended bride among the daughters of Israel, was not whom Terza had in mind.

Mordechai Dexter, then. A head as sharp as the slaughterer's knife, he will live yet to publish responsa, and to hear his name praised by the pillars of Jewish scholarship.

No, not the worthy young Mordechai either.

Nachum?

Yes, Nachum.

Rav Dovid was a little surprised. Not to take anything away from Nachum, of course, who was in every way a paragon, but he was still not exactly the son-in-law that Rav Dovid had had in mind. There would be no *yiches* in such a match. His parents were very poor, which is certainly no sin, but no virtue either. Worse, they were uneducated, "fine, God-fearing people, and may the Holy One forgive me for pointing out the imperfections in two such matchless gems, but still, when all is said and done, the boy comes from people who are barely lettered. Taking all of this into account, I ask you why you think that Nachum would be a good husband for Leiba."

"She likes him."

"She *likes* him?"

"She likes him."

A long silence followed, broken by Rav Dovid's repeated, "She *likes* him?"

Though it might appear that between Rav Dovid's first response and his second not much progress had been made, the truth is that during the space enclosed by these two questions an enormous quantity of material had been sifted through.

Talmudic opinions had been cited, refuted, revised, counterrefuted, and then the whole chain of reasoning had been overturned and swept away. Rashi had been consulted; also Onkelos and Tosefos. Far more obscure sources as well, more mystical in nature. Thousands of years' worth of written commentary on the intimate relationship of man and woman had been called into play in the silence that had separated Rav Dovid's first "She *likes* him?" from his second "She *likes* him?"

"She likes him," Terza repeated in her matter-of-fact manner. "And unless I'm very much mistaken," continued Terza, "it's my opinion that he's not indifferent to her either."

"He likes *her?*"

"He likes her."

Rav Dovid went back to pondering the sources.

"It's not *such* a bad reason," Rav Dovid finally said, stroking his beard.

Exactly two months following this late-night conversation, the plate was broken, betokening the engagement of Nachum and Leiba. And one year later, the two stood together under the marriage canopy.

CHAPTER 6

GYPSIES IN THE
CLEARING

A long caravan of Gypsy wagons had set up camp outside of Shluftchev, where the road curved into the shade of the pine forest. There was a river that ran here, dark with the color of the reflected trees, deep and cold with the water that flowed down from the mountains.

The spot that the Gypsies were temporarily claiming for themselves happened to be very well known to the inhabitants of Shluftchev. Every year, in the autumn month of Tishri, on the holiday of Rosh Hashanah, the Jews marched out of the shtetl in a disorderly little procession, toting under their arms prayer books and loaves of stale brown bread, to gather at the side of the green-black river for the ritual of *tashlich*.

"Give thanks to the Lord with harp. Sing His praises with the ten-stringed lute. Sing a new song, played skillfully amid shouts of joy."

In the folklore of the neighboring peasants, preserving the beliefs of distant pagan days, nature was everywhere running thick with spirits. There were imps animating trees, sprites imbuing animals and streams with character and purpose. Any form might suddenly reveal itself as a place of soul, its motions tracing the designs of desire.

The rabbis had instructed the Jews to avert their gaze from pagan thoughts, and so they had, or tried, resisting the pull of alien enchantments. Indoors was where the Spirit purest dwelled—in the studyhouse, holy with the smell of crumbling texts, and in the home, in the life of the family. The only time of the year that the Jews of Shluftchev ventured purposefully outside in order to pray was in the New Year ritual of *tashlich*.

"Out of the deep waters I call to Thee, O Lord."

Perhaps precisely because *tashlich* was so out of the ordinary, performed in the wildness beyond four walls, it was a great favorite among the children, inducing, despite its penitential purpose, a rambunctiousness of high adventure.

And the loaves of stale bread?

Morsels were torn off and thrown into the river, to be carried away like the sins that the Jews of Shluftchev were joyfully disowning.

"Thou wilt cast all our sins into the depths of the sea," the Jews chanted from their prayer books.

Their mothers warning them to take heed not to fall, God forbid, into the deep river, the children tore great chunks of bread from the loaves and pitched them in, watching as the pieces of pumpernickel were carried off by the dark water flowing swiftly toward the sea. The children kept begging for more bread, until their mothers and fathers would laugh and tell them that they had already cast more bread into the river than there had been sins committed this year by all the Jews of Shluftchev, than by all the Jews of Galicia and even beyond.

"Even in America, Mamma?" a little child would ask, already knowing the answer.

"Ah no, tattala. There's not enough bread in all of Poland for all the sins of the Jews in America, may the Holy One forgive them and may they live to see the error of their ways."

Fraydel had told Sorel that when the Blessed Name had commanded our father Avraham to take his son Yitzchak to Mount Moriah and there to sacrifice him, then Satan, wishing to bar Avraham's way, had transformed himself into a deep river traversing the road to Mount Moriah. Avraham and Yitzchak had plunged into the rushing waters, up to their lips that were calling out the Blessed Name, and the place had become dry land.

"This is why we go to the river to throw away our sins."

"Is it a true story?" Sorel had asked Fraydel. *"S'iz an emesa mysah?"*

"True?" echoed Fraydel, wrinkling her brow.

In only a little less than a month, the holy Days of Awe would arrive. The month of Elul had just been blessed. Every morning, the ram's horn was blown at the conclusion of the morning prayers, awakening the Jews from their spiritual slumber so that they might begin the painful process of repentance.

But for now, a band of Gypsies was camped by the side of the river, imposing their strange dark ways over the familiar ground, so that it was transformed into a foreign place, unwelcome to the locals.

One morning, they had simply appeared there. Their caravan of wooden wagons must have passed through Shluftchev in the dead of the night, before any of the men had yet awoken for the morning prayers. How the creaking wagons and high-stepping stallions could have passed right beneath the windows without waking anybody was a mystery nobody bothered to try and solve. Gypsies defied explanation.

The peasants tried to keep a vigilant eye on their animals and crops. Everyone knew the loose interpretation the Gypsies gave to the notion of ownership.

The Jews of Shluftchev, too, were suspicious of the lawless tribe temporarily in their midst, whose ways seemed to bespeak an uncleanliness of soul that was a calculated affront to God's Word. But beneath the distrust and aversion, there was a muffled chord of Jewish sympathy, which was dimly echoed back in the attitude that the Gypsies themselves took toward the Jews. These were others, different from the other others.

The Gypsies had a word, *gaje,* for all those who weren't Gypsies, just as the Jews used the word *goyim* for all those who weren't Jewish. *Gaje* simply means "peasants," and *goyim* simply means "nations," but somehow neither word was exactly a compliment. Still, the Gypsies were *goyim* who were barely tolerated by the other *goyim,* just as the Jews were *gaje* deeply despised by the other *gaje.*

The Gypsy men wore brightly colored kerchiefs knotted about their thick, strong necks, and ruffled shirts under old-fashioned suits with wide-legged pants. Their skin was the color of strong tea, and their mustaches curved upward like the lustrous wings of the seraphim. They traded horses—very shrewdly, according to the local legend—but seemed to spend the greater part of the day in Yankela's tavern, noisily toasting one another.

Sorel had only glimpsed these men from a distance, but, even from far back, there was something she couldn't name that hung about them, and that baffled her and frightened her and made her shudder whenever she imagined having one of them for a father. They had a way of standing, one hand lightly on a hip, while with the other hand they gestured in time with their speech; and also a way of moving that made you look hard and then quickly away.

The women were also strange and shameless in their ways, although somehow not so disturbing to Sorel as the men. They wore lots of brass-colored jewelry—dangling from their ears, from their necks and arms, even around their ankles. But somehow, despite all the jangle of their ornaments, they looked scruffy and destitute, most of them shoeless. Their bodices hung down loose and were cut low, and their bright-patterned skirts were very wide, down to their ankles, and of many layers, swooshing as they walked. Their hair, ink-black and gleaming, hung down from underneath embroidered kerchiefs, though some of the younger women wore their hair loose and wild. Fraydel thought these young women more beautiful than any she had ever seen, loving the dark skin and eyes of them, loving the strong white teeth. The way they moved on their bare feet and swaying hips seemed to her to be more dancing than walking, and when a girl tossed back her head in a motion for which Fraydel hadn't the words, Fraydel's breathing had stopped cold.

But the older women of Shluftchev could only look on the immodesty of these women with pity, shaking their heads at the reckless impudence of them, at the unclean thoughts they must raise up in men. The Gypsy women walked with a suggestive ease in their movements. They talked in loud voices, with a boldness in their eyes that was even worse than the peasants'.

The Gypsy women spent a large part of their day by the side of the road, while their men drank toasts to one another in Yankela's tavern.

Using an impressive array of tactics, the Gypsy women would try to get the Polish women to stop and have their fortunes told, or to buy a charm or an amulet, a pendant imprinted with symbols.

"You must guard against the Evil Eye with an amulet," a woman would urge with a fierce solemnity in her voice and eyes, strongly intimating that *you,* in particular, had urgent need for the magic she was selling.

A peasant girl, about fifteen or sixteen, fair and buxom, as pretty as any girl who had ever walked this way before, came into sight of the Gypsy women, who were gathered by the side of the road, sitting or stooping, their hands dangling between their legs, lost in the loose folds of their wide layered skirts. One of them jumped up, the black river of her hair rippling down below her knees. She was not much older than the peasant girl, who was making a poor show of pretending not to notice how closely she was being watched by the dark silent huddle of women. The Gypsy girl ran ahead a few steps and then began to walk as the other had, only much exaggerating the swinging arms and the nose in the air, so that the Gypsy women laughed with their open mouths full of gaps and gold.

The peasant girl stopped short, not certain whether she was being made fun of or not. The blood rose swiftly in the white cream of her face, until she was red-stained up into her hair.

"Pretty," said the young Gypsy girl, with the knee-length night hair, taking a handful of the bright-yellow stuff of the other. She pointed up to the sun and then back to the strands she was clutching in her fist. "You stole from it," she said, waving a finger back and forth beneath the girl's fine nose, in a sly pretense of censure.

The peasant girl smiled, a nervous, twitching smile, her wide eyes expressing the full amount of suspicion of which they were capable, and the little pack of Gypsy women all smiled back at her, a few of them even nodding, as if she had said something with which they agreed. The Gypsy girl let go of the fistful of summer hair. She reached out for the girl's wrist and grasped it. She unfolded the palm and regarded it fixedly. The smile quickly drained from the peasant girl's face.

The other Gypsies drew in closer, staring with the same expressive intensity down into the palm.

The girl looked up, her blue eyes wider than ever. "Is it good?" she whispered, her lips again twitching, and her voice sounding like a little child's. "Is it good for me?"

The Gypsy girl, still staring down into the open palm, raised her other hand and rubbed its thumb against its fingers. The peasant girl reached into her apron pocket and pulled out a bright coin.

And all of this Fraydel watched, from a little distance away.

The Gypsy women knew better than to badger the Jewish women into having their fortunes told. Jews were forbidden to consult seers and magicians, astrologers and witches. Not that the Jewish women of Shluftchev gave too much credence to the reputed powers of these passing strangers. The Jewish women repeated to one another, with little jokes at the expense of a Polish peasant's *saychel,* the predictions— cunningly vague, flattering, and insidious—that their *goyish* neighbors had paid good money to hear. A curse from a Gypsy woman, always delivered with convincing ceremony, was capable of inspiring stark terror and drastic reprisals on the part of the peasants, who deemed it highly prudent not to offend these people, while at the same time also taking care not to be fleeced by them. A peasant woman, seeing a Gypsy approaching her property, would hurry to take down the clothes drying on the clothesline. She would quickly chase the chickens and geese off the dirt tracks and into the barnyard, scolding and cursing.

But the Gypsy children who came knocking at Shluftchev's doors were given bread smeared with rendered chicken fat by the Jewish women, who clucked their tongues and shook their heads over the children's mud-encrusted bare feet and filthy necks and tattered clothes, no doubt crawling with vermin. Just to look at these little urchins made you start itching and scratching at phantom lice.

While the Gypsies camped in the clearing near the dark glassy river, Fraydel went around with eyes that sparkled and a skin that was always lightly flushed, so that Leiba kept feeling her eldest daughter's brow to see if she were sick.

"Do you feel well, Fraydel? Does your head ache you?"

And Fraydel would shake her head no and then run out the door to disappear—who knew where?

The Gypsies had their own language, Fraydel told Sorel. Romani. They traveled ceaselessly, from country to country, sneaking over borders just as soundlessly as they had crept that night through Shluftchev. (Only Fraydel had heard them, her eyes wide open as she lay beside her sisters.)

"Do they have special powers?" Sorel asked her. "Can they see into the future?"

"Maybe," said Fraydel, shrugging her thin shoulders. "In the beginning of time, the Blessed Name gave each nation a special gift. To us He gave the Torah. To the Egyptians He gave the power of magic. Perhaps the Gypsies are descendants from the ancient Egyptians."

"They *look* like Egyptians!"

Fraydel nodded.

"Do you think so, Fraydel? Do you think they're really Egyptians?"

Fraydel shrugged. She looked as if she were making ready to dash off, and, in order to forestall her, Sorel quickly asked, "Have you spoken to any of them?"

"A little. Just this morning, I was carrying some flowers, and a little girl I passed on the road made a wide circle around me. I turned and offered her one, and she almost jumped from her skin. It was as if I had insulted her. 'No flower,' she said. 'No good, flower. When someone dies. Flower, death.' Anyway," Fraydel said, shrugging, "she said something like that." Fraydel looked away, her head tilted to the side. "I think tonight I'm going to go to their camp," she said suddenly, as if she might have just decided. "Maybe she'll speak to me again."

"Can I come with you?"

Fraydel shrugged again. "Why not? But don't say anything to anyone else," she added quickly.

And so, later, after the evening soup, the two girls slipped away, Sorel disappearing with her older sister—who knew where? Chana surmised that the two were together, and it made her so angry she would have loved an excuse to scream out loud—the way Fraydel did, with no excuse at all.

Fraydel let Sorel take hold of her hand as they walked away from Shluftchev.

"Don't be so scared," she said, smiling down at her little sister as they approached the dark mass of the forest, even though Sorel hadn't murmured a word. But it was true: Sorel was scared.

"They're people, too, believe it or not," Fraydel said with a little laugh, while slightly tossing her head in a way that was new.

To Sorel's wandering eye it seemed as if she had never seen this forest before. She herself was entirely lost. She wouldn't have known her way back. As always, she put her faith completely in the superior knowledge of her sister Fraydel.

As they approached the Gypsy camp, they could see the smoke thinly rising from the many fires. Fraydel walked calmly on, her courage seeming to Sorel all the more remarkable since there were so many people from whom Fraydel ran away. There were women who lived in Shluftchev—plain, unexceptional women, whom Fraydel had known all of her life—who made her turn white and cringe—with distaste or with terror, who could say? Sorel never could understand what it was about Hadassah Willamousky or Masha Mazur that made Fraydel take off in the opposite direction, like a startled rabbit, whenever she spotted either. And how could it be that those normal Jewish housewives, as unexotic as a bowl of buckwheat groats, made Fraydel squeamish, whereas now she walked, never faltering, toward the campsite of these rough outlaws, whose unclean magic seemed to have penetrated and altered the moist woods around them?

There was a half-circle of wooden wagons, of a deep-toned natural-colored oak and heavily varnished, placed in such a way that they partly hid the camp from view from the road. The roofs of the wagons were white. They had very high wooden wheels, and three windows on either side, and double doors at the front that opened onto a wide porchlike board. Large piles of eiderdowns, covered with fading brightly colored flower-patterned fabric, lay spread about the ground.

The horses had been unhitched from the wagons, and Fraydel and Sorel could hear their snorting and neighing coming from a distance away. There were other sounds, too. Even from this far away, the loud clear voices of the Gypsies resonated with an intensity to which the girls were not accustomed. In the background, they heard the dull muffled thuds of an ax and the shrill wailing of an infant, suddenly hushed.

It was as if the two sisters had crossed foreign seas and faraway lands to come to this place that Sorel had never before seen, far more frightening and more beautiful than the little spot beside the river where she went each autumn to cast off her year's worth of sins. The evening was falling into the forest with a bluish tint to it that seemed to Sorel a Gypsy color. The smell of the earth rose up all around her, heavy and rich as after a rain, and the trees whispered so insistently above their heads that she felt she could almost make out distinct words here and there, spoken in the Gypsy tongue. Romani. She clutched Fraydel's hand even tighter, and Fraydel laughed softly in response.

The campfire smoke mingled with the forest's dark scent, and Fraydel sniffed. She liked the smell. Smells were always very important to Fraydel. She noticed the slightest change in scents, and a bad smell could make her angry, changing her mood from good into bad. Sometimes she complained about a bad odor that no one else could detect and that would make her head ache cruelly at the temples.

As they crossed the road that dipped near to the forest, three mangy-looking dogs, yellowish white and with stiff short fur, came running toward them, baring their terrifyingly sharp teeth and snarling deep down in their yellow bellies.

The two girls knew better than to run. They grabbed one another's hands and stood their ground, clutching at one another as they began to recite aloud, in panicked voices, the Hebrew prayer one makes on encountering a wild dog.

Behind them they heard low laughter. An entire pack of barefoot Gypsy children had suddenly materialized, the very small ones almost entirely naked.

A little boy, about eight or nine, with a faded magenta kerchief

knotted about his neck and a dirty white shirt that was completely but-
tonless, so that his bare young brown chest showed through, now
scooped up a rock and hurled it high off into the forest. The three dogs
immediately took off, yapping, in the direction in which the rock had
been thrown.

"*Dzenkuie*—thank you," Fraydel said in her strange whispery voice
and in her uncertain Polish, which again set the pack of children off
into gales of laughter. The boy who had thrown the rock was particularly convulsed, throwing back his head, which was topped with the
most extraordinary hair Sorel had ever seen. Though mostly dark, it
seemed to have mixed in every color possible for hair to have, and it
stood up all over his head in strange thick tufts.

Fraydel and Sorel had never heard children make such a noise. The
Gypsy children, girls and boys together, all of them only half clothed,
especially compared with Fraydel and Sorel in their high-necked, long-
sleeved dresses, pushed one another and elbowed one another so that
none remained still for more than two seconds.

The laughter at last died out. Then one of them—it seemed to be
that same tufted boy—started it up again, and instantly they were all
back to it, dancing around and pushing, a blur of motion and color and
exaggerated shrill laughter.

Fraydel and Sorel, still holding hands, watched on and smiled a little, though Sorel herself still felt weak in the knees from the thought
of the wild Gypsy dogs.

The little boy who had thrown the rock now approached the two
girls, looking intently down at their feet—or, rather, their shoes.
Fraydel quickly unlaced her black sturdy ankle-shoes, bought new for
last Rosh Hashanah but still with plenty of room in them, and handed
them over to the boy, who didn't waste a moment slipping in his own
two filthy feet.

Sorel looked at Fraydel in astonishment. What would Fraydel do if
she never got them back again? Walk around barefoot like a Gypsy?

The boy was showing off in Fraydel's shoes with silly mincing
steps, even swaying his hips slightly, so that again all the children dis-
solved into a blurring motion of laughter.

This was all the encouragement the boy needed. He launched into an exuberant dance, so fast it seemed to Sorel hardly to be possible—his legs kicking in front of him and then bent up behind him, while his hands clapped before his chest, behind his back, slapped down on his heels. And all the while his head tossed gracefully on his delicate neck, knotted with the faded magenta kerchief, and he smiled wide and wild, his teeth pure white in his dusky face.

The children around him were clapping in unison—one palm cupped, the fingers of the other hand expertly tapping. It was clapping that seemed almost to have melody. Some of the children also stamped their feet in accompaniment, while producing an eerie trill in the back of their throats.

The cadence of the rhythm, the boy's flying feet and tossing head, like nothing Sorel had ever heard or seen before, sent something strange and full of sparks rushing up through all her body. She was shocked to the depths of her being by the quick pleasure of the Gypsy heat in her blood.

Suddenly, the children halted to a dead silence, and all looked over to a spot behind Fraydel and Sorel. Fraydel and Sorel turned and saw a woman who was standing a little way off from the circle of children. Her hands were on her hips, and she had a severe expression on her strong-boned face.

She said a few sharp-sounding words to the children in a language that wasn't Polish.

Romani, thought Sorel. The Gypsy language.

The little boy, still in Fraydel's shoes, returned the woman's words with a few angry-sounding words of his own. His chin came up as he spoke, so that his head was slightly thrown back. It was a way for a child to answer back to a grown-up that completely amazed Sorel. If a Jewish child had ever dared to speak to a grown woman like that, he would have been taken to task for his lack of respect. But the woman simply shrugged her shoulders and walked away.

"You not Polish girls, she say," the boy now said to Fraydel in Polish. He stumbled over the words, clearly unsteady in the language.

Fraydel answered him in a Polish that was even more halting than his own.

"Yes. Not Polish girls. Jewish girls."

"Jewish girls," repeated the boy, seeming to take delight in the sound of the word. Perhaps it was the first time he had ever said it for himself. "You much gold. You happy girls."

"And you dance good. You happy boy."

Again the boy's legs shot out before and behind him, and he gave another enchanting demonstration of his dancing skill in Fraydel's shoes, while the children around him made music from their open palms.

"You like!" he announced, smiling widely up at the girls with a sort of showmanship that they had never before seen.

"Come," he said, "you come me. I show you something good. Jewish girls," he said again, with the same visible enjoyment at the word.

He led the girls past one of the fires that had been built downwind from the wagons. A few women were squatting near the ground cooking something that smelled very good, heavily perfumed with spice. The women barely glanced at Fraydel and Sorel.

Between two of the wagons a line had been stretched, and on it hung a fair amount of small dead animals, dangling by their hind legs. They were smaller than rabbits but definitely of the rodent family. They looked suspiciously like rats, and again Sorel clutched at Fraydel's hand. This time she was more worried for Fraydel than for herself. Even on the Sabbath and holidays, Fraydel could rarely bring herself to eat *flayshig,* or flesh. Sometimes she left the table, gagging, both hands pressed hard over her mouth.

But Fraydel now only gave a glance toward the suspended slaughter and didn't even grimace. She turned to the boy, who, looking very proud, pointed at the carcasses and pronounced some unintelligible word. The girls shook their heads, indicating that they didn't understand. He repeated the word, as well as another, rubbing his bare stomach to indicate something good to eat. When the girls still looked at him blankly, he emitted a loud explosive sound of exasperation and took them over to a small pile of debris from which he pulled out a puny dead hedgehog.

The boy crouched down and motioned the two girls to do the same. He selected a twig at random and cut a sharp point into it with a knife he also picked up from a pile on the ground. He stuck this point into the animal's hind leg, and loosened the skin around this hole until the thin bone was revealed. He then put the hole into his mouth and began to blow, inflating the hedgehog until its skin was taut. After tying off the hind-leg air passage, the little boy shaved off the quills quickly and skillfully with the knife.

As the quills fell from the hedgehog, it was transformed before their eyes into the repulsive form of the common rat.

All through this amazing demonstration, the Gypsy boy kept flashing the girls his brilliant smile. Sorel had never witnessed so much charm compressed into such a small area. In some way, although again she didn't know how to put a name to it, he reminded her of the grown-up Gypsy men, only—perhaps simply because there was less of him and therefore of that unnameable something—it didn't menace and overwhelm her. She watched what he was doing to the animal, his gold-brown hands skillfully going about their task, and she was completely fascinated and not at all disgusted, though all the time she was strangely aware of his bare brown belly.

The boy now untied the hole to deflate the carcass, and brought it over to a nearby fire, around which the women sat crouched on their haunches, Gypsy-style. The blue flames licked the bottom of the heavy iron cauldron that sat on a primitive-looking tripod. At the bottom of the cauldron, the fat was sizzling noisily, and the fumes that were rising were heavily scented with garlic.

The boy stuck a long-pronged iron utensil into one end of the denuded hedgehog and then brought the meat close to the fire, carefully turned it round and round, and withdrew it every few minutes to inspect it closely. Fraydel looked away, but Sorel watched closely, so that now the boy was clearly favoring her with his dazzling smile. Both his brown cheeks were dimpled. His eyes were very large, the lashes long. They looked like pools of black in the blue-tinged evening.

Again, from out of nowhere, his former comrades materialized. A few sat down beside the women, who began, by way of a caress, to search their heads lovingly for lice, while several others crouched beside Sorel's Gypsy boy.

Meanwhile, the flesh of the hedgehog darkened, and when the boy judged it to be ready, he deposited it onto the upturned lid of a cooking pot and offered it, again with his flashing smile, to the two girls, who wordlessly shook their heads. They grasped the insult implicit in their refusal, yet they couldn't possibly accept the boy's gift of unkosher meat.

Fortunately, one of the Gypsy women seemed to understand the situation and said a few words in the Gypsy language to the boy, who was already beginning visibly to bristle and draw back from the two girls, even from Sorel, whom he had clearly chosen as his favorite. The little boy listened, solemnly nodding now and again.

He turned back to Sorel with his former smile and dimples fully reinstated.

"You Jewish girls. No eat"—and here he repeated again the unintelligible word.

The woman who had spoken now walked over to the girls. She was carrying a large red-enameled dish, the kind that was used by the local population as wash basins. It was filled with red peppers, soaking in a vinegary-smelling brine. She gestured, with a smile, for the girls to reach in and help themselves.

Fraydel and Sorel glanced at one another. The basin that now held the peppers may have, at other times, held dead hedgehogs, or things equally *trayf*. Nonetheless, Fraydel, followed by Sorel, reached in and took out a slice of pepper. Each of them took a small bite. The pepper was sharper than almost anything they had ever tasted, bringing tears to their eyes, like the bitter herbs they ate on the first two nights of Passover. But they indicated to the women, in their broken Polish, that it tasted good.

At this almost all of the women sitting near them gave them their wide, toothy smiles. Another woman approached with some bread, but the girls had to refuse it, for fear that it had been made with lard.

Sorel and Fraydel had never before been confronted with this problem of not being able to accept food that others were offering them in kindness and hospitality. It was fortunate that some among the Gypsy women seemed to know of the strict rules that governed the diets of the Jews, and good-naturedly accepted the girls' refusals with little shrugs.

The women kept offering them different things, trying various dishes out. It soon became obvious that the girls could only accept uncooked fruits and vegetables from the Gypsy women: some small young cucumbers, dipped in coarse salt; two tin pails overflowing with blackberries that had been borrowed from a local farmer's field.

Meanwhile, the men were returning in small groups to the camp, and the women, at the sound of the approaching voices, jumped up from their places at the fire, surrendering these seats to the men.

Even Sorel, whose sense of smell was nothing compared with Fraydel's, caught the strong whiff of these men, and she wondered whether Fraydel's head would begin to ache at the temples. She took Fraydel's hand—it felt cold and limp—and she pressed it. Fraydel looked down at her, and it seemed to Sorel that an uneasiness was on Fraydel's face, now that the Gypsy men had returned. Did Fraydel also feel that incomprehensible something that the Gypsy men gave off?

The men took their places, lying back on their sides with outstretched legs crossed at the ankles, their heads resting on propped-up palms. They took no notice of the two Jewish girls, and the women now seemed to have no time to notice them either. Even the wonderful boy, who had taken such delight in showing off for them, seemed to have lost interest now in their existence. He sat down near the feet of a man who, by the smile he flashed him, was no doubt his father.

Fraydel and Sorel backed away, too shy now to say anything—even to thank the women, as they knew they should.

It was clearly time to leave. Already the darkness had fallen down from the forest, blending thickly with the smoke of the Gypsy fires. It would be a dark night. The moon was a sliver, newly blessed. The tea-brown faces caught the flickering light from the flames. Sorel looked one last time at the boy, who looked up to flash her his quick smile. He must have been very used to smiling goodbye, slipping over borders as noiselessly as they had passed that night through sleeping Shluftchev.

But how to leave when the Gypsy boy still wore Fraydel's shoes? Again one of the women came to their rescue, all at once noticing the two shoes on the little boy's feet and ordering, with a laugh, that they be returned to the Jewish girl. This time the boy didn't smile.

The girls offered their quick "thank you"s and hurried from the campsite. As they crossed the road, they could hear the terrifying shrill barking that had greeted them, but since the intruders were now leaving the campsite, the dogs didn't bother to pursue them.

The girls plunged into the farmer's field instead of taking the longer road back. Even Fraydel, who was given much more freedom than the other girls of Shluftchev, was under strict orders to be home before nightfall.

The throbbing of the crickets—like the trill of the children, only deeper and slower—sounded loudly in their ears. The air itself was heavy and sweet with the smell of the ripening grains and melons, apples and pears, and the insects were making themselves crazy in the tall singing grass.

Above the girls, in the perfectly clear sky, the new moon of Elul hung polished bright, as sharp as a sickle with which to reap the tall harvest hay. And the stars!

Fraydel had once told Sorel that the outermost sphere of the universe is a band of purest light. The stars aren't bodies but, rather, rents in the firmament, where the light of the outermost sphere squeezes through.

"Is it true?" Sorel had asked her.

"True?" Fraydel had asked her back. Yet never after this had Sorel looked at the nighttime sky in the same way as before.

Flying bugs, fat and fierce at summer's end, attacked them mercilessly as they moved through the farmer's field of buckwheat. Their legs and arms were covered by the clothes prescribed by the Jewish laws of modesty, but they could feel the welts rising anyway, as the hungry insects bored through the material of their sleeves and stockings.

Suddenly, before they had yet emerged from the farmer's field, Sorel saw Fraydel make a motion she'd never seen from her before. Fraydel threw her two thin arms around herself, as if hugging herself. Just as quickly, it was over. A strange sound, too, had escaped, like a little alarmed animal, from deep down in Fraydel's throat.

Sorel understood. She felt as if her excitement also needed to find a voice and a motion.

Leiba looked at both girls quizzically as they came into the house but asked them no questions. She and Chana were sitting at the table, sewing in the smoky light of the kerosene lamp.

Fraydel and Sorel took seats at the table and picked up some mending from the basket that lay at Leiba's feet.

Chana, whose stitches, small and perfectly even, were a source of pride to her, didn't look up from her sewing. (Often, when she saw the careless mess that Fraydel made of the mending, the threads loose and every stitch a different size, she would rip it out and, with a silent sense of satisfaction, do it over again to her standards.) But when both she and Fraydel reached down at the same moment to take a boy's shirt from the basket, she noticed that Fraydel had torn the sleeve of her own dress.

"Go take it off," she told her. "I'll sew it up right now for you."

"Here," Fraydel said, holding out the sleeve. "You can just sew it up like this."

"Are you completely crazy in the head?" Chana asked her. "Don't you know what it means to sew a garment while someone wears it? God forbid!"

"Oh, leave me alone, Chana. Leave me and my torn sleeve in peace."

Leiba caught Chana's eye and gave a very slight shake of her head. Chana looked back down at her sewing, biting her bottom lip to keep back the angry words that were in her like a bad taste, and Sorel went back to thinking over the marvelous events of this evening, which were even now swimming in visions before her eyes.

All that motion and color and noise. The vibrating voices and heavily scented food sizzling in great black cauldrons. The eiderdowns lying outside on the ground.

Imagine, to sleep out in the open, under the stars, exposed to the night!

Did the Gypsies really, then, have magical powers, to keep the unclean spirits from drawing too near? Could they stare at your palm and foresee your life—the good and the bad, the day of your death? Had they really preserved the secrets of magic the Name had once bestowed on the nation of Egypt?

She kept seeing the glint of the Gypsy boy's knife, transforming the hedgehog into a rat. Imagine, to eat such a thing!

The boy's dark eyes had held her own so steadily, and she hadn't looked away. It was shameless, unworthy, but Sorel didn't feel in the least bit sorry. In fact, she felt the very opposite of sorry! She wished she could go back and do it again. Those very same eyes that had held her own, had traveled the wide, wide world—it made her dizzy!—had taken in sights so unimaginably distant from Shluftchev. Those same eyes!

And then his dance, and the bareness of him catching the fire, and the strange Gypsy heat that had burst into her own blood. As if her body was remembering, Sorel felt her cheeks brushed with flame.

Had she really felt that—she, Sorel Sonnenberg, who sat here sewing with her mother and sisters? Was that what it felt like to be a Gypsy? If so, then the Blessed Name had given them something even better than magic, even better than—Sorel stopped herself before the full blasphemy was spoken in her mind.

Fraydel sat across from her, her gaze cast down on the sewing in her hands, her needle in her awkward fingers passing in and out of the bunched material. (Chana would have to rip it all out.) Sorel found it hard to sit so calmly, as if nothing had changed, when here they were returned from an adventure unlike any other. Like something in a Fraydel story!

It was almost impossible to believe, sitting here at the familiar table and drawing the needle in and out of the mending, that these things had really happened, that for a brief time she and Fraydel had entered into a world entirely unlike their own. Not an hour had passed since they had been standing within a stone's throw from those dark and fierce-looking men, with their great sweeping mustaches draped over the bottles they passed from hand to hand, and their voices so loud and deep that they echoed inside your chest.

She would have liked to ask Fraydel what she thought about these people, about the Gypsy women who had proved so much gentler than their impudent manner of accosting people at the side of the road would ever have led her to anticipate. But Fraydel wouldn't even allow Sorel to catch her eye. She wouldn't look up from her sewing.

It was two days later when Sorel finally got a chance to speak alone to Fraydel.

"Have you been back again to see them?"

"Yes," Fraydel answered, but offered no more.

"Do you like them, their ways?"

"If it's true that they steal, then I don't like that. But who knows if it's even true? The *goyim* say that we do all sorts of terrible things, too."

Sorel thought about this for a little while.

"Are you going to go back there again this evening?" she finally asked her sister.

Fraydel looked at Sorel for several moments.

"I'm afraid that I'll make a nuisance of myself," she finally said.

"Did you ever find that girl who spoke to you about the flowers?" Sorel didn't ask about the boy with the hair of many colors. In the two days since she'd been to the Gypsies, the shame that had refused to come that night had finally arrived. It was good that this was Elul. Sorel wouldn't have liked to carry her unclean secret for long within her chest.

"Oh yes," Fraydel said. "Tsura. I found her."

"Tsura?"

"It's her name."

"It's a little bit like my name. Does it mean something in Gypsy?"

Sorel asked, more in order to keep Fraydel with her. She sensed that Fraydel was getting ready to disappear—who knew where?

"Romani. That's the name of their language. I don't know if Gypsy names have meanings the way Jewish ones do."

And she was gone.

Late in the night, while the others slept, Sorel awoke, instantly wide awake. Beside her on one side, Chana was sleeping her undisturbed sleep. But the place on her other side was empty. Fraydel was gone!

Sorel went padding off on her bare feet to the little curtained-off place where Leiba stood singing over her dough.

Leiba looked up to see Sorel standing there and smiled. She dusted off her floury hands and lifted Sorel up to her nighttime seat on the clay oven.

It was the same as it had been every other night, only this night was different. Fraydel was not in her bed, sleeping her fitful sleep and murmuring in her dreams.

Fraydel had slipped out into the Gypsies' night, was outside beneath the stars with them. Sorel knew this, and her knowledge filled her with so many feelings that she couldn't pull them apart, like threads from different spools entangled with one another.

It was Fraydel herself who had told Sorel about the forms of darkness who roam the night.

It was Fraydel who had told her about the studyhouse, where the impure hosts argued out points of the Law and laughed at the unholy nonsense they produced!

She was wonderful, Fraydel! She was as fearless as the ancient prophetess Devorah, who had marched before an army of men!

Only what if she overheard the dangerous voices of the impure hosts?

Take care, Fraydel! Take care to stop up your ears against the terrible laughter!

Outside the window, the night pressed in as dark as the night that had once fallen on Egypt. Sorel as soon expected to see her sister's pale face staring back in as the wild-eyed leering creature she'd caught glimpses of before.

"Sing to me, Mamma."

Know that a person walks in life on a very high and narrow
    bridge.
The most important rule is not to be afraid.

Leiba gathered the child up into her two strong arms and climbed the ladder to the little loft in which the three girls slept.

Carefully, she placed the drowsy little night-wanderer under the eiderdown, between her two older sisters. Chana slept soundly, but Fraydel murmured something in her sleep.

It was two days after this that Sorel, carrying water back from the well in the darkening evening, heard Fraydel calling softly out to her.

"Over here, Sorel. Quickly. Don't let Chana catch sight of you."

Fraydel was standing behind the house of their next-door neighbors.

When Sorel slipped her hand into her sister's, the skin of Fraydel's hand felt different—not cold and damp, as usual, but hot. Perhaps Fraydel had a fever?

"What is it, Fraydel?"

"I have a secret to tell you."

A secret! From Fraydel!

"Tonight the Gypsies leave."

"Oh." The news made Sorel sad, the loss of that noise and color and motion there in the clearing by the river. Despite the burning secret of her shame, it made her sad that tonight they would go. It would be stupid now to ask Fraydel if she had ever learned the name of the boy with the strange tufted hair.

"I'm leaving with them," Fraydel said.

Sorel stared at her sister.

You never knew what would come out of Fraydel's mouth, only that it would be wonderful.

It took just a moment for everything to shift before Sorel's eyes, for all the old world to come to an abrupt end.

"I want to come with you, Fraydel."

Fraydel smiled.

"I thought you might say that."

She cocked her head to the right and thought for several seconds.

"Think very, very carefully, Sorel. You wouldn't see Mamma for a very long time. You're much younger than I am. You're more attached to her. Think carefully."

"I'm coming with you."

"So much thought?" Fraydel laughed. "So much thought you give such a big decision?"

"I'm coming with you."

It was as if she hadn't even had to come to any decision. These seemed somehow to be the only words that Sorel remembered how to say.

"All right," said Fraydel, and turned as if to walk away.

"Wait!" called out Sorel, to whom a few questions had suddenly occurred. Fraydel turned back.

"Will we have to eat hedgehogs?"

Fraydel smiled.

"No. We'll eat fruits and vegetables. There's always plenty. Their bread is *trayf*. They have a word, *marhime,* it means "unclean," just like our word *tomay*. If a woman lets her skirt pass over food, if she walks over the crops growing in a farmer's field, it's *marhime*. And you must be careful to drink water only from the women's jug. They'll teach us, the women."

"Will we have to steal from the peasants?"

"Of course not. We won't do anything that we think is wrong."

"Do the Gypsies really kidnap little children?"

"No more than we murder little children before Pesach and use their blood for matzohs."

Sorel thought about this for several moments. She didn't at all question Fraydel's mastery of the facts. Fraydel always knew things, from her books and from other places. From the air itself, it sometimes seemed, she took in floating knowledge, invisible to the eye.

Fraydel had even begun to learn the Gypsy language. Romani, Romani, she said, letting the melody of the word play over her tongue.

"And when will we see Mamma again?"

"That I can't answer you, Sorela. It may be a very long time. The *kompania* will travel very far before it passes here again. To the four corners of the world and back again."

And Fraydel threw her thin arms around herself, as she had that night in the fields of singing grass, and the sound like a small excited animal jumped from her throat.

"To America?"

"Maybe. Why not?"

"Chicago, too?"

"Maybe Chicago, too." Fraydel laughed, her strange choking laugh that made Sorel feel pity.

"But we will see Mamma again?"

"We will."

"Then it's decided," Fraydel now said. She spoke very quickly, her voice quivering, as when it took off on a wild story with a life all its own.

"I'll wake you when it's time to go. We don't need to bring anything, only the clothes that we wear. But most important, Sorela"— and here Fraydel's voice shook as if it were about to be blown apart by a wind—"most important, you must be careful of Mamma. Sometimes . . ." Fraydel paused, until she could regain control over her voice. "Sometimes I think that Mamma can read my thoughts."

All of this was hastily whispered behind the neighbors' house, in the failing light, and was interrupted by Chana's coming out of the house to call them in for the evening soup.

Fraydel gave Sorel's hand a surreptitious little squeeze, and Sorel again felt how strangely hot and dry Fraydel's hand was, as if there were a fire under the skin. If Fraydel was sick, if she got one of her terrible headaches, would the Gypsy women take care of her, as Mamma did? Would they bathe her forehead in cool wet rags?

The rest of the family was already gathered together around the table. Tatta was standing over the wash basin, pouring the water from the special tin washing cup over his fingertips, murmuring the prayer for ablution. The loaf of bread stood waiting for him on the table, and Mamma stood at the stove, ladling the soup out into the brown earthenware bowls that were so familiar that only now did Sorel notice them for the first time in her life. The dear bowls that held the nightly soup.

Everything was the same, only completely different.

Sorel drank up the picture before her. In deep, painful quaffs Sorel took in her family.

This is the last time I hear Tatta making the blessing on the bread.

The last time I sit here eating the evening soup with my family.

The last time . . . Sorel thought to herself that her chest would be crushed beneath the weight of these three words.

It was like the times when her throat hurt her only if she swallowed, and yet she couldn't keep herself from swallowing, testing and retesting for the presence of the pain. So Sorel kept repeating to herself these words, "the last time."

Bezalel slid off of his chair and toddled over to his father, who lifted him onto his lap, feeding him from his bowl. This was a nightly ritual for Tzali.

And suddenly the memory came rushing back to Sorel of how she, too, when she was very little, perhaps before she could even speak, used to climb up onto her tatta's lap while he ate his evening soup, and how he had fed her from his bowl.

And on top of this memory another quickly piled itself: Of how, when she was little, she used to climb onto her father's lap, while he sat studying from the holy books. He would move the tract of Talmud a little ways back onto the table to make room for her on his lap.

"This is an aleph," he would say, pointing to a beautiful black shape on the page: like a tall man running and waving a flag in either hand. "Aleph. It makes no sound of its own. It is of a humble nature. And for this reason it was chosen to come first in the *alephbais*."

It was Tatta who had first taught her all her letters! When had she stopped climbing onto her father's lap, and why?

Tatta! Tatta! The last time . . .

And Mamma!

Mamma, pounding her dough in the middle of the night, singing the melodies that wandered off into such sad and lonely places. Looking up, Mamma would see her standing in the doorway, and Mamma would dust the flour off from her hands and gather her up into the hush that fell around them like soft drifts of snow.

Mamma!

And yet it had to be. Sorel knew this. She couldn't let Fraydel go off into the world all by herself. If Fraydel went away alone tonight, then Sorel would lose her forever. This was the knowledge that had been there inside her when it had seemed as if all she remembered how to say were the words "I'm coming with you." She had known the moment had arrived when she might lose Fraydel forever.

But she would never lose Mamma. Mamma would always be here, waiting for her, whenever it was that she returned from wandering the four corners of the world with Fraydel.

Mamma!

And there sit Asher and Dovid. They are my brothers, and yet I barely know them. All day long they sit in the studyhouse, *chavrusas,* study partners. Soon they will both be married. When I see them next, they'll have wives of their own. Maybe even children.

And Chana. She, too, will soon be married. Sooner, now that Fraydel will be gone.

It was like a thorn sticking in Chana's soft flesh, that the older sister would have to get married first. Who would want to marry Fraydel? Fraydel, Fraydel, *da meshuggena maydel.* Would Chana have to die, God forbid, an old maid, waiting for the older sister to find a bridegroom?

Now you will marry, Chana, and have a household and children of your own. Chana! The last time.

Sorel watched the present moment slipping away into the past. This moment gone, then this moment gone. Always it was like this, she thought, only I hadn't realized. Always time is stealing away from us, snatching like a thief in the night.

And Sorel moaned softly without knowing that she did so.

"What is it, Sorela?" Mamma said quickly, reaching her hand across the table and laying it on Sorel's brow.

"Does your head ache you? Your eyes are too bright, mammala, and your cheeks are flushed. Nachum, look at the child."

Sorel's father broke off his discussion with his two sons and looked across the table at Sorel.

"Are you unwell, Sorela?" he asked, his eyes full of concern. "Does something hurt you?"

Don't break my heart, Tatta. Please, don't do it.

"Come here, little lamb. Come sit on my lap. Tzali, make some room for your sister."

Fraydel, who had kept her eyes down on the bowl of soup all through the meal, now lifted them up and flashed Sorel a quick glance, full of meaning.

Was it true? Could Mamma and Tatta read their children's thoughts?

"It's okay, Tatta," Sorel said. "I feel okay. Nothing hurts me."

A falsehood. God forgive me, a black falsehood.

"So, then, eat your soup," Mamma said. "You haven't put a spoon of soup yet into your mouth."

Sorel lifted the spoon to her mouth. The last time.

Sorel opened her eyes into the darkness, instantly wide awake. Beside her she heard the steady breathing of her sister Chana. But the place on her other side was empty. Fraydel was gone!

With as much haste as she could manage, heedless of the danger of splinters, Sorel scrambled down the narrow wooden slats of the ladder and then stood at a loss in the darkness.

Should she try to slip out the door without Mamma's seeing her, try to make her own way into the night to join Fraydel and the *kompania?* She would have to do it! She herself would have to go alone into the screaming night, filled with its unclean secrets, the leering, wild-eyed creature that had pressed itself up against the window.

She would search this black night-world for Fraydel, for Fraydel. . . . Master of the Universe, only let me not lose forever my Fraydel!

Sorel heard a noise, frightening, that was coming from the back of the house.

Silently, on her bare feet, Sorel crept toward the curtain.

There stood Fraydel—*was* it Fraydel?—choking—on laughter, on weeping, who could tell?

Was it Fraydel?

A horrible sound that was running away with a life of its own.

Fraydel's head was whipped from side to side with the brutal force that burst from her gaping mouth, so deforming her features that she hardly seemed to be Fraydel.

Was it Fraydel?

Behind Sorel now stood Tatta and the boys. Only Chana, the sound sleeper, hadn't been awoken by the shrieks and laughter, terrible.

Leiba stood, her shoulders slumped, her two strong arms hanging down at her sides, of no use to her or her child.

CHAPTER 7

COUNTING THE OMER

*L*eiba recognized that Fraydel was in danger of disappearing down the well of her own thoughts.

Fraydel was a secret keeping herself from the world. When she spoke, it was yet another way of keeping silent.

And the moods. Carrying her so far away, it seemed she might never make her way back again. These were the times when Leiba knew terror.

Flesh of her own flesh, Fraydel was a stranger in the deepest sense of the word. Leiba didn't know how to go about imagining what the world was like for her daughter, what it felt like for Fraydel to be Fraydel. Even her sons and husband, inhabiting the remote and lofty world of their high learning, were not strangers in so deep a sense as Fraydel.

Sometimes it seemed to Leiba that there was a strength forged out of some unknown metal that was hammered into Fraydel, a power to resist that bewildered even Fraydel, but in the thought of which Leiba took some comfort.

At other times, Leiba felt it was just the opposite, and she berated her own callous heart, which had chosen solace over seeing. Fraydel was so fragile she was left without any protection at all. She was a soul without a skin. Everything assaulted her. The world was flaying her raw.

A child who can't endure a touch. A mystery that won't be embraced. But a mother doesn't want a mystery for a daughter. A mother wants a Chanala, sweet and docile, a sunlit bottom hiding no sharp surprises.

With amusement, Leiba saw how Chana stared each Shabbes morning at the young married women who sat whispering together in the women's balcony of the prayerhouse. Chana, dear child, was as easy to read as a child's *mysah*.

But Fraydel had become something indecipherable, a volume written in a language Leiba didn't know—only a word here and there, and these few were such as to sicken her with fear. A pit of icy terror would open at her feet.

It took every shred of the good sense for which the people of Shluftchev praised her, for Leiba to restrain herself from falling to her knees and pleading with Fraydel:

"Is it anger that makes you do these things? And if it is anger, then—please, child—tell me why you are so angry?"

Fraydel wouldn't say. Probably, she couldn't say, for it wasn't an anger at a "this" or a "that," at a something that could be altered or erased, emended or ended. It was an anger with the world itself.

Why are you angry with the world, Fraydel? What is your *tiyna,* your complaint? Why can't you make your peace?

The girl had an unusually good head on her shoulders, this Leiba knew.

Thank God, all of her children were not lacking in this regard.

The boys, Asher and Dovid, may they be led to the wedding canopy and to deeds of loving kindness, were scholars like their saintly father, may he be granted long years, suffused with the sweet breath of his soul—*shayna menshen,* beautiful men. God grant that the baby live to follow in their ascending footsteps.

And as for Sorela, dear child, may she be blessed among the daughters of Israel: she, too, was as far from being stupid as the carp is from giving milk. A child whose head was always thick with impressions, who lived life with her eyes wide open.

For that matter, Chanala—may she live in modesty, to bear many children in good health and to educate them in the ways of God—she was far from being the dunce that Fraydel took her for. It was, rather, a matter of her having a lazier mind than her sisters and brothers, a mind that was content to grope for the nearest answer at hand.

Not that this was a bad thing. The answers surrounding Chana were good answers.

But Fraydel had been something else all over again. May the Merciful One forgive Leiba if there had been something sinful in the pride she had taken in the cleverness of the child. Should she have wished the child to have been otherwise? It had made the world over again for Leiba, to see the world through Fraydel's eyes—

—*staring up at the streaked sky, after the third meal of the Shabbes—the moment in the week when miracles are most likely to happen*—"*What do you see, Mamma Shaynala? Why do you stare?*"—"*Look, Mamma! The crack across the sky! And all the angels!*"—

The way that child could talk when she was still toddling around unsteadily on her little plump legs. Better than many an adult, in Shluftchev or beyond. A mind of her own, strong-willed as a mule—

—*I like Pharaoh the best, because always he said "No! No! No!"*—

From the moment she opened her eyes in the early morning until they finally sunk closed from exhaustion at night, she chattered away. Sometimes Leiba would even hear Fraydel continue talking in her sleep, so much had she to say about the nature of this and of that. It didn't matter if someone was listening or not, though she liked it best when her mother had time to answer. Asher was a newborn infant, and as Leiba nursed him—the only time in the day she had, of necessity, to remain still—Fraydel would sit at her feet, her arms wrapped around her little knees, pouring out such words that Leiba herself felt that she, too, was drinking.

The neighbors used to come to marvel on a Shabbes afternoon. Such things to come out of the baby's mouth. And such a memory: everybody delighted in teaching her.

If she had been a boy, they would have called her an *illui,* a prodigy. There was no denying this.

Should Leiba, then, have wished the child to be otherwise?

Even Nachum used to say, with admiration in his voice, that it was a pity that, with such a head, the child had not been born a boy, destined for a life of study. A girl with such a head, he once said, when the child was yet very young, is like the ostrich.

The ostrich, dear husband?

Yes. Like a bird that's been given wings but will never fly.

When Nachum had made this comparison, between her little daughter and the ostrich, Leiba had felt something terrible move across her, like lightning across the night sky.

She didn't have the words to describe it. Like lightning it had moved across her, and for an instant the world had looked a different place in its unnatural light. Even now Leiba remembered the look of the world in that moment.

And yet a flightless bird also has a place in the scheme of things. In time, and with the Blessed Name's help, Fraydel, too, would make her peace with the world. She would settle up her angry account.

The whole problem was that Fraydel's heart was in love only with what was marvelous and strange, with things too bright or too dark to live anywhere but in her mind. When Fraydel had, God willing, a husband and children of her own, then she would be bound through her heart to the ordinary and simple. Her every breath and her every thought would hold her fast to this life, and there would be an end to her anger.

Was it anger? Leiba didn't know how to name it, this beast that more and more possessed her daughter. No, not a beast that invaded, but her daughter herself. Maybe. Leiba didn't know. She didn't know how to speak anymore when it came to Fraydel. She didn't know how to think. Within a minute, she would change the *mushel,* the comparison, she tried to fit around her confusion.

Fraydel kept a cold distance from Leiba. Especially was this true since that terrible night, when Fraydel had stood like some demon from another realm in Leiba's kitchen. At times it seemed that Fraydel actually feared her mother. Now and again, Leiba would catch Fraydel casting furtive frightened looks her way. What did the child imagine to herself? It pained Leiba too much even to consider.

Often the word that provoked Fraydel's fury came from Leiba herself. Before she opened her mouth, she thought and rethought, then thought again. Still, she seemed never able to utter a word that didn't stir up, at the very least, a dark scowl. More and more, Leiba felt as if she sat upon a volcano.

And yet Fraydel was capable of showing a certain motherly warmth toward the two younger ones, Tzali and Sorela. Especially Sorela. Even during those terrible days when Fraydel seemed too far gone ever to return, even then sometimes Sorela could manage a gentle exchange with her. Among them all, only little Sorela was never frightened by Fraydel. She followed after the older one like the second day of a holiday follows the first.

In her own way, Fraydel also loved. And because Fraydel loved, Leiba managed to scrape up a little hope from the bottom of her deep fear, enough to pray that, with the help of the Almighty, Fraydel would be able to be lifted out of the well of her own thoughts.

The autumn Days of Awe came and went, the Jews of Shluftchev praying and weeping, weeping and praying.

> Our God and God of our fathers, may our prayer reach Thee; do not ignore our plea. For we are neither so insolent nor so obstinate as to say to Thee: "Lord our God and God of our fathers, we are just and have not sinned." Indeed, we have sinned.

During the ten days that come between Rosh Hashanah and Yom Kippur, it is the custom to go and pray beside the graves of one's relatives. The cemetery of Shluftchev was ancient. It sat on a little hill, an iron fence around it, the gravestones crowded up against one another, like old people leaning together. There lay grandparents, great-grandparents, great-great-grandparents, great-great-great-grandparents—the ancestors of generations.

On the eve of Yom Kippur, the holiest night of all the year, the Jews quickly finished their last meal, dressed themselves in white—the men in their *kittel*s, in which they had been married and in which they would be buried, the women in white dresses and white bonnets over their marriage wigs. Fathers gave their children the blessing of the high priest Aaron, and then all hurried out, in the direction of the prayerhouse.

In the road, women embraced women, men embraced men, begging forgiveness from one another.

"My friend, my friend, forgive me!"

Hinda Mandelbaum and Devorah Schick, who had not spoken to one another since before last Chanukah, when a match between their children had fallen through, now clung to one another sobbing, covering each other's wet cheeks with kisses.

At other spots along the road, similar reconciliations were being enacted. Here Reb Yisroel Samel, a man of puny body and robust opinions, and Reb Akiva Shmerl, no more disposed to self-doubt than the other, hung upon each other's necks. The natures of these men were such that they quarreled often and with heat. Their last fight, over the meaning in Yiddish of a Polish phrase, had ended in insults, for which they now begged one another's pardon.

Everywhere faces were streaming, fervent words were whispered, petty differences buried in dust. The air itself was charged as if with electricity as the sun followed the course of its descent, ushering in the Day of Awe.

In the little packed prayerhouse, the atmosphere was even thicker with emotion. Every heart was stretched as open as were the very gates of heaven on this holy night. More than one woman had brought along aromatic drops or a little cluster of spices wrapped in a rag, to sniff in the event of faintness.

Whoever has not stood, pressed in among the others in just such a prayerhouse on the eve of the Day of Atonement, cannot begin to imagine the awful mystery that then fell upon us. It was, for the twenty-five hours that followed, as if time itself were suspended, and the sensations of the physical world were obliterated, until the sounding of the great shofar that signaled the end of the day and of the long intense period of introspection.

The morning after the Day of Atonement, the Jews of Shluftchev were outside, hammering and sawing, erecting their hut for Succoss, the Feast of Booths. The peasants had their yearly autumn laugh, to see these crazy little shacks the Jews put up, only to take them down again in a week's time.

The little huts leaned crookedly against the crookedly leaning houses of Shluftchev. For roofs, the Jews piled across the beams the sweet-smelling boughs they had collected from the pine forest, arranging them all very carefully: neither too sparse, so that open space exceeds shade, nor so dense as to block out the sight of the stars; only so much, and no more; such is the Law. The women hung ornaments: fruits and vegetables, in the mood of the harvest feast, and long looping strands of cranberries, like the ruby-red beads of the highborn.

On the eastern wall of the Sonnenbergs' *succah* there hung a large and elaborate paper-cutting, a *papirn-shnit,* of a seven-branched menorah, like the one that had stood in the Holy Temple of Solomon, flanked by two lions of Judah. This was the handiwork of Chana, so skilled with her hands. She had made it to replace the one that had gotten ruined in a downpour last Succoss.

For the full week of the holiday, all the Jews of Shluftchev took their meals in these huts. Most of the men, including the Sonnenberg men, even slept outside in them, on piles of hay. And all of this to remember the forty-year sojourn in the desert and the little temporary huts that had served as shelters then. So, too, are we meant to remember how fleeting are the material comforts of this world, as few as there were of these to be found among the Jews of Shluftchev.

A golden halo, woven of warm sunshine and gentle breezes, descended on Shluftchev for the seven days of Succoss. Not a drop of rain fell to mar the holiday, and every meal was taken out-of-doors, in an atmosphere of festive well-being.

So pleasant was it in the Sonnenbergs' *succah* that the family sat out there all the afternoon, drenched in the halo, lulled into a drowsy contentment, neighbors visiting from time to time to shmooz.

"The Master of the Universe is in a good mood," the wits of Shluftchev jested, but with a little hope, too. "We must have done a good job repenting our sins on Yom Kippur, that He should give us such a golden Succoss—days dipped in honey, may all the year be just so sweet!"

A bare week after the conclusion of the festival, the first snow fell. The procrastinators who had put off dismantling their *succahs* now saw them buried beneath a thick canopy of snow.

The winter that swept in that year, with such hasty impatience, knew no mercy. Each night now, Sorela came to her mother in the back of the house with her feet half frozen.

"Sing to me, Mamma," Sorel would beg, for fear of what the quiet might invite in from the freezing darkness outside.

In the month of Kislev came the Festival of Lights, Chanukah, eight days dedicated to a small miracle, lightening the drear of the winter solstice.

The children spun wooden tops called draydels, playing for almonds and raisins. Fraydel told a tale of a demon who was invited by the children into the house to spin the draydel with them, and who won away the light of the world the children had foolishly gambled. But Fraydel's story didn't end there. What had seemed to be the story was only a long preamble to her real tale of how the world went on after its light was extinguished: the fingers with which people felt their way swelling into giant organs, like bulbous turnips, while the skin grew over the basins of their obsolete eyes.

After Chanukah, the gloom settled itself down even more heavily upon shivering Shluftchev. The forsaken months of Tayvays and Shvat seemed to drag endlessly on, a frozen mass of dreary days.

And then at last it was Adar, a lucky month for the Jews, a *mazeldika* month: the mazel, the zodiacal sign, of the fortune-beloved fish.

On the fourteenth day of Adar comes the merry holiday of Purim, the Feast of Lots, celebrating the deliverance of the Jews of Persia, in the time of the reign of the foolish Achashverus, from the destruction planned for them by a certain Haman, of the accursed tribe of Amalek, may their memory be blotted out from under heaven.

An ancient hatred, far older than the villain Haman, binds the tribes of Israel and Amalek. No sooner had the nation of Moses crossed the Sea of Reeds than they were set upon by the murderous Amalekites, descendants of Yaakov's brother, Esav. In generation after generation, the blood of Amalek has boiled up in hatred. Any slight, real or imagined, and Amalek seizes upon a scheme for wiping from off of the face of the earth every last Jew, down to the suckling child. A mysterious enmity, prolonging itself through the generations.

But in the *mazeldika* month of Adar, in the land of Persia long ago, a Jewish queen, the beautiful Esther, together with her cousin, the pious Mordechai, had been able to avert the terrible disaster poised to descend upon her people.

On the eve of the fourteenth day of Adar, and again on its morning, the Jews of Schluftchev gathered together in the little prayerhouse to hear the wonderful tale read from the Scroll of Esther, stamping with their feet each time the name of the Amalekite was mentioned. So may all those driven by hatred in their boiling blood be stamped out.

On the first day of the *mazeldika* month of Adar, a *mazeldika* event occurred: a plate was broken, betokening the betrothal of Fraydel.

The boy, Chananya, came from the nearby village of Verchnikovitz, and so the Sonnenbergs were well acquainted with the family. Fraydel herself knew who Chananya was, as Chananya knew Fraydel very well by sight.

Chananya was a good learner, a fine young man, quiet and serious, from a respectable family. He was a presentable bridegroom in all respects but one. A childhood accident, may the Lord God preserve us, had left him lame. Chananya walked dragging his twisted right leg.

Fraydel accepted the news of her betrothal quietly and without protest. The terrible scene that Leiba had anticipated, with anguish in her heart, did not, thank God, occur. With a silent nod of her head, Fraydel received the news that, in a little more than four months' time, three weeks after the celebration of the Festival of Weeks, she would stand as a bride beneath the wedding canopy.

The details of the betrothal, including the terms of the dowry, had all been worked out between the parents with the mediation of the marriage broker, Yussela Lebensohn, an enigmatic personage of

Shluftchev, with steel-framed spectacles and the ascetic mannerisms of a scholar. There was a certain something about Yussela that led people to suspect that, even while performing the God-beloved task of *shadchen,* he quietly harbored "enlightened" ideas, may God preserve us.

For one thing, Yussela loved to study maps of the world. He had acquired many such maps—who knew from where?—and had even himself drawn up others. He would present such a map to the young betrothed couple, pointing things out to the young man.

"Look. Here is Africa, and here Egypt, where our ancestors were slaves unto Pharaoh. And look, what do you think this blue here is? Yes! You guessed it: 'And the children of Israel went into the midst of the sea upon dry ground. And the waters were a wall unto them on their right hand, and on their left.' And here lie the sands of Arabia, and here—look, look: this is the Holy Land itself. Yes, my friend, you may touch it—gentle, gentle." But it was Yussela's finger that gently reached out for the spot. "Only think: here lies the beloved city, forsaken and desolate, the sacred stones plowed over. 'She weepeth sore in the night, and her tears are on her cheeks. She has none to comfort her among all her lovers.' "

It was said, by those who didn't guard their tongues with sufficient care, that Yussela Lebensohn would rather stare at the little blot of color he said was the Holy Land than at the pages of the Talmud, the study of which will speed the return to our former glory more surely than all the colored sheets of parchment.

But yet, despite his odd ways, Yussela was known to be an excellent *shadchen,* going like a lantern to light the way for destiny.

Who could deny that, more often than not, it was Yussela who first dropped a name into the ear of one parent or another?

"You know," he would say, as casual as a man remarking on the weather, the eyes, behind the steel-rimmed glasses, inscrutable, "I happened to have passed by Shimon Levy's daughter Berela only the other day. A fine girl."

More often than not, it took no more than this for destiny suddenly to open its eyes and look. And then, when it had groped forward some few paces, who could deny that Yussela knew how to work out all of the details destiny further demands: the amount of the dowry; the number of years the young couple would receive room and board from the respective parents.

For such a profession, one has to be the greatest expert in the art of dealing with people, and this Yussela Lebensohn, despite his eccentricities, undoubtedly was. Once Yussela was committed to destiny's following a particular course, he didn't give up easily. Nobody in Shluftchev could have gotten along without Yussela's interference.

In the case of Fraydel and Chananya, it was to be an unusually short engagement period. This Yussela had recommended, and nobody had disagreed. Fraydel would live for the first years of her married life in the home of her in-laws, the Bettleheims, in Verchnikovitz, a village which was a mere twenty minutes' wagon ride from Shluftchev.

All of this Fraydel took in quietly and without a murmur of protest.

Was she even pleased with the *shiddach?* It seemed to Leiba she might be, though who could say for sure?

In any case, Fraydel joined into the carnival atmosphere of Purim with a great show of high-spirited holiday joy, her face like a flower, open to the sun—

—*running, her little face pleading and her arms thrown wide, chasing after the last rays of the departing day, "Wait! Wait for me!"*—

—so that Leiba hoped in her heart that Fraydel was contented, her anger with the world appeased.

During the autumn Days of Awe, when the Jews of Shluftchev had smote their breasts while reciting the litany of their transgressions, levity of mind was one of the sins they had repented. But on Purim day, levity of mind is not only tolerated but encouraged. Frivolity falls then as a religious obligation. Even the most solemn among the Jews of Shluftchev tried to assume some tokens of silliness, no matter how feeble, if only by wearing their trousers inside out or turning their jackets back to front.

Even young yeshiva boys like Asher and Dovid would drink a *l'chayim* of schnapps or slivovitz. On Purim, the Jews of Shluftchev tried to emulate their Polish neighbors by getting rolling drunk, by becoming so *shikker,* as the saying goes, that the names of Haman and Mordechai became confused with one another in the mind.

Purim is also a day of theater, the only day of the year on which dressing up and acting out is not only permitted but applauded.

On other days of the year, public spectacle is to be avoided. The drama of a true Jew is enacted privately and with modesty: in the studyhouse and the home, the prayerhouse and the heart.

But on Purim, it's okay—it's good! it's good!—to be a little bit foolish, a little bit brash, a little bit *meshugga.*

It's okay—it's good! It's good!—to stand before others on a make-shift stage and entertain them with all kinds of *shtuss. Shtuss* itself is good on Purim. Playacting, dressing up; masks and jesters; parodies of texts, teetering perilously close to blasphemy, and comical ditties called *gramm'n:* all of this is part of the Purimshpiel, the Purim play.

In big cities like Lemberg, there were professional Purimshpielers, but in a little hidden-away place like Shluftchev, it was mostly the children, gotten up in homemade costumes, who put on the plays, sang the songs, recited the *gramm'n,* all of which had been invented in a maddened fever of creativity for the occasion.

In the Sonnenberg home, the two older boys, Asher and Dovid, delivered a lesson in which the logic of the Talmud they studied every day was turned upon its head:

"The sages ask," began Asher, in the exaggerated singsong of Talmudic learning, "in the tract *Bubba Mysahs,* what is it that makes the glass of tea sweet? If you were to answer, 'It is because of the sugar,' then I must ask, 'Of what purpose, then, is the teaspoon?' The answer, according to Tosefos, is: 'To sweeten the tea,' for which the proof is as follows: when you put sugar into the tea, it does not turn sweet until you have stirred it with the teaspoon."

"In that case," countered Dovid, "why do we need the sugar at all?"

"A good question! Tosefos also asks this! The answer is as follows: It is demonstrated that the tea is sweetened by the spoon. Now, why do we need the sugar? The reply is that sugar is necessary because it is only when the sugar dissolves that we know it's time to stop stirring the tea-spoon."

On Purim, almost anything—or, in any case, a great deal more than usual—went.

It was Chana, skilled with the needle, who had sewn the colorful clown costume out of bits and scraps for little Tzali, who, in the interim between Av and Adar, had learned to speak and, just as Fraydel had predicted, had abandoned his mystical contemplation of the puddle. Now, with the arrival of early spring, the puddle of Shluftchev was thawing, and Tzali, too, had learned to hold his nose as he went by.

In a few weeks, he would be turning three. His silken blond tresses would be snipped off, all except the earlocks, and he would be wrapped in a prayer shawl and carried off to the cheder on his mother's back to begin his life of study.

But for today, he was a clown. Chana had sewn him his costume, and Fraydel had taught him a little Purim poem to recite at the beginning of the shpiel.

Only, for the first time in his short life, Tzali had been overtaken with shyness. No matter how the others prodded and pleaded, he wouldn't come out from under the table.

It was only in the middle of his older brothers' *dr'ash* that Bezalel suddenly discovered within himself the strength to dash out from his hiding place and shout out his poem:

> Tomorrow I'll be Tzali, today I'm a clown!
> Tomorrow I'll study, today fool around.
> Tomorrow I'll be Tzali, and the day after that, too.
> But now I'm a clown, and good Purim to you!

Sorel, at nine, was really a little too old to dress up in costume, but she had anyway. She had chosen to be a Gypsy girl. Chana had gone around and borrowed, from here and there, almost all the jewelry of which Shluftchev could boast, and had sewn up, again from bits and pieces, a many-layered and many-colored skirt. Fraydel had also composed a song for Sorel to sing, though it took some doing before Bezalel, having been aroused from his bashfulness, could now be subdued back into silence.

Tomorrow I'll be Tzali, today I'm a clown!

"Be Tzali again," the family begged him, "for just a little while."

"Oy," Fraydel said, laughing, shaking her head from side to side. "What dybbuk did I let loose inside of him?"

At last Chana managed to stuff Tzali's mouth with poppy-seed hamentashen long enough to give Sorel her chance.

Sorel walked up to the little performing place before the table amidst a wave of laughter. She had managed to master to perfection the rolling walk of the Gypsy women. She sashayed a few more times around the room, her family falling over themselves with laughter, while she herself kept a perfectly straight face, so that it was a wonder. As the laughter died down, she stood calmly and waited, tossing her hair a few times over her shoulder, the way she'd seen the Gypsy girls do. Leiba could only shake her head in wonder. It hardly seemed to be little Sorela who stood there before them!

When Sorel had the complete quiet and attention of her family, she began to sing in her very strong, rather deep voice the song that Fraydel had made up for her. The melody was so beautiful and mysterious, at once so playful and so sad, that all the Sonnenberg family, with the possible exception of Tzali, heard it playing in their heads, now and then, for weeks, and even months, after Purim.

> For half a kopek I'll sell you a charm
> Or read your future from off your palm.
> La di da, di da, di da.
>
> Your extra hen, your extra goose
> Won't go to waste, I'll find some use.
> La di da, di da, di da.

Beneath the stars I go to sleep.
The night's secrets are mine to keep.
La di da, di da, di da.

You wake and hum the Gypsy's song
And look for me, but I am gone!
La di da, di da, di da.

While Sorel sang, she raised her layered Gypsy skirt slightly and danced about on her bare feet, her eyes flashing fire in the Gypsy manner. Leiba shook her head in wonder. Where did such a power come from, to slip off one's own nature and assume another's bearing so completely?

Each child, like a purse bursting with bright coins, some of foreign mint, with strange words and images engraved, so that a mother could only gaze and wonder: What is it that I have here? What is the worth of these strange bright coins? God grant me the wisdom to do right by them.

So Purim came and went, and now the arduous preparations for the Feast of Matzohs, only one month away, began. Every corner of the house, every drawer and every pocket, had to undergo a thorough cleansing, lest any crumb of bread be lurking. The road of Shluftchev now ran with sudsy water pouring out from every little house, and all the bedding of Shluftchev was dragged outside for an airing.

For Leiba, with the many obligations that pressed upon her, from both inside of the house and out, this period between Purim and Pesach was one of such physical toil that she could fulfill with very little effort of imagination the injunction recited at the Pesach seder commanding that every Jew relive in his own mind the experience of having been a slave and then freed.

At last the holiday was brought in. Somehow or other, through a string of sleepless nights, everything had gotten done. All the *chometzdika* things, the dishes and cutlery, the pots and the pans, everything had been shut away, and "sold." The morning before the holiday would begin, the children came down from their beds to find the kitchen transformed into its *pesachdika* version. With delight they saw all the dishes, like old friends, that they hadn't seen since these had been locked away on the night that the last year's Feast of Matzohs had ended.

With the second day of Pesach, the counting of the omer begins. "You shall count off seven weeks."

The time for the counting is after the evening prayer, when the new day begins. First a special blessing is pronounced, and then the formal announcement.

Today is the first day of the omer.

In the ancient days, when the Holy Temple had stood in all its glory in the city of Jerusalem, then, on the first day of the omer, a burnt offering of barley mixed with oil and frankincense, for a pleasing odor to the Lord, had been presented by the priest. The priest would take the offering in his outstretched hands and "wave it before the Lord."

Today is the eighth day, making one week and one day of the omer.

The seven weeks' time of the counting of the omer, known as Sefirah, is also a time in which certain signs of mourning must be observed. Marriages are prohibited, the hair cannot be cut, the use of musical instruments is banned.

The reason behind the mourning is shrouded in history. Something terrible had taken place during this springtime period between the Feast of Matzohs and the Feast of Weeks, something that had cast a shadow of melancholy over the counting of the omer.

Today is the fourteenth day, making two weeks of the omer.

The most common explanation given for the lingering sadness of Sefirah is the deadly plague that was said to have cut down the disciples of the great Rabbi Akivah, during the time of the Roman occupation of Jerusalem. "And they died from Passover to Shavuos." But it is possible that the mention of the plague veils an allusion to the armed rebellion of the student-soldiers against the imperial occupiers.

Just as in the summer month of Av, when there are nine days during which all Jews everywhere must take particular care because of the danger to their well-being that lurks in the world at this time, so, too, during the period of Sefirah the Angel of Death often runs amok, leaving behind a deepened sense of the sorrow of these seven weeks.

Today is the nineteenth day, making two weeks and five days of the omer.

On the Sabbaths of Sefirah, special lamentations, called *piyutt'm,* were read in the little prayerhouse of Shluftchev, and the wailing which came regularly from the women's balcony would on these occasions be joined by the weeping voices of the men. The laments remembered the medieval Crusaders who had passed through on their way to liberating Palestine, pausing to slaughter the Jews they fell across upon their way. Two waves had passed through, one in 1096 and another in 1146, and both times during the seven weeks of Sefirah; and still the memory of the massacres lingered throughout the former Pale.

Today is the twenty-third day, making three weeks and two days of the omer.

It was also during this period, already overladen with its mysterious sorrow, that the vicious uprising of Polish peasants and Cossacks, led by the blood-fiend Chmielnicki, turned their butchering knives on the Jews in their midst. Communities just like Shluftchev had then been awash in blood. Men, women, children—it is beyond all telling. And the memory of this destruction, too, finds its way into the *piyutt'm* and into the sense of the springtime sadness of Sefirah.

Today is the thirtieth day, making four weeks and two days of the omer.

Only on the thirty-third day of the counting of the omer, Lag Baomer, is the observance of semi-mourning temporarily lifted, though the reason for this, too, is shrouded in mystery. One school of thought, basing itself on a source that no longer exists, claims that on this day the deaths among Rabbi Akivah's students were halted.

Others offer the opinion that on the thirty-third day of the omer the Judeans managed to win some great, though brief, victory in their doomed resistance to the Romans.

And yet other scholars have claimed that it was on this day that the manna began to fall from the heavens.

Today is the thirty-eighth day, making five weeks and three days of the omer.

Though the celebration of marriage itself is prohibited during Sefirah, the preparations for Fraydel's wedding had been long begun.

Leiba, studying the laws of purity with Fraydel, had been once again surprised by her daughter. There was no uncontrollable weeping or fits of hysterical laughter, such as so often occurred in girls of far more robust and indelicate natures than Fraydel's. With a calm mind and great composure, Fraydel learned how it was that a Jewish woman must safeguard the precious purity of the family.

A soul cannot live without another, Leiba said to Fraydel, who listened quietly, even nodding her head from time to time. Even the Infinite, in His unspeakable Majesty, abhorred the emptiness of a universe in which the darkness lay on the face of the water. This is the foundation on which all of existence rests.

And Fraydel had nodded her head.

Today is the fortieth day, making five weeks and five days of the omer.

The spring had grown warm and lovely, the earth renewing itself in its green fields and flowering trees. The life that had preserved itself, deep down in the frozen bowels of earth's night, now stirred and stretched, and the wet earth palpitated, and the air moved with life.

Shraga the book-peddler, walking beside his beloved nag Beena on the muddy road into Shluftchev, was surprised to see no Fraydel come running to inspect the books piled up in his wagon. Worried, he had knocked on the door.

Was Fraydel, God forbid, unwell?

No, he was told. Fraydel is a *kalleh*. She will stand beneath the *chuppa* in less than two months' time.

You must come, Shraga, our dear friend. You must try to be back in Shluftchev for the wedding of Fraydel and Chananya.

Fraydel? A *kalleh? Mazel tov! Mazel tov!* By all means, I will be back in Shluftchev for the wedding of Fraydel, my very best customer and my dear little friend. A *kalleh!* Well, then, it's no wonder her head is no longer in books. God willing, she will soon produce a family of many book-lovers, and Shraga the book-peddler will also benefit by this *shiddach*.

Leiba remembered that she, too, during the time of her own engagement, had lost her passion for reading. A *kalleh* has other things to think about than stories in books.

Before, life had felt like a dress that wouldn't fit—hanging here, choking there. And then everything had altered—

—*pinching my cheeks to see if I dreamt, to think that he, resplendent among all men, was my own destined one, "How real my dream is tonight," I thought like a little fool, pinching my cheeks so that Mamma was laughing—*

—so it was not so strange, and there was nothing for which Leiba had cause to worry. But a mother's mind is like some animal foraging in the forest, sniffing one thing after another to see if it will yield food. Only what a mother's mind forages about for are reasons to worry. Even though Fraydel was calmness itself, unmolested by her moods, Leiba went about feeling that she was holding her breath and berated herself for her lack of faith.

Today is the forty-ninth day, making seven weeks of the counting of the omer.

The period of Sefirah ends in the Feast of Weeks, or Shavuos, "the fiftieth day."

Shavuos, too, had been one of the three pilgrim holidays, a harvest holiday, marking the end of the reaping of the barley and the start of the wheat.

But in addition to the agricultural cause for celebration, the Feast of Weeks is said to fall on the anniversary of the Blessed Name's revelation on the mountain of Sinai.

"In the third month, after the children of Israel were gone forth out of the land of Egypt, the same day came they into the wilderness of Sinai."

On the eve of Shavuos, it is the custom for those who can to stay up all the night studying Torah, some say in the hopes of seeing the heavens split themselves open, as they had for the Israelites gathered at Sinai. Study has the power to compel miracles.

On the first day of Shavuos, the Book of Ruth is read. It tells the story of a paradoxical marriage: between the Israelite Boaz and the Moabite woman Ruth. The paradox is this: the men of Israel had been warned to take no brides from the tribe of Moab, and yet it was from Ruth that the Messianic house of David ascends.

Chana and Sorel had decorated the house full of flowers and green plants, sticking branches of sweet-smelling pine behind the mirrors and into any cracks into which they fit. This is the custom, for Mount Sinai had been a green mountain.

Fraydel, too, had helped to decorate the house, and had produced some beautiful wild flowers that she had picked somewhere or other. But when Chana began to get too bossy and order her about, Fraydel had faded from the house.

For a short time after Fraydel's engagement, Chana had treated her with a newborn respect. Soon Fraydel would be sitting among the married women in the women's section of the prayerhouse. Already her matron's wig had been made and waited for her in a wooden box, together with other articles of her trousseau. Chana herself had altered Grandma Terza's wedding dress for Fraydel, and Aunt Fruma and Uncle Chayim, who had been living in Germany for several years, had sent as a present a beautiful wedding veil of fine old lace, shot through with a silver thread.

For the first time in her life, Chana actually envied Fraydel. Oh, to be getting married, too! Not that she would wish to marry Chananya Bettleheim. The way he went about dragging his right foot made Chana's stomach turn over on itself, may the Blessed Name forgive her.

Deep in her heart, Chana knew that for her it would be different, that it was because of what people said about Fraydel that she had to make do with a lame bridegroom. Fraydel, too, was like someone lame, someone who dragged a twisted part of herself. This is what Chana thought in the secrecy of her own heart, though it made her feel guilty to think so. But was it her fault what people said about her sister?

Fraydel didn't seem to mind a bit about Chananya. Ever since she had become engaged, she was different, quietly going about doing all that she was supposed to do, as if she had at long last come to her senses. About time! If she got too old, there would be no hope of marrying her off!

Oh, but for her, for Chana, it would be different! And Mamma had already said that she, too, would wear the beautiful veil that Aunt Fruma and Uncle Chayim had sent from Hamburg. How rich they must have become! It was all so wonderful, so wonderful, most of all wonderful that Fraydel was at last getting married! Soon it would be her turn—she would not die an old maid!—and she would get to wear the beautiful marriage veil, and how different it would all be for her!

After lunch on the first day of Shavuos, Tatta and the boys, who had of course stayed up studying all the night before, went off to take short naps. Mamma, too, who had also stayed up reading of the Book of Ruth in the *Tz'ena Ur'enah,* went to sleep.

Tzali was running around outside, together with his very best friend from cheder, Duddi, another three-year-old, who shared Tzali's view that sitting still is an unnatural state. Chana had gone off to visit with one of her girlfriends, and Sorel was sitting out on the step, hoping that Fraydel might happen by and join her.

The Shabbes after next, Fraydel's *chusun,* Chananya, would be called up to the Torah, in the celebration of his *aufruf.* After he finished reciting the weekly portion, the women and girls would shower him with raisins and almonds.

Fraydel was already different, spending more and more time doing household chores with Chana. There was a new closeness between those two that made Sorel feel like a fire had broken out in her head. Even the stories that Fraydel would occasionally tell Sorel now were different, no longer set in Chicago, no longer lurching about like a *shikker.*

Sorel knew that she ought to be happy that Fraydel was getting married, but the truth was she had to be fighting back the tears at every moment. Even though Fraydel would be living not so far by wagon from Shluftchev, nothing would ever be the same again. Now at night, when Sorel opened her eyes wide into the darkness, she didn't creep out of her bed in order to seek her mother, but instead remained lying close to Fraydel, breathing deeply of the pine forest that Fraydel always seemed to carry in her hair. Gently, she would stroke Fraydel's hair or kiss her thin white arm.

Even Fraydel's sleep was calmer now. She lay almost as still as Chana.

Sorel sometimes thought to herself that it would have been better had she and Fraydel really run away with the Gypsies. Then she would have been able to keep Fraydel with her. She could have traveled to the four corners of the world and back again with Fraydel, sleeping with her night after night under the stars, guarded by Gypsy magic.

Mamma said it wasn't selfishness to love another person so much, only confusing.

When the future arrives, Mamma had said another time, it's never as one had anticipated, neither in one's wishes nor in one's worries. So both wishing and worrying, as natural as they are, are also folly.

"You never wish, Mamma? You never worry?"

"And who ever said that I'm not foolish?"

Chana sometimes said that Fraydel never gave a thought to what other people felt, but Sorel knew that this was wrong. Fraydel had always managed—in her own way, which was like no one else's way—to tell Sorel that she did give a thought, many thoughts.

Only last Shabbes, Fraydel had told her a story of a girl, Zissela, an only child, normal in all respects but one. Sometimes when Zissela was walking along, she would suddenly halt in her path, overtaken by waves and waves of laughter, hugging herself with the joy that gurgled out of her from a secret spring. And if anyone asked her why, she couldn't say. At other times, a sorrow pressed so hard down on her that she could barely draw in a breath. And, again, she couldn't tell you why.

When Zissela's mother lay dying, she revealed to her daughter that, years before, she had had another husband and another daughter. And when that husband had died, the mother had been too grief-stricken to care for her daughter anymore, and had given her away to an old childless couple, who had promised to love her.

And so the girl set out to search for her sister. The place her mother had described was very far from her home and difficult to get to. When at last the girl made her way there, she learned that the old childless couple had long ago died. Everyone whom she asked told her a different story as to where she might find her sister. The girl remembered each of them, and, one by one, she searched in the faraway places to which the stories sent her.

At last, an old woman, with only one story left, she followed this story to the castle of a noblewoman. As she entered the castle gates, she was suddenly overcome by one of her strange fits of sadness, this one so much crueler than all the others that she could not catch her breath for several long moments and came within a glance of death.

At last, she finally dragged herself up from the ground and crawled, weeping loudly, up the palace steps. But her strange behavior attracted no attention, because all around her were guards and soldiers, courtiers and servants, weeping.

The noblewoman was her sister, and she had just died.

Sorel sat on her front step, so lost in her own thoughts that only gradually did she become aware of the noises, of the shouting and the singing, that were coming from down the road.

She looked up, shading her eyes so that she might be able to see in the glare of the strong Sivan sun. There was a little group of boys prancing around, skipping, pointing. So much excitement!

She could make out little Tzali and Duddi scampering down the street toward the frolicking band of . . .

It was Fraydel! Fraydel was in the middle of these boys, who were dancing around her and singing!

> *Fraydel, Fraydel,*
> *Da meshuggena maydel!*
> *Zie klaipt bliemen on da Shabbes!*
> *Zie iz yetzt an apikoras!*

> Fraydel, Fraydel,
> The crazy girl!
> She picks flowers on the Sabbath!
> She is now a heretic!

The strange little procession slowly made its way down the road. There was little Duddi running around with the others, laughing and trying to chant along with them.

> *Fraydel, Fraydel,*
> *Da meshuggena maydel!*

Tzali stared silently, a confused little smile on his angelic face. Was this a game? Was his sister Fraydel the leader in a game?

Sorel could now see, as Fraydel came closer, that Fraydel had made her eyes fill up with the crazy look meant to scare people away. Her lips were curled into a frozen smile, and there were two circles of deep crimson flaming on her cheeks.

And Sorel saw that Fraydel wasn't walking like Fraydel either, not like any Jewish girl or woman walked. She was barefoot—where were her shoes?—and was rolling her hips in the loose easy motions of the Gypsy women.

But worst of all—so horrible that at first Sorel thought this must surely be a nightmare and she would wake up in her bed next to a

Fraydel sleeping safely beside her—Fraydel's two thin arms were filled with the wild flowers she had picked on this day, in flagrant violation of the Law!

All had come out of their front doors and stood watching. One by one the little boys who had surrounded Fraydel, shouting their song of taunting, were called sharply away by their parents, who stared in pity and in terror at what they were seeing; so that now Fraydel walked in a complete and stunned silence down the dirt road of Shluftchev, up the step of her own house, past Mamma and Tatta and the boys who had come outside to see what all the commotion was about.

Fraydel pushed past her family, opened the front door, and walked in, dropping her flowers on the floor. Without a word she climbed the little ladder to her bed.

A few days later, the Bettleheim family, having heard of the incident of the flowers, sent back the marriage contract.

"He wasn't your intended," Leiba told her daughter, sitting alone with her at the table.

"I know that," Fraydel calmly answered her. Her eyes were as normal as those of any of the girls of Shluftchev.

Fraydel accepted the news of the broken engagement with the same quiet nod with which she had accepted the engagement itself. Such a deep calmness had sunk itself down into her. In the night, it seemed to Sorel, lying beside her, that Fraydel barely breathed. In the day, Sorel sometimes heard Fraydel suddenly drawing in a long shuddering breath, as if she were trying to get more air into her chest. Otherwise, she was quietness itself.

Sorel opened her eyes in the darkness, reaching out her hand for Fraydel.

Quickly she climbed out of the bed, not taking care as she slid down the ladder.

"Mamma! Fraydel's gone!"

"What? What do you mean, 'gone'?"

"She's not in her bed, Mamma!"

"Oh my God! Oh my God!"

Not bothering to scrape her hands of the dough that still clung to them, not bothering even to cover her head, Leiba rushed out into the night, lit bright with the full moon.

"*Fraydel!*" Leiba called out into the darkness. From the distance some dogs began to bark.

"*Fraydel!*"

More frightened than she had ever been, Sorel watched the panic overtake her mother, the helplessness with which Leiba ran first in one direction and then another, calling out Fraydel's name, her voice high and unnatural. Already doors were opening, frightened faces, expecting the worst, looking out. Neighbors, men and women, came rushing over to inquire, to try to calm the mother down.

Now her mother was leaning down over her, shaking her shoulders with her two doughy hands.

"Have you any idea where she could be? Do you know of a special hiding place?"

Terrified by the mother she saw before her, bareheaded, with a voice not her own, Sorel shook her head.

"I know!" Leiba suddenly said, slapping the side of her head, and ran off to the back, to the outhouse. But it was empty.

Men were organizing themselves into search parties, carrying wooden lanterns to light the night, Tatta and Asher and Dovid amongst them.

"Perhaps she went to look for the *kompania*." Sorel managed to get the words out, panting because her heart was wild within her, a wild animal choking the small space of her throat.

"What? What did the child say?"

"The Gypsies, she says. Maybe Fraydel went off with the Gypsies."

"Did she tell you anything about it? Did she say she was going to find them?" It was Leiba asking.

Sorel shook her head.

Leiba and the girls sat in the kitchen, surrounded by the neighbor women, while the men searched the night for Fraydel.

"Faith," the women murmured into Leiba's unhearing ear, as they tried to warm her freezing hands. "Faith in the Blessed Name."

Leiba heard and felt nothing.

—the icy blackness without a bottom—

The men said their hurried morning prayers in the forest, unwilling to lose time in their search.

—where is the bottom?

Some had gone to the churches, begging information. Perhaps a priest had managed to influence the girl. It had been known to happen before. But everywhere they were turned away, often with taunting, angry insults.

"If one of your daughters has found her salvation in our Lord Jesus Christ, then you should rejoice and seek her instruction," they were sternly chastised by one priest, who had a powerful build, and a deep voice he had made boom with indignation.

God forbid, it would not do to offend. If a forest is dry and ready to burn, it doesn't take more than the littlest spark to bring on an inferno.

The priest's response left little doubt in many minds that Fraydel, long known to be strange in the head, may God preserve us, had become an apostate. The thundering priest clearly knew something.

She was always disappearing, God Himself had only known where. Perhaps she had long been meeting in secrecy with a priest, either that one or another, who had filled her poor distracted mind with the poison of self-hatred. A pretty story, such as they well know how to tell, might have sufficed for Fraydel.

What was to be done? What was to be done?

Who was there who might intercede in their behalf?

They must begin immediately to compose letters—but to whom?—appealing for help.

In the end, it wasn't one of them, one of the Jewish men of Shluftchev, who found Fraydel.

Igor Sweitchetkow, a young peasant who lived near the village of Tchervov, more than fifty kilometers away, came to the house. It was late into the second day of searching, the sun already sinking.

Igor held his cap in his hands. He was a tall strapping fellow with clear blue eyes and a slow smile. Not yet married, he was a danger to the virtue of many a girl.

The moment Leiba's eyes fell on him, her shoulders slumped, and she covered her face with her hands.

Late that night, in the tavern, his speech slurred by the vodka he mechanically threw down his throat in shot glass after shot glass, Igor told his drinking companions how it had been when he had told the Jewish woman, slumped in her chair, never once looking up or making a sound the whole time he spoke. The other Jewish women hovered silently around her, like waiting dark buzzards.

He had known immediately it was the Jewish girl. He'd heard that a group of them had come earlier in the day, making insulting accusations to the priest. The fellows who had told him had also said that they were planning that night to teach the Christ-killers some respect. Nothing more than a few bashed noses and broken-in doors. A few shorn heads and beards. Only the men. To pay them back for their damned insolence to the priest. The spokesman for the group spat and cursed. "*Psia krev*—dog's blood."

Would Igor join them for a little Jew fun?

Sure, why not? He was game. Just tell me where and when.

He had been on his way to the forest in order to chop some wood. It was the color of the skirt, the blue in the blackness of the river, that drew his eye.

Dark hair streaming downward with the current.

Near the side of the river, in the reeds. The water here no more than knee-deep for him.

Must drag it to the bank. . . . Might free itself and get carried off to the sea. . . .

Igor didn't look too closely at the face. Even as he told his story that night in the tavern, he had felt the wave of bitter-tasting sickness rising in him.

Seeing his desperate gulp, his friends had jeered.

Why was he getting all choked up over one drowned Jewish slut?

Didn't the Jews themselves murder little Christian children all the time? More times than they got caught for it.

Igor had to acknowledge that this was so.

Still, a drowned body is a terrible sight.

Caught in the reeds . . . the dark hair flowing downward with the current . . . and the arms . . . the arms wrapped around itself . . . hugging herself . . .

Almost impossible it had been to drag that corpse up onto the bank, even for a young fellow like Igor. Heavy as bricks.

Had to throw his arms around it from the back, under the arms. When he finally managed to get it onto the bank, he discovered the reason why the corpse, small as it was, had weighed so much.

Heavy rocks sewn into the bottom of the skirt. Mother of God, as I sit here before you: a line of stitches across the blue skirt, so small, and even—a line of stitches holding in the heavy rocks.

Igor shook his head, in his blue eyes a look that was a little lost.

Later that evening, he took Lyuba, who worked in the tavern and had sullenly listened to his story, back to his bed with him.

The girl was dull-witted and bad-smelling. Igor had never before felt the urge to come near her. But tonight he wanted the feel of a live body beneath him, the cow warmth the girl gave off.

The girl herself, though she was stupid as a pig, seemed to guess something of his state of mind. For, when Igor was finished with her, he saw that there was a smirk on her face.

He rolled over so that he faced the wall.

Let her smirk. She hadn't seen it. She hadn't dragged it, slippery with slime, from the river.

If only he hadn't looked at the face.

Although it is the custom for a suicide to be buried near the fence, away from others, nobody had the will to raise this question in relation to Fraydel Sonnenberg.

Even those in Shluftchev who had an endless appetite for discussing the subtleties of the Law, allowed that the girl had been out of her senses and let the question go at that.

Neither when she had transgressed the Law and picked the flowers, nor when she had transgressed the Law and taken her own life, could she be held accountable. The Talmud itself provides for numerous extenuating circumstances. Even despair is cited as a reason to excuse.

Despair or madness, either one or the other—the girl was not accountable.

All the rituals for the dead were observed, the honor was given. She was laid beside the blessed bones of her ancestors, in the little crowded cemetery on the hill.

"May you be comforted among the mourners of Israel."

So each visitor, upon leaving, had softly murmured to each member of the family.

For seven days, the family sat on the earthen floor, in their white stockings, their clothes torn. The neighbor women carried in pots of food that went untouched, and men and women took turns sitting with the mourners. From early morning until late evening they sat, mourners and visitors mute with shared grief.

Children had died before. Infants, of course. The cemetery was crowded with dead infants. But older children, too—young people on the thresholds of their lives. There had been many who had met with untimely ends, from diseases, from accident.

Still, never had the Angel of Death assumed so cruel a shape in their midst.

What words could be offered the mourners? Silence itself sat *shiva* in the house.

When Leiba got up from the seven days of mourning, she had become an old woman. Her hair, once fair beneath her wig, was now pure white, and her step was slow and faltering.

PART III

Warsaw, Poland

*T*he King of the land where the poor tailor's apprentice lived had but one child, and this a girl, and this girl a heartache to her father and mother. She was very beautiful but so brilliant that the conversations of all the young men who sought her hand bored her to tears, and she remained unmarried.

At last the princess herself said, "I will marry the man, no matter his rank or circumstance, who can engage me in a conversation. But lest this be mistaken as an open invitation for all to come and torment me with nonsense, let me add that all who fail shall be beheaded."

All the highborn eligible men, who, having education as well as birth, lacked nothing in the high regard they paid themselves, came calling at the castle. But none of them proceeded very far into the grand speeches they had prepared before they were marched off to the executioner.

Those who lack saychel think either too highly or too poorly of themselves. The tailor's apprentice, however, knew precisely his own worth and therefore decided to risk a meeting with the picky princess.

He knocked on the castle's front door, declared his intention, and was led down a maze of corridors until he was brought to the room where the princess sat with her lady-in-waiting. The princess turned to look at the boy with ill-concealed indifference, and he returned her stare just as coolly, making certain that his eyes didn't reflect any delight in her beauty, because the boy had saychel.

—To be continued

157

CHAPTER 8

MARCH DAWN

Sorel opened her eyes, not knowing what it was that had jolted her awake. She usually had a great deal of trouble bestirring herself in the morning.

"Not yet," she'd think, blindly clutching the last shreds of torn sleep.

But this morning she opened her eyes to find the world rushing in at her, as if something had tilted sharply in the night. Everything seemed momentarily to have lost its place . . . *and to be rushing in at her.*

She sat up in her little cot in the corner, steadying herself for several moments until the strange sensation passed. Still, the world had an indescribably different look to it.

She wrapped the quilt about her shoulders, hugging it around herself like a long trailing robe, and went to kneel before the small low casement window of the darkened room.

The great gray presence of the buildings rose up silently, reducing God's own heaven to that poor thin excuse for a sky, smeared now with dawn.

"What *serious* buildings," she murmured to herself, suddenly taking in the full dimensions of their weight and substance.

No crookedly leaning homes of unwhitewashed wood sinking half buried in the mud. Where was there even a patch of naked earth to be turned into mud? Not a tree, not a blade of grass dared to show itself here. Everything was forged of massive pale stone and great slabs of concrete.

Serious buildings, which took *themselves* seriously, too.

How remarkable to have so transformed the naked earth that nothing of its original state remained! All had been done over according to the needs and desires of man, who was either a creature of absurd audacity or divinelike aspirations. Maybe a little of both?

Sorel thrust the window open. It was early March. The winter hadn't yet loosened its icy grip on the city. Great mountains of blackened snow still stood, erected by men with shovels, called out like an army with each new white deluge delivered from above.

The chill in the air, still with the raw taste of winter in it, fell on Sorel with an intensity that was itself a pleasure.

She took it in, suddenly thirsty for this air, drew it deep, deep down into her startled lungs. Like honey wine! Like honey wine, it went straight to her head, and she was drunk—drunk on the sweet, chilled air of March!

It was still too early for the trolley car to be running, or the droshkies, with their high rubber wheels and hired drivers. But she saw a few dark figures scurrying here and there in the straining light, pious Jews carrying their prayer-shawl bags under their arms, hurrying off to an early dawn *minyan.*

The little strip of sky bordering the rooftops grew a half-shade brighter, and she caught sight of others, dressed in modern clothes, in overcoats and fedoras. Instead of prayer-shawl bags, these men carried the first newspapers of the day, purchased at the corner kiosks that opened at the crack of dawn.

She had a sudden fierce desire, vivid as a sense impression, to read these newspapers—Polish and Russian, as well as Yiddish.

She was now completely comfortable in Polish. Yiddish was the language of instruction at her *gymnasium,* but lessons in Polish and Polish history were conducted entirely in the Polish language, for this was the law. She had also learned German—which was anyway, at least in its vocabulary, very similar to Yiddish—and also Russian and a smattering of English, a language she loved above all the others, carrying the magic of the New World in its hard-edged syllables.

She would have loved at this moment to read all the newspapers in all the languages, to be given the widest view possible of this very day. She wanted God Almighty's own view of this day!

This is mine! I am here and this is mine!

The street below was slowly coming alive. Hawkers and beggars were bestirring themselves, taking up their positions, which were as fixed as the shops themselves.

There below was the family of bagel sellers—a mother, a father, a child—that stood each day near the entrance of the building that lay directly across the street. They carried their bagels in straw hampers. The child, a boy, must have been about eleven or twelve.

Other peddlers, selling loaves of bread, smoked herring, hot peas, brown beans, apples, pears, plums, would soon crowd the streets— adding their voices to the background hum, the vast and distant din that had enclosed Sorel's silence.

A few wooden wagons, piled with goods and pulled by the poor city horses, for whom Sorel's heart always went out, moved over the cobblestones, making a racket that was carried up to her window like music, like a galloping polonaise of Chopin.

So loud, so unspeakably, beautifully loud! It was all the music she could have borne right now. Real melody would have cracked her soul wide open!

The light now was seeping into the room, rippling at the baseboards and bubbling up in the corners, impressions crowding out impressions, too vivid to be caught, too swift to fit themselves to expression.

Outside, a boy drove a noisy cluster of turkeys down the middle of the street, expertly running alongside them with a stick, first this side, then that side, to keep them from scattering.

Men and women, pious and emancipated, were now rushing off to meet the morning, in a rich blend of noise and color and motion. They,

too, seemed to feel the urgency of this new day, *here it is, never to be repeated, this moment.*

A red trolley car came clanging, people piling aboard, all destined
for different destinations, so many possibilities. . . .

Possibilities! As if the walls of a room suddenly and swiftly moved
back, melted away, vistas in every direction.

This is mine! I am here and this is mine!

The light was strong now, crackling like fire—was it outside her or
inside her, this crackling light?

She had never seen such light as this, certainly not in Warsaw,
which had always seemed to her clogged with the shadows cast by the
tall buildings. A city composed of layers of dimness and muffled
sounds, as if you were seeing and hearing under water. Nothing had the
sharp edge of reality, so that afterward you could hardly remember
what was real and what wasn't, and the distinction didn't matter much
anyway.

But now the light . . . the light was everywhere, and every place it
touched burst into clarity!

It was already time for her to be getting ready for school. She could
hear the noises of stirring coming from the other room of the apartment, where Mamma and Tatta slept.

Tatta would be getting ready to go off to the little prayerhouse that
he preferred, a tiny hole in the wall that smelled of old books, like the
studyhouse of Shluftchev.

After the morning *shachris* prayer, he would return and open his little shop, down on the ground floor of the building in which they lived.
The shop also smelled of old books, for that was what was offered for
sale there.

It was Aunt Fruma and Uncle Chayim who had helped Tatta to
purchase the store. Perhaps there was still money being sent from Germany, for it seemed to Sorel that Tatta never sold a single book. He sat
in his little dark store always bent over an open tract. So long as he
swayed over the long columns in the holy books, then maybe it was as
if he were still back in his beloved studyhouse.

It has been stated: if a man desires to dig a pit close to the boundary, between his field and his neighbor's, Abaya says he may do so and Raba says he may not do so. Now in a field where pits would naturally be dug, both agree that he may not dig close up. Where they differ is in the case of a field where pits would not naturally be dug. Abaya says he may dig, because it is not naturally a field for digging pits, while Raba says he may not dig, because his neighbor can say to him: Just as you have altered your mind and want to dig, so I may alter my mind and want to dig.

This is true, Nachum thought, looking up from the tract. Raba was right to add into his reasoning the fact that a man may always alter his mind.

Of course, Leiba still continued to run here and there, buying and selling, scraping and scrimping. Poverty wore a far more terrible face here in the city than it had back in the shtetl, where everybody had been poor but nobody had ever literally starved to death, as they did here.

This past winter, two old people who lived on this very block had frozen to death. It was nothing so unusual to hear of such things.

Sorel's school uniform was draped neatly over the back of a wooden chair. The books from which she had studied until late the evening before were gathered together into a neat stack on the floor beside the chair.

And all of this, too—the uniform, the books, the entire room that became her bedroom only at night, when the little cot in the corner was unfolded—all of this Sorel now stared at, her eyes darting to look at this and then that.

For the first time, she noticed that the leather band that held her books together was brown, frayed at the holes where the metal prong poked through.

She saw the shade of gray of the school uniform she wore each weekday, ran her hand over the nubby texture of the wool.

Looking into the little dark smudgy mirror that hung on the wall as she put a ribbon to the long braid of her hair, she stared, startled at her reflection.

"Pretty," she thought. "If I saw such a girl in the street, I would think that she was pretty."

Her hair was a heavy mass of ash blond that lay in a thick braid down her back, and her eyes were gray and long, with a slightly Slavic tilt to them. Her high cheekbones also gave a very distinctive cast to her face.

She glanced downward at the long stretch of her body. She was tall. Tall, and still growing. Every week, it seemed, her mother had to add on to her skirt.

She placed her two outspread hands at her waist. Her fingers were so long and her waist was so narrow, she could almost encircle herself entirely.

She glanced back down again. Her legs started very far up on her body.

"I'm some long noodle," she thought.

She laughed out loud. Her laugh was very deep for a girl her age, a deep strong laugh just like her voice.

But at the sound of her own laughter, she froze. A dead stillness and dark.

"I must stay back here," she thought, stricken. "How can I leave her here all by herself?

"Master of the Universe! Only let me not lose forever my Fraydel!"

In the flash of that clear moment, in the dazzle of consciousness into which her reawakened faculties had delivered her, Sorel knew, once and for all, that Fraydel was lost.

Fraydel was lost, never to be reclaimed—and the full sadness of this, too, was finally and fully hers.

Sadness came with the clarity of everything she experienced this morning, yet Sorel was determined to withstand it. She yearned, above all, to have the clarity of the world back again.

Behind her she left years she wouldn't have been able to recall even if she had wanted. They were years too deadened to have impressed themselves on memory. Only sometimes a certain sense of them would overtake her, and then she would feel that she couldn't draw enough air into her lungs.

She had managed to learn Polish and Russian and German and a little smattering of English; had managed even to charm some of her teachers, those who didn't hold against her the Galitzianer pronunciation to which she clung out of sheer stubbornness. Yet, in some sense, she had not been entirely present in that classroom a single moment of a single day.

She knew the names of all her schoolmates, knew even that there were some whom, at least in theory, she liked a little, and others whom she didn't. But, out of their sight, she couldn't have ever called forth a single one of their faces, or a single comment they had ever made to her. Really, she hadn't taken very much care over them, neither smarting over their little snobbish cuts nor feeling any interest in their lives. Her existence here must have involved a countless number of daily little adjustments. Somehow she had accomplished them—had studied grammars, memorized dates and mathematical operations, taken examinations—much like a sleepwalker who doesn't take a false step.

But suddenly she was wide awake.

The night that had restored to Sorel the vivid keenness of perception, the wild force of desire and will, had deposited deep within her the knowledge that it was now time for her to step out of that unlit place where she had tried to cling to her dead sister.

All her life, she would never know what it was that had transpired during the night, so that she awoke one chilly morning in early March with her sense of the world reinstated; awoke with the knowledge that there *is* no clinging to the dead; that death, which is unclean, must be contained—therefore, choose life.

So Sorel chose life. Sorel chose life with a vengeance.

She was twelve years old.

CHAPTER 9

MANY WORLDS

*W*hen Nachum Sonnenberg began to pay very close attention to the people around him, he saw, with great astonishment, how different a world it was, depending on who was looking at it, and when.

The Master of the Universe had created heaven and earth, and all that stood and moved thereon. But when, on the sixth day, He saw fit to create a creature in His own image, on that day He had brought into existence a great vast number of separate worlds. Here, too, stood firmaments dividing one world from another.

Now, at last, Nachum felt that he had come to understand a passage in the Talmud that before had always baffled him.

The puzzling passage occurs in the book of Sanhedrin. Each person, says the text, has been created absolutely unique as regards his appearance, his voice, and his mind. Therefore, each person should believe that the world was created precisely for him.

A baffling passage, no? Nachum was to believe that the world was created *for him?*

But now he saw: the Master of the Universe has created for each person a world that he alone inhabits.

What is this one's world like, and what is it like for that one? More and more, Nachum found his mind occupied with such questions, even though for the most part he was at a loss to supply the answers. Warsaw was a city filled with people whose lives Nachum couldn't begin to imagine. Even the Jews of Warsaw were strange beings to him. There were Jews here who didn't look like Jews, who didn't *think* like Jews. What would it be like to be one of these moderns, who spoke Polish more fluently than Yiddish, and knew the world at large as Nachum had once known his Shluftchev?

For the first time in his life, Nachum found himself paying close attention to all manner of people. Rich and poor, Jew and non-Jew, male and female. What was it like for this one and for that one?

Take, for example, his wife's sister Fruma Pomeranz. She had become a modern. In fact, Nachum's sister-in-law was no longer Fruma, but Frieda. Her husband, with whom Nachum had once been a student in the home of his beloved father-in-law, Rav Dovid Broder, of blessed memory, was now known as Heinrich rather than Chayim. They had brought a different world back with them from Germany, the world of the so-called enlightenment.

"Enlightenment" was, of course, the name its advocates gave it. Others believed such thinking emanated from darkness and chaos, the evil breath of Asmodeus, or Satan, which overcame its victims with an arrogant confusion.

For Nachum, light was a concept fraught with mystical associations, allied to the wondrous mysteries of Creation.

Still (so he reasoned to himself), one person's light is another person's "darkness and chaos." One person's place of shelter is another's airless dungeon.

Fruma/Frieda and Chayim/Heinrich, as befits people who were almost German Jews, were now living life on a very grand scale. Even Frieda's Yiddish had progressed to something much closer to German. When a person came to visit her in her elegant apartment on her very elegant street—no, not a street, a *boulevard,* wide as the whole of Shluftchev had been long, and planted with such fine, big chestnut trees—she would invite you graciously to *sitzen sich* on her red silk sofa, not to *zetza avec.* She would offer you *ein Bischen* of this and that, instead of *a bissella* this and that. Where another person would say *azoy,* with her it was always *so* or even *javohl!*

Fruma/Frieda and Chayim/Heinrich had returned from Germany only six months ago. Their three married sons, Velvel/Wolfgang, Meyer/Maximilian, and Leibel/Ludwig, had remained in Germany to take care of the business from that end. Nachum himself, who had no head at all for business, was very vague on the nature of Heinrich's enterprises. There was some sort of product that Heinrich's sons bought in Germany and that Heinrich then sold in Poland. Or maybe he bought the product in Poland and it was then sold in Germany— though what did they have in Poland that they didn't already have in Germany, and a thousand times better-made?

About all of this, Nachum held no opinion. However, from paying close attention, Nachum had come to the conclusion that not only Heinrich but even Frieda herself was overjoyed, despite what they might say, to be back in Poland, shoddy and inferior as they told us it was in its every little detail.

In Poland, even in such a city as Warsaw, the elegant Frieda and Heinrich had instantly become people of the highest importance, mixing with the most elite members of Jewish society.

Who among us wasn't proud to be able to say that he or she was an intimate of the Pomeranzes, recently of Hamburg and now of the Marshalovsky Boulevard?

In Germany (so Nachum reasoned to himself), of what social value is a *javohl?* A carp is nothing to stare at in the midst of the ocean. But if this same carp should suddenly emerge from the kitchen faucet, then *s'iz a wunder.*

For Nachum, who still could not get over the tumult of Warsaw—he always stayed on the few streets he knew, as if he could cling to the *shtetl* in all the confusion—for Nachum, his sister-in-law's assurances that, compared with a real city, compared with Hamburg or Frankfurt or Berlin, Warsaw was no more than an overgrown Shluftchev—such talk could only make him shake his head in wonder.

The noises of the wagons and the trolleys rattling over the cobblestones made his head ache. Even in the apartment, the babble came pouring through the walls: not only the living voices of one's neighbors, but famous *chazzonim* singing as if in the synagogue; and women, too, may God forgive them. This was the doing of the Gentile *gaon* in America, Edison, the inventor of the phonograph. Nachum had read an article about him in the Yiddish paper.

Between the crowds and the streetcars and the inventions of Mr. Edison, it was difficult for a man to think. And this overwhelming confusion—a maze of so many streets you could live your whole life in Warsaw and never see them all—this, according to his sister-in-law, was no more than an overgrown Shluftchev? How much more noise and tumult could there be squeezed in between the heavens and the earth?

No, no, Frieda had corrected him. In Germany, even though there is so much more of everything, yet this more is accomplished quietly and with *ordnung*.

When you began to pay close attention to people, then there was often much to smile about. People had their funny little ways. The important thing was to remember that this was not the whole story. You don't stop with the smile. Nachum knew that Frieda's kindness was many times more substantial than all the innocent little airs she might put on. Nachum knew that in her heart she, too, still spoke a good plain Galitzianer Yiddish. And who was to say that all the things she loved so much—the books and the music and the plays—were not very fine things, and maybe even worthwhile? Maybe yes, maybe no. Maybe light, maybe darkness.

Frieda herself was determined to contribute, if only by the multitude of her opinions, to the general improvement of the Yiddish cultural life of Warsaw. She had taken on this life by storm, bringing Sorela with her. Sometimes even Chanala would leave her four little boys, over whom she fussed like a mother hen, at home with her husband, Mendel Bayrish, and go out for an evening on the town with her aunt Frieda.

In the past six months, Frieda had attended every play, every concert, every poetry reading, or, as they sometimes billed themselves, "word concerts." She had begun by finding fault with everything, but her natural propensities soon overcame her critical reviews. Frieda's talent lay not in criticism but in exultation. Sorela, with her talent for impersonating, loved to imitate her aunt describing the latest genius of

Warsaw. About a young pianist: "He's the Jewish Paderewski!" About a new poet: "He's the Jewish Goethe!"

From paying close attention, Nachum saw that often, when it seemed as if Frieda was being foolish, she was really making fun of herself, exaggerating her nature so as to make it into a good joke. She enjoyed it when people had a good laugh at her expense, especially Leiba. It seemed to Nachum that this was a very exalted level of generosity, a form of charity of one of the highest orders.

The more Nachum paid attention, the more he grew to admire this woman whom he most certainly would once, in his ignorance, have shunned—in the old days, before he had learned, through sorrow, to pay closer attention to how the world looked through this one's eyes and through that one's.

CHAPTER 10

ALL THIS AND
CHUTZPA, TOO

"What presence the girl has," Aunt Frieda had murmured, when her sister's family had come to her home to greet her and Heinrich on their return to Poland.

The change in her sister—of course she had come to stay with her for a few days shortly after the tragedy, may everyone be spared from such, but then she hadn't seen her for at least another five years, over the course of which she had forgotten—had probably made herself forget—the terrible changes that sorrow had wrought in her sister—well, of course, it broke Frieda's heart. Anything she could do, anything at all, would be done. Any distraction that she could offer.

But her niece! Here was a sight on which to feast the eyes! She was lovely, enchanting. A goddess. If Frieda had had a daughter—and, dear God, how much she had always wanted a daughter, not that her three sons weren't wonderful, wonderful boys, and her three daughters-in-law . . . all right. But if Frieda had had a daughter, she would have wanted one just like this niece of hers.

Only look at how tall and well formed she was, and such a lovely, but still such an *interesting* face. The cheekbones! Where in their family had anyone had such cheekbones? You can *see* the personality shining out from her every feature, speaking as with a voice.

And speaking of that voice: such a voice! Like something delicious,

171

something spiked and expensive to drink, that warms your *kishka*s in a tingling afterglow.

"What presence. And that voice," Frieda had murmured. "She ought to be on the stage."

Once uttered, the thought immediately gathered potency for Frieda, so that now she repeated it, but with far more vehemence, with a tone, even, of accusation.

"Really, Leiba, this exquisite niece of mine should be on the stage!"

To Sorel it seemed that Aunt Frieda herself was on a stage. Behind her there were three great windows, draped in a rich red velvet, held back with golden tassels.

On another wall there was a huge fireplace—unfortunately without a fire, but with a screen and andirons and a mantelpiece on which stood various statues—items Sorel would have thought forbidden in a Jewish home, with its prohibition of graven images. Of course, Aunt Frieda *was* a modern, a married woman who didn't cover her hair. Though she had assured Sorel's mother that her home was strictly kosher, Sorel noticed that her father didn't touch any of the fancy pastries that Aunt Frieda had laid out on the delicate round table with the curved little legs. All that he asked for was a glass of water, not even accepting the tea that Aunt Frieda had poured from an enormous silver samovar that sat on a sideboard on yet another wall.

In the center of the room, which Aunt Frieda had called her parlor and which was immense, were clustered a circle of armchairs and a beautiful sofa, all uphostered in a deep-red silky fabric. On the highly polished parquet floors there were several Oriental rugs.

It was all so clean, so spacious and uncluttered, it was like something Gentile. Sorel's eyes were drawn to everything—so this is what it meant to be rich!—but Aunt Frieda's wide-eyed gaze kept itself fixed entirely on Sorel.

Leiba had laughed at her sister Fruma's pronouncement on Sorel. She might be Frieda and oh-so-fancy, but it was still the same old Fruma about whom Mamma used to say that the thoughts were like little birds, flitting from tree to tree, never resting for a moment, twittering their meaningless melody from dawn to dusk.

"Yes, of course, Fruma, right away. How had I not thought of it? Quick, Sorel, finish up your tea and *kichel*. We're off to the stage. You must become a star this very night. How have we neglected this, Nachum?"

"Laugh away, Leiba," countered Frieda, although laughing herself. "But, really, I am telling you, and I think I know a little something about the theater. Theater, music, poetry—tell her, Heinrich, what these have become to me! They are the life force of my soul! And, believe me, I have been exposed to the best. I myself heard the legendary Dietrich Mussenkavitzy play his violin. Not a dry eye in the entire concert hall. And those were Germans weeping! What I wouldn't give to myself be an artiste. Don't laugh, Leiba! You know, had things been different, had I been exposed at an earlier age, then who knows? But what did we know back then about anything? Nonetheless, there was always something in me, something that struggled to express itself, that . . . Ech, what's the use of talking now?

"But at the least it has been given to me to know how to appreciate. And this niece of mine I know to appreciate! I see the dramatic potential! Tell me, darling. Have you ever been to a theater?"

"No, Aunt Frieda, never. Will you take me?"

"Chutzpa!" Frieda had laughed. "All this and chutzpa, too! Good! Everything is right for the stage! Of course I will take you. With the greatest of pleasure. Believe me, my treasure, you have in store for you a richness of pleasure you can't begin to imagine. How I envy you! You will get to taste it all now, for the first time! And believe me: the first time, mmmmmmwah!" Aunt Frieda put the fingers of her hand to her mouth as if she was tasting something delicious and then kissed them. Sorel watched her aunt's performance with unmixed pleasure. It, too, had been given to Sorel to know to appreciate.

"I will take you everywhere, to everything! And you also, Leiba. You also, Nachum! You are going to have the culture coming from out of your ears! Heinrich, darling, go and get for me—what did you do with it—the newspaper I'm looking for. Nu, get, now. Let's see what this Warsaw can offer my promising niece in the way of cultural experience!

"Look at this! Ech! Whoever heard of these names? Who are these *shtikeleh* actors strutting and fretting their hour upon the stage. That's Shakespeare, darling. Herr Wilhelm Shakespeare. Have you heard of him perhaps?"

"Yes, Aunt Frieda. An Englishman, of the Renaissance period. He wrote the plays *Romeo and Juliet*, *King Lear*, and *Hamlet*."

"Oh, but my darling! This is beyond belief! You are educated! Leiba, I didn't know. You have an educated daughter!"

Nachum and Sorel looked quickly at Leiba, who remained expressionless.

Frieda, feeling a hot rush of regret, saw that in her hasty stupidity she had stepped on the grave.

Fool! she berated herself. Thoughtless, blundering nincompoop!

Leiba, seeing the fluster on Frieda, immediately came to her rescue. She smiled calmly.

"Yes, indeed. A most educated daughter. Sorela, give your tanta Frieda a taste of the world to come. Say a few words of Shakespeare in English for your aunt and uncle."

Sorel instinctively chose the most romantic of the passages she knew:

> See how she leans her cheek upon her hand!
> O that I were a glove upon that hand,
> That I might touch that cheek!

"I never heard anything so ravishing in all my life! Heinrich! What have you to say? What words have you for this niece of mine? My own niece! My own flesh and blood! In Warsaw she learned this? In Poland? Only, darling, quickly tell me, what does it mean?"

And when Sorel had translated the passage into Yiddish, and explained how Romeo, watching Juliet on her balcony from below, had spoken these words, then Aunt Frieda had been too overcome for a few moments even to speak.

Her large and luminous eyes had welled up with tears that she had blinked back with her long dark lashes.

"Come here," she finally whispered. "Come to me, that I might touch *your* cheek."

Sorel was amazed at the sweet-smelling softness that enfolded her. Aunt Frieda seemed more a fragrant cloud than a woman.

Aunt Frieda was still very pretty, her face smooth-skinned and finely powdered. How different from the feel of Sorel's own mother, who looked so many years older than the sister who was only two years younger that she. Sorel felt a little guilty in so admiring her aunt, the pampered feel of her.

And there was no denying to herself that she was enjoying to the last degree the heady adulation her aunt was lavishing on *her!* Just like the luxury of that flat on Marshalovsky Boulevard, her aunt's compliments were an extravagance that Sorel could very easily imagine herself growing accustomed to.

Aunt Frieda held Sorel out at arm's length and said to the others:

"I am telling you, as I live and breathe, this girl will stand yet upon the stage. She will make audiences weep as I am weeping now. Sorela, you will be another Sarah Bernhardt. Have you heard of her, the Frenchwoman all the world called 'the divine Sarah'? When she died, a million sobbing French people came to her funeral.

"You, Sorela, will be the *Jewish* Sarah Bernhardt!"

"The Jewish Sarah Bernhardt, Fruma? But wasn't the woman herself Jewish?"

"Oh, for heaven's sakes, Leiba! You *know* what I mean!"

CHAPTER 11

A LITTLE YIDDISH
THEATER

*B*ecause her niece was an expert on the English playwright Wilhelm Shakespeare, the first play to which Aunt Frieda treated Sorel was a revival of *The Jewish King Lear*, a classic in its own right, adapted from the original by Jacob Gordin.

When Gordin had died, across the wide ocean in New York City, a quarter of a million mourners had followed his coffin on foot. For the enlightened Jews of his era, Gordin had been not only the greatest of the Yiddish playwrights. He had been the rebbe, the teacher, the preacher—bringing to his faithful flock the great good news of education, secularization, and progressive politics.

"Come, come," his sonorous voice could be heard coaxing gently beneath the surface of his plots. "Come into this playhouse, this studyhouse of laughter and tears. Come, my good friend, into the great wide world. You have been living in a cage, closed in by heavy bars forged of superstition and fear. But look, my dear friend, the door of your cage is open! Turn the handle for yourself and step out. It's a pretty fine place, this wide world!"

When Gordin had first begun to write for it, the Yiddish theater was still in its brash and spirited adolescence. Avraham Goldfaden, the "father of Yiddish theater," had figured he knew his audiences pretty well. What they wanted, he was fond of saying, was a song, a jig, a kiss, a happy ending.

But Gordin, a Russian intellectual who wasn't even entirely comfortable in the "Jewish jargon," had set about putting an entirely different sort of production before these audiences, one that would take their impulse toward enlightenment and cultivation—if they had had no such impulses, why would they be there in the first place?—and raise it to a higher order.

It was true that, for these people of the book, any theater, good or bad, smacked strongly of the forbidden. Of all the arts—music, letters, painting—drama is the only one that receives absolutely no recognition within the rabbinical sources. How could it have been otherwise, when the true drama of a Torah Jew is always enacted inwardly and with modesty: in the studyhouse and the home, the prayerhouse and the heart?

Still, long before there had been anything that might have been called a Jewish theater, there had been Jews who had found their way to the stage. In England and France and Germany, there had been playwrights and directors, actors and actresses. Just think of it: Sarah Bernhardt herself. And even further back, before the divine Sarah, there hovers the slight girlish figure of the actress whom Sarah herself had revered: Rachel. That's how famous she was: she didn't need a last name.

If there was anybody who singly managed to embody the transformative powers of art, it was she. The daughter of poor peddlers from Alsace-Lorraine, Élisa (Rachel) Félix had been discovered singing with her little sister in the streets of Lyons, and had gone on to rescue, single-handedly, the moribund national theater of France. Papa Félix's impure French and (exaggerated?) vulgarity were everywhere lampooned. Yet Rachel's voice gave a startlingly new life to the classic plays of Corneille and Racine. The pristine purity of her delivery, joined to a terrifying passion, had seemed to some of her contemporaries to place her beyond the bounds of the human. She had inhabited the text as no one else had ever done and had made it over as her own. She had *possessed* France itself. Reciting the "Marseillaise," in the heady days of the Republic, sinking to her knees and wrapping herself in the tricolor, she had transformed herself into the very image of France embodied—no small feat for anyone, least of all a girl who had stepped forth from the most obscure and despised margins of European society.

Rachel's triumphs and transfigurations, however, had belonged, as had Sarah Bernhardt's after her, to the world at large. It would be something quite different to have a theater that the Jews could call their very own.

The first Yiddish play, *Serkele*, was written by an enlightened Lemberg doctor named Solomon Ettinger, in the early thirties of the nineteenth century. *Serkele*, the story of an ambitious woman, was never produced in Ettinger's lifetime. Instead, copies of the manuscript were privately circulated, daringly read in the salons and parlors of the Polish Jewish intelligentsia.

It was 1862 when Avraham Goldfaden, a young rabbinical student, participated in an amateur production of *Serkele* at his yeshiva one Purim day. He himself took the leading female role, since there were no females at the yeshiva—and that was the end of Avraham's rabbinical career. He managed to get together a troupe of performers, even eventually a few women daring, or shameless, enough to lay aside the modesty that is said to be a Jewish woman's special virtue.

Under Goldfaden, a Yiddish theater of enormous vibrancy began to emerge. He was impresario, manager, producer, author, composer, and scenic artist. His show tunes were accepted as authentic folk songs, sung at cradles and weddings. Almost all the leading players of the early Yiddish theater passed through his hands, and even those who went on to become his rivals (and deplore his high-handedness) proudly traced their roots to him.

Goldfaden hadn't been the sort to be overly impressed by the reforming impulses implicit in Jewish theater. He wanted to entertain and, in the process, make a living. He succeeded, but Jewish intellectuals stayed aloof from these efforts, which they ranked as, at best, middle-brow.

When Jacob Gordin—a worldly man, a journalist and political reformer—was first taken to see a performance at a Yiddish theater, he was appalled. "Oy vay," he recalled, years later, having groaned to himself from his seat in a theater on New York's Second Avenue. "Everything I saw and heard was far from real Jewish life. All was vulgar, immoderate, false, and coarse. 'Oy, oy,' I thought to myself, and I went home and sat down to write my first play, which at its *bris* was given the name *Siberia*. I wrote my first play the way a pious man, a scribe, copies out a Torah scroll."

But by the time that Sorela was taken to *her* first play, at the newly built and quite magnificent Nowosci Theater, the Yiddish theater had passed well beyond the Gordin era—so well and self-assuredly beyond that affectionate revivals of his work were now entering the repertoire. Even some of Goldfaden's plays, such as *The Two Kuni Lemels* and *The Witch*, were being revived in fond, if somewhat campy, productions.

For the first time in its short history, the Yiddish theater was actually coming into possession of something that could proudly be called a repertoire. There were plays that could now be considered "classics," and an exuberant vitality was feeding new productions each season. And, then, of course, the irresistible riches of the great wide world were brought to Yiddish audiences in lovingly rendered translations. Molière and Ibsen, Schiller and Strindberg, Hugo, Hauptmann, Gogol, Gorki, and, of course, the beloved Shakespeare.

Jews and theater may have come together belatedly, but once they were together, it was a match of real love. How could it have been otherwise? You step onto a stage . . . and *become somebody else!* How could Jews *not* have loved it?

Of the more than one hundred plays that Gordin had turned out, only a few were still thought to be dramatically viable. In many of them, the high didactic purpose shines through too glaringly. In fact, even while Gordin had lain on his deathbed, in 1909, the Yiddish New York daily, the *Forward*, was publishing an unflattering series of retrospective articles that, at least according to Gordin's *patriot'n,* hastened the great man's death.

Still, the Gordin name continued to be so famous that even a man as unworldly as Nachum Sonnenberg was not completely unaware of its significance.

"Aha, Gordin," he had said to Sorel when she had told him where she was going this evening—and so dressed up!

Never in his wildest dreams had Nachum ever imagined stepping foot for himself into a theater. To him, such a place smelled unpleasantly from Hellenistic corruption. Nachum only prayed that the Jewish actors and actresses didn't carry on the way the pagans had, ranting and raving so that it would have been an embarrassment for Nachum to have to sit there and listen. Surely a Jewish playwright would have the sense not to put his performers through such excesses, though who could say? To Nachum, a Jewish play was a paradox in itself. What could be Jewish about men and women getting up on a stage and carrying on before the eyes of strangers?

Still, there was no denying that many Jewish people took enjoyment from these productions, so who was Nachum to say? Jewish Warsaw was filled with talk of theater. The poorest worker set aside money for a show—alas, often going on the Shabbes. The streets were plastered with posters announcing the appearance of the legendary star so-and-so, now appearing in the immortal play such-and-such. One troupe had even hired a wagon that all day long rode up and down the busy streets.

"Aha, Gordin," is all that Nachum said, looking at his Sorela, who had come dancing over to where he sat before his open text. Her eyes shone so brightly they put to shame the little smoking lamp at his elbow. Who would have the heart to dampen such lights?

Outwardly, Nachum had not changed much over the years. His fair hair and beard remained unstreaked by gray, and an air of unworldly innocence clung to him, almost as if he were still a young and painfully shy student, boarding in the home of Rav Broder of Lemberg, of blessed memory. Somewhere it had been written in his body that it would resist the signs that time and misfortune inscribe. Though he was almost exactly the same age as his wife, he looked many years younger.

"Give my best regards to Reb Gordin," he said, kissing his daughter on the top of her head. She had to stoop low for him to reach her.

Of all the children, only Sorela still lived at home. Tzali, the baby, was studying in the prestigious Ramalyes Yeshiva in Vilna. The other children, thank God, were married, and themselves parents. Chana was the proud mother of four fine sons. Asher's wife, Sima Sora, had last month given birth to her sixth child and her first son. What a celebration that circumcision had been! And Dovid's delicate wife, Menucha, who for some years had been unable to conceive, so that it had seemed that the marriage might be, God forbid, barren, had finally given birth to a beautiful, golden-haired little girl, Malka. The child would soon be two years old. From morning until night, she chattered away, having the most comical ways of stating her mind. She was the light of Nachum and Leiba's life.

From the window, Nachum watched his daughter making her way down the darkening street. It was a freezing-cold evening in the dead of Shvat. He only prayed the child was warm enough in that coat and shawl. Thank God, the theater would be certain to be well heated. Nachum himself sat in his overcoat, warming his hands around a glass of tea while he studied.

When he could make her out no longer, he bent again over his open tract of *Baba Bathra*:

Our rabbis taught: When the Temple was destroyed for the second time, large numbers in Israel became ascetics, binding themselves neither to eat meat nor drink wine. Rav Joshua got into conversation with them and said to them: My sons, why do you not eat meat nor drink wine? They replied: Shall we eat flesh which used to be brought as an offering on the altar, now that this altar is in abeyance? Shall we drink wine which used to be poured as a libation on the altar, but now no longer? He said to them: If that is so, we should not eat bread either, because the meal offerings have ceased. They said: That is so, and we can manage with fruit. We should not eat fruit either, he said, because there is no longer an offering of first fruits. Then we can manage with other fruits, they said. But, he said, we should not drink water, because there is no longer any ceremony of the pouring of water. To this they could find no answer, so he said to them: My sons, not to mourn at all is impossible, because the blow has fallen. To mourn overmuch is also impossible, because we do not impose on the community a hardship which the majority cannot endure.

Nachum, his forehead resting on his open palm, let his eyes drift sideways off the page. The tears that came so easily to him these days, just as it used to be with the saintly stepmother of blessed memory who had raised him, clouded his vision.

Sorel caught the trolley that let her off not far from her aunt's apartment building. It was one of the few residential buildings in Warsaw that had an elevator, though this enchanting conveyance was reserved solely for the occupants. All others were directed to the less-than-enchanting stairs. But there now occurred one of those pleasant exceptions to tiresome rules to which Sorel had been growing a little more accustomed these days, though never so accustomed as to cease to feel pretty damned pleased. The doorman, who in more characteristic moments was encased in the icy dignity of doormen the world over, was suddenly reduced to an ingratiating attention. He himself, in all the importance of his gold-braided uniform and military bearing (he must have been a retired army man), escorted the girl to the elevator, all but clicking his heels together as she stepped in.

At seventeen, Sorel was still getting used to the tributes. Here were grown-up men, before whom only a short time ago she, as a mere child, had stood respectfully subdued. Now they fell all over themselves, like cheder boys!

Was she beautiful? She couldn't really decide. She often stared into the little smoky mirror, the only one her family owned, trying to make up her mind as to whether "beautiful" was really the word to sum up what she saw. She liked her long gray Cossack eyes, the prominence of her cheekbones, the thick blond mass of her hair. She liked that she didn't seem to look like anyone else. She just wasn't at all certain that these attributes added up to "beautiful." Maybe she was beautiful, without being pretty?

Was it a matter of the "presence" her aunt was always exclaiming over? Or was it because she looked so very un-Jewish?

People were always telling her this. She was, to be perfectly frank, perfectly sick of it. People always said it as if it constituted a compliment of the highest order. Well, Sorel didn't consider it such. It rankled in her, this dismissal of Jewish beauty. Her sister Fraydel had been a Jewish beauty: her frame slight, her bones small, her eyes large and liquid and luminous, filled with an eloquence that bypassed the clumsy speech of lips. She would pull her dark heavy hair across her face as if it were a veil.

The elevator operator (too old to be affected by Sorel's "presence," but clearly the doorman's underling) closed the open-grilled gates with a crashing clang. The noise awoke a sense of terror Sorel had known before. Sorel felt that she couldn't get enough air into her lungs, that she would suffocate, that . . . Fortunately, the trip to the third floor didn't take very long, and the doors were reopened for the white-faced passenger. From now on she would take the stairs.

The door of Aunt Frieda's apartment was painted blue. A small brass plate was hung, engraved with the name "Pomeranz."

Aunt Frieda herself, and not the uniformed maid, answered the buzz of the bell.

She hugged Sorel with great warmth, and again Sorel was amazed at the softness of her aunt. It was like being embraced by a fragrant froth. Sorel guessed that it must take many zlotys, and many hours, to achieve such a degree of insubstantiality. Even the scent of her aunt's perfume—Sorel guessed that it must be French—set off vague little half-wishes and half-thoughts in Sorel's head—half only because she had no idea of how to complete them.

Her aunt seemed tonight to be even younger than she had the evening before. Her dark eyes shone, as if she were almost as excited about this night out at the theater as Sorel herself.

Of course, privately Frieda didn't expect to be overly impressed by what she and her niece would sample at the Nowosci Theater. Having lived so many years in Germany, Frieda was out of touch with any recent developments in Warsaw's world of Yiddish drama. She couldn't anticipate too much. After all, she had seen the dramas of such Germanic geniuses as Wedekind and Hauptmann, performed by the greatest tragedians of the German stage.

On the other hand, sitting and watching a good Yiddish play, she couldn't keep her heart from kicking up like a Chasid at a wedding. Somehow—and completely in spite of her own better judgment, you should understand—she ended up having such a wonderful time. It was like when you go back to the old neighborhood after you've, thank God, made good. You get all *ferputzt,* change your dress a million times before deciding, wear your fur even if it's ninety degrees in the shade, just so there shouldn't be the slightest bit of doubt in anybody's mind. And then what happens but that the sight of the old places and the old faces makes you go limp with memories, and before your better judgment can step in and slap some sense into you, you're actually overcome with the bittersweetness of nostalgia.

It was only the two of them going out tonight. Heinrich was away on business, and Leiba had declined the invitation. "Go and enjoy" was all that Frieda could get out of her sister.

Frieda would have liked for her sister to come along, of course, but she also welcomed this chance to become better acquainted with her enchanting niece, whose reaction to the stage Frieda was very anxious to see. Wait, wait. If Frieda was any judge of character at all, then that niece of hers was a genuine kindred spirit, as artistic and sensitive as she herself. Sorela, too, just like her, had a soul that disdained everything that was petty and mundane, a soul that vibrated with the music of the higher spheres!

And that voice!

They would begin with a little Yiddish theater, and then Frieda would lead her artistic niece onward and upward. To Wedekind! To Hauptmann!

Frieda's eyes couldn't get enough of the girl. She was dressed as simply as could be: a black pleated woolen skirt and a simple white satin blouse, her Sabbath best. Only, on Sorel, these prosaic clothes took on the strains of purest poetry! Who needed a fancy gown when one had been blessed with such a complexion? Who needed diamonds with such eyes?

Aunt Frieda stood in her parlor, exclaiming over her niece—not a bad experience for either of them. Sorel had already caught on to the fact that her aunt went in for embellishments on everything, not excluding the truth. Still, if she were only a fraction so wonderful as her aunt Frieda seemed to think her, she was a creature to be envied.

For herself, Sorel wouldn't have minded such a gown as her aunt Frieda was wearing, a deep-green velvet that almost swept the floor. And the emeralds at her throat! Seeing Sorel's eyes on these, Aunt Frieda rushed out of the room and came back with a black velvet choker adorned with a large and beautiful antique cameo.

"I'd gladly lend you these," she said, putting her fluttering hand to her throat. "But, with what you're wearing, this will produce more of an effect."

After fastening it about Sorel's long graceful neck, she stood back to admire.

"Exquisite," she murmured. The choker was the very line needed to complete the perfect poem.

Sorel's coat . . . Well, no flight of imagination could endow it with poetry. It was an object that had long ago seen better days.

Wait, Aunt Frieda had just the thing. She pulled out of the front closet a great flowing sweep of a black velvet cape, lined with white fur, that extended itself into a border for the charming caul-like hood.

Arranging the cape and hood about her niece, Frieda pronounced Sorela the image of a romantic heroine out of a Russian novel: a member of the aristocracy, off to a ball—or, better, making ready to flee into the night, before the approaching hordes of unwashed revolutionaries!

"It's yours," Frieda said firmly. "You and this cape were clearly destined for one another. I never knew why I bought it, since it makes me look like a walking display in a drapery store. Now I know that I was but the blind instrument of your fate."

Finally, the two were ready. Arm in arm, like two sisters, they swept out of the apartment, past the following eyes of Sorel's vanquished doorman, and out into the starry night.

The beauty of the clear cold night came to meet Sorel, now that she had discarded the little worn-out coat for the luxurious folds of the fur-lined cape.

In the soft glow cast by the streetlights, their breath hung before them in heavy blossoms of mist.

And the sky! Rent full with stars, it seemed nearer to earth, almost within reach.

It was January, the month that looks both ways, though tonight it was turned toward winter with an undivided face. But even if the night was cold, it was without bitterness. The winds that often blew off of the Vistula, to whip with so much savage hatred up the boulevards and across the squares of the city, tonight were stilled.

In the winter snows, horse-drawn sleighs replaced the droshkies. Aunt Frieda and Sorel stepped into a sleigh that was waiting at the curb. The driver was wrapped in an enormous greatcoat and had on a huge cap of dark fur that was pulled down low.

The two women buried themselves beneath the heavy tattered blanket provided, and the horse, a poor skinny martyred creature who was covered with nothing but a thin coat of ice, set off, its tiny bells tinkling, its hoofbeats muffled by the new layer of yet-unfrozen snow. From here and there came the silvery tinkling of other sleighs, calling to one another.

Riding in such a sleigh, leaning up against the deep fur coat of her aunt, and breathing in her perfume, Sorel looked out on the wonderfully stilled body of Warsaw. Few people were out on the streets in the frigid air, though the restaurants and cafés they passed were brightly lit, no doubt crowded, and there were short lines of people before the movie houses.

The glowing windows of the great fine residential buildings they passed provoked something sharp with the ache of longing in Sorel, as she imagined to herself the cultivated existence that must go on in such places: book-lined walls, artful talk, refined tastes and pleasures. So many lives going on simultaneously! It was wonderful somehow just to know this was so, even though you couldn't hope to partake in all these lives. . . .

She had dreamt of such nights, had lain in her pulled-out cot in the corner, dreaming.

It was as if she had long felt the presence of this other self of Warsaw. Like a patient older lover, it had waited, ready to teach her when she herself became ready to learn.

Was it a madness—to love a city as she was prepared to love this Warsaw?

Aunt Frieda chattered away, but Sorel only half took in the content of what she said. She let her mind drift off to the rich fantasy her aunt's words had let loose in her imagination. A heroine stepped forth from a Russian novel, she rode out into the night, a privileged but doomed child of the nobility, clinging feverishly to her old world, while a tomorrow cold and cruel as an ax was waiting to fell her rightful future. A tear, half frozen, hung on Sorel's eyelash.

The sleigh pulled up among many others that were converging before the grand edifice of the Nowosci Theater. Sorel alighted, not yet quite relinquishing the character born of her aunt's words.

Carried along by the crush, they entered one of the three wooden doors that stood in the façade, each door flanked by sculpted pillars. The lobby was plush with red velvet, and a crystal chandelier cast its warm glow on the lively crowd. *What* a crowd: worldly and wonderful! It was an honor to be crushed within its midst! Around her, Sorel heard only Polish. Had Sorel's mother consented to come with them, she would have been the only woman in the Nowosci Theater in an old-fashioned matron's wig.

Aunt Frieda noticed the heads turning their way. Her niece, tall and aristocratic in her velvet cape and hood, was creating a sensation. So Frieda was not alone in thinking she had something quite extraordinary here. Wait, wait.

Where in the world had the girl learned to make such an entrance? In Shluftchev?

Look at how she carried herself, so regally, as if she were oblivious to the attention! She looked like one of the Polish debutantes who rode horseback along Ujazdowe Allee and in Lazienki Park.

Aunt Frieda saw people whispering, their eyes on Sorela.

Aunt Frieda would have been prepared to bet several hundred zlo-tys, then and there, that they whispered: "Give a look at the beautiful shiksa. What brings her to *The Jewish King Lear?*"

In confirmation of Aunt Frieda's speculation, the crowd actually parted for them. And Sorel sailed through, oblivious!

Only here Aunt Frieda was wrong. Sorel was not the slightest bit oblivious to the impression she was making in her debut as the fatally doomed Russian heroine, now mounting the red-carpeted stairs to take her seat in the box, and to lean her head so affectingly on the arm that rested on the carved wooden balustrade.

It was only when the lights dimmed, and the orchestra started up, that Sorel was wrenched out of the role she had assumed, wrenched out of all awareness of anything other than the actions taking place on the stage.

Here is a family, obviously very well-to-do, gathered around the holiday table, celebrating the joyous feast of Purim. There is drinking and singing and many affectionate jokes made at the expense of Shammoi, a servant.

This Shammoi is a real character, with a voice like a badly blown shofar. On Purim, everyone drinks, even Shammoi. Especially Shammoi. He keeps going behind the handsome heavy drapes to take another little nip, so that his speech gets ever more slurred and his legs are bending underneath him in a way one wouldn't have thought was humanly possible. Every word he says sends the family into laugh-ter.

The father of the family, Dovid Maysheles, is clearly a patriarch of the old school, devoted to his family, if also somewhat tyrannical in as-serting his authority over his wife, Chana Leah, and his three daugh-ters.

The two older daughters, Ettela and Gittela, are married and al-ready not so young. They sit with their Orthodox husbands, Avraham Chariff and Moishe Chossid. Ettela and Gittela both wear elaborate matron's wigs and fine-lace scarves, and are dripping with jewelry. Though they and their husbands sprinkle their speech with pieties, there's something insincere and grating in their voices. The funny thing is that only the foolish servant Shammoi seems to hear the heavy and oily insincerity.

But the youngest daughter, Toibela, is altogether different. Dressed in a very simple dress, whose short sleeves testify to her modern thinking, she's quiet and looks distracted, in the midst of all the chattering, and she keeps glancing at the empty seat next to her. When she hears footsteps, she jumps up and opens the door, joyfully leading in a young handsome man, Mr. Joffe, who is also dressed in a modern suit and hat. He is welcomed and takes his place in the seat beside Toibela.

Dovid Maysheles orders Shammoi to bring him his jewelry box, and tells his daughters he has Purim gifts for them all.

"For you, Ettela, my eldest daughter, who has such golden hands— for these hands on this happy day I give you two diamond rings!"

Ettela is overjoyed and kisses her father's hands. With a great deal of showy emoting she blesses her father, wishing him and her mother long years of health and happiness, "till a hundred and twenty-five!"

"For you, Gittela, my next daughter," continues Dovid Maysheles, "who has such golden ears—I give you for a Purim gift a pair of diamond earrings!"

Now it's Gittela's turn to exclaim her love, to kiss her father's hands and wish him and her mother long years and every good fortune.

"And for you, Toibela, my youngest daughter, who has such a golden heart," continues Dovid Maysheles, "for you, I have on this Purim day a diamond brooch!"

Toibela sits, staring down at her lap, as if she hasn't heard a word!

"Now speak!" her father orders. "Give your father a blessing!"

"What's the matter with you?" her two sisters simper. "Why don't you thank our dear father, who shows you so much love? Is this the kind of behavior you learn from all those books you're always reading? You see, Father, you see what comes of allowing a girl to study from books?"

Dovid Maysheles orders Toibela to get up from the table and to go stand before him.

Quietly, she gets up, her eyes cast downward, and stands before her glowering father.

"Why do you keep silent?" he thunders like an avenging angel. "Can't you accept my gift to you?"

"The brooch is beautiful, Father," Toibela says in her low and refined voice. "But, Father, I don't like ornaments. I don't need it. I don't understand why humanity needs to decorate itself in this way, putting so much love into cold pieces of jewelry."

"A woman must do as she is told!" Dovid Maysheles fulminates. "She musn't indulge in philosophy like a man! A woman must have beautiful things!"

"Of course, Father," chime in the smirking Ettela and Gittela. "Who could argue with the truth? Especially when the truth is so pleasant to accept!"

"You see, Mr. Teacher," they accuse Mr. Joffe. "You had to go and teach her how to read!"

"I don't have any trouble loving ornaments," Ettela continues, smiling in such a way that she seems actually to ooze with her love of herself. "When I go to the synagogue on Shabbes morning, wearing all of my pieces of jewelry, and the other women all look at me and turn green with jealousy, then I couldn't be any happier. What can be more pleasant than having things so that others turn green?"

"Oy, daughters," Dovid Maysheles now says, reversing himself with the capriciousness of the despot. "My Toibela is wiser than both of you. It's all right, my dear youngest daughter. If you don't want to wear the brooch, nobody is forcing you. Now, here, sweet Toibela. Take a drink of wine and give your father a blessing."

"Oh, Father, I gladly give you my blessing, but, please, I cannot drink the wine. It gives me a headache."

"Drink!"

Toibela drinks, and then quietly goes back to her seat.

Dovid Maysheles drinks also with Mr. Joffe, and tells him, "I love a wise man, though he may be a modern!

"As long as I live, children, you must obey my will. That is the way it has always been, and that is the way it must always be!

"When I say it is daytime, then, even though the moon is out, it is daytime!

"When I say it is nighttime, then, though the sun may be shining, it is nighttime!"

"Yes, Father."

"Of course, Father."

"This is only right, Father."

"What is there to argue about, dear Father," Ettela and Gittela and Chariff and Moishe Chossid all clamor together.

Now Dovid Maysheles sits back, placated and benevolent.

"I have been blessed in having such good, such devoted children."

"And now, my dear children, I have something very important to tell you. For my entire life, I have devoted myself to my affairs, to my family, and to God. But from this day forward, I devote myself entirely to God!

"I give over to you my entire fortune. I will go to Jerusalem, to spend my last years in the Holy Land, walking where our blessed ancestors of old walked, seeing the hills and the valleys that they saw."

"Better he should see what goes on in his own house!" the drunken Shammoi cackles to the servant girl, who hurriedly shushes him.

Dovid Maysheles's announcement is greeted with loud exclamations of approval from the older daughters and their husbands.

Chariff says how much he has always revered his father-in-law, and how now he stands in such awe he hardly knows what to say, although he keeps saying.

Moishe Chossid says, with his exaggerated Talmudic singsong and gestures, that it is given only to the most pure and pious to be worthy of seeing Jerusalem in their lifetimes.

"All others must roll there, mile after mile, only after they have died!"

Dovid Maysheles tells Chariff that the paper he is now giving him makes him the lawful caretaker of the entire fortune: the house, the granaries, and cash amounts up to three hundred and ten rubles.

"You, my dear eldest son-in-law, a man of pious faith and of God-fearing honesty, will administer my fortune for me. You will see that all of my children receive their equal share."

"Just like the fox sees that all the little chicks are well provided for!" wheezes Shammoi.

"I give you my fortune, but remember!" Dovid Maysheles intones. "My will shall always rule you!"

Dovid Maysheles's wife says, in a somewhat plaintive tone, "You didn't tell me you were going to give away all your wealth."

"Wife!" he thunders at her. "What I say goes! That is all you ever need to know! Even if I had announced that tomorrow we pack up and move to the farthermost reaches of frozen Siberia, you would follow without a word!"

Only Toibela and Mr. Joffe remain completely quiet in the midst of the family's turnabouts. Now Dovid Maysheles shifts his attention to his solemn youngest daughter.

"You, Toibela, will now be the richest prospective bride in all of Vilna! Your brother-in-law Chariff will choose a husband for you. All the girls of Vilna will envy you. Speak! What have you to say about your good mazel?"

"Oh, Father, I beg you! Do not do what you are contemplating! Do not give me over to that false Chariff and do not give away your fortune! I implore you with all my heart! Listen and take my advice!"

But at this Dovid Maysheles explodes, now finally giving vent to the full thrust of his temper.

"Do as I say, or get out of my sight! Do you hear me, daughter? Get out of my house!"

While poor Chana Leah sobs, and Toibela leaves the room, Mr. Joffe stands before Dovid Maysheles.

"Have you ever heard of the famous Shakespeare? He has written a drama by the name of *King Lear* in which a father orders from his house the friend who truly loves him. That is exactly what you are doing now. You are the Yiddish King Lear!"

"*Oy vay iz mir, oy vay iz mir,*" Chana Leah is weeping. "Toibela has packed her things and is leaving!"

Dovid Maysheles, gathering the reins over his anger, sits back down at his place at the head of the table.

"It's Purim! Sing, sing!"

The remaining daughters and sons-in-law begin a Purim song, and with that the curtain falls and the house lights come on.

Aunt Frieda saw that Sorela was gripping the red balustrade in front of her so that her knuckles were white. And when her niece turned to her, Frieda saw the child's face was bathed in tears.

Of course, Frieda's face, too, was streaming. She took out a little gold compact, inspected the damage, and carefully repowdered her face. She knew that this was shmaltzy melodrama, little more than *shund,* trash. But go tell that to her gushing eyes!

"Is it over?" Sorela asked in a stricken voice.

"Over? Of course not. This was just the first act. You're an educated girl. You should know about acts."

"It's just that the lights are on. And everybody is getting out of their seats."

"This is what you call the intermission. Now is the time to get up, stretch your legs, look over the audience. Come."

Reluctantly, Sorel got up to follow her aunt. Intermission seemed like a very bad idea to Sorel. Why break the magic spell by reminding the audience who they were and where they were—by letting so-called real life intrude? Still, it was not in Sorel's nature to turn down an opportunity for seeing and being seen.

By following the general flow, they soon made their way to one of the two buffets. There was a crush of people before it. Again heads turned. And then one of the greatest tributes that can be paid to someone, especially when performed by Jewish people waiting in line to get food: the crowd parted for Sorela.

There could be no doubt: everyone assumed she was a young Polish aristocrat, a beautiful shiksa. Sorel, just like a real aristocrat, gave away not a hint that she noticed the tribute paid her. But of course she noticed it all and in every little detail. To be thought worthy of notice in the midst of such an elegant, Polish-speaking crowd was almost more astonishing than it was gratifying.

Aunt Frieda purchased two little china cups—demitasses, she

called them—that held a rich and scalding coffee. There were luscious-looking pastries and chocolates, but Sorel was not in the mood for these.

Aunt Frieda looked at her with wonder.

"This I can't understand. I am never not in the mood!" Aunt Frieda gave one last look, full of longing, at the buffet. She had put on some kilos since coming back to Poland. The food here—well, it was what she was used to, what she had been raised on, and she found it irresistible. But she had made up her mind to put up a better fight, especially after Heinrich, embracing her the other morning, had said that he was glad there was a little bit more to love these days. So even he had noticed! Looking at her niece's slender waist was a good inspiration.

"Hurry, drink up," Aunt Frieda warned her, as a great gong was struck by one of the uniformed ushers. "We have to get back to the box now."

They were again carried by the flow, this time in reverse, back into the theater. The two had barely resettled themselves into their box when the lights dimmed, and Sorel was once again swept up into the actions on the stage:

The curtain rose to reveal Toibela sitting in a poor but colorfully decorated room, crowded with books. She has a roommate, Tova, to whom she explains that the letter she is reading is from her parents, who have gone off to live in Palestine, without even a farewell to her. She is very hurt, almost crying, as she says this. But then Mr. Joffe comes into the room and announces to the two girls that they are all to go off to St. Petersburg, there to pursue their studies in medicine.

Chariff, sitting in the former house of his father-in-law, the scene of the fatal Purim feast, is now approached by Toibela and Mr. Joffe, who demand that Toibela receive her share of her inheritance, so that she will have something to live on while she studies. But Chariff, assuming his arch stance of offended piety, denies Toibela her inheritance.

"I won't allow the family money to be used for the support of impiety and foolish *narrishkeiten.*"

"Do you think you have the right to dictate my life to me? I only ask for what is rightfully mine!"

At this Chariff says, with a smile oily enough to fry latkes, that he'll give Toibela some rubles, but only if she signs a paper he has prepared that promises she'll make no more claims to any money.

She and Mr. Joffe depart indignantly.

Now Gittela and her little Chossid enter the room. Moishe Chossid is completely tipsy, tripping over his own feet and singing a garbled version of a Chasidic tune. Chariff makes some cruel remarks, at which Gittela flares up.

"You give us barely enough money to live on! My poor Moishela has nothing to do with himself all day! It is the humiliation that has made him a *shikker!*"

Chariff laughs for a few moments at his brother-in-law's drunken antics, then orders the two from his room, so that he may get back to his work . . . and the curtain falls.

When the curtain next comes up, here is Dovid Maysheles returning from the studyhouse to his wife, Chana Leah. The room they sit in has none of the former glory of their house in Vilna, although through a window one can see the Wailing Wall of Jerusalem. They, too, have not been receiving the money Chariff is supposed to be sending them in order that they may live. Chana Leah reads a letter that her daughter Toibela has sent from St. Petersburg, reporting the shabby way in which Chariff is conducting himself.

"Now do you see to whom you have entrusted our family's fortune and fate?" the poor wife wails.

"We shall return to Vilna at once!" the old father declares.

When the curtain next comes up, we are again in the house in Vilna. Shammoi sits rocking a cradle, a task to which Ettela has assigned him.

"Now, in my old age, I am made into a nanny!"

Ettela comes storming into the room. She is missing a spoon and accuses Shammoi.

Her mother comes in, and she, too, is accused.

"What? A spoon? Yes, near your father's book; he used it to stir his tea. What is so horrible?"

Dovid Maysheles comes back from the studyhouse, and Chana Leah goes off to prepare a little refreshment for him. She comes back lamenting that her daughter has now put locks on all of the cupboards!

Ettela, still making noises like a devoted daughter, brings her father a meal that consists of a piece of bread and a radish.

"Here, Tatta, look at what I have prepared for you myself. Eat in good health."

"This is how you treat a father!" Chana Leah cries out. "A father who never could do enough for you, to his own everlasting harm!"

Dovid Maysheles, summoning some of his old authority, informs his son-in-law that, according to Russian law, a donor is allowed to retract a gift.

Chariff turns pale and begins to tremble.

But, no, Dovid Maysheles has not been in earnest. He tells his son-in-law that, no matter what the Russian law says, he, Dovid Maysheles, would never go back on his word. For him, his word is the law.

Just now, Toibela and Mr. Joffe come to the house, both of them now doctors, or, as Ettela says contemptuously, "the doctor and doctoress." Chana Leah is overjoyed, but Dovid Maysheles tells his daughter that she's already forgotten her Jewish faith.

"I want to be independent!" she answers him. "I want to be useful!"

"Come," Dr. Joffe tells her, leading her away. "We'll show these fanatics they can't extinguish the light of science!"

Chana Leah, heartbroken at losing her daughter yet a second time, sobs and protests, and now Chariff orders both her and Dovid Maysheles to leave the house!

Cast out, penniless, from the house he has given away, Dovid Maysheles becomes a beggar, taking the fool Shammoi with him. His mind seems to have been broken by his heartache, and he calls out, as he takes his beggar's pouch over his shoulder, "Respect for the King! Make way for the new king beggar! Give charity to the Jewish King Lear!"

Toibela finds her mother living in poverty and brings her to live in her own house.

And now it is Toibela's wedding. She and Dr. Joffe are getting married. An uninvited Ettela and Chariff suddenly barge in, Chariff showing off the heavy gold chain he means to give them as a wedding gift, but they are both told to leave by the outraged bridegroom. Gittela and her Chossid, however, are welcomed into the *simcha.*

While Toibela and Dr. Joffe can be heard taking their vows off to the side, a blind Dovid Maysheles is led into the house by Shammoi.

"Where are you taking me? What kind of people live here? I didn't feel a *mezuzah* on the doorpost."

"Don't worry," answers Shammoi. "These are good people. You can't tell everything about a person by what he hangs on his doorpost."

"How good it feels to sit here in the warmth," sighs the broken old man.

What a reunion takes place after this!

"Let me just stay in a little corner of your house," Dovid Maysheles weeps as he holds his youngest daughter, the glowing bride. "I promise I won't make any trouble for you. I only want to be somewhere near you, and when I die I want to die at your feet."

"Please, Father, don't talk like that. You will always have a home with me."

"What is happening?" asked the helpless old man. "Am I awake or am I dreaming?"

"You're awake," answers Shammoi, laughing. "After years of sleeping, you're awake."

"If God wants to punish someone, He takes away his sense," says the trembling old father. "I thought I could see better than all the world, so God made me blind. I thought I could understand better than all the world, so God made a fool of me. Oh, God in heaven, give me back my eyesight for a few minutes so I can see my dear children!"

Dr. Joffe, examining his father-in-law's eyes, diagnoses the problem as not serious, curable by a simple operation. Not only this, but Chariff and Ettela return, loudly wailing that they have suffered financial ruin!

And on this happy scene, the final curtain comes down.

Who would ever have thought that Warsaw could be so quiet, broken only by the silvery tinkling of the horse's bells, calling out to one another in sweet unintelligible phrases. Above the silenced city, the clear night sky was a chill glittering dazzle of stars.

Stars! Gashes slashed through the covering of sky!

Sorel had glimpsed the outermost sphere of light before—brief glimpses, now and then. But those stars she had seen moving across the stage tonight: they must take the cold fire in and out of themselves, as others breathe the air. Yes stars, really and truly. Though they spoke her mother tongue, still how they had spoken it! In their mouths it had become a language as otherworldly and pure as the Hebrew in which her father and brothers conversed with one another on the Sabbath. And then how those stars had been able to make their every gesture and every expression take on unvoiceable meanings. Every flutter of the eyelid or sweep of the arm had charged the air around them with suggestions, absorbed into the unnatural glow that bathed them. That's how it is for people to live—to move and speak and feel—when it has been given to them to be rents in the firmament, to draw down to earth the distant light—cold and clear and utterly without comfort—that speaks with a strange soft voice and smells faintly of the pine forest.

"Are you crying, Sorela?"

"Only because I'm so happy, Aunt Frieda. Thank you so much!"

Sorel nestled up close to her mother's sister, burying herself into the deliciously deep fur of her coat. Impulsively, she gave her aunt a kiss on her soft powdered cheek.

"Oh my darling, you are a million times welcome! I knew you would take to the theater as a *shikker* takes to drink."

"It's a good comparison, Aunt Frieda. I feel as if I'm drunk."

"I know exactly what you mean.

"You know, darling, we should read the Shakespeare version of the play," her aunt continued. "I'm curious now to see how Gordin changed it. Do you think Shakespeare's King Lear is as ox-stubborn as that Dovid Maysheles? Really, you felt like shaking him by his shoulders. I'm sure Shakespeare's hero didn't give up his kingdom in order to go off to sit and learn in Jerusalem! But he was very convincing as a Jewish father, that Yiddish King Lear, a patriarch of the old school, of a type

I know all too well. I'm sorry to say that he reminded me a little bit of my own father, he should rest in peace."

"Really? My *zayda?*"

Sorel had, of course, heard stories from her mother about this grandfather, whom Sorel had never known. All of Leiba's stories extolled her father for the rigors of his piety and learning, and Sorel knew that her own father (her paragon of virtue) had revered his father-in-law and teacher. It had been to Rav Dovid Broder that the dead man had come, mournfully petitioning that he be allowed to be buried among his own kind.

"Well, never mind that," Frieda now said hurriedly. "I've gone and spoken where I shouldn't have. Your grandfather certainly wasn't the fool that that Dovid Maysheles was. And one thing I'll give my father. He had the highest respect for my mother. So, there, let's change the subject and not speak any ill of the dead, may they rest in peace."

Sorel's mind again sought out the visions of the play, gazing in wonder at scene after scene, each one linked through a hidden logic to the tear-drenched radiance of the final reconciliation between the blind, enfeebled father and the daughter he had so misjudged. If only life could be like that! If only we could all be made to see before the final curtain comes down and it's too late.

"So what do you think of it, darling?" she heard her aunt demanding of her.

"I'm sorry. What do I think of what, Aunt Frieda?"

"The name Sasha. As your stage name. What do you think?"

"Isn't it a man's name?"

"A man's and a woman's, too. That's the beauty of it!"

"Yes, I see what you mean," Sorel said slowly. "Yes, I like it. Sasha Sonnenberg!"

"No. Just Sasha. Like the great French actress Rachel. Sasha and nothing more."

"I know, I know," said Sorel, laughing softly. "I'll be the Jewish Rachel!"

"Go on, darling, laugh at your silly Aunt Frieda. But I tell you, I have only the greatest expectations."

This was certainly true. With Aunt Frieda anticipation was a constant state. Frieda had always lived, even when she was nothing but Fruma, expecting something that exceeds all expectations to turn up, momentarily. Given her disposition, she never entertained a doubt that it would be something wonderful. Given her preference, she hoped it would be something wildly romantic, though, of course, not of such a nature as to compromise her marriage, God forbid.

And now, riding home beside her enchanting flesh-and-blood, Frieda had the sense that she at long last knew what it was she had been breathlessly awaiting since as long as she could remember; that extraordinary Something that would lift her life above the accidents of circumstance—happy as these were in her case—and transform it into an existence distinctly its own, unexchangeable with that of any other Polish-Jewish woman of modern point of view and moderately comfortable means. When she had been a girl and her *yichesdika* marriage with Chayim Pomeranz had been arranged, she had believed that it had been to this dazzling match that those expectations of hers had been all along mutely pointing. Yet still there had lingered—or been revived, after the blissful delirium of her first years of marriage and motherhood—the sense of Something even beyond Chayim, even beyond the *naches* of having borne three sons—each one, in his own way, all that a mother could ask—on whom she and Chayim had been able to lavish advantages she could never have dreamed of as a girl. Still, a happily married bourgeois existence, as pleasant as it was, was not that fateful Something she had always sensed to be carrying inside her, as a fruit has its core.

Engrossed in their intertwining fantasies, Sorel and Frieda were transported, amidst the silvery music of the suffering horse, to the street of the Sonnenberg flat.

"Good night, darling Aunt Frieda!" Sorel whispered into her aunt's fragrant hair.

"Good night . . . Sasha!" Aunt Frieda answered, her voice husky with its caught throb.

CHAPTER 12

A MOMENT IN TIME

*W*hat a city Warsaw was at this moment in time. What a city Jewish Warsaw was.

Sorel wasn't alone in being drunk on her vision of the light from beyond the sky. All of Warsaw seemed to be wildly teetering . . . reeling . . . tilting at large and improbable angles.

All across the former Pale were Jewish parents having their Jewish hearts broken, as sons and daughters broke away from the old ways, made a blind run for the light.

Not Leiba and Nachum, though, since their hearts had already been broken.

The world that now opened up before Sorel couldn't have been more alien to her parents, and yet they said not a word against it, offered up no obstacles to the strange future she was running toward, her arms thrown open to the glowing western sky.

From scattered little places indistinguishable from Shluftchev on the Puddle, places tucked away in ritual and folklore, untouched for centuries, there now came young people so hungry for the world at large that, no matter how much they took in, they still felt themselves famished. It was a hunger that would be felt unto the seventh generation.

This is mine! I am here and this is mine!

But there was so much to catch up on. While the Jews of the shtetl had been living from one Sabbath to the next, one feast day to the next, praying only to be left alone, the great, wide world had been accumulating one triumph upon another.

Visionaries of science had uncovered the laws governing the movements of all things in heaven and on earth. Prodigies of music had brought echoes of the harmonies of the spheres to human ears. Philosophers had voyaged to the outer limits of human knowledge, to peer beyond in vivid wonder and longing.

How could there be time enough to touch it all, absorb it all, and then—yes—contribute something of one's own? A piece of melody, an equation, a theory, a canvas—something of one's own that will make a difference. It doesn't have to be big, though all the better if it is. But *something* to show that one is there, *there,* inhabiting the text itself, no longer stranded in the despair of those despicably narrow margins.

And, speaking of texts, what literature the great vast world had been churning out while our forebears hadn't been looking—pages filled with the poetry of the anguished spirit, words stretching to enclose the impossible predicament of being human.

But surely not the last word. Surely there is something more to be said—now, and by me. Because I will no longer be confined in the narrow, grimy margins, where my father and mother were born and will die, having never even learned the language of the text.

They, but not I!

No wonder so many we passed on the street had the feverish look of consumptives. Desire for the world at large was consuming us alive.

And it wasn't only the great ideas suddenly placed within our reach—no farther away than the many bookshops of Warsaw or Bresler's Library on Nowolipke Street or the municipal library on Koszykowa Street—that made our souls threaten to shatter into pieces with the force of raw desire.

Breaking away from the old ways, we were breaking away also from the hateful rigid segregation between the sexes, from being married off, most probably before we were eighteen, to a partner our parents had designated, taking every consideration into account except our struggling inclinations, the inexpressible stirrings of our barely awakened souls.

Enlightenment brought with it all the heady varieties of romance, from delicious dalliances to *la grande passion tragique.* Here, too, there was a tremendous amount of catching up to do, since the rest of Western culture had discovered the existence of romantic love at least several centuries before.

"What can you do?" a young and spicy actress named Rosalie was to ask Sasha late one night, in a rare moment of introspection.

Rosalie, with her mass of corkscrew-curled red hair and her perpetually changing reel of animated expressions, was altogether barely five feet tall. Yet those five feet were carried with such a manner that they could give unchaste thoughts to a dead man. Rosalie longed to play tragic roles, but the very distinctive timbre of her voice—a theater critic in one of the Yiddish dailies once tried to describe Rosalie's voice in an expression that translates roughly as: "a ram's horn with an attitude"—made her suitable only for comedy.

"What can you do?" Rosalie shrugged her beautiful bared shoulders. "This is our youth. Even if the times themselves are not so hot, this is our time to live it up."

What life there was in the streets and cafés, the theaters and cabarets, a flushed and tireless life dancing in the arms of grim-faced reality.

"Hey, Hershel, do you have a story about poverty?" one of the Bilbulniks called out to Hershel Blau late one night in the Café Pripetshok.

We were all there that night at the Pripetshok, crowded in around some tables pushed together, Hershel and the members of his struggling theatrical troupe, the Bilbul Art Theater, as well as a few others who were more or less of an artistic bent. Jascha Saunders, the composer who despised melodies, happened to be there that night, though this was, for him, unusual. He didn't often squander his time, especially not in the company of these erstwhile Yiddish actors, with their misplaced dreams of spinning a high and noble culture out of the jargon.

Though Jascha was, like all of us, an ardent atheist, he had somehow retained intact the more severe aspects of the spirit of religion, so much so that Hershel sometimes jokingly referred to Jascha as "our local Isaiah," a secular incarnation of the magnificently castigating prophet of old.

But something had put Jascha into a mood of unusual forbearance and expansion tonight, and here he was, his stern dark gaze behind his wire-rimmed glasses a little softened, speaking the jargon, and even indulging in some frivolous gossip.

In fact, it had been he who had reported that he had seen a "Grabski hearse" outside the home of that patron of Yiddish theater, Feliks Zakauer, which was very bad news, not only for Zakauer, but for the whole *mishpocheh.* Their tab at the Pripetshok was often picked up by Zakauer, who in this way justified his *gruba* capitalist presence within the circle of artists and idealists.

"Are you sure it was Feliks's home the hearse was visiting?"

"Yes. There is no doubt. I myself saw Feliks standing on the curb, looking as if he were saying *kaddish* for a beloved."

"Eh, not to worry. Somehow or other our friend will land again on his feet."

Grabski was the Polish Minister of Finance, and he had imposed such high taxes on the Jews, with the intent of forcing them to leave, that many found themselves unable to pay. After a while, one or more of the wagons that the Jews had dubbed "Grabski hearses" would come from the tax collector's office and remove all the householder's belongings.

It was the sad tale of Zakauer that prompted one of the Bilbulniks to ask their director whether he knew any good *mysahs* about poverty.

"Of course, I have a story about poverty," Hershel answered, his round, somewhat soft face already showing amusement at what was to come. "How could such a familiar of mine not be represented by a story or two?"

"Is this by any chance one of your father's stories, Hershel?" someone asked.

"So who else's?"

Hershel's father was a *maggid,* an itinerant Chasidic preacher, who interlaced his homilies with an inexhaustible stock of parables and allegories, some of which, at least if Hershel could be believed, which was debatable, had an almost satirical edge to them.

"Once upon a time, a poor man noticed that there was a naked stranger in his house and tried to throw him out.

" 'Don't you see I'm naked? How can you drive me into the streets like this?' the naked stranger demanded.

" 'You're right,' said the poor man. 'That would be a sin. But tell me who you are.'

" 'You don't recognize me? I'm Poverty.'

" 'Oy vay,' said the poor man. 'I have to get this one out of my house.'

"So he went to a tailor, gave a description of Poverty, and ordered a suit. The tailor wrote down the measurements and went to work.

"To pay for the suit, the poor man had to sell everything he owned. But he gritted his teeth and did it, because anything is better than having naked Poverty as a permanent guest.

"Finally, the tailor delivered the suit and Poverty put it on. . . ."

"And it didn't fit!" This was Mayer Saunders, Jascha's younger brother, who was also there that night at the Pripetshok. Actually, by this time he had already taken to calling himself not Mayer but Maurice (his inspiration, of course, Maurice Chavalier, the debonair Frenchman). All of us, however, still slipped up, now and then. Only Jascha (who himself had once been Yossela) never forgot to call the younger brother by the preferred name.

Maurice was still at *gymnasium,* and happened to be a great darling of the actors and actresses—especially the actresses—who hung out at the Pripetshok. He was, at sixteen years old, a kid so bursting with brains and good looks and charm, he still didn't know what to do with it all.

"Yes, Mr. Wiseguy," Hershel said, grinning. "And why not?"

"Obviously, because, while the poor man had been paying for the suit, Poverty had been getting fatter and fatter!"

"Oy, is this one smart. Come here, *tsatskeleh,*" said Rosalie, patting her lap. "I have to reward you."

"Rosalie, Rosalie, don't encourage him like that! He already thinks far too well of himself. And with rewards like that, no wonder the kid would rather hang around with the likes of us instead of staying home with his books."

Maurice was supposed to take the exams for university at the end of the next school year, and he carried the hopes of a great many, including his entire *gymnasium,* on his young shoulders.

Very few, if any, Jews would be accepted. Each year, the quota, the *numerus clausus,* was tightened. In addition to the written exams, there was an oral examination, and here the examiners had a great deal more liberty in granting their marks. Still, if any Jewish kid had a chance, it would be Maurice Saunders, who breezed through all his studies, having an equal facility for the mathematical sciences and the humanities, with a photographic memory to boot.

The strange thing was that Maurice's own determination to beat the system and enter the university seemed to have been wavering over these last few months. He ought to have been cramming like a demon, and instead here he was, night after night, shmoozing it up in the Pripetshok.

The truth was, Maurice knew all too well that he could study from now until the final redemption but, if he had the luck to get one of the notorious anti-Semites on his examining board, it would all come to nothing.

And suppose he did get in? Then the fun would really begin! He'd have to sit against the back wall, on one of the "ghetto benches." He'd probably also have to see his head used now and again for a soccer ball by one of the more sporting student clubs.

So, undecided, he didn't overstudy. (Even so, a teacher could weep with joy at his essays.) The bulk of his time was spent hanging around the Café Pripetshok or one of the other cafés where the girls were lively and beautiful and the talk was almost as juicy.

Jewish Warsaw, which was roughly a third of Warsaw proper, was a city of rabbis and swindlers, capitalists and poets; but, most of all, it was a city of talkers. There were so many ideas in the air you could get an education simply by breathing deeply.

Eavesdropping on a conversation taking place on the next park bench, in the row behind you in the theater, at the next table in a restaurant, you had a good chance of overhearing something astonishing.

One ravishing spring morning—the sky deep blue, the scent of the fields and orchards lying around Warsaw blending with the odors of newly baked bread, bagels, roasted coffee, and milk fresh from the udder, so that the fragrance that resulted had the effect of raising desire to an impossible pitch—Sorel was hurrying down Leszno Street, not far from the Yiddish Writers' Club. She was just passing by a couple strolling more leisurely—she tall and slender, blond, and elegantly dressed; he a redhead with a yeshiva boy's gait, looking as if he had only that morning snipped off his earlocks.

Suddenly, in the middle of this dazzling day, just as Sorel was walking past the two, she heard the young woman say, "We Jews are damned. Why?"

Sorel slowed her steps so that she could hear what the newly modernized yeshiva boy would answer.

"Because we love life too much," he said.

Later that evening, over coffee in Aunt Frieda's parlor, Sorel mentioned this snatch of overheard conversation.

"Oy," Aunt Frieda said, laughing, "I'd bet my last zloty I know who that yeshiva *bocher* was. Itzkele Singer. His brother is the writer Singer. And, by the way, that young man is a yeshiva *bocher* like I'm a yeshiva *bocher*. I've heard he's keeping at least three women, one of them old enough to be his mother. Someone told me he scribbles, too, though how he can find either the time or the energy, I ask you. So, maybe let's give him the benefit of the doubt and say he's acquiring experience for his future masterpieces."

In the few months Aunt Frieda had lived here, she had gotten to know everybody in the tight little world of Yiddishist writers, philosophers, actors, and social critics (this last category, of course, being understood as including the whole bunch).

"Oh, but I forget myself! I've made you turn the red of my upholstery! You give off such an air of sophistication, I sometimes forget you've still got one foot back in Shluftchev!"

"It's not at all true, Aunt Frieda," Sorel protested, turning redder. "I've got both my feet in Warsaw."

"It's all right, darling. It's nice to know how to blush. You will use it to good purpose someday, of that I have no doubt.

"But now enough of coffee and gossip. To work!"

Sorel, who had been sitting quite comfortably, her shoes off and her long legs folded beneath her on the deep-red silk of Aunt Frieda's divan, got up with a slight sigh, and went to stand at one end of the gleaming parquet floor of her aunt's long parlor, placing herself before the thick red velvet drapes that had so reminded her of a stage the first time she had seen them.

Her escaped sigh was no indication that she disliked the work at hand. The truth was, she loved it. It absorbed her as nothing else ever had. Still, each time, before she plunged herself deep down into the role she was preparing, she felt a sort of aversion, a fleeting fervent wish to hold back. She had discovered that there was, in the middle of the exhilaration, also a certain terror at this disciplined obliteration of self.

The aunt and niece had been working for several weeks now on the speech that Sorel would deliver at her audition before Hershel Blau, the young director whom Aunt Frieda had already dubbed, without a flicker of a doubt, the Jewish Stanislavski.

The speech was taken from the role of Ophelia, a character in Shakespeare's *Hamlet.* That's the *real* Shakespeare, not an adaptation by Jacob Gordin.

After their transfiguring night out at the Nowosci, Aunt Frieda and Sorel had gone over to Bresler's in order to read Shakespeare's *King Lear* for themselves. It was quite a different play, they had discovered. Shakespeare didn't bring down his final curtain on a happy bride and groom and a chastened father's sight restored. His play ended with a stage so littered with corpses that just reading it froze the blood in the veins. So much tragedy!

Still, with all the drama, they hadn't found a female part there that had appealed to them. Cordelia, who was Shakespeare's version of Toibela, hardly opens her mouth to speak, and when she does, it's in a voice "soft, gentle, and low, an excellent thing in women."

Well, maybe. But not, Aunt Frieda thought, such an excellent thing in an audition. Cordelia is such a lady, she even dies offstage.

No, the good roles, Sorel and Aunt Frieda had both agreed, belonged to the King and also to his Fool, Shakespeare's Shammoi. Sorel was all for attempting the King's rantings and ravings in the storm—what theater!—but Aunt Frieda stood firmly opposed. Sorel needed a part that would play up the incalculable gifts of her youth and good looks. Where would be the sense in playing a *farblondjeta* old man?

A bespectacled young man working behind the desk—he happened to be Bresler's own son, very knowledgeable—had suggested that, if Sorel wanted a Shakespearean role in which she could rant and rave and still look pretty, she should take a look at Ophelia. So that was how it came to be that Sorel now stood before Aunt Frieda's drapes, cast her eyes off toward the wall with the samovar as if she were following the retreating form of the prince, and cried out in a tone of heart-piercing despair:

Oy sara geyst eyn eydeler iz daw tzeshtert!

O, what a noble mind is here o'erthrown!

Such a voice! A voice that had been created for the theater! And now it had been made even more theatrical by its mastery of the Daytshmerish that was Aunt Frieda's own prized possession, a Yiddish so highly Germanized that really it was hardly even Yiddish anymore. How could Hershel Blau fail to be impressed?

Sorel's pronunciation was really all that Frieda could personally take credit for. So far as the rest went, the child was a natural, born to act as some are born to make money, others trouble, still others both. Frieda had known from the first moment she had laid eyes upon her niece that the girl had been destined to take center stage.

"How do you do it?" Aunt Frieda asked her.

"I'm not even sure. It's make-believe, but then it's not make-believe. The feelings are real even if the story isn't."

"Yes," Aunt Frieda agreed. "I suppose that's the way it's done. After all, when I watch, my feelings are real, too."

Sorel progressed through the scenes that they had strung together into one long dramatic monologue (because, after all, an audition should make a big impression).

Ophelia, poor child, was going mad. Her father had been murdered, a senseless death, a blunder, but still a tragedy for the orphans. Hamlet, who had before professed his love, was now cold and distant, completely unavailable to the poor child in her grief. Of course, he had his own problems. But despair left Ophelia no place else to go but toward craziness.

Her voice became more hesitant, wavering. A sad smile flitted on and off around her lips, like a candle about to go out. Her eyes became filled with a look that made the goosebumps rise up along Aunt Frieda's arms and legs.

There's rosemary, that's for remembrance; pray you, love, remember. And there is pansies, that's for thoughts.

Ophelia reached out her arm as if she were distributing flowers, her lips smiling, her eyes wild and lost. Nowhere else to go.

There's rue for you, and here's some for me.

By the time Ophelia delivered her final, distracted line and wandered off, still cradling her flowers, toward the dark cold river, God forbid, Aunt Frieda's cheeks were bathed in tears.

Wait, wait.

CHAPTER 13

A MOUTHFUL OF
DISTASTE

*J*ascha Saunders was in a foul mood on this fine morning. It would have been far better to sleep it off, the whole miserable stink of consciousness into which he had awoken, after some four hours of shallow, unrestorative sleep. Even in his sleep he had been aware of his disgust.

He had finally gotten back to his room here on Stawki Street, not far from the railroad tracks, past four in the morning. Idiot! And now he had the devil of a head to pay for it.

He was senseless with stupidity this morning, unable to find his way back into the work of the day before, his faculties dry and dull, with the taste of cinders in his mouth. His digestive system, delicate under the best of circumstances, was in shambles, and he had an evil taste in his mouth.

Regrettably, however, he was constitutionally incapable of sleeping past nine o'clock in the morning, no matter what the abuses of the night before. This had been true of him since he was a boy, a self-discipline that was no longer subject to his will.

And so he was up—and even out in the oppressively glaring April day. A beautiful day, goddamn it.

Jascha had stayed up into the small hours, wasting time in drunken drivel with that pack of deluded ideologues at the Café Pripetshok, engaging in the kind of discussion for which he harbored nothing but unambivalent abhorrence. He had ventured out in a fit of self-deluded camaraderie last night, for which his abstemious system was less than ill-prepared. He had drunk, he had gossiped, and, before he knew it, he had sunk into speechifying idiocy along with the rest of them, had allowed himself to be drawn into one of those rambling, irrational, irresolvable debates—hard even to say what it had been about.

Ah, but of course: the eternal question of "Jewishness." What else.

Yes, he really had made some fine speeches, especially when that idiot Zev Ben-Something-or-Other, a rabid Zionist, had arrived on the scene, to add his own vociferous lunacy to the Pripetshok clamor.

But if the "eternal-question-of-Jewishness" bunch were idiots, how much more so was Jascha? All his annoyance had by this morning been converted into a passionate pitch of self-disgust.

It was the unpleasant hangover from this discussion, more than from the vodka that he had stupidly drunk on an almost empty stomach—what *had* he been thinking?—that now lingered in his brain and poisoned his sense of all existence, as he made his way to Bresler's on the crowded sunny streets, filled with pretty women in summery dresses carrying packages tied with colored strings.

The librarian had promised to try and get him a copy of the *Tractatus Logico-philosophicus* of Ludwig Wittgenstein, a philosopher with whom Jascha had felt an immediate affinity; and also the *Principia Mathematica* of Bertrand Russell and Alfred North Whitehead. The mathematical philosophy of the Cambridge philosophers, who cultivated an admirable clarity and intolerance for metaphysical jargon, was underrepresented on Bresler's shelves, which instead heaved with all the dialectical long-winded outpourings of the various German schools: Kant and Hegel and Fichte and Schelling and Nietzsche and Schopenhauer and Marx—as well as all their lesser, though no less turgid, epigones.

Since he wouldn't get any useful work done today, at the least he would drop by Bresler's and see if his books were in.

Jascha had an overwhelming horror of wasting time. Well, today would be wasted. It would be a day of abject idleness paid out in recompense for last night's folly—and it was a damned shame, too, since his work had gone uncommonly well yesterday, and usually the morning hours yielded his most productive time.

But this morning, he had stared, at a loss, at the pages written yesterday. His state of mind was such that he had trouble even *hearing* the music.

Yesterday, the logic of his composition had emerged in a vision of shining transparency. Today, he hadn't a clue. Fool! *Shlimazel!*

Even the student exercises Professor Konstancze had handed over to him yesterday—the marking Jascha did for Professor Konstancze was essentially his only source of income—even these elementary student pieces were quite beyond him this morning.

His garret room had seemed suddenly intolerable. Its one small window faced a back alley, and the squalid purposes to which the inhabitants of Stawki Street put this place found their way into the stench that drifted upward from it. At least when it was winter, everything froze—although then, as his sister, Henya, had once remarked, you could almost see the tubercular germs thickly hovering in every corner.

Under better circumstances, when his faculties were in working order, his mind immersed in the glorious complexities of his work, the room, the whole of Stawki Street, didn't bother him much. But now his non-immersed mind couldn't help pronouncing summarily on its surroundings:

Sordid.

"How *can* you bear it?" his sister, Henya, had involuntarily exclaimed the first time that she had defied her father's orders and come in secret to visit her eldest brother. Jascha had moved out of his father's house after the last of their arguments, during which his father had accused him of being an enemy of his people, and Jascha had countercharged that his father, who was the head cantor at the Great Synagogue and had his degree in musicology from a German university, was as pompous as he was parochial.

"And how can *you* bear it?" Jascha had shot back at Henya, immediately to regret it, because, of course, the remark had instantaneously found its target. Wounding Henya was the easiest thing in all the world.

She had looked at Jascha, her brown eyes, the only features of any loveliness in her otherwise quite homely face, softly begging their mute appeal.

The philosopher René Descartes wrote in his *Meditations on First Philosophy* that man is profoundly finite in his understanding and infinite in his will. In Henya, this order seemed reversed. It was her will, not her understanding, that was profoundly, cripplingly, finite.

Still, she defied her father each time she came in secret to visit Jascha. Of course, *such* defiance, tendered in the service of *another,* was perfectly in keeping with her nature. It was in matters having to do with herself that she was entirely and utterly without will. And because of this fatal absence of will, all of her talent, all the music she was God-ordained to deliver to the world, was locked up soundless within her. Music unexpressed goes sour and sick, poisons the system in countless insidious ways. Under the tyranny of their father, the only inclinations Henya was free to develop with abandon were her scores of nervous ailments, the twitchings and grimaces that came and went, and which, at their worst, made almost a freak of this infinitely kind and infinitely intelligent sister.

Only when she played the piano was Henya free from her afflictions. Within the music, she existed whole and harmonious. Her face—with its great high forehead and sunken cheeks and long, thin nose—rested in repose; her fingers flew with perfect control over the keyboard. She stopped playing, and her organism was once again the scene of grotesque, almost mocking, mannerisms.

This is why, finally, she had been allowed the hours and hours she spent each day and night at the piano, because of the respite the music-making gave, not only to her, but to the rest of the family, their father especially. He, of all of them, seemed the least able to bear the sight of Henya's twitchings.

Was there, then, some method in her malady? No, Jascha could not imagine that this was so, that she was capable of manipulating any-thing, even the processes of her unconscious, for the purpose of at-taining something that she wanted.

And she had asked him how *he* could bear it! He would live in physical surroundings a thousand times more degrading than his garret room on Stawki Street, if such was the condition demanded for free-dom!

Yes, he had told her that, even though he was well aware that by doing so he was simply changing the terminology of the question she had mutely begged him not to put:

How, Henya, can *you* bear it?

But today he found that he could not—not quite—bear it. He walked more swiftly than he felt like walking down Smocza Street to-ward Nowolipke Street, passing the strolling throngs who were quite shamelessly luxuriating in the sensuality of the day. The air was unendurably redolent—a blend of lilacs, the scent from the forests of Praga, and something else, unidentifiable. It was the kind of day, thought Jascha, that had driven Thomas Mann's Tonio Kröger into his own state of desperate exasperation.

"*Gott verdamme den Frühling. Er ist und bleibt die grässlichste Jahreszeit.* Goddamn the spring. It is and remains the most atrocious time of year."

Jascha Saunders was a very tall young man, well over six feet, who carried himself with the slightly hunched shoulders a man develops when he towers all too self-consciously over others. Nonetheless, he made a striking, even imposing, figure, with his great mane of very thick, very wavy black hair. His face was habitually pale, almost rigid with seriousness, with a strong, tense jaw, hollowed cheeks, and large, heavily hooded, dark eyes. His eyesight was poor and he wore wire-rimmed glasses. His mouth was rather thin, though the upper lip was sensuously curved. It was the only extravagance in his otherwise rigor-ously ascetic face.

"*Man arbeitet schlect im Frühling, gewiss, und warum? Weil man empfindet. Und weil der ein Stumper ist, der glaubt, der Schaffende durfe empfinden.* Yes, it's certain, one's work goes badly in the spring. And why? Because one feels. Only a bungler believes that someone who creates must feel."

Fool! *Shlimazel!*

It had been an attack of happiness, of groundless, giddy, self-delusional happiness, that had prompted last night's excesses. And why the happiness? Because he had had a few superficially pleasant words with her yesterday, with Katya Konstancze—a few meaningless if cordial words, in the early afternoon, in the anteroom of her father's house. And upon this inconsequentiality there had followed a surfeit of happiness, and from that surfeit other follies, which now arranged themselves before his disgusted mind like a proof in formal logic.

She had been leaving just as he was entering, and they had stood in the narrow space of the anteroom exchanging slightly stiff greetings.

"Ah," she had then said. Her delicate eyelids—he had never before seen a skin that was so translucently white as Katya's, you could see through it to the pale tracery of delicate blue veins—her eyelids had fluttered in the direction of the sheaf of staff paper he held in his hand, and she smiled that indefinably mysterious smile of hers, one of the few sights he had ever seen on this earth capable of making him wish that his talent lay in pictorial representation rather than music. "Is that your latest composition?"

She herself was carrying her flute case. No doubt she was off to the Conservatory.

"Yes," he had answered, shrugging a little, in a gesture meant to suggest a casual indifference, and even allowing the extravagant curve of his mouth to follow its impulse toward a smile. "Another composition for your father to despise."

"Despise?" she had said, a low voice but exceptionally clear, so like the timbre of her instrument that it was truly astonishing. Had he had the courage, he would have loved to question her on the direction of the causality: whether she had chosen the flute for her flutelike voice, or whether her voice had, rather, come to resemble the instrument. "But I don't think so. At least, that's not what Father tells me. He tells me you are full of promise."

"Promise? Well, perhaps if I myself promise to write only the kind of pretty things that your father thinks are alone worthy to be called music."

Oh, God! Listen to the pomposity of him! How could she not turn on her heel and flee?

And yet she hadn't, and—though it had come out all wrong, so vilely pompous and embittered—still, the frustration he voiced was all too real.

Nothing would have been easier for Jascha than to produce the sort of melodically lush music that would have aroused Professor Konstancze's admiration. Jascha could almost have produced such music in his sleep. In fact, he did sometimes awake in the morning with a new melody, facile and pretty, playing in his head.

He had always had this easy skill for melody. In the old days, when he had sung in his father's choir, the two of them would sometimes collaborate on new *niggunim,* prayer melodies, and on the High Holidays, when he and his younger brother had sung together with their father in the Great Synagogue, it had been almost impossible to obtain tickets. The Great Synagogue would be packed with non-Jewish music-lovers, as well as the cream of Jewish "enlightened" society. And their father, Lazar Saunders, a man who greatly prided himself on his dispassionate objectivity, could not help feeling a certain sense of gratification. On one occasion, he had even gone so far as to express this to his elder son.

Jascha had long since outgrown his effortless talent for melody. Music that came so naturally had very little to do with his more matured conception of his art: rigorously formal and abstract, deriving from the most complex and cerebral impulses, and inducing a pleasure equally complex and of the mind. *That* for Jascha was music—purged of the pretty and facile, the melodic impulse that brought forth a pleasure merely sensual, and just as superficial and short-lived as all such ripples of sensation.

Jascha was finally producing a kind of music that didn't disgust him, yet Katya's father continued to extol Jascha's juvenilia. The little sonata for piano, for example, a simple theme and variation that Jascha had submitted when he was seeking admission into the Conservatory: Professor Konstancze could not stop praising the stupid little piece, urging Jascha to go back to such conceptions. Back! That was not the direction one was usually urged to travel in one's artistic development!

Still, Jascha hadn't meant to let the bile escape into the vicinity of Katya. What an ingrate she must think him—and justifiably.

Yet Katya had only smiled her enigmatic smile—a transformation of lips and eyes that was maddeningly and exquisitely ambiguous.

Jascha had never before taken cognizance of the supreme mystery of the human face. It speaks. Dear God, how it speaks. A language so subtle and suggestive—perhaps even more subtle and suggestive than music itself.

"Is Father really so dictatorial as all that?" she had asked gently, so gently that he had been utterly and hopelessly confounded. He had only stared at her with his fatuousness loudly proclaiming its vast dominions.

Under the powerful sway of this stupidity, his brain offered no rejoinder. What exactly could he say? No, he's not so dictatorial as *all that*. What an admission of gratitude that would be.

Of course, beneath it all—beneath Jascha's profound disagreement and frustration with Professor Konstancze's implacable hostility to Jascha's latest efforts—Jascha *was* grateful: unspeakably grateful.

Professor Konstancze had taken him on as a private, and nonpaying, student, after the Conservatory—for reasons too obvious to bear mentioning—had rejected his petition for admission.

The two most powerful personages at the Conservatory happened to be notoriously anti-Semitic. Professor Konstancze's own position would be compromised should any of them find out about the arrangement between him and Jascha Saunders.

No, Jascha was not such a barbarian as to be without the deepest sense of gratitude toward Katya's father. He was a man of great moral principle and personal courage, a man whose sense of fairness wasn't cut off at the boundaries of self-interest.

But when it came to music, Professor Konstancze was profoundly, hopelessly nineteenth-century. He was at a loss to appreciate the possi-

bilities of atonality that drew Jascha. Where Jascha felt himself to be
discovering virgin forms of music—pure and lean and supple—the
older man heard only noise.

It was ironic, really. At every juncture, Jascha had to fight the old
men. At every damned juncture.

So, when Katya had asked him, in her low and flutelike voice,
whether her father was really as dictatorial as all that, he had stood
there, tongue-tied, in the anteroom.

"Well, I must be off," she had finally said, her gentle smile wavering into uncertainty.

"Yes," he had answered. Having committed himself to stupidity, he
had been, at the least, consistent.

He had not been able to forbear watching her as she turned to
leave. Her long silky hair, white-blond, like moonbeams—she was
made more from the delicate stuff of the moon than from the sun—had
swayed with her motion. When she turned back again, his eyes had
been fastened helplessly upon her.

"You must take heart," she had said, the perfect essence of her
smile—like Smileness itself—finding its realization in the fineness of
her features. "Father has the highest respect for your talent. I know this
for a fact."

She had paused, looking into his face as if she was perhaps searching for something there. Had she found it?

"And anyway, even if he hadn't," she had continued, "it would perhaps prove no more than that he isn't yet capable of appreciating the
authentic originality of your music. Anything authentically original
must meet with initial resistance. Isn't that so?"

Again, nothing had come to his now blissfully befuddled mind to
offer in response—only wordless wonder at the divine kindness of this
divine creature.

And then she was gone, she and her moonlike substance and her essence of Smileness; and for the rest of the afternoon and evening, Jascha
had been unable to compose his mind and get even so much as a good
quarter-hour's work out of it.

He had tried doing some mathematics. He often found this to be a very effective means for calming his faculties when they became over-excited. He kept some textbooks—complex variables, differential geometry—to be used precisely as the situation demanded. There's nothing like a good stiff dose of complex variables when one's cognitive arteries have become clogged.

But even these proven remedies had failed him on this occasion. His mood of ecstatic idiocy had lingered, in fact deepened to a more generalized longing for human companionship.

Yes, that was it. He had had some sort of pressing, inarticulate swell of yearning for contact with his fellow creatures.

He really couldn't remember the last time he could have said this of himself, despite the almost unrelievedly solitary existence he led. Aside from the secret visits of his brother and sister, no one ever came to the garret room on Stawki Street. Ah yes, once his mother, a pitifully weak woman, who had long ago given up laying claims to any will or identity distinct from her husband's, had paid him a hasty, noticeably nervous call.

The itch of gregariousness had persisted, so that, when his little brother, Maurice, had stopped by to say hello on his way to one of the cafés he loved to frequent, Jascha had impulsively offered to accompany him.

And that was how he had come to be that night at the Pripetshok in the first place, deposited there by the grinding mechanisms of de-meaning causality.

At first, actually, it had been rather pleasant there in the café. Con-vivial and all that. The Café Ziemanska, over on Gesia Street, was the hangout of the more mainstream literati, who were loosely grouped around the weekly *Wiadomosa Literackie*, or *Literary News*, edited by Grydrewski.

But Hershel Blau and his sort mostly stayed away from the Ziemanska in favor of the Pripetshok. They were all there already, in the back room of the Pripetshok. The front room, where the bar stood, was thick with droshky drivers, who went about the business of drink-ing quietly and efficiently, throwing their heads back.

But the back room, huge and bare and harshly lit, was another matter entirely. Here drinking and eating—breathing, even—definitely took a back seat to talking.

What talkers these were! Others might distinguish between words and actions, between thought and passion, but such distinctions didn't exist here at the Pripetshok. All the passion in the world went into thinking, and words themselves were actions: not something you heard, but something you *felt,* like a blow on the head, or, at the least, a pinch. You proved your mettle, you proved your *manhood,* by the way you could wield an argument, crack a witticism, punch a line.

Under normal circumstances, Jascha had a musician's disdain for words. They were clumsy things, words. And yet it was congenial, somehow, to be here, in the midst of this bantering, word-intoxicated bunch. Blau was in fine form.

Jascha had rather mixed feelings about Blau. Because Blau was by no means a fool—because he was, on a personal level, a very fine fellow, full of integrity—it wasn't as easy to dismiss him for all the absurd things he had the misfortune to believe. And what were these absurdities? Blau was a disciple, a veritable Chasid, of secular Yiddishism— yet one more ism churned out by these indefatigable word-meisters of Jewish Warsaw.

This particular ism, insofar as Jascha had bothered to understand it, devoted itself to the disentanglement of the condition of Jewishness from its unfortunate and embarrassing theological underpinnings, thereby to weave it into a high and noble culture: radically and uncompromisingly secular, but still, somehow or other, Jewish.

Blau's father, Jascha had once heard, was a Chasidic storyteller, a *maggid,* who wandered from village to village preaching, primarily to women and children.

The son had left all that behind; or, rather, he had and he hadn't. Rationality had drawn the conclusion, but sentiment had balked at following. He had left his father's simple-minded narrowness in favor of his own convoluted, highly knowledgeable . . . narrowness.

Hershel Blau and all the other Yiddishists, who hung out at the Writers' Club on Leszno Street and here at the Pripetshok, were all stuck in some untenable middle-ground, stalled halfway between the past and the future, trying to think of some means or other of being good Jewish sons and daughters, even though they no longer believed anything their fathers and mothers had taught them. The Bundists and the Zionists were the same at heart, none of them able to follow the path to the simple, unavoidable conclusion.

Last night, they had accused him of advocating yet another ism: assimilationism. What arrant rot! Assimilation was no ideology but simply the fulfillment of the natural processes of history, once the artificial obstacles have been cleared away.

Yes: there was no reason to keep oneself separate and cut off any longer. The world at large, or at least enough of it, had freed itself from the steel-trap dogmas and pieties of the past, so that there was room at last to enter: without conversion, without hysteria and martyrdom and guilt; with nothing but one's faith in man's perfectibility and reason. The Bundists and Zionists spouted politics—the "brotherhood of workers," the "Jewish homeland"—the Yiddishists babbled on about a Jewish culture forged of a bastardized language and a history that consisted primarily of persecutions: why did Jews think there was something noble in this? But at heart they were all the same. Bundists, Zionists, Yiddishists: they were all men and women stalled halfway on their path to clear thinking, overcome by the centuries-weighted pull from the past.

Yes, yes, Jascha was of Jewish origins. But he could not for the life of him see why this fact ought to have any consequences. One's origins were the place where one had begun, not where one ended up. Surely, no one could demand, on the basis of a man's origins, that he, for example, must compose a different sort of music? If you thought about it clearly and rationally, as Jascha had, the whole idea of "Jewish art" made about as much sense as the idea of "Jewish science." And so far as Jascha knew, it was only the frothing madmen goose-stepping their way toward German lawlessness who ever spoke in terms of "Jewish science."

It was a shame, because Hershel Blau was otherwise an extremely intelligent person, with good intuitions, a largeness of soul. It was only when he spoke his vision of the future that he became like a geometrician who draws his circles in the water.

But none of the talk at the Pripetshok had really bothered him until that rabid Zionist Zev Ben-Something-or-Other had shown up.

He was the brother of that shameless little flirt of an actress. Rosalie Chernikov. The one who kept petting Jascha's brother as if he were her lapdog. What was wrong with the woman, to flirt with a schoolboy? Jascha himself was more than once on the point of saying something, even though he noticed how astoundingly comfortable Maurice was with the woman's attention.

Rosalie and her brother were both red-headed live-wires, though the sister was pretty and the brother was not. A tough little guy in a leather jacket, as if he were a Communist, a Cheske, with a nose that had been bashed more than once and now sat strangely twisted above his thin, tense, and never-for-a-moment-quiet lips.

Rosalie and her brother had come from a Chasidic family, escaping from a large brood of maybe ten or eleven children, buried away in poverty somewhere or other. The brother was the most insufferable sort of an ideologue, like a dog with a bone, gnawing away. He was off in the morning for Vilna, to organize an agricultural, kibbutz-style collective there. Somehow, Jascha couldn't really picture this tough guy planting and weeding, tending tender little shoots of green. But if his ideology demanded that he be a farmer, he'd be a farmer—if not yet in Palestine, then in Vilna.

So far as Jascha was concerned, Zionism was the worst of the various ideological diseases that had lately been infecting Warsaw's Jews on a very large scale.

Nonetheless, he ought never to have permitted his temper to become engaged. Yet somehow it had. Somehow he had suddenly felt this man's lunacies on a deeply personal level. It seemed to be his—Jascha's—very own domain, and the freedom that it enclosed, that this Zev Ben-Something-or-Other was challenging, in the name of some invidiously vague notion of collective destiny.

That's what all of them—Yiddishists, Zionists, Bundists—had in common, despite the vitriolic differences. They were united in believing that some collective destiny hovered inescapably over each and every one of them, merely by virtue of their having been born of Jewish origins.

And the stupendous idiocy of this idea—especially when voiced in the blunt arrogance of that Zev Ben-Zion—right, that was the Hebraicized name he went by—had finally caused Jascha to erupt, so that, before he knew it, he himself was delivering a long and livid diatribe of his own.

"Homeland?" He had turned the word contemptuously back on the odious little firebrand.

"I suppose by this you mean some wilderness on the other side of the globe, on which I have never laid eyes, and which I don't even know how to picture, but which, from its description, even by those who profess themselves its eternal lovers, can promise me *nothing.*

"And yet, if I am to believe the arguments of people like you, it is that place, and not here in the Europe of my birth, and of my father's birth, and of my father's father's father's birth, that I am to think of as my authentic homeland. And why? Because, several millennia ago, my ancestors were deprived of that place. And this is now supposed to have something to do with me, with my own personal destiny. Yet those ancestors exist for me only in a very removed and, so to speak, theoretical manner, whereas not a day goes by when I am not conscious of the legacy left behind to me by those I recognize as my masters and mentors. Bach and Beethoven and Brahms, not Avraham, Yitzchak, and Yaakov. So I would ask you please not to impose upon me a destiny that I could never experience but as entirely forced and artificial and external—I would even say inimical—to my own given nature."

Anger invariably turned Jascha pedantic. Somehow he had let this little fanatic pull a hidden cord in his psyche. Why, he couldn't really understand. You simply rejected the nonsense of the world, coldly and dispassionately. You didn't go out and drink vodka with it and engage it in dialogue.

Because, of course, Jascha's long-winded statement of his rejection of the principles of Jewish nationalism had not been the end of it. One fine diatribe invites an infinite sequence of others. And so on it had gone, until the early hours of the morn; so that now Jascha awoke with his brain shot to pieces, incapable of a good day's work.

Idleness immediately called forth an assault of self-doubts, a replay of the litany of voices telling him he was dead wrong in his conceptions.

He was pitifully isolated from the community of musicians. His only contact was Professor Konstancze, and Professor Konstancze offered him nothing but benevolent discouragement.

"You are seduced by your theory to abandon your talent," Professor Konstancze had told him last week, in his habitually amiable tones, though slowly shaking his rather magnificent head.

This head, somewhat squarish and very grand, adorned by a mane of silken yellowish-white hair, seemed to give Professor Konstancze an incommensurable stature. His eyes behind his thick spectacles were extremely large, slightly protuberant, a warm shade of blue. The head was such that one tended to think, until one actually stood beside him, that Professor Konstancze was a taller man than he in fact was.

Perhaps the professor was right. Perhaps the music Jascha had been producing was, beneath its technical razzle-dazzle, basically sterile and vapid.

"Anything authentically original must meet with initial resistance. Isn't that so?"

That low and flutelike voice had spoken the only words from which Jascha had been able, in a very long time, to extract the living warmth of encouragement.

Well, of course, there was his sister, Henya, who consistently encouraged him. She sat in his garret room reading through his latest work, her poor homely face intent and serious, hardly twitching at all.

Suddenly Jascha was overcome with a pity for this kind and intelligent woman, his sister, greater than he had ever known for her.

He had never before thought of her in this light: as a woman. And, thinking of her so, he couldn't help pitying.

Would any man ever think of her as he himself thought of Katya Konstancze?

Would any man ever torment himself over the meaning of poor Henya's smiles?

If only Jascha knew better how to understand the subtle language of Katya's face. Why was she so kind to him? Was it the compassion she had perhaps inherited from her father? (Her mother, whom he had only glimpsed now and then, seemed a different, less extraordinary, sort.)

He saw that face again, the exquisite and maddening ambiguity of her smile.

And suddenly, right there on crowded Nowolipke Street, a few steps away from Bresler's Library, Jascha halted. A woman heavily laden with packages, a few steps behind, bumped into him, and he barely noticed.

He stood, stunned, people walking around him on the crowded sidewalk in the bright sunshine of the glorious day.

It was a melody.

It rose up in him, complete and perfect, overwhelming all his scruples, flooding his faculties with sheer loveliness. The most beautiful melody he had ever in his life been offered.

Jascha stood on the sidewalk, the austerity of his face washed over by wonder, as passersby, glancing curiously, made their way around him.

Jascha Saunders stood, as if turned to stone, his entire being ravished by melody.

CHAPTER 14

A VOICE LIKE
NO OTHER

$\mathcal{S}$orel set off all by herself in the late afternoon. She had decided to walk rather than take the trolley, even though it was a good long hike to the tailors' union hall. Walking might do her some good, silence some of the crackling static in her head. In any case, she had more than two hours to kill before her meeting with Hershel Blau of the Bilbul Art Theater.

Aunt Frieda had assumed that she would accompany Sorel to her audition. After all, she was her niece's coach, her mentor—her self-appointed manager, even, since it had been she who had arranged for Sorel to meet the director.

Leiba, too, all of a sudden and out of the blue, had asked if Sorel would perhaps like for her mother to come along for moral support.

This offer from her mother—such a mother!—touched Sorel so deeply her eyes welled up, and she threw her arms around Leiba in one of those bone-crushing squeezes to which she sometimes resorted on the rare occasion that words failed her. She squeezed so hard that Leiba cried out that she couldn't breathe.

Still, if Sorel was going to make a fool of herself—and what else but?—then let her at least do so before an audience of strangers, to whom her fiasco would matter as much as last year's snows.

Sorel placed enormous confidence in her gut feelings, and the gastrointestinal message of the moment wasn't so promising. In fact, it strongly suggested that she should turn herself around and go back home.

Aunt Frieda waxed ecstatic over Sorel's Ophelia, it's true, and Aunt Frieda was no doubt a maven of the theater. But Leiba, who was not so impressed with her sister's highfalutin Yiddish as she perhaps ought to have been, had suggested a more natural pronunciation for Sorel's audition, a suggestion that Aunt Frieda had vigorously pooh-poohed.

"Theater isn't supposed to be natural, Leiba! That's where you make your mistake. What person would pay out good money just to sit and listen to people like you could hear them yammering on Krochmalna Street?"

The day was overcast. It had rained on and off since yesterday, and now, though the rain had stopped, the sky hung down gray and low, and the pavements glimmered with wetness. On the streets there were rainbow-colored puddles from the gasoline that had leaked from cars and trucks. Droplets still dripped from the shimmering spring trees Sorel passed under, and the special smell of a wet Warsaw that blanketed the city gave it a certain sweet intimacy.

Having no theater of their own, the Bilbulniks used the hall of the tailors' union building over on Freta Street, all the way past the Krasinski Gardens.

The room was huge and bare, with a concrete floor and rows of backless wooden benches. As a theater, it was, to say the least, less than ideal. Plaster pillars rose up at inconvenient intervals to obscure the views, and the acoustics couldn't have been worse.

To overcome these obstacles, Blau was endlessly experimenting with various techniques. For example, he dispensed with a stage and instead dispersed his actors all over the cavernous space, with its tricky echoes. There were even actors sitting on the benches amidst the audience, so that a spectator would be startled when suddenly the spotlight swept down to illuminate his anonymity and a neighbor rose up into the action, not a real person at all, but an *actor!*

The Bilbulniks were very young and experimental, still very much feeling their way. Among themselves, they referred to their troupe as the *mishpocheh,* or family, and this was no accident. Most of them had come from pious families, from whom they had broken away, some more wrenchingly than others. They looked to each other, and especially to Hershel, their director, in order to fill the gaping place in their lives.

Hershel understood this very well, and though sometimes the neediness of his actors threatened to overwhelm him, he had a nature that reveled in taking care of the members of his *mishpocheh,* whose average age was twenty. Hershel, at twenty-eight, was the old man, the *zayda,* the grandfather.

All had agreed from the beginning that there would be no so-called stars, that the *mishpocheh* would be what is called an ensemble or a repertory troupe. Unlike most other art-theater groups, they had no interest in adapting the Western classics for the Yiddish stage. "To hell with universality," was one of Hershel's most ardent beliefs. Almost everybody had a hand in the writing of the material, though Hershel was always the first among equals, if for no other reason than that he was the most obsessive.

Their current production was called *Golem.* Aunt Frieda and Sorel had seen it three times, though they still couldn't have told you exactly what it all had meant.

It was, to say the least, a strange play, hard to follow, the actions disjointed and the speeches long and trailing off into uneasy, inconclusive silences. Perhaps there was something a little artificial, a little forced, a little too theatrical and straining toward Significance? Nonetheless, both Aunt Frieda and Sorel had found the play deeply, and even terrifyingly, effective.

There is a young man, called only K., who is studying medicine in Prague. He is a modern, an unsentimental man of science, and an advocate of metaphysical materialism, according to which man is nothing but a collection of physical particles in motion. Consciousness, purposiveness, aspiration, desire—all these are by-products of the motions of mindless atoms.

"Someday," K. proclaims, "science will have progressed to the point where the so-called privacy of mental life will be eradicated. We will probe a man's central nervous system and know precisely what it is he is perceiving, remembering, hoping, dreading. The few distinct words by which a man speaks his thoughts to himself, awash in the vague inexpressible sense of the moment: every nuance of his consciousness will be rendered transparent to scientific observation."

Many—far too many, for Aunt Frieda's tastes—of the rambling speeches trailing off into inconclusive silences were disquisitions on metaphysical materialism, in which such names as Epicurus and Lucretius and Hobbes were portentously dropped. But the drama picks up considerably as K. gradually becomes obsessed with the legend of the famous *golem* of Prague.

A *golem* is an artificial man, a ghoul, created out of dust through the use of holy names. According to legend, there had been a *golem* created, sometime in the sixteenth century, by the rabbi of the Altneushul of that time, Rabbi Yehuda Loew. The *golem* had served the rabbi and his community, even delivering them from the dire consequences of a blood libel. But eventually the *golem* had begun to run amok, and even to endanger innocent people's lives, and the rabbi had been forced to return him to his inanimate dust. There were many in Prague who still believed that, among the old holy books that had found their final resting place in the garret of the Altneushul, there lay the lifeless form of the *golem.*

K. first learns of the ancient legend from a friend, a fellow medical student named Max. Max, whom K. dismisses as a romantic, rejects K.'s metaphysical materialism in the name of the fundamentally irreducible nature of the human psyche.

"Look at these eyes," he says, gently lifting the face of his sister, a beautiful girl named Dora. "Look at the soul that stares out from them! Can you possibly maintain that what you see here is the random product of the dance of mindless particles?"

Neither to Aunt Frieda nor to Sorel was it exactly clear how all this philosophizing fit in with the legend of the *golem.* But for some reason or other, K. becomes more and more obsessed with this legend, until eventually he is scheming as to how he might gain access to the garret of the Altneushul.

In the final, terrifying scene, which happened to make the entire play, metaphysical materialism and all, worth the price of admission, K. discovers that everyone he has been dealing with, even the beautiful Dora, whom he has come to love, is a *golem.*

"What do you think it all meant, Aunt Frieda?" Sorel had asked the first time they had seen it.

"Meant? Who knows? Maybe that modern man has been reduced to something not quite human. That sounds pretty likely, doesn't it?"

"To me, the way the ghouls were marching at the end, they looked like the fascists, may they soon burn in hell."

"Yes, that, too," said Aunt Frieda, and her pretty brow had creased into a frown.

The letters from her sons and daughters-in-law in Hamburg were filled with more and more accounts of the unbelievable. What Sorela said was very true. You thought you lived among human beings, and then discover they are something else altogether. Ghouls. The entire family was making plans to move back to Warsaw by summer's end.

"That, too?" said Sorel with a laugh, seeing her aunt's frown, and trying to dispel the understandable gloom. "How can both be true?"

"True?" Aunt Frieda, still distracted, had asked her.

Sorel had suddenly stared at her, so strangely, with such a stricken expression on her face, that Aunt Frieda had immediately forgotten her own troubles.

"What is it, darling? Why do you look at me like that?"

"Oh, Aunt Frieda, you so reminded me of my sister for a moment."

"What? Of Chanala?"

"No. My other sister. My sister Fraydel." She spoke the name very softly.

As intimate as the two of them had become over these last months, it was the first time that Sorel had ever mentioned the name of Fraydel to her aunt Frieda, and both women quickly looked away.

The next step, having already determined that her niece was destined for the stage, was to convince the stage, in the person of Hershel Blau. Aunt Frieda liked it very much that the Bilbul Art Theater had not yet been exactly discovered. It was enough that she had discovered them. She may not have been able to tell you what they had been up to in *Golem*. But she knew they were brilliant. And so young, so young. Aunt Frieda didn't exactly equate youth with beauty. She recognized that there might be, at least in theory, a few exceptions. But the extreme youth of the Bilbul Art Theater was, in her eyes, its crowning glory, bestowing on it something better even than greatness itself—namely, the *promise* of greatness, "whether or not Warsaw yet knows it."

So far, Warsaw didn't know it in the least. None of the major Yiddish newspapers—or, for that matter, the minor ones—had bothered to review *Golem*, and the audiences at the tailors' union hall were consistently scant. Of course, as Aunt Frieda pointed out, you yourself had to be either very young or a voluptuary of discomfort to endure sitting on those wooden benches.

Nonetheless, they were a pack of geniuses, Hershel Blau was the Jewish Stanislavski, and Sorel must hitch her wagon *immediately* to their star.

Sorel walked quickly, even though she had so much time, because such was her habit. She usually adored this smell of a wet Warsaw, but she was oblivious to it now. She stared down at the shimmering pavements, trying to remember a line from Ophelia's speech.

"And I of all ladies . . ." Was it *unt ich* or *int uch?*

Every painstaking subtlety of expression and gesture was blotted out as if with black ink.

God forbid, Sorel might even begin to speak in her old Galitzianer accent!

Unt ich fun alla froyen . . . No, no. *Fin allie friyen?*

Her palms felt as wet and clammy as the day itself. No, she emphatically did *not* have a good feeling about this audition. Perhaps Mamma had been right to suggest a more natural delivery? Mamma, after all, was a sensible person.

So, what was the worst that could happen? She would make a fool of herself before some strangers. Maybe she would provide them with a good laugh, not such a bad thing in itself. She would far prefer that they enjoy themselves, even at her expense, than have them feel pity for her. That would be hard to take. But even in that case, nobody so far had ever yet died from such causes.

She could pretend that she wasn't even herself, that she had no particular connection with the person hacking the immortal poet to pieces.

Yes, from the outside she would look at it. From the vantage point of somewhere else completely.

But the one thing she *would not do* was yield to the impulse that was begging her—on its knees it was begging her—to turn herself around and forget the whole thing altogether. Ignominious impulse!

She walked up Lezsno Street to Tłomackie, passing the magnificent synagogue where the great people went to pray. Its domed roof was shaped to look like the crown placed on the Torah scrolls. On either side of its steps stood two menorahs, lit up at night. People said that it was like going to an opera to go to the Tłomackie Synagogue, which some called the Great Synagogue, some the German Synagogue.

Of course she got to the tailors' union building far too early, and retraced her steps back to the Krasinski Gardens. This was the park which belonged primarily to the Jews, especially the poor Jews. On nice days, the old men and women would come and sit on the benches, the men constantly arguing about politics. And on Shabbes, almost everyone came here for a promenade, except the more wealthy Jews, or at least those with aspirations, who went to the grander Saxony Gardens, where, in the old days, Jews hadn't been allowed. Even now, you couldn't dress like a Jew if you wanted to promenade in the Saxony Gardens, whose very grand entrance, right behind the eternal flame to the unknown soldier, stood on Piłsudski Square.

As Sorel neared the much less ostentatious entrance to the Krasinski Gardens, she caught a glimpse of the castle. The park was almost entirely deserted, forsaken even by the old men, who must have been arguing their politics in some dry café or other. The benches were too wet for Sorel to sit down.

She walked along one of the paths that led to a little pond, where the swans were gliding about, unbothered by wetness or anything else. How wonderful to be an animal, to be swanlike if one were a swan, fishlike if one were a fish, and not to carry the burden of ambitions.

Unt ich, unt ich . . .

Finally, though still too early, she made her way back to Freta Street, and into the courtyard that led to several institutions, including the tailors' union. She entered a long dark corridor and walked up a flight of stairs, leading to the large bleak room.

The murkiness was like twilight, the light struggling in from a few high and filthy windows. The Bilbulniks didn't waste their zlotys on electricity unless they had to. Sorel made out the figures of a few people at the other end of the shadowed room, some sitting, some standing, almost all of them holding lighted cigarettes, glowing in the dimness like fireflies on a summer's evening. There was talking going on, but it was hard to know whether they were working or shmoozing.

Anyway, she was too early. She clung to the doorway, overcome with the luminous perception of her age and inexperience.

"Hey!" someone suddenly shouted out to the tall blonde girl who looked as if she couldn't make up her mind whether to come in or run away. "Are you looking for someone? Or are you just very eager for tonight's show?"

Several people laughed.

The sense of her own idiocy dropped down around Sorel like a heavy curtain. What was she doing here? She was an actress like . . . like . . . like who knew what?

"Hershel Blau," Sorel said, her voice seeming not her own to her ears. It flew out from her head like a wind out of an empty house.

"You want Hershel Blau?"

"Yes."

"Are you sure about that? You look like a nice kid."

Again there was a little smattering of laughter. Sorel managed a not very convincing smile.

"All right, all right, shmendrik. Can't you see the girl has better taste than to find you amusing?" said another man, who looked slightly older. He got up and came over to where Sorel still clung to the possibility of escape. He was of average height, a little broad, with a face that was intelligent and gentle and thoroughly homely. It had a sort of punched-in look about it, his nose short and snubbed, his lips thick.

His hair, dark and curly, was beginning to recede around his forehead, and his ears stuck out prominently from the sides of his head.

"I'm Hershel Blau," he said to her with a nice smile.

There was something open and reassuring about his smile. It brought you in somehow. His homeliness, too, had the effect of making Sorel feel a little more comfortable, a little more certain of herself.

He extended his hand to Sorel for a handshake, a very modern gesture. Her own hand was icy in his. And still she remained dumb, her head abandoned, the wind sweeping through the bare rooms, in and out of the gaping windows.

"What can I do for you?" Hershel gently prompted her.

"I'm Sasha?" she said, though not very convincingly.

She felt thoroughly ridiculous, almost like a liar, introducing herself by this dreamed-up name.

"My aunt, Frieda Pomeranz, spoke to you about me?" she added in a very hurried, very young and uncertain voice.

"Ah yes," said the guy whom Hershel had called "shmendrik." "The enchanting Frieda Pomeranz! She picked up our entire tab at the Pripetshok the other night, may she have long and prosperous years!"

"That's Mendel," Hershel said to Sorel, rolling his eyes in the direction of the very small and wiry figure still lurking in the shadows. "Don't pay any attention to him. He's just trying to impress you—but, poor fool, he has no idea how to go about it."

"Touché!" someone or other called out from the far end of the cavernous room—a young man's voice, with a strange and piercing timbre.

"Come, let me introduce you to everybody. As far as Mendel is concerned, just do as the rest of the world does and ignore the fact of his existence!"

"I'll get you back for that one!" Mendel called out to Hershel. *"En garde!"* He leapt up onto one of the benches, assuming a fencing position.

"You see how it is with the poor man," Hershel said, laughing, tapping his index finger to his head.

Besides Mendel and Hershel, there were five other young men there, and four women—not the hundreds of coldly staring strangers that had figured in the worst of Sorel's nightmares, but still more than she had bargained for.

Sorel thought she recognized one of the men, Viktor, as the actor who had played the young medical student, K., even though he looked a good deal younger from up close. What was oddest, however, was how real he looked, how unextraordinary—just a tall, dark young man, with well-formed, softish features, prominent cheekbones, perhaps a slightly brooding cast to his face.

Mendel was grinning broadly at her. He had a small and lively monkey's face: enormous gaping eyes, a tiny cleft chin, a wide and mobile mouth. His brown hair, straight and slick, was parted down the middle of his head.

Sorel also thought she recognized one of the girls, slim and dark-haired, as Dora. She, too, looked extraordinarily ordinary without the lights and makeup, though she was certainly pretty, with straight dark brows above her serious deep-set eyes. Hershel introduced her as Naomi and the girl who stood beside her, whose fair hair was fluffed out around her baby face, dimpled cheeks and all, as Helena.

Another girl, Clara, squinted at her in a nearsighted fashion, a girl who needed glasses but didn't like the way she looked in them. Angular in both her body and face, she had a certain sharpness in her look that kept her from being pretty, though she looked plenty smart.

There were two young men, Shimmy and Effrim, who had the yeshiva look about them, thin, pale, and studious, though they were both, of course, bareheaded and clean-shaven. Effrim was the better-looking of the two, with curly fair hair and an angelic smile.

A young man introduced as Jerzy was so small and thin he looked like a boy, except that he had a very slight stoop. His face also was that of a solemn child, with enormous eyes.

A few steps behind everyone there was a girl introduced as Rosalie. Something drew one's eye to her. She, too, must have possessed this famous mysterious "presence," though with her it couldn't have been a matter of her height. She was the shortest person here, a little shorter than Jerzy. She had the most amazing bunch of red hair that Sorel had ever seen, and a complexion that, even here in the murky light, seemed to glow, along with her long green cat eyes. Her hair was so startling a shade that the equally startling idea—that the effect might have been produced from out of a bottle—suddenly occurred to Sorel. Normally, she would never have leapt to such a thought, but an actress . . . It was a possibility, no?

Somehow this Rosalie, smiling at her with a slightly tilted head as if sizing her up, intensified Sorel's feeling of being too young and thoroughly out of her depth.

Unt ich or *int uch?* And then after that . . . *what?* The wind was sweeping through room after vacant room, an unimpeded swooshing in and out of the shattered windows.

"So, Sasha," Hershel said, smiling. He had a nice homey voice, nothing fancy or theatrical. "Your aunt tells us that you are blessed with an unusual talent. So let's not waste any time. As you can see, we're not very formal here, and we couldn't be accused of being elitist either. After all, consider the case of Mendel!"

All laughed, most especially Mendel, his two thin arms crossed over his narrow chest, his laugh high and manic.

"Still, believe it or not, we really don't just accept anybody. In fact, we accept almost nobody."

"You speak like all the world is clamoring to become part of the *mishpocheh!*" Rosalie laughingly said. Though she was, to look at, the most creamily feminine concoction, she had the voice of a young man. It had been she who had, a few moments before, called out *"Touché!"*

"Soon, soon. Anyway, we're all learning here together. The truth is, what we're trying to do here, nobody knows how to teach."

Nobody was laughing at this.

"So, as usual, I'm talking too much, when we're really hear to listen to you."

"What are you going to give us?" Rosalie asked. "Please, say it's not Goldfaden!"

"Shakespeare," Sorel managed to answer.

"Shakespeare! Ai, ai, ai! Well, that's certainly not Goldfaden!"

"To be or not to be!" Mendel recited in a quite beautiful Oxford English, with his hand placed theatrically on his breast, "that is the *fraga!*"

"No, Mendel," a young man who had been introduced as Aleksander said. His was a serious and determined-looking face, with a chin that was squarely cut, dark hair neatly parted at the side. He had a muscular build and carried himself with the physical ease of an athlete. Sorel recognized him as the actor who had played K.'s friend, Max. "The *fraga* is how you can be such an untiring ass."

Unt ich or *int uch,* and then . . . *what?*

What?

Meanwhile, they had all seated themselves together on the benches and were facing Sorel. A cluster of faces turned upward toward her. . . .

What?

"So, Sasha."

"You want me to just do it right now?"

"Right now," said Hershel, smiling.

"Right here?"

Hershel nodded, folding his arms over his chest.

That's what finally did it: his folding his arms over his chest in that fashion.

Terror.

The winds sweeping through the barren rooms whipped themselves up into a fury, hissing and whistling. Lost in the din was every line, every syllable, every plotted nuance of pronunciation.

"Are you waiting for the music?" Mendel laughed.

Dying . . . dying . . . Must get out of here. . . .

"Did you want us to feed you some lines?" asked Hershel, his brow furrowing. He unfolded his arms, but it was far too late for gestures of that sort. Everything was lost to the angry winds.

Dying . . .

Rosalie glanced sideways at Hershel, who sat next to her. They had once been lovers, for a week that had somehow, strangely, only deepened their friendship. There was nothing that the one wouldn't do for the other. But what was Hershel going to do right now, to ease this lost little girl out—out from *her* misery and *their* midst?

Hershel, full of *rachmones,* Jewish pity, for this very pretty girl who was all too visibly suffering before them, was just about to say something, kind but final, when she opened her mouth and began to speak.

"There's rosemary, that's for remembrance. Pray you, love, remember." Her voice was quivering, its pathetic quality laid so bare you felt guilty for hearing it. It was an entirely different voice, the lisping Galician accent extremely pronounced. "Pray you, love, remember," she repeated. "And there is pansies, that's for thoughts. . . ."

The voice was so halting, the pauses so painfully elongated, that it was possible to believe—to hope—that she wouldn't continue.

"For thoughts. No flowers," she continued. "When someone dies, flowers."

Again she paused, at a loss, so that everyone fervently prayed she would simply give up, wander out the same way she had wandered in.

"In the middle of America, there is a city called by the name Chicago."

What was this?

"Chicago, Chicago." Her strange voice shook with the wonder of the word.

"In Chicago there lived a girl whose name was Fredericka Bodayda, the only daughter of Reb Mayer Laybish. Reb Mayer Laybish was the wealthiest landowner in all of Chicago. His vineyards covered the hills of the surrounding countryside, and the wine that was made from his grapes was the sweetest that had ever been tasted."

It certainly wasn't Shakespeare. God Himself only knew what it was.

"Every moment, she had the feeling that she had lived that exact moment once before. 'Only that other time,' she would think, 'I was happy. Or else I was sad. . . .' "

Hershel had never before heard a voice like this. She stood leaning slightly forward from her waist, but otherwise quite rigid, with her eyes fixed on some distance. The effect was altogether unsettling. But it was the quivering Galician voice that stirred him to his depths. . . .

"It was time for Frederika Bodayda to find a husband. But for such a daughter, Mayer Laybish found it very difficult to accept anyone as suitable."

Was she crying? Her eyes were glistening, the look in them impossible to read.

"And it was then that Mayer Laybish saw that Elazar's words were on fire. The moment they left the boy's mouth, they sprouted wings of flame and flew upward. The boy's moving lips, his beardless face, his crooked body—everything vanished behind a wall of fire, leaping toward the sky."

Lord of the Universe, she *was* crying. How she was crying! The tears simply spilled over the glistening eyes and kept coming and coming. He'd never seen anything like it. If this was acting, it was near genius.

"And the strangest thing is that all of these rumors turned out to be true. Mayer Laybish had spared nothing for the wedding of his only daughter."

The unanalyzable element of her voice seemed to be growing stronger. It was a voice that wouldn't let you go, that held you fast, even when it crouched down into a whisper. And the tears, the tears.

"There was a loud commotion as the men, singing and dancing, led in the bridegroom, who was pale and trembling from his fasting, and also from the fear of seeing his bride for the first time.

"Elazar looked down at the young woman, sitting so calmly beside her mother, and he became lost. All of the pages of his learning flew out from him, like startled white doves.

"Fredericka Bodayda looked up at her betrothed, at the moment before the foaming veil was dropped before her face, and all that she could think was, 'Only the last time, I was happy. Or perhaps it was that I was sad.' "

Rosalie wasn't even aware that she had taken Hershel's hand, and that the other hand was bunching the filmy material of her brand-new dress into a tight ball.

Even Mendel, the eternal jokester, sat without a smile on his mobile lips, wondering: What the hell?

Something extraordinary was happening here. . . .

"In the room it grows hotter by the minute, from all the dancing and from Mayer Laybish's sweet red wine. The breath of the guests fogs the windows, so that nobody can see out."

Sorel herself had lost all sense of where she was, of why it was that she was standing before these people and telling them the story she had heard one Sabbath afternoon, in the summer month of Av, so long ago. . . .

"And now it is that a grinning man enters, tall and thin, and so pale and handsome that three girls immediately lose their hearts forever with the first glance that falls on him. Each girl will die an old maid, mourning the life she lost in that one glance."

She was aware of nothing, not even of her own voice speaking. . . .

"Each person silently prays to himself, as he watches the badchen approaching his table, 'I beg of you, God of my fathers, let it not be me he chooses.'

"They glance at the head table, wondering why it is that Reb Mayer Laybish, or the seven rabbis from Jerusalem, don't order the badchen to stop his versifying, for now they are all trembling. Everybody's head has begun to ache at the temples, with a dull steady pounding that can almost be heard."

Her voice was whispering up against Sorel's ear, that strange voice that shook and trembled as if it were carried by a wind, so that there was no other sound in all the world. . . .

> I've walked beside you, every step,
> And filled your dreams while you have slept. . . .

. . . Never in all the years another voice like it . . .

> And whispered in your ear: No choice!
> You knew at once your husband's voice. . . .

Rosalie felt herself shudder, and Hershel felt the tickling sensation of his hairs rising on the back of his neck. . . .

> That whispered in your ear: No chance!
> Come . . . dance with me your bridal dance!

Silently, she began to circle before them, looking up as if into the eyes of the tall figure who held her. And still the tears coursed unceasingly down her cheeks, her voice now sunk to just above a whisper, but still sustaining its strange hypnotic power. . . .

"Mayer Laybish and Pesha Sima and the seven rabbis from Jerusalem pull out their hair and cry out their hearts, as Fredericka Bodayda and the badchen slowly circle the room in silence, each holding a corner of the gleaming white scarf.

"The two dancers make no noise, but all around them the groans are piling up, the room is thick with them, as the Jews of Chicago see the young girl they've known since her birth slowly taking on the face of the badchen, her eyes dissolving into shadows of black, and her bloodless lips giving way to the grin that rises up from behind them."

The spell the girl had cast with her story was such that it seemed to Rosalie that she did indeed see the young face transforming itself before her into a mask of death, and hear the groans of the Jews dim in the background. An icy finger seemed to be tracing a pattern up Rosalie's back, her heart thrashing as if she were in terror—pity and terror.

"Only Elazar, the bridegroom, never looks up, but sits rocking on his seat, back and forth, back and forth, muttering meaningless words and laughing like a boy of three at a spot of sun that dances on a wall."

The voice, which had sunk to the faintest whisper, now faded off into silence.

The members of the Bilbul were completely silent for several long moments, as each of them continued to watch the bride and her bride-groom silently dancing.

And then they were standing up, clapping for her.

The women had faces stained with tears, their mascara running.

Sorel still held her pose, still dazed, only slowly coming out of whatever it was that had held her.

What had just happened? She looked at the transfigured faces before her and she could only wonder:

What was it that had just happened?

She had heard Fraydel, as if she had been there, whispering up against her ear, a voice like no other come from out of the lonely wind. And now it was gone, perhaps forever, so that she wanted to scream out: *Fraydel!*

"*Mazel tov*," the beautiful red-headed actress was saying in her deep throaty voice, standing on her tiptoes so that she might give Sorel a hug. "*Mazel tov* and welcome to the *mishpocheh!*"

Fraydel! Sorel was screaming in her heart. *Lord of the Universe, only let me not lose forever my Fraydel!*

There were people all around her, strangers, asking her questions; the women had been crying, she could see that.

The man with the kind and homely face was grasping her hand. He, too, had been crying, his eyes puffy and red, his face homelier than ever.

His two hands clasped her own, which were no longer moist and cold, as they had been, but hot and dry, as if there were a fire under the skin.

CHAPTER 15

SLEUTHING ON
STAWKI STREET

*F*or Jascha, artistic creation was the most private activity in the world: the soul's sacred and solitary communion with itself. For him, the moments of sweetest intensity were always lived alone, inside his head, where the music was first heard.

He resented in his innermost being the fact that a composer cannot live a life of pure and inviolable self-containment—that is to say, a life of freedom, at least as the philosopher Spinoza had defined it, which was the definition that Jascha, too, had adopted.

The most private activity in the world must issue into something public: heard music. Music must be relinquished to performers, to listeners, or it is doubtful that the composer is even a composer.

For this reason, as well as for many others, Jascha considered Hershel Blau a man of paradox. Granted, Hershel's métier was theater and not music. But even so, his methods astounded.

Hershel's creative processes were not introspective and monadic but, rather, extravagantly, raucously, communal. The man couldn't write, he couldn't *think,* unless he was at the same time talking, arguing, laughing, flirting, among a bunch of people, all of whom were just as noisily, though never quite so intensely, engaged in this selfsame task of collective creativity.

Was such a nature incompatible with serious work? So one would, quite justifiably, suppose. And yet Jascha had seen some interesting theater emerge from Blau's paradoxical School of Shmooz.

Difficult as it was to comprehend, Hershel Blau was not devoid of talent. Not by any means. Misguided, yes: supremely. Yet not ungifted.

Of course, from Jascha's point of view, the proposition that he should personally be drawn anywhere into the vicinity of a Blau collaboration was patently inconceivable—as he had, in no uncertain terms, told the man the first time he had approached Jascha. For some reason or other, Blau had become fixated on the idea that Jascha should compose the music for a new play that he and his Bilbulniks were hatching, amidst even more commotion than usual.

"It's out of the question, Blau. It interests me not in the least."

"How can you know that, before you know anything about the work?"

"I know the kind of music I'm interested in composing. Believe me, it's not suitable for your purposes."

"I disagree."

"So now I'll turn your own question back on you. How can you know that, when you don't know anything about my work?"

"Ah, there's where you're wrong. I've heard your music."

"When? Where?"

"Your sister, Henya, has played your music for me."

"Which pieces?"

"Well, your piano sonata, for one. It's beautiful, Jascha. Simply and wonderfully beautiful. It's moved me to tears—more than once."

Jascha's thin lips smiled in a way that was painful to behold.

Self-containment. If only it were possible for a musician to live a life of absolute self-containment. The soul's communing with itself— and the hell with the rest of the world!

He was as ready to join into the raucous communal creativity practiced by the Bilbulniks as he was to volunteer himself to the Polish army.

Which was precisely what he told Blau the next time that the director came nudzhing him . . . and the next time after that.

Blau, the *posgunyak,* was prepared to sink so low, apparently, that he even enlisted Jascha's little brother in the cause of enticing Jascha down to the tailors' union hall. Or perhaps Maurice had taken it upon himself. Jascha's brother seemed to be spending more and more time with the actors. Or was it more and more time with the actresses? He couldn't stop talking about some new girl, Jascha couldn't remember her name, because frankly he never really listened when Maurice started rhapsodizing in this ridiculous fashion.

Jascha suspected that Maurice—who wasn't even seventeen yet—fancied himself to be in love, which half amused and half annoyed the older brother.

Jascha was quite passionately devoted to this younger brother of his. In fact, he was, if anything, even more ambitious for Maurice than he was for himself. The boy would be a scholar of the first rank one day, a seminal thinker in one field or another. Already, though still a schoolboy, he could toss off links between subjects, could grasp patterns that were startling. Most important, there was an element of playfulness in his thinking, the mark of the true original. Jascha adored him. And why not? He was adorable—perhaps too adorable for his own damned good. Perhaps a little too quick-witted for his own good as well. He hadn't yet been exposed to a subject that could make him feel the puniness of the human intellect, which is why it was so absolutely imperative that Maurice be admitted to university. That's what the boy needed, and not a love affair with an actress! Maurice Saunders had been made for better things than *that.*

"I'm telling you, Jascha, it's not anything like that!" For a moment Maurice's voice, which had long ago settled down into its manly baritone, rose perilously near to a squeak. "Just come down for yourself and see. I'm telling you, it's not like any theater you've ever seen before. Blau is inspired. They all are. I don't know what it is about this new play, but it's pulling something brilliant out from them. They're all carrying on like a pack of raving geniuses."

Jascha visibly winced at this offhanded abuse of such words as "inspired," "brilliant," "genius"—the most sacred terms in man's vocabulary—but all he muttered was, "I'll accept without question the 'raving' part of your description."

Maurice had seen the wince.

"Look, I know how you hate the way those words are thrown around so much. I hate it, too, you know that. 'Wiesenthal, the genius of hat-blocking, whose latest work, Mr. Feldblum's black felt homburg with the nice little feather, has brilliantly redefined the meaning of "That's a nice hat, Feldblum." ' But, really, I'm telling you . . ."

"Yes, yes. You're telling me that you're not in love with that new actress."

"What are you talking about, you big lummox? Of course I'm in love with her! I'm going to grow old with her!"

"Aha!"

"Aha! The Jewish Sherlock Holmes!"

Maurice, tall for his age, but still not quite up to his lanky brother, stood laughing up into Jascha's face, at which Jascha tried to tousle his little brother's hair, an act of provocation that immediately resulted in the sort of horseplay the two brothers had never given up. Jascha had the advantage in height, but Maurice was the athlete and soon had Jascha pinned down beneath him.

"Say you'll come to the theater!"

"Never!"

"Theater!"

"Never!"

At this point, the old man—by profession a ragpicker—who lived beneath Jascha's garret room began banging on his ceiling with his broom.

The two grinned a little shamefacedly at one another and got up from the floor.

"So you're going to grow old with this woman?"

"I am going to grow old with this woman. Nothing else in my life is a certainty . . . but this I know for sure."

Jascha examined Maurice's face for traces of irony and found none.

Maurice's hair, as dark as his brother's but straight where the other's was curly, was wildly disheveled from his little bout of wrestling. Long wisps of hair fell down over his forehead and into his eyes, and this had the effect of making him look once again like a very little boy.

Jascha could clearly discern the child this used to be, and not so long ago, suddenly staring out at him from the midst of the solemn declaration.

And it *was* solemn. Maurice, who was never serious about much of anything, was in deadly earnest now. His extraordinary eyes—icy blue and piercing—stared steadily into Jascha's, and there was nothing of the ironical in them.

"I suppose," said Jascha, looking with a certain sense of wonder back into those eyes, "I suppose I shall have to go to that blasted theater after all. And by the way, Sherlock Holmes *is* Jewish. He changed his name. I'm surprised you never guessed it."

"What about Dr. Watson?"

"Are you kidding? Of course Watson's a *goy.* The thing I've always wondered about is whether or not Watson ever suspected. My dear friend Holmes: a filthy Yid."

CHAPTER 16

THE WAY A SWAN
GLIDES

*M*aurice left Stawki Street feeling more than a little amazed by himself. Self-avowals weren't at all his style. The fear of appearing ridiculous was always strong in him; in fact, he considered it one of the most ridiculous things about himself. And he particularly dreaded seeming absurd before his brother, the person he most respected in all the world. To Maurice, Jascha was the standard by which all men were judged and found wanting.

He had really taken Jascha aback. Jascha had stared at him, waiting for the quip to come. With Maurice, the quip always came, sooner or later, usually sooner. Maurice had felt at least half a dozen ready to spring to his lips, but he had let them wither away into silence.

Instead of going straight over to watch the *mishpocheh* rehearsing, as he had been intending, he headed over to the Krasinski Gardens and sank down onto one of the green benches.

There was only one swan gliding about in the little muddy pond in front of him. What an extravagance of nature such a creature was. Maurice had lately developed a passionate appreciation for extravagances of nature.

He felt a slight tightening around his heart even before he realized why. This odd white bird, like something dreamt up by a whimsical mind, reminded him, of course, of Sasha. Just like the swan, Sasha, too, glided. And, just like Sasha, this swan couldn't have cared less that Maurice stared at it in stupefied admiration.

And yet, only a half-hour before, Maurice had declared, with a conviction that had rung true to his own ears as well, that he was going to grow old with that woman!

There had been a certain exhilaration in saying those words aloud, but now the giddiness had dissipated, and all that he felt was intense embarrassment. He didn't know why it was like this for him, why he felt himself so compromised whenever anyone got a glimpse inside of him. He couldn't even tolerate anyone's ever knowing when he was sick. Just having a thermometer put into his mouth made him feel enfeebled, as if he were the biblical Samson getting a trim.

Once, not so many years ago, at the age of ten or eleven, he had gotten up for school one morning feeling horrible but determined to ignore it. He stood up and was immediately sick all over the floor. Before he could run and get the mop, he heard his mother at his door, so he picked up the throw rug and acted according to its name. His mother stood there on that rug, sniffing suspiciously, asking him questions to which he breezily lied: "No, *I* haven't been sick." "*I* don't smell anything at all." What a commotion she had made when she had finally lifted up that rug. Though Maurice had begged her please, please not to, she hadn't been able to stop repeating this story to everyone, intimates and strangers alike, seeking their interpretation of its deeper meaning, as if it were a mystical text.

For each of her three children she had one such story, recounted again and again. Henya's and Jascha's stories were no more uplifting than Maurice's.

A nice analogy, Maurice had to admit, sitting there on the park bench while Sasha the swan glided past without so much as a glance. A real inspiration, comparing Jascha's now knowing that I'm hopelessly in love to my mother's discovering the sickness under the rug. Love has obviously turned me into a poet of no mean power.

Love. So this was the distinguished thing at last. And, yes, the poets, no matter how gaga, hadn't been exaggerating. It's quite a thing, this love. It takes over your breath and your blood, your mind and your body, with the little bits of life that are left over clinging to the edges in dry flakes, so that you can just flick them off like this.

"Like this, Sasha," he demonstrated to his cygnet surrogate as she circled once again, barely parting the unworthy waters.

What had his life been up until now? He had been a schoolboy, with a schoolboy's wants, a schoolboy's shallow mentality. He liked to do well in his classes, earn the respect of his teachers and classmates, score goals in soccer, carry away the prizes at the end of the academic year. This is what he had wanted, and it had come to him, so that he had had every reason to feel quite pleased with himself.

Well, no, he was trivializing his former existence, just because it now seemed to him that everything that had come before must have been utterly, utterly trivial. He had never really felt quite so sure of himself as he liked to let others believe—exactly why, he couldn't say. The sickness-under-the-rug business in another guise.

Only last week, his father had called him into his study for an "interview," taking him to task for his "pernicious flippancy."

Lazar Saunders was not a tall man. Jascha towered over him, and Maurice was already taller and still growing. Still, he was a substantial figure, his bald head large and shiny, his chest extremely broad, giving great power to the tenor voice that filled the palatial sanctuary of the Great Synagogue each Sabbath.

"Isn't there anything at all that you really care about?" he had demanded of his younger son.

"I care about everything, sir," Maurice had responded, taking care to show no flippancy. His father was clearly in a mood in which any motion in the wrong direction would be pounced upon.

"To me that means you care about nothing," his father had answered, with a contempt that he had allowed quite deliberately to show through. Maurice had had to recognize the degree of truth in what his father said.

For his brother, Jascha, there was music, only music. Jascha awoke in the middle of the night hearing symphonies. Genius in a person was like a weed that takes over the entire garden, that won't allow anything else to grow. Ah, yet another image of dubious poetry. In any case, to

Maurice, the very fact that he found himself equally interested in so many things showed—to himself, as it did to his father—that he had no particular talent in anything.

When Jascha was sixteen, it had already been obvious that there would be no life for him outside of music. But Maurice could imagine himself easily into a great number of mutually exclusive lives.

He would have liked, at one and the same time, to be both a *talmid chachem,* a disciple of the wise, and also to be one of those bright lights who danced away every night at the Astoria Hotel, buying drinks for the prettiest and fastest girls in all of Warsaw.

He would have liked to be a thorough-going rationalist, a professor of physics or philosophy at some famous German university, and at the same time to be a Cabalistic mystic, seeing divine emanations in every puddle.

He would have liked to be an American millionaire, but also a kibbutznik living in collective penury in Palestine.

Every single one, and more, of these imagined lives called out to him, and he would, if he could, gladly take hold of them all. But the thing was simply impossible. The *talmid chachem*'s existence would run counter to the bright light's. The rationalist and the mystic would trip each other up. The millionaire and the kibbutznik could not possibly keep house in the same puny precincts of his person.

One life is definitely not enough, which is why the Cabalistic idea of reincarnation had always appealed so much to him. Or, if reincarnation wasn't in the metaphysical cards, there was always the theater, where at least a person could *pretend* to try on one life after another.

The thought of the stage of course brought him within wincing distance of that other thought, the thought of all thoughts.

He sighed.

Of all the lives that had clamored out for his attention, he had never once thought of acting out for himself the role of the Yiddish Romeo, which was, to his mind, a slightly ridiculous character, even *with* a Juliet who was willing, which his certainly wasn't.

Now he had ventured closer in to that thought of all thoughts, radiating its deadly energy like a rod of pure uranium. He had passed over from the wincing region into downright laceration.

Maurice was a person who was used to reasoning with himself. The philosopher at the famous German university hadn't yet been placed at such a far remove that Maurice didn't still try to enlist his powers of cerebration.

A person is just a person, after all, even if she's a beautiful girl whose voice sends shivers so deep down you could almost swear they were penetrating the soul. (The rationalist, of course, didn't really believe in souls.) And what is a person but a species of ape that has been taught some fancy tricks by that old subtle magician, evolution? (The rationalist was, needless to say, a disciple of Darwin.) The poets, the whole rhapsodizing pack of romantics: it was nice stuff that they had written, but they had simply gotten it *wrong.* They were like the ones who sit in the audience and don't even *suspect* the cards up the sleeve, the false bottoms and the trapdoors.

Why should he allow this girl just to come loping into his life— but he stopped right there, stopped dead with the image of the lope. That heart-lacerating, life-displacing, reason-resistant, poetry-in-motion lope.

"Sasha, Sasha," Maurice called out in the silent chambers of his heart to that form of sheer loveliness that was tracing its elegant path across the surface of Krasinski's brackish pond.

"Turn and give me a look," he begged. "Just one little cold glance and I'll be content."

But the snowy creature glided past, swanlike and oblivious, a heartrending perfection that wouldn't—in a truly rational universe—be allowed to exist at all.

CHAPTER 17

THE BOOK OF
ROSALIE

*R*osalie, Rosalie. Oy, was this a Rosalie!

This girl was an education in herself. What Rosalie didn't know on certain subjects wasn't worth knowing.

And what subjects were these? Don't ask!

How did a girl like Rosalie come to be the daughter of a pious family? How did a girl like Rosalie come to be at all?

There was nobody's conversation that intrigued and tickled Sorel more than Rosalie's. Her talk about men—and of what else did Rosalie talk?—was to Sorel like the Book of Revelation.

"He looks me in the eye and tells me he wants to have children by me. 'What?' I say to him, giving him a look like my own sister Masha." Among the large Chasidic brood from which Rosalie had somehow or other originated, she had a sister named Masha, whose stupidity, according to Rosalie, was unequaled anywhere, any time. " 'You got children you want to board by me?' 'Rosalie,' he says, 'don't play dumb with *me.* I want you to be the mother of my children.' Just like that, he comes out and says it! 'And what goes along with this charming proposition?' I ask him. 'What else are you throwing in besides the *mamzarim?*' And he starts to laugh like a *meshuggena,* saying, 'Oy, is this a Rosalie' . . . !"

More often than not, Sorel had no idea what Rosalie was talking about, though that didn't stop her from relishing every unintelligible word, rendered in that highly inflected voice that had doomed Rosalie never to play the great tragic roles to which she aspired.

"Don't go near that one," Rosalie warned Sorel, hooking her thumb toward a very elegant and refined-looking gentleman who had nodded to the two girls with a dazzling smile from across Leszno Street. "Not unless you want a nice case of the crabs. And that one over there, who's looking at you like you're a nice fresh roll and he's just getting ready to break his Yom Kippur fast, that one has a tubercular wife and maybe ten or eleven children, they wait at home for their darling father; men are such dogs, always sniffing where they shouldn't be sniffing!"

Rosalie had the role of Sorel's mother in the new play the *mishpocheh* was rehearsing; and even outside of rehearsals, there had crept something just a little bit maternal and proprietary into her relationship with the younger girl. The two were always whispering together conspiratorially, like two Bolsheviks plotting.

"You see that woman over there, the one who's so skinny, *nebech,* it looks like her two cheeks are glued together. She's a Yiddish actress, or at least she *was,* when your grandmother and my grandmother were still pishing in their diapers. They say that there was once a crazy writer by the name of Kafka—not from Warsaw, I don't know, maybe Vilna or Białystock—and that this Kafka was so madly in love with that creature there that every night he'd come and watch her act and stare and stare and not say a word, such a shmuck!"

Sorel, too, now stared.

"Strange, no?" Rosalie said, grinning.

Sorel grinned back, in agreement with everything Rosalie's grin had said, which was plenty. It was next to impossible to imagine anyone's ever having been in love, madly or otherwise, with the fleshless woman who was sitting across the room at the Writers' Club in an unbecoming hat.

"Of course, they say that this Kafka was *dafka* a crazy man, he wrote all sorts of *mishegoss* that nobody can make heads or tails of, but even so . . ."

Sorel continued to watch the woman, who was slowly consuming a *kichel* that she first dipped into her glass of tea.

"It all goes to show you," Rosalie now summed up the situation expertly, "when the penis stands up, then the brains fall down."

This came from Rosalie's stock of dirty Yiddish sayings, which constituted a long, long chapter in her Book of Revelation. Rosalie had even produced some excerpts out of this amazing text that were written expressly about Sorel herself.

"It didn't take you so long, *tsatskeleh.* Only yesterday, it seems to me, you thought every Jewish girl and boy got married through a *shadchen.* Now look at you!"

"*What,* look at me?"

"No, no, *tsatskeleh,* not with Rosalie can you play coy! With Rosalie there are no secrets!"

"Oy, Rosalie," Sorel groaned. "It's so obvious?"

"Obvious? I wouldn't go so far as to say that. I'd say it's only obvious to someone who's not, God forbid, blinded in both eyes and maybe a little bit stupid on top of that."

"So you think he knows?"

"Didn't you hear what I just said? From him you're safe!"

Poor Sorel groaned again—and her face! It was a face for an actress who aspired to tragedy to study and memorize.

"Where are his eyes? Where are his eyes?" Rosalie murmured. "Oy, darling, don't look like that, you break my heart! But that's what you get for falling in love with a man as dry as last year's matzohs. Love is all very well, I'm all for it, as I don't have to tell you or too many others, but you have to have a little *saychel,* too!"

"So, then, it's hopeless!" Sorel moaned, with an intonation that so perfectly carried the hopelessness of it all that again Rosalie took notes and tried to commit to memory.

"Hopeless? Never! Where there's life there's hope. The only question that remains is: is that man alive? You know, there are two schools of thought on this question. Bais Hillel says . . ."

"Rosalie! Have some *rachmones!* I love him! Can I help it? To me, he's . . . he's . . ."

"What? I'm waiting to hear what it is you see in that unleavened soul. For myself, I can't take a humorless person. God knows I'm willing to overlook any number of faults in a man, you name the fault and, believe me, sometime in my life I've overlooked, only not that one."

"He's a genius!"

"You think that's an excuse for no sense of humor? You think a great man doesn't have to know to laugh? God Himself has a sense of humor—and how! All right, so next time you'll know better."

Next time? There would be no *next time* for Sorel, no time in which she would love the composer Jascha Saunders no longer.

She wasn't a Rosalie, who could take out the old love and bring in the new, like the Passover dishes.

Rosalie's dislike for Jascha was sincere, though perhaps she laid it on a little thicker for Sorel's benefit, in order to talk the poor girl out of her miserable infatuation.

And it *was* miserable. It had been misery at first sight, from the first moment that she had been introduced to him and had felt his eyes brushing over her with such a cold indifference.

And why, dear God, should it be that such a dead coldness made Sorel start to smolder like a high priest's burnt offering?

Sorel had immediately felt the justice of his dismissive glance. Yes, it was true that men were everywhere tripping all over themselves to impress her these days, ever since she had acquired her mysterious "presence." But Jascha Saunders was not like these others—which is why she was so utterly, utterly lost. With that first cold glance of his, she was lost!

How, she sometimes wondered, could she even *aspire* to the love of such a man? Yet such wondering didn't put out the fire. She had only to picture his white, aristocratic hands, the fingers so extraordinarily long and sensitive, to feel sensations she'd never dreamt of before. Those hands played piano, violin, cello. Every finger pulsed with genius, and when she saw or even imagined them, she pulsed, too. Oh my God, in what strange ways and strange places she pulsed!

So, all the time that Rosalie was reciting passages to her from out of her Book of Revelation, Sorel's thoughts had been on him. Everything she was learning these days fed into her feelings for him. Her love for the wide world itself had become her love for him.

And why not? He *was* the world, because he had mastered it, had made it his own.

No, he was *more* than the world, because of the music he would yet give it.

That's what it was to love a genius: it was to love something that was larger than life itself. So let Rosalie make fun until the final redemption!

Every time Rosalie asked her what she saw in Jascha Saunders, Sorel struggled to make her friend understand.

"I love him because he's so angry all the time," she said once.

"Ai, ai," said Rosalie, laughing, "now at last I understand. How can a girl resist a bad temper? That makes it clear. Clear as borsht with sour cream."

Yes, let Rosalie laugh. She didn't see—she couldn't possibly see—what it was that Sorel saw in that gaze that stared out so implacably from behind the steel-framed glasses.

Jascha's wasn't an anger at a "this" or a "that." It was an anger at the world itself.

And, oh, how Sorel loved! When she saw him and when she didn't—it didn't matter—at any moment, a rush of longing would suddenly overtake her, streaming through the long stem of her body, to end up in her eyes as hot tears.

And every passage that came out of Rosalie's Book of Revelation— every startling little detail about the ways in which men and women carry on with each other in this world—it all went straight into Sorela's pulsing—her blood on fire with what she called to herself the Gypsy heat. (She had never forgotten that Gypsy boy's dance.) Her body, her very own body, was constantly shocking her these days.

It had been misery at first sight, and it only deepened and bulged with every subsequent sighting. Jascha was often among the *mishpocheh* that spring, having been drawn, by some mysterious process, into the new production. So Sorel had plenty of opportunity for heartache.

He sat at the new piano, Aunt Frieda's gift to the Bilbulniks, his long fingers either caressing the ivory keys—oh, to be one of those keys—or thrashing them savagely. Oh my *God!*

His personality was carved out in ice, frozen away into a reserve so deep it was hard to believe the man was really Jewish. But in the music he was writing for the Bilbulniks this spring, the soul was in flames— here flickering with muted snatches from ancient prayers, here flaring up into the sounds of Jewish celebration and Jewish mourning.

Yes, she'd think, her ear catching an old Chasidic cadence: he and I are of the same people, the same story. His soul is not so unimaginably different from my own.

All day long, Sorel went about with this music blending into all the other million and one things that were going on in her head. At night, she closed her eyes hearing the ache of the melody that was her own haunting theme—the heartrending music he had composed for the tragic girl that she played—and it would be waiting for her in the morning.

During her last dance, she was supposed to grow slowly more lifeless, but Jascha's music, caressing her from within, made her cheeks burn and her eyes blaze so that sometimes Hershel had to halt the action until Sasha cooled down. She would glance over at Jascha, who would return her gaze with icy indifference, his eyes passing over her without a flicker of interest. This look of his was often quite helpful in making her feel as good as dead, so that she was able to play her role convincingly, and Hershel was happy.

And yet Sorel didn't judge her beloved's dismissal to be in any way unfair. She was incapable of any judgment insofar as Jascha Saunders was concerned. She accepted his indifference as the verdict justly passed on the present state of Sorel Sonnenberg.

Nonetheless, she wasn't prepared just to sit back and gush tears and see stretching out before her only the dark, dense doom of unrequited love, forever and ever, amen.

As Rosalie herself had said: where there's life, there's hope.

And there was even more than hope here, for, after all, Sorel was *changing*. So, too—it only stood to reason—would Jascha Saunders's opinion of her.

She had known nothing, *nothing,* before; she knew a little something now; and who *knew* what she would know tomorrow?

So, though Jascha Saunders might dismiss her today as unworthy of his notice, who was to say he might not like her a little better next week, or maybe the week after that?

Alone among all of the Bilbulniks who found themselves in love this spring—and they happened all to be in love this spring—only Rosalie was happily in love.

Feliks Zakauer had been after Rosalie for as long as any of them could remember. But it was only after he had become a ruined man, his worldly possessions carted off by a Grabski hearse, that Rosalie suddenly felt herself melting at his entreaties. And before you knew it, it was Feliks and Rosalie!

Sorel had been at first completely incredulous. The man was at least forty, maybe more. And ugly—oy, was he ugly: a beefy nose, greedy lips, even greedier eyes; a face drawn by a talented anti-Semite.

And yet Rosalie swore that beneath that unpromising exterior dwelled the soul of a sensitive man, misunderstood by all the world.

"And passionate? *Tsatskeleh,* you wouldn't believe it!"

No, frankly, Sorel wouldn't have believed it, at least not before. But now she was ready to believe almost anything when it came to this strange business of love.

So Rosalie and Feliks came together during that Warsaw spring in what Rosalie swore to her friend was that most elusive of all miracles: perfect love. But for the rest of the *mishpocheh,* perfect love remained that spring as distant as the light of the outermost sphere.

Hershel, more obsessed than ever by the demands of the new play, still managed to grab an hour here or there so that he might pay a brief visit to the rather formal Saunders household.

He would sit in the parlor, where the grand piano was, his hands folded in his lap, listening intently to the music that came pouring out from beneath Henya's fingers. Her face rested in perfect repose inside the music, and she seemed not even to be aware of the way in which the director's sad, hooded eyes stayed on her.

She sat playing out her heart, beside the long, open window, graced with elegant fine-lace curtains. The outdoor air wafted in, fraught with the scent that had lingered on through all the late spring, maddening our dreams and desires, so that simply to breathe was to suffer.

Did Henya, sitting at the piano, the breeze fluttering the curtain beside her, also long? And for whom? For whom?

In the midst of all this love and longing, spoken and unspoken, the Bilbulniks went on working. There was a new play in production, about which the Bilbulniks weren't as yet saying too much, but they were all clearly infected with Hershel's fever of inspiration. Everything was all hush-hush and whispers, a great air of significant secrecy to be maintained until the curtain went up. As if all of Warsaw were simply dying from the anticipation!

Hershel Blau, son of the Chasidic wandering preacher, was not yet so distant from his father's world that he didn't know deep in his soul the yearning to fly. What is a Chasid's dance but one long, sustained attempt to arch away into suspended ascension, beyond the laws of bodies, a thing of air and light and fire?

When Hershel had been a little boy, he used to go with his father on all the important holidays to the court of the rebbe whose Chasidim they were. It was a fairly small sect, not as prosperous and influential as some of the other Chasidic dynasties, like the Bobover or the Tshortkever, whose rabbinical courts were like palaces spread out on grassy acres. In contrast, the sect to which the Blaus belonged had been dwindling, ever since the death of the old rebbe, who, even till the end, when he was well into his nineties, had had a certain fiery charisma. His son, who had inherited his position at the age of fifty-eight, was still known as "the young rebbe," even though his beard was by now gray and sparse and his shoulders were stooped. Still, neither the present rebbe nor his followers had altogether lost their gift for ecstasy, the longing to fly with which they all danced.

There was one holiday in particular, the springtime festival of Shavuos, when Hershel, then perhaps seven or eight years old, had known that he himself could have flown had he chosen. He had danced and danced that night, in the room that was hot and crowded with the singing, swaying men and boys, all gradually working themselves up into exaltation on this night when the sky is said to split wide open in revelation.

After hours of dancing, never tiring for a moment, Hershel had felt his limbs growing strangely weightless, porous with light. With each leap he went higher and hovered motionless for several seconds longer. He *could* have flown, but he had held himself back. It would only have taken a voiceless inner consent, which he had withheld. It wasn't the fear of flying itself but, rather, the fear of changing his life irrevocably with his flight. You could not fly on Shavuos night in the rabbinical court of a Chasidic rebbe, however obscure, and then go on with things as they had been before. The Chasidim might even have deposed "the young rebbe" and made Hershel himself the new leader of the dynasty!

He could have flown, and he yearned to fly, but he didn't want to be known among the Chasidim as the boy who had flown on Shavuos night. And yet, without the other Chasidim dancing and swaying and singing all around him, levitation was impossible. No matter how long and ardently Hershel danced by himself in the days and weeks and months that followed that Shavuos night, whirling and leaping himself into exhaustion, he never could attain that moment of possibility again.

Not until this spring, which found Hershel with no fear at all. He couldn't have stopped himself had he tried.

CHAPTER 18

SANDAL-WEARERS

*A*re all great artists egomaniacal? Jascha tended to think so. A delusion of grandeur might very well be a necessary component in the mysterious process of creativity.

Just to embark at all upon some daunting imaginative project—an opera, a symphony, a novel—a man must be filled with a quite unjustified sense of his own powers and importance. Otherwise, he simply does not presume to write that first sentence, that first measure. Those whose egos maintain perfectly normal dimensions don't set out to recreate the world according to their own conceptions of content and form.

It's therefore quite imbecile to criticize, say, a Tolstoy for being less—all right, a great deal less—than a saint. Jascha had read an article just the other day, printed in a Polish academic journal he had happened to pick up at Bresler's, which had crucified Tolstoy for his "overweening ego, his aspirations to the state of God's older brother," etc. etc. Not only this. The writer seemed to be arguing that Tolstoy's life should be taken as some kind of proof that intellectuals are at their core base hypocrites, assuming the responsibility of telling all the world how it should live, while at home they make their wives and children miserable with the overflow of their vastly ghastly egos.

What rot, Jascha had thought, setting the article aside with an expression of distaste just at the point where the author, with puerile delight, began to plunge into the more unseemly details of the great man's home life.

After all, who but an egomaniac would ever attempt a masterpiece on the order of *War and Peace?*

The unfortunate fact was not that great artists are great egoists. What is unfortunate is that great egoists are not necessarily great artists. There's a good deal more pomposity out there than there is talent.

Jascha had always held Blau to be a paradoxical exception: a man of truly creative impulses who yet preserved a very high degree of modesty. But in the last few weeks, Jascha had observed, with a certain amount of amusement, that he had been dead wrong. It was not simply that for Hershel nothing else really existed except the work at hand. This was no more than one would expect, this inversion of reality that was a given in the creative life. No, it was more than this. Hershel's heightened exhilaration this spring had blown the cover off his vaulting ambition.

Blau suffered from a mild case of messianism, an ailment as common among Jewish males as nearsightedness. This wasn't just theater to Blau, not by a long shot. Of course, the director was very good at concealing his messianic illness under his *menshlichkeit* and *mysah*s. Even when he came right out and argued his point, he didn't exactly come right out and argue his point.

"Once upon a time, a peasant lost his way and found himself in a desert."

It was in the very early hours of the morning. Only Hershel and Jascha and Sorel still remained at the Pripetshok.

The rest of the *mishpocheh* had finally called it a night, going off to lonely beds in rented rooms—all except, of course, Rosalie and Feliks, who were anything but lonely. These two had excused themselves much earlier in the evening, their arms tightly linked about each other.

But Hershel and Jascha were still going at it, and Sorel stayed on simply for the sake of remaining in the proximity of Jascha.

Oh yes, and Jascha's little brother, Maurice, was also still there.

Maurice Saunders wasn't all that much younger than Sorel, though she considered the gap between them immense and unbridgeable. So far as she was concerned, he was a mere pest. Even for his age, he was immature—always looking for attention, always showing off how smart he was. It surprised Sorel to see how the others indulged him.

Nobody else connected with the *mishpocheh* irked Sasha so profoundly as that little showoff of a schoolboy. It's not that Sasha was crazy about each and every one of the actors and actresses. Clara Gowinska, for example, was no great friend of hers. The girl was a bitch, no doubt about it, wallowing up to her nose in envy—though, of course, in theory, there could be no envy among the ensemble. But, theory or no, Clara was a real *farbisseneh,* a person who was as if bitten up. So what could Sasha do about it? There had been girls at her *gymnasium* who had likewise decided to hate her, on whatever grounds: her blond hair, her long legs, whatever. Who knew? Who cared? When it comes to such people and their hatreds, there's only one thing you can do, and that's to know the right moment to hold in your breath as you walk around them, as everyone in Shluftchev had known how to walk around the puddle.

But when it came to Maurice Saunders, Sasha found it impossible to take the high road of ignoring. He simply annoyed her too much for that. Although she made a great show of *pretending* to ignore, as extravagantly as she knew how, everything he said—she had taken upon herself, since nobody else seemed ready to assume the responsibility, the task of bringing Maurice Saunders down a peg or two—Sasha actually always took great notice, for the sheer exquisite agony of having a raw nerve jabbed. He was the only member of the *mishpocheh* whom Sasha really couldn't stand—not that he was *really* part of the *mishpocheh.* They said he would go to the university, that he was a regular Einstein when it came to books. For her part, Sorel suspected that this rumor had originated with none other than Maurice Saunders himself, who knew how to promote himself like nobody's business. Personally, Sasha thought it was probably having a brother so extraordinary as Jascha that had turned the younger brother into the obnoxious little showoff that he was.

"Suddenly," Hershel was saying, "there was a windstorm that caught up the dust and the sand and a mixture of all sorts of things and sent them whirling around and around. Eventually, the storm died down, and the peasant continued on his way.

"But as this peasant walked on, he discovered something amazing. With every step he took, he found himself becoming smarter and smarter. He could understand all manner of things: how the birds stayed up in the air, why it was hotter in the summer and colder in the winter. All the things that had always baffled him before were suddenly revealed as crystal clear. Even questions he had never thought to ask before, he now had the answers to.

"After a while, he grew tired and so sat down to rest, taking his sandals off. The moment he did this, he felt himself becoming just as boorish and befuddled as before. Yet, the minute he once again slipped on his sandals, all the confusion lifted like the darkness at dawn, and he became again a clever and sensible person. So it was clear to him that the sandals had brought all this about.

"The explanation was that the windstorm had blown a leaf from the Tree of Knowledge out of the Garden of Eden, and the leaf had become stuck on the bottom of one of his sandals."

At this, Maurice, the little showoff, began to laugh in that superior hoot of his that raised the hackles up all along the long stem of Sorel's body.

"So, Mr. Big-Shot-Who-Doesn't-Even-Use-a-Razor-Yet," Sasha inwardly sneered, "you have to let us all know that you already foresee the end of the story."

Sorel had vowed that she would religiously ignore Maurice, but she couldn't restrain herself from shooting him a glance, dripping with venom, at the sight of which the poor boy quickly quieted down.

"The peasant came to a town in which the King's daughter was very sick. All the doctors had already despaired of her life, and now there was nothing to do but wait for the inevitable. Then word was brought to the grieving King that a crude peasant had come to the palace, promising to cure the princess.

"The peasant prepared various remedies and began to treat the princess. In a few days, she had regained consciousness; a few days after that, she was running around as if she'd never been sick.

"The King, of course, rewarded the peasant royally. He also requested that the peasant stay a few more days in the palace, so that the court physicians could have the opportunity of studying the peasant's remedies. The King was anxious to determine whether there had been real knowledge there, or only some kind of sorcery.

"The King's doctors testified that the remedies had been well and wisely chosen.

"So the King asked the peasant how it was that he, a mere peasant, had come by so much medical knowledge.

" 'It's my sandals,' said the man.

" 'What kind of joke is that?' demanded the King.

" 'No joke,' protested the peasant. 'I'm telling you, all my wisdom comes from my sandals.'

"The King promised half the kingdom and even more if the peasant would present him with these sandals, which the peasant did.

"But it stands to reason that a king can't wear dirty sandals. So he gave them to his servants to be cleaned, and the servants, of course, scraped away the leaf from the Tree of Knowledge along with the other *shmutz,* and when the King put them on he was no wiser or more sensible than before."

Maurice had restrained himself from delivering the end of the story, which he had indeed more or less foreseen at the point at which he'd started laughing. He wasn't going to risk another glance from Gehenna.

Jascha sat with his eyebrows raised, his smile almost audibly delivering its caustic commentary. Obviously, he hadn't thought too much of the story.

"A good story, huh, Yossela?" Maurice said to his brother, trying to provoke him. He alone could get away with calling his brother by his discarded Yiddish name.

"Not so bad, Mayer," the elder brother responded in kind. "But a story is only a story. It proves nothing."

"Says who? If a story rings true, you think that doesn't count for anything?"

"Not much," said Jascha, shrugging. Then he turned back to

Hershel. "You say there's wisdom buried somewhere in all the *shmutz* we've picked up along the way. I say *shmutz* is *shmutz*."

"But what about your music?" Sorel suddenly burst out.

"What about it?" Jascha's voice was so cold, a blast from Siberia, that poor Sorel wished to God she had kept out of it. But Maurice rushed to take up Sasha's point.

"Isn't the kind of music you're working on now exactly the sort of thing that Hershel's talking about?" he asked his brother.

"Whether it is or isn't, I couldn't say for sure. But, in any case, the music I'm working on now is only a fluke. It's nothing serious, it has nothing to do with my life's work."

"I think it's beautiful! It's the most beautiful music I've ever heard!" Again Sorel couldn't restrain herself from exclaiming, her voice so charged and her face so flushed with passion that poor Maurice felt he might die on the spot for all the longing she unleashed. But Jascha only gave her a tight smile that was even worse than if he had glared at her, so that again she slumped back in her chair and cursed her rash tongue.

"Listen, Hershel. You tell me your father's falsehoods, clothed in his pretty *mysahs,* in exchange for which I'll give you the naked truth. If they didn't hate us, there would no longer be anything like this anachronism you call Jewishness."

"Only hatred?" It was Maurice who asked.

"It's enough," Jascha answered him. He turned back to Hershel. "Here, you have told me a fairy tale, I'll tell you another. Imagine that there is a place on this earth—who knows, maybe it's America—where a person can really wipe the *shmutz* off of his ancient sandals, once and for all, and nobody will tell him he can't. He can throw the sandals out altogether with the morning garbage, put on the shoes his neighbors choose to wear, and live among them with no difference."

"And you accuse Hershel of telling fairy tales?" Maurice said with a laugh.

"So," said Jascha, smiling at his brother, "how do you foresee the end of my fairy tale?"

"Oh, I know how *you* think it will end," said Maurice. "There won't be anyone left who still wears sandals."

"Precisely. In a few generations, three or four at the most, nobody will even remember who was a sandal-wearer and who wasn't."

"So," said Hershel, finally pushing back his chair and reaching for his hat, "we will have to see whose is the more improbable fairy tale."

"We will never see it," Jascha said.

They stepped out onto the quiet street, setting off in the direction of Sasha's apartment. The trolley cars weren't operating at this hour. Once again they would have to walk.

They hadn't gone three blocks from the Café Pripetshok when they heard, from down the darkened street, the sound of rowdy voices, speaking in Polish. University students, most probably.

Without a word, the four of them melted into the darkness of the first courtyard that presented itself. They certainly preferred not to have to test Sasha's proven talent for projecting the air of a Polish aristocrat.

They waited for the joyful voices of the students, about four or five in number, deep in their cups from the sound of them, to pass down the road and fade into the night, before they ventured out once more beneath the street lamps and continued toward home.

CHAPTER 19

MISHA OPINES

*I*t was madness to think that the new play would really be ready to open three weeks after Shavuos. But sometimes there is a strange convergence of different madnesses, and the result wreaks havoc on probabilities.

Opening night in the tailors' union hall was unprecedentedly well attended, and this was largely the work of one person, Aunt Frieda, who had gone from being the coach and manager of Sasha to being the publicist, as well as surrogate aunt, for the entire troupe. And in the art of publicity, Frieda Pomeranz had found, at last, the artiste she had long known herself to be.

She had always been a charming person, but now her charm had method. It had technique and discipline. Like everyone else connected that particular spring with the *mishpocheh,* Aunt Frieda, too, was *inspired.*

She had devoted herself these past few weeks to becoming acquainted with *le tout* Warsaw, and into every influential person's ear she had dropped a suggestive word, always remembering to insinuate that surely the ear's owner had already heard *something. . . .*

Aunt Frieda's nature could be at times—let's be frank: affection doesn't have to be sightless—just a little bit ridiculous. Her exuberance sometimes so overstepped itself that you wondered whether she was perhaps being a little bit tongue-in-cheek. But this spring, Aunt

Frieda handled herself with finesse. From start to finish, it was a virtuoso performance.

And as proof of her virtuosity, there, on opening night, sitting inconspicuously toward the front of the tailors' union hall (the fourth row, to be exact), was Misha Zaks, the cultural critic for *Nasz Przeglad*.

Misha generally had little use for Yiddish theater. His Polish-language newspaper appealed to a more sophisticated Jewish reader, middle-class and well on the way toward assimilation.

Misha himself—a small man, with a wisp of a mustache, a weak chin, and a nervously alert expression—would never be taken for a critic, except for the little bound notebook and pen that he kept discreetly in an inside coat pocket, and which he was furtively reaching for at this very moment. He had more the look of a timid furrier—or perhaps, even more strikingly, the look of the furry small things who had donated their pelts—than a critic.

But a critic he was, and a force with which to be reckoned. On the pages of *Nasz Przeglad*, Misha was anything but timid. There he raged indignantly, not only against the "artistes" themselves, but against the pack of driveling critics who worked for all the other Warsaw Jewish newspapers, whether in Yiddish or in Polish.

Three times a day, *shachris, mincha,* and *maariv,* another Jewish genius is proclaimed. The number of geniuses currently living in Warsaw is, according to the last census count, roughly double the number of its legal inhabitants.

Misha's domain was all of Warsaw's cultural life, but he devoted a large proportion of his columns to the theater, because he happened to be an ardent theater-lover. And here, too, Misha's timorous looks belied his tastes, for Misha loved theater that was full of risks, on the cutting edge of the avant-garde.

"Where are our Max Reinhardts?" he queried his readers.

So how did Misha Zaks come to be sitting in the fourth row of the tailors' union hall on opening night?

He had happened to be, only last week, in a restaurant, and had made the acquaintance there of a very cultured woman by the name of Frau Pomeranz. The way that this had come about was really quite remarkable, since Misha generally did not go out of his way to speak with strange women.

But there she was, by the most remarkable coincidence, sitting at the very next table, with a younger woman, both of them speaking fluent German with a word or two of the jargon sprinkled in every now and then. The younger woman, it turned out, was the daughter-in-law, only recently moved back with her husband from Hamburg. She was a handsome young woman, very well dressed, but stolid and conventional, with none of the flair and sparkle of the older woman, who was doing most of the talking. She was describing, with a tremendous amount of relish, a performance that she herself had witnessed, some years back, in Hamburg, of the immortal Rudolph Schildkraut in his legendary rendition of Shylock.

And so, although usually Misha would as soon willingly disturb his anonymity as he would go out and contact typhus, before he knew it he was sharing reminiscences of other great moments of German theater with this very cosmopolitan woman.

It was only as Frau Pomeranz was getting ready to leave that she had offered a few words about a new play that was in the making, a troupe of wildly talented young people, using the jargon but very influenced by German expressionism, surely Herr Zaks had heard *something.* . . .

As Aunt Frieda emerged from the revolving door of the restaurant, she gave her daughter-in-law a healthy nudge with an elbow, which made the younger woman wince, more with annoyance than with pain.

There's such a thing as mazel, but there's also such a thing as using your head.

The consequence of this wisdom was that now Misha Zaks sat in the fourth row of the tailors' union hall. And already, even before the lights had dimmed, he was scribbling furtively in his brown leather notebook.

Only Aunt Frieda noticed him, and she kept the observation to herself. Everybody was just a little bit on *shpilkes*, on pins and needles,

Sorela especially. The poor child was convinced she could remember nothing of her lines. This was the famous stage-fright of which Aunt Frieda had heard, and from which even the divine Sarah herself had suffered.

Better perhaps they shouldn't know that the mighty Misha Zaks sat out there, for all the world like a timid furrier.

Misha scrutinized the program, which was printed, he noted, on very inferior paper.

The Bilbul Art Theater presents
The Bridegroom
AN ORIGINAL PLAY
based on a story by Fraydel Sonnenberg

Fredericka Bodayda	*Sasha Sonnenberg*
Mayer Laybish, her father	*Aleksander Meisel*
Pesha Sima, her mother	*Rosalie Chernikov*
Elazar, her bridegroom	*Jerzy Ruppin*
The badchen	*Viktor Friedlander*
Shmulik, the town lunatic	*Mendel Goldstein*
The rabbis of Jerusalem	*Effrim Schoenfeld*
	Shimmy Sofer
	Ilya Berenson
Wedding guests	*Naomi Meyerson*
	Clara Gowinska
	Zygmunt Zeiten
	Zanvil Braun
	Dvasha Braun
	Helena Margolis
Director	*Hershel Blau*
Original music by	*Jascha Saunders*
Sets and lighting by	*Michal Pfefferberg*

The badchen? The rabbis of Jerusalem? Oy vay!

Misha had been led to expect a play that would break the ground wide open with the seismic force of modernism, the genius of German expressionism finally brought to the Yiddish stage.

That was what that woman had suggested, wasn't it?

Already Misha felt the first paragraph of his review forming itself.

We have waited many years for a play of the first rank to be produced by those who till the rocky field of Yiddish theater. Last night the Bilbul Art Theater presented an original play, *The Bridegroom*, and it looks as if we're going to have to wait a few years longer.

He would be certain to get in something about these miserable benches as well.

CHAPTER 20

AND OPINES AGAIN

*T*he article that Misha finally ended up writing the next morning for *Nasz Przeglad* was only the first of the five articles that he would devote to the play over the course of that summer and autumn.

And if you added in the number of times that he slipped mention of *The Bridegroom* into other contexts, well, then, the tally came up to maybe thirty or forty.

Part of the reason Misha kept returning to the play at the tailors' union hall was his own frustration at not being able entirely to put his finger on the source of the long-lingering effect it had produced in him.

It was true that all the elements of the play worked together in the way good theater must. The troupe performed with great passion and intensity, especially the young Sonnenberg and Friedlander. The stage direction was brilliant; the music and the lighting were also of the highest rank, serving to darken and deepen the play's gathering mood of doom. And yet, when all was said and done, were all these tricks of the theater, as susceptible to these as Misha confessed himself to be, still sufficient to explain the effect produced?

For weeks and weeks, Misha had found that he couldn't dislodge himself from the velvet grip of the play. He closed his eyes and saw the final eerie dance, the young mesmerized bride in the arms of a grinning Death, and heard the music, half Chasidic, half Schoenberg, blending in with the moans, until finally, imperceptibly, it had changed to nothing but moaning.

The play had at once exhilarated and depressed him, and it continued to do so all through that unusually warm Warsaw summer. The artistry was superb, and yet the net result of all this artistry had been to induce in Misha an overwhelming sense of life's futility.

> The drunken lift their cups to Life,
> To strange powers of unseeing and forgetting. . . .

Misha wasn't able to get these lyrics out from his head.

It was true that existence more than ever required just such a strange power of living in the moment and willfully ignoring.

Was it because Misha knew this truth that the play resonated within him as it did? How can a critic distinguish what is essential and timeless in a work of art from what is merely fleeting and of the moment? So Misha mused publicly in the pages of the *Nasz Przegląd.*

One thing Misha knew for certain was that he hadn't experienced an aesthetic response of such proportions since the summer of his fifteenth year, which had been spent prone in a hammock strung up between two trees on his parents' summer property, a book of Dostoevsky propped up before him. Then, too, his soul had been flooded by just this tragic sense of life. And this bit of personal history, Misha also shared with his readers.

> But I am no longer fifteen! And the work in question, despite its obvious merits, is not—let's be honest—*The Idiot* or *The Brothers Karamazov*! No! It is a rather simple tale, derived from the backward life of the shtetl, wrapped up in childish superstition and ignorance. . . .
>
> What an irony, that from such primitive materials should come the first genuinely authentic contribution the Yiddish theater has yet made to world drama.

And who in the world was this Fraydel Sonnenberg, credited in the program with the original story? Was she related to the young actress

Sasha Sonnenberg? At first it was almost impossible to get any information about her out of the members of the troupe.

Finally, Frieda—she was now Frieda to Misha, and not Frau Pomeranz—told him that, yes, Fraydel had been Sasha's sister and that she had died under conditions that Frieda would only describe as tragic.

The unspoken tragedy would, of course, have made for excellent publicity, but such practical concerns were, in the circumstances, unthinkable. In any case, they hardly seemed needed. The mystique surrounding the Bilbul Art Theater continued to mount throughout that hot Warsaw summer.

By now Misha knew all about Frieda's connection with the *mishpocheh.* He had more than forgiven her her little subterfuge. He was really quite ready to forgive Frieda Pomeranz everything. What a woman she was, with her beguiling wiles and smiles—a person larger than life itself, just like Misha's first love, the theater. Misha, who had never married, sometimes wondered how it might have been had . . . Ech, what was the use of such thinking?

Misha Zaks's personal musings on the strange power of *The Bridegroom* in the pages of the *Nasz Przeglad* certainly contributed their share to what happened to the *mishpocheh* over the course of that warm, wilting summer. But not even Misha flattered himself that he alone was responsible.

The pack of critics from Warsaw's other nine Jewish newspapers, both Yiddish and Polish, had, one by one, over the course of the summer, discovered the Bilbulniks for themselves.

"So yet another Columbus is discovering America," was the way Aunt Frieda put it, clipping out one more rave.

By the time Rosh Hashanah rolled around, in late September, the days finally growing a little crisper, almost all of the non-Jewish Warsaw papers, with the exception of those that were virulently anti-Semitic, had written up something about *The Bridegroom* as well. And once this happened, then a few Gentiles themselves began coming by the tailors' union hall, mostly those who belonged to the more artistic and Bohemian circle.

All through that autumn and winter, there were rumors flying through Jewish Warsaw that the legendary Russian-born impresario, *he* whose name could only be whispered with the awed hush of the once pious, had himself been sighted in Warsaw: disappearing into the recesses of a Rolls-Royce limousine, into the gilded aviarylike elevator at the Astoria Hotel. Here, there, everywhere, his elegant, diminutive figure was reportedly spotted, only always disappearing, never apprehended face to face. What else could have brought the impresario nonpareil, the very framer of the current sensibility of Europe, *here*, argued Jewish Warsaw, if not our very own Bilbul Art Theater? Perhaps, the Jews speculated, he has plans to take the troupe to Paris? Some argued the case for Berlin, but they were drowned out by the majority, who maintained that it must surely be Paris the great man had in mind. A visionary of his stature would see the dramatic validity of presenting the first authentic masterpiece of the Yiddish stage (only to quote what even some Gentile newspapers had said) to audiences that had themselves beheld the divine Sarah, as their grandparents had Rachel. Even non-Jewish Warsaw gave a degree of credence to the fantastic rumors making the rounds and felt itself appropriately impressed, even a little bit proud. The Gentiles who now came to see the play were no longer restricted to the more outré artistic class. Even a few aristocratic young people were spotted, now and again, on the hard wooden benches of the tailors' union hall.

Not all of these Gentiles, of course, understood Yiddish. And even among those who did, it was rare for them to respond as, say, Misha Zaks of the *Nasz Przeglad* had. Why should they, after all?

"When the bride can't dance," said Aunt Frieda, shrugging, "she complains that the musicians can't play."

But for the Jews in the audience, no matter how enlightened and assimilated, the story of the young bride meeting her doom on the very night of her wedding cast a long shadow of meaning. So that, by the time Chanukah came around that year, the trolley-car conductors had simply taken to calling out the stop before the tailors' union hall—to which Hershel superstitiously clung, refusing to move to a proper theater—as *"The Bridegroom."*

Misha Zaks was altogether right. Who can tell what is timeless, and what is merely of the moment?

And who, in the moment, really cares?

The fact was that this moment had given the young Bilbulniks the theatrical triumph of their lives.

CHAPTER 21

SECOND AVENUE
IS CALLING

*H*ershel had received a highly flattering letter last week from the legendary Maurice Schwartz, the great Yiddish American actor who had been struggling for years, amidst the sentimental *shmalzgrub,* or tub of fat, on Second Avenue, to offer Yiddish audiences a theater at once of substance and delicacy. Mr. Schwartz had invited the Bilbulniks to bring their great "international triumph," *The Bridegroom*, to his own stage, the Yiddish Art Theater.

You will find here, in this golden land, a great hunger for the Yiddish theater, a hunger that would as soon gorge, I don't deny it, on all sorts of *chazerei* as on the choice bits, but, then, who can you blame for that, the starved masses or the cooks . . . ?

I would myself be tempted to make the journey now to Warsaw, for the sole purpose of seeing for myself the play that is on everyone's lips, were I not bound hand and foot to my obligations here in New York City, where I am in the midst of a season that has been called by many magnificent, although I hesitate to use such a word in addressing you. . . .

And so, as they say, since Mohammad, *l'havdil,* can't come to the mountain, perhaps the mountain would be so kind as to take an ocean liner and come to Mohammad? Especially since the terms that I can offer will not, I think I can safely say, be insulting to even so lofty a mountain as the Bilbul Art Theater. . . .

One thing for certain, I can promise you, my esteemed fellow artist, and I know that this will mean more to you than all the haggling over dollars and cents. You will have here audiences who will cheer you nightly, until they are so hoarse that they will only be able to whisper your praises the next morning. . . .

Frankly, audiences who cheered nightly were nothing new to Hershel and the Bilbulniks. But audiences cheering in English!

Yet not everybody in the *mishpocheh* jumped at the chance to go to America. Rosalie, in particular, seemed to find very little to excite herself over in the idea of taking *The Bridegroom* to Second Avenue. For one thing, she didn't like to leave Feliks, and Feliks couldn't be budged from Warsaw. For another, she was completely sick of *The Bridegroom*, which had been running for close to a year now.

"Enough is enough. You can have too much of anything, even of blintzes."

Rosalie's nagging set off the internal *kvetch* inside Hershel himself. What artist doesn't have such a *kvetch*, who permanently resides in his head, and remains unimpressed with any amount of success? "Okay, not so bad *this time*. But let's see what you're capable of *next*."

Hershel didn't want, God forbid, *The Bridegroom* to be the last good thing he ever did.

Frankly, the question of "the next play" was more than a little bit daunting. The *mishpocheh* was constantly tossing ideas for "the next play" around, but nothing had surfaced yet as absolutely right. So much would be expected this time. A failure would be so much more a failure lit up in the glare of the spotlight. How different it had been when they had enjoyed the great luxury of being nobodies with nothing to lose.

Could Hershel even hope for a repeat of that singular strangeness that had gone into the making of *The Bridegroom*? Everything had happened so naturally and in so unforced a way as to seem almost inevitable, as if there were nothing at all to wonder about—that suddenly his limbs had become porous with light and he had flown without fear.

Well, of course, Jascha Saunders had required a little prodding. But then he, too, had been drawn in, so much so as to write music that went against all he believed. The score Jascha had written for *The Bridegroom*, whether or not the composer approved of it, was beginning to make his name. He even had a few private students of his own now.

Who would deny that without the brilliant score of Jascha Saunders *The Bridegroom* would not have been *The Bridegroom*? Yet it was highly doubtful that Hershel would ever be able to entice Jascha back into collaboration. Highly doubtful? It was a mathematical impossibility! Even before this last, sad business—Hershel couldn't think about Jascha's betrayal without a terrible sense of grieving—Jascha had taken tremendous pains to distance himself from his music for the Yiddish theater.

That collaboration with Jascha Saunders had meant everything to Hershel. It had been like the hidden hand, holding him up in his ascension. How could he hope to reproduce anything like *The Bridegroom* without Saunders?

And why, after all, rush things? Why not, rather, take *The Bridegroom* on the road—Vilna, Odessa, maybe London's Whitechapel? And then on to Second Avenue and the wonders of Manhattan!

Rosalie was right, of course. Sooner or later, the *mishpocheh* would have to begin work on "the next play." But for the moment, nobody really seemed to want anything else from them but *The Bridegroom*. Maurice Schwartz himself wanted *The Bridegroom*! No, the moment was not yet over.

Who would ever have dreamt that Hershel would one day be facing such decisions as these, trying to cope with the problems that too great a success had created? Had Hershel time, within the exigencies of this moment, for indulging in retrospection, he would most certainly have regarded that bygone obscurity with a bit of wistful longing. But he had known, even when he had been a little boy dancing among the Chasidim, that you can't fly, even among the most obscure of the Chasidic sects, and then hope to go on with things as they once had been.

CHAPTER 22

MADAME ZUTA AND
THE FUTURE

*M*aurice and Sasha sat alone in the back room of the Pripetshok, in the midst of the tables that had been crowded together and had just been vacated by the rest of the *mishpocheh.*

They had all gone rushing off, at the suggestion of Rosalie, who hadn't even meant it seriously, to consult Madame Zuta, a Gypsy employed at a restaurant in the old town called The Gypsy Cauldron.

"She's a Gypsy like my grandmother Zeitel is a Gypsy. She's been there nightly for at least the past three years. What kind of a Gypsy is that to show up regularly for work? Still, she's told me plenty of things that my grandmother Zeitel could never have told me. You know, she told me years ago about Feliks." Here Rosalie huddled down into the form of an old shifty-eyed crone and croaked out: " 'I see true love is waiting a little way down the road for you.' "

"Did she mention this true love by name?" Mendel asked, grinning widely.

"If she had, genius, would I have wasted my time with all those others? So, of course, you're going to ask me how I know it was Feliks that Madame Zuta predicted. For one thing, she told me that this true love of mine would appear from the outside the most unlikely of all candidates for the role of Mr. Don Juan. Now, isn't that as good as calling Feliks by name?"

"It's good enough for me," said Mendel. "Come on, Hershel, let's go ask Madame Zuta to tell us our future."

"Wait a minute," said Maurice. "Don't you see the problem here?"

"What? Don't tell me you're going to say it's forbidden by the Torah?"

"God forbid I should say such a thing. No, my problem is more metaphysical."

"How did I know that?" Mendel asked, throwing his hands up in melodramatic despair.

"If Madame Zuta sees the future, then how can going to her help any? The future will happen no matter what."

"But maybe only because we go to Madame Zuta!" said Mendel, his malleable monkey-face screwed up into triumph. "So, Spinoza, answer me that one!"

"I wouldn't even attempt it," Maurice said, laughing. They were all on their feet now, all except for Sasha and Maurice.

"Aren't you coming, *tsatskeleh?*" Rosalie asked. "Really, I promise you a good show." Rosalie grabbed Sasha's hand and peered down into her palm. "Hmmmm, so interesting," she croaked, at the same time holding up one of her hands and rubbing her thumb against her other fingers.

"Is true love also waiting down the road for Sasha?" Mendel whispered, peering down at the palm with Rosalie.

"So what else should be waiting for our Sasha?" Rosalie answered. "Only I think it's getting a little bit tired waiting. I think its feet are beginning to ache almost as much as its pining heart."

Sasha remained unmoved, gesturing with her hand for them to leave her.

"Maurice is right for once," she said. "The future will happen without our trying to see it. What's the sense in spoiling the suspense?"

So the rest had left, taking all the commotion with them, and Maurice and Sasha remained sitting alone together in the Pripetshok's back room.

This room had, by an unspoken rule, become more or less reserved for the celebrated troupe, of whom the Pripetshok's proprietors, Zanvil and Dvasha Braun, were parentally proud. They had put up for years with the raucousness and penury, and now were entitled to *shep* a little *naches,* derive a little prideful pleasure (in addition to making occasional appearances as "wedding guests" in the play).

The Brauns had even created a special dish in honor of Sasha, the famous Blintzes Sasha. It was an extravagant concoction, the thin pancakes filled with cherries that had been marinated in kirsch, and on top of this a brandied sauce that would be ignited at the table in a spectacle of flaming blue that always brought applause.

Sasha was forever ordering Blintzes Sasha, and Maurice hoped with all his heart that she would get disgustingly fat. Maybe if she waddled like a duck instead of loping in that maddening way he would be granted some peace yet in this lifetime. But so far Blintzes Sasha had added no discernible kilos to any part of her, with the exception of her bulging ego.

This ego had plenty more than blintzes on which to gorge these days. The *mishpocheh,* of course, was philosophically opposed to the whole idea of a star, but who listened to philosophy? All of Jewish Warsaw was in love with Sasha. In the public's mind, she was completely identified with her role as the doomed bride, even though off the stage she—so unlike the great actress Rachel, so unlike the divine Sarah— had no interest in perpetuating the aura of tragedy.

Sarah Bernhardt used to sleep in her coffin. Rachel went even further and actually died a tragic death at the age of thirty-eight—from consumption, no less. But Sasha took a much more pragmatic attitude toward her art. What, after all, was the use of being young and famous if you didn't go out and enjoy?

Lately, she had even been forsaking the *mishpocheh* for other company, for what Jewish Warsaw called the *goldeneh yugnt,* the gilded youth. These were the young men who actually had some superfluous cash in their pockets, and too often they spent it on Sasha, taking her off to the posher restaurants and cabarets, the *kleinkunst* theaters, which served up a mixture of song and dance and sketches, none of it in the least worthy of her, so far as Maurice was concerned.

Or, even more to her liking, and less to his, she'd go off dancing.

Dancing had become a regular passion with her. She was shamelessly in love with the tango. She would almost rather tango than tease, though—how lucky for her—the world was so designed that she didn't ever have to choose between the two. Men without souls got to hold her and dip her backward, to whirl her about until she was dizzy and she fell against them laughing. And then these gilded *golemim* went on with the rest of their lives, as if there could be more that was worth experiencing after this.

She was developing all sorts of vices in the company of these bastards. She would drink champagne all the time if she could. It was like drinking the stars, she announced. When she drank champagne, she insisted, it didn't at all go to her head, no matter how much she drank. What happened instead—and to hear Sasha describe it, it was almost a religious experience—was that the people around her started acting more and more tipsy the more *she* drank.

Maurice, who happened to tango quite as well as any one of those *goldeneh yugnt,* had never yet once danced with Sasha. In exactly six more weeks, he would take those accursed exams for the university in which everyone but he was certain that his true future lay. If, against all odds, he managed to gain admittance, at the celebratory party that would be his he would demand a tango from Sasha. It was, at this point, the only good reason he could come up with for being granted admission to the university.

The teachers at his school, whose hopes for him oppressed him no end, kept giving him thumps on his back, hearty words of encouragement: "Unless they have reduced the quota for Jews to the null set, then you will surely be admitted."

Maurice had come to regard it all as a sick joke. The exam itself would be an ordeal that would last for five solid days—including the dreaded oral examination, delivered by a firing squad of three. Maurice had heard war tales about the sorts of questions they asked the Jewish students who came before them. Albert Frankel, known as gifted in mathematics, had been asked last year, during his oral examination, to solve a problem he later found out has never been solved. In fact, the professor who had posed the question had several doctoral students working on it.

Still, although Frankel—who happened to be a good friend of Maurice's—had been denied admission, another mutual friend of theirs, Josef Selig, had been accepted. So there was just enough hope to provoke anguish. If Maurice was really serious about that tango, then he ought to be home at this very moment, prepping himself like crazy. It was madness to be sitting here at all, exposing himself to yet more heartbreak—couldn't he ever get enough?—when it was his head that he ought to be breaking.

But everything, from Spinoza to Sasha with the rest of the world thrown in between, had conspired to make a committed fatalist of Maurice. So he continued to sit there in the back room of the Pripetshok, the noises from the front, where the more serious drinking took place, intruding every time Zanvil or Dvasha opened the door on the way to or from the kitchen, which was right off of this room.

Otherwise, it was quiet. Sasha was thinking, or maybe even brooding, which seemed strange. Not, of course, that Sasha was a non-thinking person. Maurice, who studied Sasha with even greater application than he did Spinoza, never mistook for frivolity her determination to grab at life with such fierceness. Sasha was far from frivolous. She had greater depths than anyone but he—he was certain of this—suspected. People, especially men—who were almost always, Maurice had come to the conclusion, dolts—have such a deluded tendency to deprive beautiful women of any dimensions that go beyond gawking observation.

It wasn't, of course, that Maurice didn't gawk, or at least didn't long to gawk. If she had let him—if she hadn't cast her looks of venom over him whenever she met his glance—he would have feasted his eyes on her with abandon. Perhaps there were more beautiful women in Warsaw, but there was no one at whom he would rather stare, no one whose changing expressions so unfailingly moved him, even while he remained totally in the dark as to what lay behind.

No matter how much he studied her, she continued to confound

him. Night after night, she gave herself entirely over to that play that
had transformed them all and for which she was the one most directly
responsible, and then she went off to guzzle champagne with soulless
idiots. Maurice wasn't even able to say how Sasha really felt about her
spectacular success, other than that she seemed glad for the opportuni-
ties for high living it provided. Sasha, Sasha. Maurice suspected that
she, too, had something like his own sickness under the rug.

In any case, Maurice was more than disposed to take everything
that Sasha said with the utmost seriousness, even if it had only been
said in the spirit of contradiction. For example, a few weeks ago,
Maurice, in the course of arguing a point of philosophy with
Aleksander Meisel, had declared that everything in the world connects,
a fundamental axiom of Spinoza's. All of a sudden, Sasha, who Maurice
had thought wasn't even listening, had whirled around and almost
hissed at him, the contempt in her voice hitting him like a knock in
the head, *"Nothing connects!"*

And would you believe that ever since then Maurice had been pondering these words? A few times he had been on the point of ques-
tioning her about her meaning, though he had backed off before the
vastness of the vehemence he so well knew could be unleashed.

He had never inspired such a passion of hatred before, at least not
so he was aware. With Sasha, there was no chance of remaining ignorant. Why she so disliked him he had no idea. He knew, of course, that
she considered him conceited. Perhaps he once had been as arrogant as
she persisted in thinking him. But how much of his former vanity
could have survived the ordeal of loving that woman?

Maurice also knew that Sasha had suffered for Jasha as Maurice continued to suffer for her. It hadn't really bothered him so much. He had
taken some comfort in the fact that at least it was in the family. Sasha,
however, had long ago gotten over *her* infatuation. She, who had no desire to play even a leading tragic role off of the stage, was even less enthusiastic about settling for this kind of minor comic part. The glacial
genius, encased in his tomb of icy solitude, whom she would someday
melt away with her volcanic love: that was the image that she had more

or less had in mind. She wasn't going to waste her passion on a Jascha who was in love with a Katya who was in love with a Jascha.

The great secret had come out, right around Chanukah-time. Katya's mother had given the girl, at least according to the rumors, a difficult time, but Professor Konstancze was prepared to accept Jascha as a son-in-law, even without the benefit of a conversion.

Nonetheless, in order to placate Katya's mother, and because he himself didn't really care one way or the other, Jascha had undergone a formal conversion to Catholicism. The wedding of Jascha and Katya was planned for this coming autumn, to be held in the great cathedral that stood on the square in the old town.

This was one of the many reasons Hershel was so anxious to be off on tour as soon as possible. He had no desire to be here in the autumn, no desire to attend the magnificent wedding in the beautiful medieval cathedral. Of all of them, including even the members of Jascha's own family, it was Hershel who seemed to take Jascha's conversion the hardest. For the life of him, the director couldn't understand how a man who had written the music that Saunders had for *The Bridegroom* could be capable of such treachery: yes, that was how Hershel thought of it, and it had seemed almost to break his heart.

The elder Saunderses had, following the Orthodox tradition, sat *shiva* for their son, as had Henya, who had caved in, as always, before her father's awesome authority. But not Maurice. Not even his father's terrifying severity could induce him to tear his clothes as if his brother had died, and to sit on the floor for the seven days of formal mourning. He had fled the house, staying away for the entire week, sleeping on the floor of Jascha's garret room. More than anything, he had been unable to endure the sight of the grim satisfaction that had seemed to him to underlie his father's observance of the rituals of mourning. The father's dire predictions for his firstborn had come to pass.

All in all, his brother's apostasy had bothered Maurice much less than he would have thought. Jascha, basking in the love of the beautiful flute-playing Katya, seemed happy for the first time in his adult life. And Katya was a fantastic girl. How could Maurice not love someone who so clearly loved his brother? It wasn't as if Jascha had really abandoned his true religion. His religion had always been, and still remained, music.

Maurice, his eyes ever trained on Sasha, had seen how, in the past, Sasha's eyes had kept registering Jascha's entrances and exits. But now that Jascha had executed, in a certain sense, his final exit, Sasha had simply looked away, dry-eyed and unmoved. And Maurice, watching, had learned more about Sasha from this than from anything else.

He, unfortunately, was far more at one with the tragic sense of life than was she, acclaimed tragic actress though she was. For here he was, still faithfully courting heartbreak.

It was a beautiful night in the first week of April. It had been a particularly severe winter, but now the days were regaining their strength, like a recovering invalid, and tonight Sasha was wearing a soft and summery sort of dress, a vivid blue that gave her long gray eyes an overtone of blueness that was just like the shimmery sea.

Maurice liked her best in just these sorts of dresses, though he had to admit that she was irresistible, too, in the trousers that she had recently taken to wearing, causing a commotion she relished. What a sensation Sasha created, loping down Jewish Leszno Street in her trousers.

Maurice, giving voice to that unfortunate sense of the tragic that he was forced to own, sighed deeply. Sasha looked up from her thoughts, as if startled to find him there still.

"Why didn't you go off with the others, to Rosalie's Gypsy?" she asked him, stubbing out her cigarette as she spoke. The *goldeneh yugnt* kept her supplied with expensive American-made cigarettes.

"It's foolishness," he said.

"Yes, it is," she answered, surprisingly tame, and then went back to her own thoughts.

"You want to know something?" she suddenly said. "I once almost ran away with the Gypsies."

"It doesn't surprise me."

"No? Why not?"

"You're the same girl who came to an audition all prepared to recite

Shakespeare and instead told a story about a bride and a badchen. Why should anything about you surprise me?"

Something happened now that gave the lie completely to Maurice's words. Sasha smiled at Maurice. It left him speechless.

"It was with that sister that I was going to run away with the Gypsies."

"With Fraydel?"

"With Fraydel. She had already begun to learn their language. Romani, it's called. She had a theory that perhaps the Gypsies had descended from the ancient Egyptians."

"Why the Egyptians?"

"They know magic."

Maurice nodded.

"Why not?" he said.

"Why not?" Sasha answered him back, and then returned to her strangely pensive pose.

"I've wished so many times that we really had run off with the Gypsies," she suddenly said, so softly that for a moment Maurice wondered whether he had only imagined it.

Zanvil, carrying a tray of dirty plates, passed through the room, disappearing into the kitchen. Then it was quiet again, quieter than it had ever seemed before in the world. Maurice sat and pondered Sasha's strange words.

"She took her own life. She drowned herself in the river."

She was staring at him, and he stared back into her long gray eyes, overlaid with their shimmering sea-blueness, and it was hard to shake off the sense that this moment wasn't happening at all.

"She could have been anything, my sister Fraydel. She could pull knowledge from out of the air, even there in the shtetl. You don't know what it was like there"—her voice suddenly became fierce—"especially for a girl like Fraydel. Fraydel, Fraydel, *da meshuggena* . . ."

Sasha's sobs cut short her sentence.

When Maurice, who was also crying, just a little, reached out his arms to her, she collapsed into them and clung, clutching him, so that, for the first time in his life, Maurice Saunders forgot to think.

The two of them were still sitting there when the rest of the *mishpocheh* came trooping back into the Pripetshok after midnight.

"Did you miss something!" Mendel announced. "A fat little *yenta* in a greasy turban, about as exotic as a bowl of *lukshun!*"

The hilarity swirled around the two, one Bilbulnik after another taking turns impersonating the fortune-teller, elaborating on her predictions, which, by the way, had been very encouraging in terms of finances and romance—the two issues on which she had been pressed— though a little vague on the specifics, so that Mendel argued that Madame Zuta had definitely foretold that they were off to the provinces, and Rosalie swore it was just the opposite.

But even as she kidded, Rosalie took in how the two of them, Sasha and Maurice, sat with almost the same dazed expression on their flushed faces, so that it was really almost comical to contemplate them.

And she saw, too, how every once in a while they shot quick little glances at one another, so that Rosalie knew everything.

"So . . . finally!" Rosalie congratulated herself. "Finally, they pull out a chair!"

She was referring to a Yiddish expression that she liked and found many occasions for using, even though it wasn't in the least off-color: *Ven mazel kumt, shtelt im a shtul.* When mazel comes, pull up a chair for it.

PART IV

Vilna, Poland;
Vilna, Lithuania

$\mathcal{T}$*he tailor's apprentice, wishing to provoke the disdainful princess, did not address himself to her but to her lady-in-waiting, declaring that he had a story about which he desired her opinion.*

"Once upon a time," he began, "there were three friends who lived in a village. One was a woodcarver, the other a tailor, and the third a teacher. Because the village was too small to provide much work, the three decided to seek their fortunes in the greater world.

"They set out, and by nightfall they had arrived in a great forest. Fearing wild animals, they agreed that each of them would stand guard for two hours while the other two slept.

"The first watch fell to the woodcarver. He soon grew bored and looked around for something with which he could whittle away the empty hours. His eyes fell on a log, which he set about carving into the statue of a woman. At the end of the two hours, the wooden form of a beautiful woman sat on the ground, and the woodcarver woke the tailor.

"The tailor, too, cast his eye about for some way to shorten the stretching hours and soon noticed the wooden woman. Producing his shears, threaded needle, and cloth, he set about stitching together some clothes for the statue. At the end of his two hours, the wooden woman was all dolled up, and the tailor woke up the teacher.

"The teacher, too, looked about for something to enliven the silent hours, and immediately noticed the beautiful, fashionable woman. He tried to engage her *in conversation, but she made no reply. Feeling that it was a shame for so exquisite a creature to have nothing to say, he decided that he must teach her. And before the two hours were up, the teacher, through skill and patience, had instilled the power of speech.*

"*When the woodcarver and tailor awoke, they found their companion speaking with a beautiful, elegantly dressed woman. They soon recognized their own handiwork and wanted the woman for themselves.*

"*'I am the one who formed her from a log,' said the woodcarver. 'She belongs to me.'*

"*'What?' yelled the tailor. 'When I found her, she was a naked piece of wood. Now she is the very model of style, so she belongs to me.'*

"*'I gave her the gift of speech,' argued the teacher, 'without which she would have remained just a beautiful dummy in fancy clothes. She's mine.'*

"*So," concluded the boy, with a smile to the lady-in-waiting, "what is your opinion? To whom does this wonderful woman belong?"*

The lady-in-waiting was at a loss, but the princess quickly put in her two kopeks' worth.

"*Of course she belongs to the man who made her talk. He made her into a person."*

And the princess bestowed upon the boy one of the rarest treasures of the kingdom: her smile.

There were servants posted at the door, waiting to hear if the princess should be interested enough to speak. But because this particular suitor was lowborn and uneducated, they harbored no expectations for him. They stood at the door, barely paying attention, making foolish jokes amongst themselves, and they didn't hear that the princess had been drawn into conversation. Assuming that he hadn't succeeded where his social betters had failed, they marched the young unfortunate off to his doom.

—To be continued

CHAPTER 23

A DRUNKARD'S DANCE

*E*ven after such weeks as these had been, the Bilbulniks could never have anticipated what awaited them in Vilna.

These had been days of living at such a pitch of intensity—a feast of experience, seasoned with excitement, noise, motion, commotion, even the sharp, sharp pungency of danger. For each of them, ordinary life would have seemed ever after just a little bit bland and dry.

It was nearing the end of August. The countryside they traveled was ripe and golden, lush with the sweet heaviness of harvest. Rosalie, who hadn't been acting herself for several weeks now, would suddenly become inexplicably weepy at scenes of Mother Nature doing what it is she does, the melons and apples and pears sweetening under the sun, the peasants singing in the fields as they reaped.

"So beautiful," she'd sigh.

"Just like Kletchava," she'd murmur, meaning the shtetl that she had fled as if from the cholera, but which she now mentioned as if its name were blessed.

And Sasha would glance at her friend and shrug. Perhaps it was the absence of Feliks that was making Rosalie go suddenly soft in the head.

Since the middle of June, the Bilbul Art Theater had been on the road, never staying for more than two or three nights at any one place, traveling the width and breadth of Poland.

They had thought themselves well celebrated in Warsaw. But Warsaw, they now found, had been a chilly lover compared with the ardor of the provinces. My God, but these provincials knew how to receive the stars!

You would have thought that, with all the drama being mounted on the greater stage of the world—the saber-rattling and fiery words, the ultimata and counter-ultimata—you would have thought that the make-believe of a mere pack of players would have been the very last thing that Jewish audiences had on their minds.

But, strangely, the exact opposite was the case. No matter what the madness screamed out by the headlines of the day, the audience was there to pack the theater that night. They waited, breathless with anticipation, and then hung on every word and gesture, a gift of attention that still arrived each time to startle those on the stage with the generosity of its love.

For many who held their breath out there in the dark audience, it was the first taste ever of the forbidden fruit of theater. Some came to the playhouse in a mood of Purim merrymaking, whereas others were as somber as on the most solemn of Jewish fast-days.

Yeshiva boys, in Brest-Litovsk and Grodno, in Łódź and Pinsk, risked the wrath of the Presence, not to speak of their rebbes, to sneak into the darkened playhouse. Sometimes even a rebbe or two was there, ostensibly so that he might better know how to warn his students against the pagan temptations. But the rebbe, too, laughed out loud at the antics of Rosalie and Mendel and wept at the final scene.

The fame of the Bilbul Art Theater had gone before them. Wherever they went, there were hordes of admirers to greet them. The troupe would ride into the railroad station and find almost the entire town, with the exception of the religious fanatics, turned out to welcome them, with flowers for the actresses, flowery words for one and all.

In Lemberg—Sasha's very own Lemberg, where her mamma used to go to buy up this and that so that she could then sell it to the women of Shluftchev—the crowd had been so enthusiastic that the men had lifted the actors onto their own backs and thus borne them in triumph to their hotel. In the case of Mendel, it had been a woman—a solid mountain of a woman, over six feet tall and wearing men's boots—who had hoisted him off, as he screamed for dear life. He had never, so he told his friends later that night, been so terrified in all his life.

"I didn't know whether it was a flesh-and-blood female or a succubus that was carrying me off to beyond the Mountains of Darkness. I kept trying to remember some special blessing to ward off a demon, but all I could think of was that one about a wild dog. Thank God it worked!"

In place after place, in big famous cities like Kraków and Białystock, or towns that Sasha had hardly even heard of before, they turned out to cheer the arriving players. The theater in some of these smaller places was sometimes little more than a barn. It didn't matter. The Bilbulniks were used to putting up with less-than-ideal conditions, and the response of the audiences more than compensated. The lights came on after the final scene, and still the audience sat there stunned, sometimes sobbing as if on Yom Kippur.

After the performance, the leading citizens of the town would take it upon themselves to entertain the players. The whole troupe would be invited back to whichever home was considered the finest, or, if it was a city, to a restaurant.

What a collection of characters Sasha had been treated to at these gatherings. However cramped the external circumstances of a person's life may be, there's no relationship to how much space his inner being occupies.

There were old-time amateur actors—some whose only claim to fame was the yearly Purimspiels—but who were yet so full of themselves you would think that maybe Boris Tomashchevsky had been their understudy.

And then, of course, there were the ladies' men. If only Sasha could have had as many years added onto her life as the lines she had been offered over the course of this summer. She collected at least one proposal of marriage at almost every stop they made.

In his hotel room in Lublin, early in the morning, Hershel had been visited by a pious-looking man in a caftan and beard. He turned out to be a marriage broker, representing a prominent widower who had been in the front row the night before and by this morning had the terms of his offer to Sasha all ready and official.

Mendel, looking over the papers, asked Hershel to find out if the prosperous widower would maybe agree to take Mendel instead.

In Warsaw, Rosalie would have been the life of the party along with Sasha, but being on the road had put her out of sorts. She was, by turns, sentimental and sullen. More often than not, she skipped the parties altogether and went to sleep immediately after the show.

And she complained, she complained. She couldn't sleep in the strange beds, the strange food had upset her system, she was sick to death of *The Bridegroom*, she missed Feliks.

Sasha missed Maurice, too, at least every once in a while, when, with a sudden spasm of remorse, she would picture him languishing— she *always* pictured him languishing—alone in Warsaw, missing her to distraction, while he awaited the results of the accursed exams.

Poor Maurice. She'd make it up to him when she got back.

But until then she wished with all her heart that they could travel to the ends of the world and back again. As it was, they were only going as far as Vilna. Their plans for Second Avenue had fallen through, at least for now. Not even the legendary Maurice Schwartz had been able to pull all the diplomatic strings required for the whole troupe to cross the ocean at this time. Still, Sasha had great hopes and worked diligently on her English, making sure to see every American movie that crossed her path.

The life of a vagabond star couldn't have suited her better. The constant stream of new sights and new faces, always replenished: she couldn't have found it more to her liking. Everybody everywhere was touched by the glimmer of mania this summer. It was as if Sasha had drunk too much champagne—far, far too much champagne—enough so that all of Poland was tilting and reeling, dancing a drunkard's dance.

It wasn't just the celebrated Bilbulniks who were living life at an unprecedented pitch of intensity this summer. Poland itself had been stirred up, so that it became something more than itself, was roused into a posture of heroic proportions. Everywhere you looked there were Polish flags flying, and the music of Chopin, which all Poles agreed was the purest expression of the Polish soul, poured out of loudspeakers onto public squares.

What was going on? Not just the triumphant tour of the Bilbul Art Theater, as it happened. The spotlight of the world was focused on Poland, and Poland was, at least for the moment, *inspired.*

The villain in Berlin, whom all the world leaders had tried to placate with gifts of first this piece of Europe and then that, was now carrying on about Danzig/Gdańsk and the Polish Corridor. And in response, Poland—thrice-partitioned and threatened again—was united as never before, exploding into a frenzied performance of nationalism and pride.

Even the Jews, inhabiting those much-despised narrow margins, were swept along by their country's proud spirit of defiance. From the far right to the far left, Jews were everywhere pronouncing the great word of the moment, "honor," and declaring their readiness to spill their blood for Poland.

"We in Poland do not accept the concept of peace at any price," Foreign Minister Beck had declared. "There is only one thing in the life of men, nations, and states that is without price, and that is honor."

Such words turned even the most phlegmatic of souls into ardent patriots. And those who were already patriotic became certifiably crazy.

A partial mobilization had been called, and everywhere the Bilbulniks traveled they saw great long convoys of military trucks.

And in the midst of all of this, strange to say, audiences still found the time to wax ecstatic over the arrival of the Bilbul Art Theater and to sit in raptured silence while the players acted out the story of the dazed and beautiful bride.

Who knows? Maybe the blurring of the lines around the real, the unthinkable, made the make-believe of mere actors seem suddenly more significant. The world had gone marvelous and strange, so that all the rules for the suspension of disbelief had themselves been suspended.

The Bilbulniks themselves, being people of the theater, didn't, of course, find it in the least remarkable that so much excitement should swirl around them, even in such times as these. What artist ever questions the attention he gets? But it was remarkable. It was more than remarkable.

And also in the midst of all this—Jascha would have been amused: can *nothing* pierce the artistic solipsism?—Hershel still found the time to agonize over "the next play."

He had seen the shadow of an idea rising up before him. It was all too vague yet to share with the others, he was afraid even a whisper would make the tentative thing take flight, but it was there, the obscured shape, slowly taking on a little substance, a shade here and there of color, a splash of light.

And Hershel, ever the patient lover, waited.

And also in the midst of all this—in fact, it was on the train riding into Vilna, the fabled city—a radiant Rosalie, looking almost bashful, announced to the *mishpocheh* what they perhaps should all have already guessed.

Rosalie was pregnant.

CHAPTER 24

VOICES THROUGH
A WINDOW

*I*t was a far quieter and more dignified welcome they received in the railroad station at Vilna than the tumultuous greeting to which they had become accustomed over the course of the summer.

There was no crowd of breathless admirers waiting to embrace the stars, to gush and to kvell. Only a dignified little group waited on the platform, a few of the leading lights of Vilna's cultural life, speaking in the slightly lisping accent of the Litvak, the Lithuanian Jew. Just as a Litvak is not a Galitzianer, so Vilna was not a Lemberg, to be overly impressed with whomever.

Vilna gave off the air of a city that had been sleeping through the centuries. There wasn't the sense of inexhaustible life contained in Sasha's own beloved Warsaw. For Sasha, to be crushed in among the throngs of humanity that moved as one through the streets of Jewish Warsaw—that was life as she wanted to live it.

Vilna, in comparison, looked drowsy and decorous. Decorous it was. But drowsy? Hardly. Vilna—Jewish Vilna—the "Jerusalem of Europe," was legendary for its scholars, whether yeshiva students or committed secularists. Some of the most sophisticated minds in all of Europe would be in the audience that night. It wasn't by accident that Hershel had planned that Vilna would be the last stop on their tour before they returned to Warsaw. Their appearance there would be—at least that was the hope—a sort of culmination to all their triumphs.

The little bunch of dignitaries waiting on the platform may have presented the very picture of decorum, but the troupe which disembarked was anything but. Even for actors and actresses, they seemed to be in a highly overwrought state. They were laughing, they were crying, they all seemed more than a little *meshugga*. All the women's makeup was running with tears, and everybody was talking without listening. The little actress with the flaming hair, Rosalie Chernikov, was the spark in the center. Whatever it was they were all worked up over, it clearly focused on her. All in all, the renowned Bilbulniks—too true to their name—presented quite a sight to the astonished spectators.

The troupe of shooting stars managed to get themselves settled into their hotel, and then, trying to compose themselves to the business at hand, went off to inspect the theater where they would be performing for the next few days.

The stage was in the Conservatory, a beautifully ornate gem of a building—the stage a little small, it was true, but no matter, the Bilbulniks were experts at adaptation. They made the adjustments—to their sets, their movements—that had to be made, and then dispersed for the afternoon, some of them to go exploring, others to return to the hotel and grab a few hours of rest before the performance.

Sasha went back to the hotel with Rosalie. They talked for several hours, thinking up various scenarios for how Feliks would respond to the news Rosalie would bring back with her to Warsaw. They imagined everything, from his packing up his belongings and stealing off in the middle of the night for America, to his insisting on inviting Rosalie's entire brood to come to live with them. The truth was, as Rosalie now confided, Feliks had long been begging to be allowed to make an honest woman out of her.

Finally, Rosalie announced she wanted to sleep a little before the show, and so Sasha went off for a bit of sightseeing.

Vilna was set like an antique jewel in the valley carved out between the rivers Wilenka and Wilja, a city of crooked and narrow cobbled streets, climbing up and down steep hills, an occasional medieval structure still arching overhead.

On one of the highest hills surrounding the inner city there stood the remains of a medieval castle fortress, built by the Grand Duke Gediminas, whose dream of a howling wolf donning an iron shield had led him to establish the city of Vilna. Now it was a tourist attraction, surrounded by a park, the perfect place for picnics and lovers' trysts.

On another high hill stood three towering iron crosses, looking stark and—to Sasha's Jewish eyes—brutal, etched white against the cloudless sky. The place marked the spot where Gediminas's son and successor, and the last of the pagan rulers of Lithuania, had put seven Franciscan monks to death. When Olgierd's son, the Grand Duke Jagiełło, married, he converted to Christianity, and his kingdom, the last pocket of paganism in Europe, converted along with him. King Władisław Jagiełło himself led a procession out into the ancient grove of oak trees, which had been worshiped as deities, and he took an ax to them. Where the Franciscans had been martyred, he placed three crosses.

Sasha knew nothing of the history, the long struggle between paganism and Christianity, that was represented on the hilltop known as Trzy Krzyze, the Hill of the Three Crosses; but the sight of the three massive iron crosses aroused a kind of chilled wonder in her nonetheless.

She was most interested in using the little time she had to explore the crowded and ancient area that was the heart of legendary Jewish Vilna. The Jewish area was shaped like a triangle, bounded on one side by German Street, on another by Jews Street. In the very center was the *shulhof,* or synagogue courtyard, the heart and soul of Jewish Vilna.

The *shulhof* was a world unto itself, dense and humming with life: alleys running off into alleys, leading to prayerhouses, studyhouses, schools, charitable institutions, libraries.

Somewhere in this maze was the famous Strashum Library, which housed perhaps the largest collection of Jewish texts in the world. At its long wooden tables, modern, worldly men and women sat reading almost elbow to elbow with bearded rabbis.

She passed one little prayerhouse that had the date "1440" etched over its doorway. Nearby was the prayerhouse where the Vilna Gaon himself had prayed, the legendary eighteenth-century genius who had, more than any other, impressed his spirit onto Jewish Vilna, so that his conception of Judaism still persisted to this day: scholarly and rational, rigorously intellectual.

It was late in the afternoon. Even here, in the hilly city of Vilna, the late-August day was close and oppressively warm.

Through an open window came the singsong chanting of little che-der boys still at their study. Like the droning of honeybees, their sing-ing drifted out the window.

Sasha paused a moment and listened to them. She didn't know why. Usually she had scant patience for these old ways.

How much better for these little children if they could have been outside in the fresh air, hiking in the countryside on this summer day, taking a swim in a stream. Just hearing them made Sasha feel a rush of the choking claustrophobia from which she sometimes suffered. Still, she stood and listened.

They must have been very small boys. Their soprano voices sang the ancient monotonous melody—the same, no doubt, that had been sung when that date "1440" had first been etched over the doorway Sasha had just passed.

"And Lavan had two daughters." First they chanted the Hebrew, and then they translated it into Yiddish. These old ways, these old ways.

She was tempted to take a peek through the slit of a window, though she knew the sight of a young modern female would have been less than welcome—she would have been chased away like something unclean. Anyway, she didn't really have to look. She could well imagine the little white pinched faces gathered round the table, the stunted bodies and the large sad eyes.

"And the name of the older one was Leah, and the name of the younger one was Rachel." The girlish voices sounded so weary, so bored, the words blurring indistinguishably into one another.

Sasha heard the voice of the *melamed,* the teacher, chastising the poor baby scholars for their inattention, and her heart went out to them.

She was already too stirred up by everything that was happening during this drunkard's dance of a season. And now, on top of everything else, came Rosalie with her announcement. Rosalie, Rosalie. Was it any wonder that Sasha was slightly undone?

It felt to her as if her heart had been thrown wide open, that there was nothing at all that stood between it and the world, so that the tired voices of those unseen children fell straight into it, and she would hear them forever.

CHAPTER 25

THE OUTERMOST
SPHERE

*T*he play had been called *The Dybbuk*, a dark and brooding drama about a dead lover who possesses the soul of his intended bride, after she has been betrothed by her father to another man. A play about possession, it had indeed possessed. Its author had been a Yiddish folklorist named Shlomo Rapaport, who had written under the name S. An-ski. Rapaport had based his play on an old Chasidic legend that he had recorded during one of his ethnographic expeditions, but he had never been able to convince any of the Yiddish actors that he'd known to perform it.

It had only been after his death that the still-obscure Vilna Troupe had decided to produce their friend's play as a memorial to him. They had put everything together in great haste, wanting to open on the night that marked the end of the thirty-day period of mourning. When they opened, they had found themselves with a smash hit. For a few brief years, they had lived at the feverish pace of fame, there within the nimbus of the limelight. They had toured Western Europe and then gone on to America. And there, in America, they had somehow or other fallen apart, a *mishpocheh* no more, each of them going his or her own separate way and claiming to represent, in his or her very own person, the former Vilna.

More than one critic had claimed that the Bilbul was the spiritual heir to the legendary Vilna Troupe. It was a piece of well-meaning flattery that Hershel could frankly have done without. The history of the Vilna—their rise and their fall—didn't exactly reassure him.

There were many in the audience that night at the Conservatory who could still call forth, in the most vivid of visions, the incandescent performances of the original Vilna Troupe. But nowadays almost all the theater that Vilna saw came to them by way of Warsaw. So, although the audience in attendance tonight was among the most scholarly and sophisticated of any that could be brought together in a Yiddish theater—an audience of Litvaks, notorious for the sharpness of their highly critical minds—it was also an audience that was extremely receptive and grateful for what it got.

Still, that night in Vilna, even after all the laurel wreaths with which the Bilbulniks had been crowned, came to both the actors and the audience with something of the unexpectedness of love.

It happens sometimes like this, although very rarely: a collaboration between spirits that steps over the footlights, drawing the spectators up out of their seats and into the art, so that they are as inspired as the players, and an entirely new work emerges between them.

Out there in the dark were sensibilities refined by the untold generations of scholars from whom they had issued. They were worldly men and women, dressed like any other citizens of Europe, and informed by Europe's culture; and yet they were unworldly, too. What they took from the world was meshed with that sensibility which was their birthright, which they could no sooner have put off than their own faces. There was a sort of subtlety sitting out there in the darkness this night that had been centuries in the making, and it was from it that these spirits had soared over the footlights, to join themselves with those on the stage, creating an entirely new work. And even Hershel, with all the torments of his ambitions, knew a moment of complete and perfect satisfaction.

The ovations went on and on, nobody in the room wanting to relinquish the moment just yet, everyone holding on to it for as long as possible and then just a little longer.

Dovid Kaplan-Kaplansky, whom the troupe had already met earlier in the day, at the railroad station, now came to sweep them off to a party he had organized in their honor. It was held in a restaurant called Velfkah's, which looked to be Vilna's counterpart to the Pripetshok, also with a back room that was largely reserved for Vilna's more artistic and Bohemian sorts.

Dovid was a tall and handsome man, perhaps in his early fifties—an accomplished charmer, as Sasha soon learned. His dark hair was beginning to recede from his forehead, and he had a large dark mustache, a well-trimmed Vandyke beard, and a smile that showed a mouthful of white teeth and a knowledge of his own charm. He had been born into wealth, but bothered himself little over the family business. Vilna's leading patron of the arts, he had only this past year organized a Jewish symphony orchestra that had enjoyed some moderate success.

His wife, Tobya, was also at the party: a trim woman in beautiful clothes, with an air of intelligence and sophistication—but there was a certain restraint to her which was almost a tightness, showing itself most severely around her mouth, so that she was not as attractive a woman as she would otherwise have been.

Tobya excused herself from the party somewhat early, and Sasha then discovered the most likely explanation for the woman's severe mouth. The moment the wife left, the husband's flirtations, only in the gallant vein before, began in earnest. This was not exactly a new story for Sasha, and it wasn't one that she altogether minded either. She always enjoyed an accomplished flirt, and Dovid Kaplansky was extremely good, though she emphatically removed his hand from her knee beneath the table.

In the midst of the party, as boisterous as any the Bilbulniks had ever enjoyed, a young boy suddenly entered the room, looking as out of place as a priest in the studyhouse. He was dressed in a typical yeshiva boy's garb, a plain black suit and white shirt, with a black hat pulled down over his forehead.

Everyone stared in amusement.

The Bilbulniks had seen yeshiva boys sneaking into the theater, but never before had one ventured to approach the actors themselves. Had he come, perhaps, to deliver a piece of his rabbi's *muser* to them, to preach to them of the evils of their pagan playacting?

"Tzali! Oh my God, it's Tzali!" Sasha, who was not a shrieker, came close to shrieking.

Bezalel grinned and even allowed his sister to cover him with hugs and kisses.

He was twelve years old, very tall for his age and well built, blond like his sister. The two of them, in fact, looked very much alike, favoring their mother's side. Placed on a chair between Sasha and Kaplansky, Bezalel was at first a little shy in the midst of these strange worldly people. But with a little coaxing, he soon threw off the shyness and enjoyed the attention that Sasha and the others showered on him.

He described, extremely pleased with himself, how he had managed to sneak out of the yeshiva that night, and the trouble he would catch tomorrow for missing tonight's study session.

"And just to see me!" Sasha exclaimed.

"Well, to see you and also the show."

"What? You were there at the theater? Some yeshiva *bocher!* And what will happen if your rabbis find out?"

"Even then it would have been worth it!" he said, with an expression on his face that made his resemblance to his sister all the more striking.

He grinned a slightly lopsided grin that Sasha could remember from when he was still a baby.

"You want to hear something? In the first psalm, King Dovid mentions the 'seat of the scoffers.' We had a *muser* sermon this morning, in honor of your arrival, that warned us that the seat of the scoffers is the theater!"

"You don't say? It makes you proud to be an actor!"

"If only all the critics would take us as seriously as the rabbis do."

"So," Hershel said, grinning at the yeshiva boy, "after such a sermon, you come to the theater anyway?"

"I'll tell you the truth. If I wasn't determined before, the sermon itself would have brought me."

"Now I know he's your brother!"

It was early in the morning when the party finally broke up.

"Come, I'll walk you back to the yeshiva," Sasha said.

"Let's just walk around for a while," said Bezalel. "I can't go back yet."

"It's late, Tzali. You're not tired?"

"I'm wide awake. I won't sleep tonight."

"As I remember, you never liked to sleep."

"I still don't. I need less sleep than anyone I know."

Sasha smiled. She hardly knew this brother of hers. The boys in her family had been swept away on their lives of scholarship so soon, when they were still babies, and she had never really gotten the chance to know them.

"Is it always like this for you?" Bezalel was asking her. "Is there always this much excitement?"

"Well, this was a particularly good night, I have to say. Something special happened tonight in the theater. But, yes, it's an exciting life."

"It must be wonderful. Maybe I'll become an actor, too. What do you think? Could you people use me? I think I have some of your talent, Sasha. Everybody's always begging me to imitate the rabbis for them. I didn't really realize until tonight that you can make a living just from that."

"That's all Tatta and Mamma need," Sasha said, laughing, "that you leave the yeshiva to become a vagabond like me."

"How are they . . . Mamma?"

"They're both okay. Mamma . . . Well, of course, she's nervous. Tatta is exactly the same: God will help."

They walked a few paces in silence.

"Look at those stars!" Bezalel was suddenly exclaiming, throwing back his head and at the same time catching his hat so that it didn't fall to the ground. "Look at them, Sasha! You feel like you could touch them!"

He stretched his arm straight up toward where he was gazing.

"Are they always like this in the middle of the night, so close to earth?"

"They're also particularly fine tonight."

Sasha was just on the verge of sharing with Bezalel what their sister Fraydel had once said, about the outermost sphere of light; but somehow she kept her silence. After all these years, she was still jealous of her memories of Fraydel.

When Sasha finally got back to the hotel, it was almost four o'clock in the morning. There, sitting in the lobby, with the letter of acceptance from the university resting on his lap, sat Maurice.

He had come to claim his tango.

How—Sasha asked herself over the course of the next few hours, every now and then, when she came back long enough to ask herself anything at all—*how could I have put him* for a moment *from my mind?*

Sasha was the one who had always been known as tireless, but there must have been unknown powers in that letter of acceptance. Maurice at eighteen was now fully grown, no boy at all; he had suffered for this woman and now took nothing, nothing for granted.

And, yes, they did dance, too. She sang him "The Gypsy's Tango" and he spun her and dipped her and whirled her around until she was dizzy and she collapsed against him laughing, naked and laughing, so that who but a *golem* would have needed champagne?

They finally fell asleep past eleven that morning, and at eleven-thirty Rosalie was pounding at their door.

CHAPTER 26

LAUGHTER IN THE STUDYHOUSE

*L*et the drunken dance themselves into oblivion, and those with the strange power of living in the moment keep their eyes turned away. Still, the night waits outside the window, the unclean hosts have occupied the studyhouse, and the laughter is terrible beyond all words.

Rosalie didn't register any surprise at seeing Maurice. She looked at him as if she had known he was there. It was the end of being surprised.

Even after an entire year of unthinkable events, nobody was prepared for this last trick the world was playing them.

Hitler's Germany and Stalin's Russia, the two arch-enemies, had signed a treaty of nonaggression. It was clear that the two intended to carve up Poland between them.

On the streets of Vilna, which the day before had been so quiet and sleepy, today there was pandemonium. Before every store stretched long lines, everyone anxious to stock up on food for the war that was now inevitable, maybe only a matter of days away.

The reservists had all been called up. Everywhere you looked, there were men in uniform.

Anything attached to wheels, every truck, every car, every hand wagon, had been requisitioned by the army.

The *mishpocheh* had to drag their suitcases all by themselves down to the railroad station, which was crowded with husbands and wives, parents and sons, tearfully saying goodbye.

Hershel and the others had actually debated staying on for just one more performance in Vilna. But then even they had to concede that this would be madness. War could come at any moment.

Sasha and Maurice had gone down to the railroad station to see the others off on the late-afternoon train to Warsaw, the summer sun still shining and the air sweet with the ripening fruits in the surrounding countryside.

Rosalie, with the unleashed torrents of emotions for which they now at least had the general explanation, had burst into tears as she said goodbye to Sasha and Maurice, those two as crazy as young lovers were ever known to be, which is saying a mouthful. They had promised Rosalie that they would follow in two or three days at the most, but she was carrying on as if she might, God forbid, never see them again. And Maurice and Sasha, so shameless it did your heart good, could only stand there on the platform and glow, giving each other such looks that Rosalie, in the midst of her sobbing, took notes and committed to memory.

Even though the streets of Vilna were now filled with so much commotion, it seemed to Sasha and Maurice to grow suddenly quiet once the *mishpocheh* had gone. The troupe had taken all their noise with them.

Tzali's yeshiva was sending the boys back home, so the next day Sasha and Maurice were at the railroad station once again, this time saying goodbye to her little brother.

Now the only one they knew from Warsaw who still remained in Vilna was Zev Ben-Zion, Rosalie's brother, who lived at the collective farm he and the others of his organization had set up in a little country village not ten kilometers outside of the city.

He, too, would soon be gone: he had an exit visa for Palestine. Sasha and Maurice met him once in the street. He was still organizing, trying to get as many Jews as he could out of Europe on the few exit visas his Zionist group had been able to procure from the British.

Anyone with a visa who wasn't married took along another as a counterfeit spouse, to squeeze a few more past the watchful British. Zev mentioned this to Sasha, saying that he himself might be able to take her along on his visa. But she, feeling the heat of Maurice's body beside her, had only half paid attention to what the Zionist bore was saying. Maurice, as it turned out, had been paying much closer attention, asking Zev question after question while Sasha, like a child, tugged impatiently at his hand.

They would always keep the secret between them, Sasha and Maurice, for as long as they lived. It must mean that they were very selfish people, that they could have grabbed at happiness in such times as these, greedy in love, as all around them the world was crashing down.

Friday, September 1, they awoke in their little bed to the news that the Germans had already invaded Poland. The newspapers that had been printed the night before were already outdated.

At 4:00 A.M., the Germans had opened fire on the Polish post office in Gdańsk and on other places in the Polish Corridor. At 5:40, Hitler had addressed his armed forces, in that rabid stream that Mendel impersonated to perfection.

By the end of the second week of war, Warsaw was already encircled. By the end of the third week, it was all over, and Hitler and Stalin helped themselves to Poland.

Sasha and Maurice were now in a city that had been declared by the occupying Red Army to be the capital of the Lithuanian Soviet Socialist Republic.

And Warsaw, the beloved city where every soul they cherished was living, was in the hands of Amalek.

PART V

Again, New Jersey

*T*he sword was poised over the boy's neck when Mazel turned with a smirk to Saychel and spoke:

"Well, now, my dear brainy friend, you see where intelligence alone will get you in this world. Let me have a try, and you'll see that within a few minutes I'll do more for this poor boy than you've been able to get done for him over his entire lifetime."

No sooner had Mazel bestirred himself than the princess, looking pensive, strolled out onto her balcony. Seeing the intelligent apprentice with his neck stretched out beneath the sword, she quickly called down:

"Stop, you idiots! That's my destined one you're about to behead!"

The King ordered that the incompetent servants themselves be executed, while the young man was brought to wed the princess.

And, with Mazel, the two of them lived happily ever after.

—A Yiddish folktale

CHAPTER 27

THE VIEW FROM BEHIND
THE PARTITION

Sasha gave Chloe's hand one of those bone-crushing squeezes to which she resorted on the rare occasion when words failed her. Chloe, glancing sideways at her mother, squeezed her bones back. Sasha heaved her shoulders upward in one of her more eloquent shrugs. It was time to go back in.

Chloe lifted her hand toward the bell of the house on Stellar Road, but was prevented by her mother's timely intercession.

"Not on Shabbes."

"Oh, right." Chloe smiled. "I keep forgetting."

"Go on. Forget I reminded you. We'll give them something more to talk about."

"Dare we?"

"Of course we dare! Don't let the likes of Beatrice Kantor cow you into submission! Who the hell *is* she?"

"She's Phoebe's future mother-in-law," Chloe answered quietly, raising her hand to knock.

"Well, maybe I did give her enough grief for today," Sasha muttered, relenting, although rolling her eyes heavenward as only she knew how.

Debby, Jason's younger sister, opened the door for them. A sweet girl, this Debby, very natural and interested in other people, and not at all stupid, even though she submitted without a murmur, as docile as a lamb chop, to her mother's constant bossing. This was one of the odd-est things: what truly *nice* children Beatrice had produced.

Debby was fairly tall, like Beatrice, and in fact looked—and even sounded—like a much softer version of her mother. She was just about to graduate from Stern College, the women's branch of Yeshiva University, in Manhattan, having majored, like her brother, in computer science.

"Did you have a nice walk?" she asked now, smiling warmly as Sasha and Chloe stepped into the entrance hall, done up very fancy in Italian tiles. The entire house is, as Sasha puts it, *ongepotchket,* overdone, just like the hostess with the mostest herself.

Sasha, not ready to concede anything, not even to this lovely girl, simply shrugged, but Chloe answered that it had been a very nice walk.

"Mom and her friends are still pretty much where you left them," Debby said with a little laugh that just skirted the edge of banter. So maybe there was some private commentary going on inside that head, after all?

Debby led them to the den in the back of the house, where Beatrice and a thinned-out crowd of her chosen few sat huddled together, deep in a conversation that halted to a tell-all silence the moment the three-some appeared in the doorway.

And the faces! Beatrice and her friends might just as well have an-nounced that they had been in the midst of verbally trashing either Sasha or Chloe or both.

Actually, it had been both.

Chloe, it had been decided, was really more to be pitied than judged. (Had she *ever* been married?) "Eccentric" was one of the words that had been used, in the spirit of generosity that was being exercised.

"Anyway, Beatrice, console yourself with the thought that Jason is marrying the girl, not the mother."

"And he's certainly not marrying the grandmother . . . !"

Oh, but that grandmother!

"Really, Beatrice, you didn't exaggerate one little bit about her."

"*Exaggerate?*" Beatrice's tone was deeply offended. "Are you kid-ding? I haven't told you the *half* of it . . . !"

"Ridiculous, a woman of her age . . . !"

"She's more like a rebellious teen-ager than a woman in her seventies . . . !"

"Those pants . . . !"

Those pants had, in fact, been part of the grief to which Sasha had just now been referring. This morning, Sasha had gone off, in a perfectly respectable navy-blue dress and hat, to the synagogue services that were the reason she and Chloe were here in Lipton in the first place.

It was Jason's *aufruf,* the last Shabbes before his wedding, and, as was the custom, he had been honored by being called up to the Torah. Phoebe wasn't here, as was also the custom. Phoebe and Jason weren't allowed (*allowed!*) to see one another for the entire week before the wedding.

So it was just Sasha and Chloe here for Jason's *aufruf,* with Chloe feeling more than slightly lost, knowing little or nothing about the customs of the land—and Sasha knowing all too much.

"Pants, Sasha?"

Beatrice had intercepted Sasha before anyone else had yet seen her, just as she was coming down the stairs from the guest room, where she had gone to change the moment they had returned from the synagogue.

"And black leather, no less?"

Sasha hadn't deigned to answer. She had simply stared Beatrice down, as brazenly as she knew how, which was considerably.

"Well, it's up to you, of course. After all, I certainly wouldn't presume to tell you what to do, Sasha."

"I should certainly hope not, Beatrice."

"But you probably just don't realize that women simply don't wear pants here on Shabbes."

"So *stone* me, Beatrice," Sasha had answered, her tone so grim that even Beatrice had slightly faltered before pursuing her case.

"Lipton isn't Manhattan, Sasha."

"You're telling me?"

"I really think you'll feel very uncomfortable."

"I really think I won't."

For several long moments, the two of them had hung fire. It would have been anyone's guess which way it was going to go. But it was Beatrice who had finally yielded, giving up with a smile that had been a wonder to behold, managing to convey the negation of all that smiles were ever intended to convey.

"I can't understand it," Sasha repeated more times than was necessary to Chloe over the course of this weekend. "I had always taken for granted a certain *level* of *enlightenment.* What kind of fiendish mind could have dreamt up such a thing as Lipton? Suburbia isn't bad enough?"

Phoebe had told her mother that Lipton was sometimes called the "Jerusalem of New Jersey." Of course, being Phoebe, she had said this with no irony at all.

There were five different Orthodox congregations. Three of the five were housed in more or less proper-looking synagogues, but Beatrice and Nat were partial to the one that met in the gymnasium of the local Jewish day school, which was half a block away from their home on Stellar Road. It had been here that Jason's *aufruf* had been held earlier today.

The basketball hoops had been retracted but were still very much visible. Seating was provided in the form of metal folding chairs. A temporary wooden partition ran almost the entire length of the gym, separating the men and the women. In the front of the room, on the men's side, was the ark that held the Torahs, a blue velvet curtain strung across it, embroidered in gold with the lions of Judah.

Walking down the aisle of the women's section to get to her seat, even Sasha, who after all was used to getting her fair share of attention, had deemed the amount of scrutinizing being directed their way just a bit excessive. A *little* discretion, *please.* Eyes were looking Chloe and herself up and down with such a thoroughness it was as if you could actually feel them pawing you.

Little places, little minds, Sasha had thought grimly. Still, the rapt attention of her audience couldn't help inspiring her, and she had executed an entrance worthy of the former star of the Bilbul Art Theater.

Chloe, on the other hand, couldn't sink down onto her seat quickly enough.

The two of them had taken their places near Beatrice, who sat as close as it was possible for a woman to sit to the reading table on the *other* side of the partition, where all the action was going on. This, Chloe had assumed, must be the women's version of the seat of honor.

Beatrice, truly superb in yet another designer suit and a matching complicated hat, had played to the hilt her role of doyenne of Lipton, nodding graciously to one and all, accepting the tributes that were her due—*always,* but most especially now.

Yet how odd, Chloe had thought, that such a forceful presence as Beatrice—surely the dominating factor in any interaction that remotely involved her—should be content to sit as a nonparticipant on the wrong side of the partition. It had made Chloe think fleetingly of the women of ancient Athens, who had lived out their lives in the dark and cramped women's quarters of their homes, hidden from public view, probably all but entirely ignorant of the wonders of their civilization. It had made her think of the *purdah.*

She was only surprised that a woman like Beatrice would stand for this sort of marginalization. Was it conviction or merely habit that reconciled a personality of Beatrice's proportions to peering passively over the partition?

Chloe had peered, too. She had never actually seen men wrapped in prayer shawls, although, of course, she'd seen pictures. Maurice hadn't owned one, she was pretty sure. In any case, she'd certainly never seen him in one.

Jason had stood with a Torah scroll unrolled before him, chanting in an eerie monotone. The sounds of the ancient Hebrew had thrilled Chloe, as all ancient tongues did.

She stared down into the prayer book. She had once known how to read Hebrew quite well. Of course, Yiddish had been her first language. Sasha had always claimed that that was what had given Chloe her taste for dead tongues. But by the time Chloe was learning how to read, she had switched entirely to English. It was Maurice who had taught her how to read the Hebrew script. She must have been about six or seven.

Staring down into the prayer book, trying to recall the sounds of the letters, brought him vividly back to her.

Her handsome, mysterious father, always a book in his back pocket, heavily underlined and annotated. He would appear, unannounced, full of anecdotes about the people he'd met on his last junket, the odd jobs he'd taken to support himself. When he had exhausted his supply of fresh tales, he'd be gone again. At least that's how it used to seem to her: that his stays were so brief and his absences so long.

But Sasha had always disputed this. She always claimed he had been with them more than he had been away, which could very well have been true. Time has that horrible trick of accelerating just when you want it to freeze.

Chloe had been almost four years old when he had first suddenly appeared in her life. All the years when he had been fleeing from Europe, trekking through the better part of Asia, he hadn't known he had a daughter, born in a kibbutz in Palestine. The history of all the missed messages that Sasha and Maurice had sent to one another was a story in itself.

Maurice had taken the long route out of Vilna. After he had finally persuaded Sasha, using every form of entreaty his inventive mind could offer, to leave the occupied city on Zev Ben-Zion's visa, he had traveled more deeply into Russia, spending long months in prison when he had been caught with false identification papers. He had thought he would rot there, but a Jewish jailer had finally bribed the right people, and Maurice had made his way eventually to Japan and then, by steamer, to Calcutta via Shanghai. From India he had taken a ferry via the Suez Canal, where he had been shelled by German guns. The plan had been for Sasha and Maurice to reunite in Palestine, but Maurice was three years too late, and Sasha was gone. She had despaired that Maurice was alive and, not finding kibbutz life exactly to her liking, especially with the importunate Zev Ben-Zion making life uncomfortable for her—it turned out he had been in love with her the whole time—she had finally gone with her little daughter to New York.

Chloe could still recall everything about her first encounter with her father, right down to what both of them had been wearing, the special hair ribbons her mother had put on her braids. Meeting her father was, in fact, her first perfectly distinct memory, as if her consecutive history had started then. From her life before—the kibbutz, the voyage to America—she had only a jumble of fleeting impressions, so vague she couldn't even say what they were about.

She could remember the funny sandals her father had been wearing, with socks underneath them. These sandals had struck her as unbelievably odd. Still, except for the sandals, she had immediately approved of him. He was better-looking than any father she'd ever seen, and she had approved.

He had told her she should call him Maurice. He had solemnly shaken her hand, bowing slightly from the waist in a very Old World manner.

And then he had begun slowly to smile, a grin that had just kept coming and coming, and that had filled her with the fine wonder of knowing she had somehow pleased him.

You would think that, once he had finally located them, his own family, he would never again want to leave them, but it hadn't been like that. Transplanted from Poland, he seemed to have gotten the wandering into his blood.

For a while he'd stay with them, finding some sort of work in New York. Sasha had connections, knowing everybody in New York's tight little circle of Yiddishists, among whom she found the jobs—either in acting or other things—with which she supported herself and Chloe. (Then, too, there was always "Uncle Felix," who, once again, had landed on his feet and who continued his prewar practice of helping out when needed.) But Maurice had had little patience for the Yiddishists and relied on his own resources.

One year he'd been an usher at Radio City Music Hall and became great friends with all the acts. He'd take Chloe to visit backstage, where the Rockettes would all make a big fuss over her, doing fancy things with her hair and polishing her nails.

Gradually, he'd grow restless. Staying put for too long brought out the sadness. He'd leave, always for someplace cold.

He never could sit out a New York summer. Once, in desperation, he had joined a freighter headed for Iceland, offering himself as a cook's assistant. He had figured that all he'd have to do was stir the pots and peel the potatoes. But then the cook had gotten seasick, and he had been ordered to take over. Discovered as an impostor, he had been relegated to swabbing the decks until they reached Reykjavík, where they had put him ashore. He had eventually made his way back to New York by way of Labrador, bringing home a bunch of good stories, filled with his wonder at the endless variety of human lives to be found on this planet. No person was too quirky or marginal for Maurice not to want to know how the world looked through his eyes. In fact, the more quirky and marginal, the better. Maurice himself had a great weakness for life in the margins.

He came back once, after an absence that had seemed particularly long, and told Chloe of the months he had spent driving a calèche, a horse-drawn carriage, in old Quebec. His horse, a temperamental nag, he had named Miessa, the Yiddish for "ugly."

"The tourists all thought my accent was typical French Canadian," he had said, laughing. "Miessa and I, we were very popular with the tourists."

Miessa hadn't gotten along so well with the other horses, and Maurice had also initially been kept at a distance by the other drivers, all of whom were French Canadian, a clannish group, "like a bunch of Satmar Chasidim." Eventually, though, they had warmed up to Maurice—

—Chloe hadn't doubted it; who could resist Maurice for long?—

—so that they had all become great pals. What characters they were, each and every one a philosopher.

"There are horse-and-carriage drivers in New York, too, Maurice," Chloe had said softly. It was as close as she would ever come to asking him to stay.

"Oh no," he had said, grinning. "In New York I have to do a New York kind of thing. Maybe a jazz singer. What do you think, baby?" And he sang her his jazzed-up version, à la Louis Armstrong, of "Mack the Knife."

She had never questioned his nomadic ways. Her mother never had either, so far as Chloe knew. Neither of them had ever doubted for a moment that eventually he'd make his way back to New York, a city he hated.

He'd come back and always, the very first thing, he would question Chloe closely: What are you learning in school? What books have you been reading? Every answer would be followed up by more questions. Even as she got older, it seemed to her that her father, who had spent the years he ought to have been at a university wandering, had read everything.

And then, at last, after all the questions and answers, the slow, slow grin that would keep coming and coming, and the bliss she'd feel in knowing she'd pleased him.

He had always said she'd be a professor someday, though he hadn't lived long enough to see it. The first day of her graduate classes at Columbia, she'd gotten back to the apartment on Riverside Drive to have Sasha fling open the door before Chloe could fit in her key. Sasha had stood there, wild-eyed, unable to find her voice, finally just thrusting the telegram out before her.

Maurice had died of a heart attack on his way back to them from Nova Scotia.

For weeks, Sasha had stayed in the apartment, not even bothering to repair with makeup the damage that grief was doing to her face. For the first week, Aunt Harriet had come to stay with them. And Felix, too, had sat in the apartment with them for the seven days that none of them had openly acknowledged as the period of *shiva*.

Chloe missed him still, until this day, missed him all the more terribly because she knew that she'd never really known him—the handsome man, with his piercing blue eyes, his wanderings and stories, his heavily underlined books. Sometimes Sasha would say something that made it sound to Chloe as if her mother were still imagining that he was making his way back to them.

The ancient script, Jason's chanting: they brought Maurice back to Chloe. For a moment, she could see him: as he was that first time, bowing solemnly to his little daughter; as he was at thirty-nine, the last time she'd seen him.

Jason had reached the conclusion of his Torah reading, and a scene that looked like a re-enactment of the seventh plague of Egypt had erupted: the women pelting Jason with little plastic bags filled with candies, upon which the many, many children came swarming down, as if in a reinterpretation of the eighth plague of Egypt.

To Chloe it was all fascinating—wonderful, really, all these communal rites. She wished she knew a bit more about them. She thought fleetingly of the May Day festival she had once witnessed in Padstow, a small village in Cornwall: the hobbyhorse processional that had wandered through town in a route that had perhaps been fixed for centuries, with all the villagers singing a haunting melody, something about uniting, uniting; and all the themes of fertility and resurrection. If a woman gets caught under the hobbyhorse's hooped skirt, the legend goes, she'll be pregnant within the year. And at one point in the processional, the hobbyhorse lies down as if dead, and all the villagers sing a song asking where St. George is. And then the horse bounds up, alive once more.

Chloe had felt that same spine-tingling awe, the sense that one was tapping into rituals that, despite any modern accretions along the way (the plastic bags, for example), reached far back into something authentically ancient and therefore thrilling.

What, she had wondered, did this sweet, though potentially hazardous, assault on the bridegroom signify? Did it, too, have something to do with fertility?

She had considered asking her mother, who probably would know. After all, Sasha had come from this sort of background. But a glance at Sasha, sitting with her arms folded tightly across her chest, an unceasing fount of acidic incredulity, had convinced Chloe to forgo immediate enlightenment.

"I haven't felt this claustrophobic in years," Sasha had whispered fiercely to Chloe. "Make my apologies to Beatrice if I should happen to pass out."

After the services, the festivities surrounding Jason's *aufruf* had continued at the house on Stellar Road, spilling over into the backyard. Although this weekend was ostensibly for Jason, it seemed all about

Beatrice. Her admirers, and they were many, were all there to pay her homage—while Sasha, in black leather, looked on in withering contempt. Finally, Chloe, none too comfortable herself in this setting, had suggested to her mother that they escape for a bit and go for a little walk.

It was a beautiful day, with lots of people out strolling—many, many young people, pushing carriages or walking hand-in-hand with multiples of children. If any of those rites Chloe had just been witnessing had anything to do with fertility, they certainly seemed to have been working.

Many of the people Chloe was seeing had a very different look to them from the older crowd paying court on Stellar Road. These younger people, even Debby and Jason, reminded Chloe just a little of Phoebe. They seemed to be quite entirely without the Yuppie pretensions of their elders. Perhaps Chloe was simply projecting—she herself considered this more than possible—but still she did seem to see in them something of her own daughter's almost unbearably poignant innocence, the air-sweetening breath of the very wise child. Chloe wondered how many of them had chosen for themselves to return to this way of life, just as Phoebe had. She wondered what it was that they saw in these old ways, so at odds with the life and spirit of our times.

"Look at that!" Sasha exclaimed, pointing to the door of a suburban château, which had clearly just been built. In fact, it was so new, the lawn hadn't yet been planted.

"Yes?" Chloe asked. Was Sasha simply outraged by the materialism?

"Look at the door!"

There was a bit of red—it looked like a ribbon—tied around the handle of the massive wooden door. Perhaps, Chloe speculated, the husband had symbolically "wrapped" this present to his wife and family.

"It's a bendel," Sasha said to Chloe, in such a tone as to suggest this was Chloe's fault. "Blessed by a rebbe. To protect against the evil wishes of the envious. A bendel on a New Jersey French Provincial: it says it all."

Did it? Chloe didn't know. She lacked the translation.

Most of the people they passed, including the children, had hesitated before wishing Sasha and Chloe "good Shabbes." Chloe, still in the clothes she had worn to the synagogue and not carrying a pocketbook, had, more or less, looked the part; but Sasha, in the much-disputed black leather pants, hadn't. Nonetheless, almost everyone, after a slight hesitation, had offered the two the traditional greeting, which Chloe, completely charmed, had returned. If Chloe hadn't had other things to distract her—Sasha's aggressive bristling, Beatrice's flattening superiority—she might actually have enjoyed herself this weekend.

Phoebe described herself as Orthodox—to Chloe's ears, an unfortunate term—but there seemed to be a rather large range of value-systems lumped under the rubric of that one word. No wonder that "the Jerusalem of New Jersey," as small as it was, had five different Orthodox synagogues. For Beatrice and her friends, this life really did seem to mean something akin to "Mrs. Vanderbilt and her Four Hundred." But Phoebe, of course, had been drawn by something entirely different. Phoebe had found something here that she loved, and Chloe was trying her damnedest to see what it might be, if only for the sake of understanding her daughter. She was trying to peer past the limits of irony, a difficult enough enterprise in itself, and she was determined not to let distractions such as Beatrice's condescension or Sasha's counter-condescension get in her way.

Chloe and Sasha had walked down wide Stonystream Avenue, which ended in a little downward slope heading toward the railroad tracks. At the side of the road were tennis courts, and right near these was a little excuse for a park: a bit of well-trodden grass with a few swings, some seesaws, a picnic table. Most of the people around here simply referred to it as "the Shabbes park," and it was, on this beautiful spring day, literally swarming with overdressed children of all ages. Sasha had given it a withering glance.

"Well, you know, darling," Chloe had said, with a daughter's intimate cunning, "there's such a thing as mazel."

It had been, of course, a rather brilliant thing to say—so brilliant, in fact, that Sasha hadn't even answered. She had given Chloe's hand one of those bone-crushing squeezes to which she resorted on the rare occasion when words failed her, and Chloe had felt that perhaps the confrontation that was waiting to happen had been averted.

And then they had stepped into that den, where Beatrice and her friends were all too clearly engaged in the act of trashing either one or the other or both of them. There was a long moment of uncomfortable silence, but Beatrice soon recovered herself.

"Did you have a nice walk? Come, sit down. Can I get you some tea?"

"Thanks, no, Beatrice. We're fine."

Again some silence, as the two women found places in Beatrice's den.

"So," began one of Beatrice's friends, smiling brightly at Sasha. "What do you think of our Lipton?"

Chloe's heart sank.

"Lipton?" Sasha said with a dismissive little laugh. "Well, since you asked, I'll tell you *exactly* what I think of Lipton."

She paused dramatically, letting the tension palpably mount, her theatrical instincts still very much intact.

"Lipton, New Jersey," she finally pronounced, her glance sweeping the room, her delivery professional enough to have circumvented the tricky echoes of the tailors' union hall, "is Shluftchev . . . with a designer label."

CHAPTER 28

SEALED TOGETHER, WORLDS APART

"Shluftchev?" someone finally asked, after several moments of an uncomfortable silence. Of course, nobody—with the sole exception of the despairing Chloe—could possibly have known what Sasha was talking about.

"It's the shtetl where I was born. Shluftchev on the Puddle. It had a puddle that never disappeared. In summer it grew smaller, in the winter it froze over, but always it was there, with a terrible stench hanging over it. I had an older sister who used to say that all of the memories of Shluftchev had sunk to the bottom of that puddle, and these memories were of such a nature as to give off just such a stink."

This again was not a comment from which the conversation easily flowed. Clearly, Sasha's comparing Lipton to Shluftchev was not intended to be flattering.

"Well, I think Lipton seems quite wonderful," Chloe suddenly said, smiling as serenely as a goddamned saint. "There seems to be such a unique feeling of community here."

A chorus of agreement began to sound, but it was cut off, brutally, by Sasha's professionally commanding voice. When Sasha so desired, nobody, not even the likes of Beatrice, could prevail against that voice.

"Of course, you *would* find it *wonderful*," she almost hissed at Chloe. "You're nothing but a *pagan*. You're ready to accept anybody's gods!"

This again had an immediate and devastating effect on the flow of conversation. Finally, Beatrice was asked by one of her friends—as if she didn't already know—who was going to be doing the makeup for the wedding tomorrow, and the conversation flowed off into safer channels.

Chloe had to acknowledge to herself that, in the midst of her mother's grand theatrics, there resided a certain degree of truth. Chloe *was* rather nonexclusive when it came to accepting gods, and it probably did have something to do with her being more or less a pagan. Up until almost a year ago, when Phoebe had made her startling announcement that she had begun to keep kosher, being Jewish had seemed to Chloe to be nothing more than an incidental feature in both her own and her daughter's biographies.

It had been in the back pages of the family history that being Jewish had figured. It was because they were Jewish that Chloe had had no grandparents, no cousins—only poor dear sweet Aunt Harriet, with her odd twitchings and grimacings.

There was also, Chloe knew, a woman named Katya who had been married to Chloe's uncle Jascha, who had been a composer—a genius according to both her father and mother. Katya, who wasn't Jewish, had stayed on the outside when the Jews had been ordered into the ghetto. Jascha had died in there in the last days of the uprising, one of the legendary ghetto-fighters. His was the only death they knew something about. The rest of both Sasha's and Maurice's families had vanished without a record. Katya had eventually remarried. Sasha and she used to exchange Christmas cards, but eventually Sasha had lost track of her.

These family stories had been what had constituted Chloe's elusive sense of herself as Jewish. Her mother and her father had lived through extraordinary events, largely because they had been born into a Europe in which being Jewish was no incidental feature in a person's biography. The world from which these stories had derived had always seemed so remote to Chloe, existing almost at the level of mythology. And this was true even though Chloe, of course, had been conceived right in the middle of all that inconceivable history, just as the old world had come crashing down around her father and mother.

Most remote of all to Chloe was that mythological place where her mother had begun her own life. Shluftchev. Her mother rarely mentioned the place, and then only with an ironic shudder. Shluftchev on the Puddle. Sasha had hated shtetl life: close and narrow, shut off from that great wide world with which Sasha has been, ever after, carrying on her impassioned love affair. Sasha only has to think of the shtetl to feel, so she swears, a rush of the old claustrophobia.

For herself, Chloe could call forth no real mental image of the shtetl; only something shadowy and gray, scrimmed over by a curtain that looked vaguely like a prayer shawl, black-striped and fringed. To her that world was far more distant and inaccessible than the world of the ancient Greeks.

So she was startled, of course, when Phoebe seemed suddenly to start taking being Jewish so very seriously, insisting on removing it from the level of mythology. Chloe had no idea whether this was, in itself, a good thing. But she did find herself believing, increasingly, that it was a good thing for Phoebe. In fact, she couldn't help feeling that Phoebe—who had always been an extraordinarily gifted problem-solver, first as a little chess prodigy, and then as a mathematician—had hit upon a quite brilliant solution to the problem of being Phoebe.

When Phoebe had first announced to her mother, over lunch one day in Butler Terrace, high over Columbia University, that she was keeping kosher, Chloe hadn't known anything at all about what this proposition might entail.

Phoebe had ordered a plain green salad, and then, all of a sudden, while Chloe spooned up her lobster bisque, announced, very, very softly, that she had recently become kosher. This was the first that Chloe had heard anything at all about it.

Of course, there had been that time, several months earlier, when Phoebe, suddenly and out of the blue, had asked Chloe whether Oliver Crittendon had been Jewish. Chloe, flabbergasted, had simply interpreted Phoebe's question—quite wrongly, it later appeared—as a request for the facts of her existence.

"No, he's not, as a matter of fact," she had finally gotten around to saying, after she had spilled out a great deal more of the story than Phoebe had apparently been seeking. "Does it matter, darling?"

And Phoebe had smiled, her face as cryptic as one of those strings of mathematics she was endlessly scribbling on her long yellow legal pads. Clearly, Chloe—never quite so good at deduction as her mathematically gifted daughter—had bungled this first clue.

But the second had left no margin for misinterpretation.

"I've started to keep kosher," Phobe had quietly announced, with that slight air of self-consciousness she showed whenever she said anything of a directly personal nature.

"Kosher?"

"Yes. I've really just started. Wednesday will be my first full week."

She had smiled across the table at her mother. Her little heartlike face was suffused with that mysterious glow that would sometimes overtake her, so that Chloe would feel something lurching terribly inside of her.

"Why?" Chloe had asked.

"I don't exactly know," Phoebe had answered slowly. "It just seemed logical."

Logical? Maybe so. Chloe herself didn't see the logic, but, then, she wasn't the daughter of a (Gentile) logician.

Chloe was, of course, highly accustomed to being somewhat mystified by her daughter. Phoebe, even as a child, had combined an almost aggressive streak of logic—"What do you mean by that? That doesn't make sense!"—with something almost impossibly tender. The logic didn't exhaust what there was to Phoebe. There always had been some unplumbable realm in Phoebe, and it was to this realm that Chloe had attributed Phoebe's announcement that she had suddenly become kosher.

She had mentioned Phoebe's announcement to Sasha that evening.

"Guess what. Phoebe's decided to keep kosher."

Sasha had hit the roof.

First she had called Phoebe up in order to harangue her, and then, early the next morning, she had gotten herself down to Penn Station and onto a train out to Princeton, surprising Phoebe in her office on the ninth floor of Fine Hall, the great tower of a building for math and physics that defines the Princeton skyline.

The door was open. Phoebe was standing facing her blackboard, chalk in hand, staring up at her equations.

"I can't *understand* you!" Sasha had greeted her. "You're an educated woman! A *professor!* Why would you want to start up all over again with those *old ways?*"

"You know that story you used to tell me about my great-great-grandfather?" Phoebe had answered her, speaking very low, but gazing up at Sasha in that intense way she had.

"What—with the dead man?"

"Right."

Phoebe often had the habit of speaking with elongated pauses, most especially when there was emotion behind her words; so that, if you didn't know her better, you would think that she wasn't going to go on. But Sasha knew her better.

"With the dead man. I always loved that story the best."

"Well—it's a good story."

"I always loved what the dead man said to Rav Dovid. That even the dead need the comfort of their own kind."

Phoebe's childlike face, gazing up into her grandmother's, was flushed with that terrifying purity that so affected Sasha.

"Grandma . . . I think I've always felt like that dead man."

CHAPTER 29

AN OLD ARGUMENT

*I*t wasn't only Chloe who had been visited by a vivid sense of Maurice while sitting there within the claustrophobic confines of the women's section of the gymnasium-prayerhouse in Lipton, New Jersey.

Sasha has always continued, sometimes more, sometimes less, her habit of addressing Maurice, bringing him along with her as the past went rushing into the present. It was a habit with a long history, going all the way back to the train ride from Vilna to Odessa, where she and Zev were supposed to get themselves onto a boat. Maurice, the sense of him, had stayed with her; the sight and feel and wonder of him as he was on that last night, when their child had been conceived. A woman knows. She had known that what went on between them on that last night would issue in a soul. She had known it already on the train ride out of Vilna, pressed in with all the pandemonium, the near hysteria packed into that train. And she had spoken it to him as if he stood beside her and seen how he had smiled. The slow, slow grin that had just kept coming and coming. She had seen it.

She had kept her certainty all through her pregnancy and the ordeal of the birth, when both she and the baby had almost died there in that primitive kibbutz: she had never doubted for a moment that Maurice was alive and making his way to her. It was only after almost three years of waiting, no word from anyone coming from Europe, all of the hundreds of unanswered letters, that Sasha had despaired and had told herself that there is no clinging to the dead.

So she had left Palestine, the harshness of the life there for which she hadn't the ideals to make it tolerable. Unforgivably, as it had turned out, because Maurice had finally arrived there to find her gone. All their life together, from beginning to end, she had made things difficult for him. She wishes with all her soul that she could say it had been otherwise, but it hadn't.

It was a funny thing, though, that back then, when Maurice had actually been alive, Sasha had managed to kill him off completely in her head; whereas for these past thirty-five years she's kept the sense of him safe.

And now, in this hideous place that their granddaughter had chosen out of all the possibilities offered by the wide, wide world; sitting in a women's section—a women's section!—struggling to get enough air into her lungs beside the oxygen-grabbing presence of this future *machetayneste:* Sasha had suddenly been visited by a sense of Maurice so strong that she had actually turned in spite of herself to scan the faces of the men wrapped in their *talaysim* on the other side of the *mechitza.* Like a superstitious old *bubba* who had never wandered far from darkest Shluftchev, she had searched to see if her beloved were really there.

"Everything connects," Maurice had mouthed to her silently through the swaying forms of the davening men. "There's always a reason."

She had slowly shaken her head in answer. For Maurice she had no more of the vehemence with which she had too often tormented him. But even so, with all of her tormenting, he had always made his way back to them, back to New York, a city he had hated. There was something in the life here that had oppressed him. Sooner or later he'd begin to feel the sheer colossal waste of it all. He liked cold places, sparsely populated. Even human life is worth something more in places where there's little of it.

She had never tried to keep him from leaving, that much she could say for herself. That much of a good wife at least she had been. It was hard for her, it was harder for Chloe—too hard for a child, even a rational little creature like Chloe. Maybe especially a rational little creature like Chloe. But even that Sasha had forgiven him.

It had been harder to forgive herself. She had much to answer for, right down to that spring before Maurice had left for the last time. He had lost weight and his color was terrible. There were mornings when he had woken up looking almost haggard, years older than he was. She had caught sight of him, once or twice, rubbing his chest as if something hurt. Of course, he had denied that anything was wrong. A stomach virus was the most that he would admit to. But that was Maurice. The boy who had hidden his sickness under the rug. Afterward, in the the pitilessness of her own grief and remorse, she had realized that he had known, that he must have known from the way that he had acted, from things that he had said. For the first time since she knew him, all that he had seemed to want to talk about was the past, going back, again and again, to stories of Jascha and Hershel and Rosalie and Aunt Frieda.

One evening, they had strolled over to a favorite little coffee-and-pastry shop, on Amsterdam Avenue, owned by a middle-aged Viennese couple. It had been the three of them: Sasha and Maurice and Chloe, who was in her last year at Barnard, hiding her prettiness behind thick glasses and baggy clothes. They had all sat close together around the little round glass table, on the wrought-iron chairs that were painted white. Sasha had ordered the most extravagant confection on the menu, something called a Spanische Windtorte, layers of baked meringue held together with whipped cream. Watching her consume it with impassioned gusto, Maurice had smiled.

"Did she ever tell you about Blintzes Sasha?" Maurice had suddenly asked Chloe.

Chloe, looking up from her bowl of vanilla ice cream, had smiled back at him. "Numerous times."

"Oh my God," Maurice said, grinning a little more broadly, "could she put those away!"

"They were delicious," Sasha said, licking the whipped cream from her fork.

"I can't remember exactly how they tasted. I don't think I liked them very much. But I did love Zanvil's air of drama as he struck the match and ignited the slivovitz. *That* was something to see."

"It was kirsch."

"You're right. It was kirsch."

"Here," Sasha said, pushing her plate with the remains of her Spanische Windtorte over to him. "Finish it up." All that Maurice was having was black coffee. As far as Maurice and Sasha were concerned, the Viennese couple made the best cup of coffee in New York.

"It's too rich for me," Maurice said, pushing the plate back toward Sasha.

"You're tired, Maurice. Come, let's go back home."

"No, not at all!" he said, grinning again, and signaling Frau Holzapfel for more coffee. "The night is so young it hasn't even said its first word." This had been an expression in Warsaw.

He just hadn't wanted to leave, although he looked so tired it had hurt Sasha's heart. He kept ordering cup after cup of coffee and telling story after story, all of them of the past.

At one point, he and Sasha had gotten into an argument over whether his brother, Jascha, had had a sense of humor.

"Listen, Maurice, I grant you that your brother was a great man, a genius even. But humor he didn't have. Rosalie used to say he was as dry as last Pesach's matzohs."

"No," Maurice had insisted. "You girls were absolutely wrong. Jascha was extremely funny. *Extremely.* You just didn't see that side of him. He showed it to very few people."

Sasha had given him one of her extravagant shrugs, her eyebrows eloquently skeptical. "Next thing you're going to tell me that that ice princess he married was also a wild comedian."

Suddenly Maurice had started to laugh—*really* to laugh.

"What?" Sasha had asked him, but he had only shaken his head and continued laughing.

"What?"

"No, it's nothing." He was still grinning. The laughter had done him a world of good; the strained look was almost gone from his blue eyes.

"*Tell me!*"

"It's just that I suddenly realized that you've never forgiven him."

"I don't know what you're talking about," Sasha had said huffily, turning her attention back to what remained of her second piece of pastry.

"Oh yes, you do!" He was still grinning, looking so much like his old self that Sasha had felt all of her vehemence suddenly melting into tenderness, and Maurice, seeing her face, had forgotten to breathe. Meanwhile, poor Chloe, looking at both her parents, had wished to God that she could just disappear into the Viennese woodwork.

Sasha had laid her hand on the side of Maurice's head and drawn his head to her, whispering into his ear.

"There was nothing to forgive."

"You'll never convince me, Maurice," she answered him now over the *mechitza* in Lipton, New Jersey, shaking her head gently at him, no longer so vehement but still not willing to concede him the point. "There's no reason. Mazel, Maurice. Only mazel."

CHAPTER 30

MAY DANCE

*T*here are people who don't have a good word to say for the late sixties. They look back on the excesses of those times as on a sickness in the soul, like maybe a hernia, some kind of a rupture. Not Sasha, though. There had been something in the largeness of those times that had healed her, closed up the wound that had bled years. Maurice had died—alone, alone, in some frozen wasteland, where no one had known him from Adam. If he had said a last word, who had heard? Yes, all true, but still. Here was the world, endlessly shifting, so that if you looked away for too long, who knew what you would miss? The curtain was going up on some new sets that looked like they might have been drawn up by Shmulik the town lunatic when the moon was full. And the players, too, were all raving in fine form, putting poetry in their lunacy, like Ophelia, such a show!

The students had closed Columbia University down. Sasha, dressed in blue jeans, sandals, and a flowing purple Indian shirt, had been standing in her kitchen, washing some fresh strawberries for Phoebe's lunch, when she had heard the news of the Columbia University uprising on the all-news radio station, the one that always promises, "More of these and other stories, after this," and then either forgets or never really meant it.

"Right on!" Sasha had said to little Phoebe, whom she was babysitting.

"Go on," Sasha had coaxed the little girl, who was sitting at the kitchen table blowing her soap bubbles. She was the easiest child in all the world to take care of, as sagacious as a little Aristotle. You almost *wanted* to hear her, just once, throw a temper tantrum, or at least whine a little.

"Go on, darling, you say it, too, just like Grandma. *Right on.*"

"Right on," Phoebe had repeated dutifully, with little of her grandmother's heart, and then had turned back to contemplating the shimmering, shifting forms she was holding at the end of her bubble wand. This was the one distinctly childish activity that could absorb her for hours.

Sasha babysat Phoebe during the day, while Chloe was up at Columbia, teaching her classes and doing her research. But today Chloe had arrived home early, her classes canceled, by reason of the Revolution.

Sasha had by now gotten used to being baffled by her daughter, who would rather sit out any event, *even a revolution,* reading those plays that were written in yet another dead language, and engaging her brainy little daughter in brainy games. Chloe seemed to be entirely unswept up by the spirit of the topsy-turvy times, even though it was *her* generation that was leading the psychedelic May dance. Chloe alone kept her head entirely on her shoulders, untempted by any form of unreason, refusing to be anything less than objective, sensible, and fair. Her mother couldn't have felt more sorry for her.

Chloe had even gone about getting pregnant as if it were a research project.

"Celibacy isn't an alternative life-style!" Sasha had tried to tell her, before she finally gave up trying to talk any sense or nonsense into her.

"Why not?"

"Because *it's not a life!*"

Chloe had grinned, but—this was one of her most maddening ploys—had said nothing.

So it hadn't exactly surprised Sasha that Chloe had decided to skip the drama unfolding up on Morningside Heights and instead had taken advantage of the Revolution to pick Phoebe up early from Sasha's.

"What's it like?" Sasha now asked her.

"Chaos," Chloe answered.

"I'm on my way!"

The Powers That Be (though who knew for how long?) had sealed off the campus, trying to keep out the notorious Outside Agitators. (Like *me,* Sasha thought.) The only gate that was still semi-open—but controlled by guards—was the one at 116th Street and Broadway. Sasha emerged from the subway to find a fairly sizable throng milling around this gate, some just trying to get a look at the action inside and others disgruntling in one way or another. There was a little half-hearted attempt at chanting and a few homemade placards:

COLUMBIA IS RACIST AND ELITIST!

COLUMBIA OUT OF HARLEM!

That sort of thing.

Sasha had had the foresight to borrow Chloe's faculty ID card, which she flashed to the guard at the gate; he respectfully waved her in. Inside the gates, it looked less like the ten days that shook the world, and more like Purim. So much color, and motion, and noise. Sasha felt the old rush of excitement rising up through the long stem of her body. It had been a while.

There were groups of hyper students everywhere, and everyone seemed to be wearing a different-colored armband. You needed a color code to know which side was which. The statue of *The Thinker* that sat in front of Philosophy Hall was wearing at least five different-colored armbands. Sasha wanted to get a look at the leading man of this pro-duction, the charismatic Mark Rudd, leader of the SDS, but nobody seemed to have any idea where he might be.

The other stars of the takeover, the Leibela Trotskys from Columbia College, the Emma Goldmans from Barnard, were sitting up on the ledges of the liberated buildings, soaking in the bright springtime sun, and engaging in revolutionary dialogue with those who stood on the ground below, both supporters and hecklers. The hecklers (almost all of whom were reputed to come from the School of Engineering) were the only ones who looked genuinely pained by the whole situation.

Sasha didn't for a moment doubt the sincerity of the students happily sprawled up there on the ledges. She knew that the anger and grief they felt over the war and racism was as authentic as her own. Still, you couldn't help seeing that, there at center stage, backdropped by their belligerent banners, they were also, at least for the moment, having an awfully good time.

And *why not,* Sasha would have liked to know. She was constantly having this argument. So many of the old lefties that she knew were more purple than red these days, going apoplectic at the high-spirited politics in the street. Sour grapes, was Sasha's opinion, which she of course didn't hesitate to share with the over-forty fogies who just couldn't stand it that anyone should be having so much *fun* with their Revolution.

Sasha always, always sided with the young. Even if the times themselves weren't so hot, this was their time to live it up, and it did Sasha's heart good to see that they were. At the sundial, there was more ardent dialogue going on. It reminded Sasha, just a little, of the Café Pripetshok, where the ideas used to be so thick in the air that you could get an education just by inhaling.

"We don't have to clarify our demands!" a pixie girl with hair almost to her knees was arguing with a beautiful passion from up on the sundial. "Being specific is a liberal cop-out!"

"Bullshit!" yelled a young man whose veins seemed about to explode. His short hair and good physique proclaimed him a jock. "You assholes live in a dream world!"

Sasha had been on the verge of saying something on the side of dream worlds, but then she heard music drifting up from the great lawn below, which was bordered by red and yellow tulips and crowded with the radiant young in their jeans and Gypsy costumes. The music sounded vaguely familiar to Sasha, distinctly European. Someone had brought a record player outdoors, and it was blaring a medley of mandolins—a folk song from the Balkans, of all things!

Sasha looked down at the lawn to see that the children were forming themselves into a long line of dancers, slowly snaking their way beneath the windows of Furnald Hall. Sasha hurried down to the lawn and placed her hand on the shoulder of a long-haired boy in front of her. It was an easy, repetitive dance, everyone caught on quickly, and the snake grew in length and grace so that it was undulating all across the wide expanse of the South Lawn.

"Oh," the boy in front of her suddenly turned around and said. "You've changed."

"Yes," Sasha answered him, "I suppose I have. We all have."

"You're so beautiful," he said, when he turned back again after a while.

He was a slight boy, with very narrow waist and shoulders, although he may still have been growing. Yes, he was probably still growing. His delicate, fine-featured face was framed by his shoulder-length silky blond hair, and his very blue eyes were just the slightest bit unfocused.

"Thank you," Sasha said, laughing, "and you're so stoned."

"Well, we're both right. I'm Owen MacArthur III," he suddenly introduced himself, too somberly to be kidding. Sasha had to repress the urge to gather him up into her arms, to stroke the silken locks and reassure him that it would all be okay someday, that these things truly do have a way of working themselves out.

"I'm Sasha," is what she said.

"Sasha," he repeated. "It's perfect."

"That's always been my opinion."

They danced some more in the snaking line. It was Marty Koenig who had brought out the record player and taught the dance, thinking to calm everybody down just a little. For years and years, after the Revolution had come and gone, a subculture of Balkan dancers would persist up on Morningside Heights.

Owen suddenly turned back again to Sasha, having grown disaffected with the dance.

"This is beginning to feel like some sort of form of fascism," he complained to Sasha. "Everybody falling into step. Come on, let's you and I do our own thing."

He broke off from the line, bringing Sasha unreluctantly with him. Owen must have endured, sometime in his not-too-distant childhood, a very complete set of parentally imposed dance lessons. He knew them all, all the square, middle-aged, country-club sorts of steps, the fox trots and the waltzes. He and Sasha tried them all out, trying to make them fit to the Balkan melodies, a thankless task.

Then Sasha, inspired, whipped off the tie-dyed bandana she was wearing on her head and she held it up between herself and Owen, who was such a natural, so lithe and brilliant on his feet, that he caught on immediately. You would have thought that Owen MacArthur III had grown up seeing brides and bridegrooms dancing the handkerchief dance at Jewish weddings all of his life.

He held a corner and she held a corner and they twirled and circled, while many of us on the lawn gathered round to watch. It didn't take us very long to catch on, and soon Marty's snake was embroidered with many more handkerchief dancers, holding corners of scarves, of streamers, of revolutionary armbands.

Several days later, there came the shock of the police arriving at 4:00 A.M., swinging their clubs with a vengeance. They weren't pretending in the *least,* and this came as the profoundest shock of all. For many of us, the sweetest moment of the ephemeral Revolution had been that dance on the South Lawn with Sasha, the beautiful older woman with the amazing voice and the presence that had made us all wonder, we eighteen- and nineteen- and twenty-year-olds, who she was and how one might possibly get to be like that.

It had been a good moment for Sasha, too, and she always kept a soft spot in her heart for that season of sweet chutzpa. For a brief time, she had really believed that the kids were going to do it, to make everything over again in a way that had felt for all the world like Purim.

CHAPTER 31

LIKE CIRCLES DRAWN
IN WATER

*P*hoebe sat, a radiant bride, between her mother and Beatrice, up on a little raised platform.

The room here at the Sheraton Meadowlands, right off exit 15 W of the turnpike, was thronged with guests. The cluster of well-wishers before the dais was constant and changing.

Off in another room were more guests, men and boys, keeping the bridegroom company while the business of the marriage contract, the *ketuba,* was being conducted, with rabbis and witnesses.

When Phoebe had first brought up the subject of the Hebrew name which would appear on the *ketuba,* Sasha had kept herself out of it.

Chloe and Phoebe had been curled up together on the couch in the living room on Riverside Drive, each with a glass of kosher white wine in her hand, while the sun set behind them on the Hudson.

"I thought, since my name means 'shining' in Greek, that maybe I should use the Hebrew equivalent."

It was funny how all of a sudden something Phoebe would say would make Chloe see the child's face superimposed over the woman's. Was it like this for all mothers?—

—"*Phoebus is my favorite of all the gods, because he loves math and his name means shining just like me*—"

Just like you.

"Is there such a name?" Chloe had asked.

"Ora."

"It's beautiful."

"You like it?"

"I think it's beautiful."

Sasha had been listening, off in her little shoe-box kitchen, stir-frying some vegetables and tofu in the separate wok she now kept solely for Phoebe.

" 'Fraydel,' " she had said, suddenly stepping into the living room. "I want you to use the name 'Fraydel' for your *ketuba*."

And so "Fraydel" was the name used for the bride in the *ketuba* that Jason had just this moment finished signing.

And with this the moment for the veiling ceremony arrived. The musicians—two clarinets, a trombone, a fiddle—came bursting into the room, where Phoebe sat waiting for her Jason, her face like a flower, open to the sun.

Jason—his father, Nat, beaming beside him—was surrounded by a pack of wildly singing and dancing young men, leading him to his bride.

Sasha (even though she and Maurice had been married quietly by a justice of the peace in Brooklyn) had plenty of experience with traditional Jewish weddings. She was, after all, that Sasha who had once stood center-stage, playing the role of the beautiful and doomed bride in the Bilbul Art Theater's triumphant production of *The Bridegroom*. But Chloe had never before seen anything like this. Her heart was pounding inside her chest as the men approached the dais, and her face was wet with tears, so that all the makeup that had been applied by the expert at Beatrice's insistence was streaking.

Jason was led up, and now he stood, looking down at Phoebe, and Chloe offered up a silent fervent little prayer to Hymen, the pagan god of marriage.

Hail, Hymen. . . .

Jason leaned down over Phoebe's upturned face, whispering something into her ear, before drawing the foaming veil down over her face. And with that, the crowd moved quickly off to yet another room.

Jason and Phoebe had prepared a little booklet, placed on each seat

in this room, explaining various aspects of the Orthodox wedding ceremony for those among their friends and relatives who didn't know. The
bedecking which had just taken place, Jason and Phoebe explained in
the booklet, is a custom that can be traced back to the experience of our
forefather Yaakov, who worked for seven years in order to win his bride,
Rachel, only to have been tricked by his father-in-law, Lavan, into marrying her older sister, Leah, whom he hadn't recognized beneath the
thick veil. In order to avoid any repetitions of such painful deceptions,
Jewish men pull the veil down over their brides' faces for themselves.

In the front of the room was the beautifully decorated *chuppa*. It
was Beatrice who had seen to the flower arrangements, as she'd seen to
everything else, and all of her friends had to admit that once again she
had completely outdone herself. They'd never seen anything like this,
a *chuppa* clustered with an abundance of white roses, the whole thing
giving the effect of a Viennese garden.

The musicians began to play. Some of Jason's friends marched
down the aisle. . . . Jason's two sets of grandparents . . .

And now Jason, his lips moving in prayer, as he walked between
Beatrice and Nat, who both held candles. Each row—the men on the
one side, the women on the other—stood as he walked by.

The *chuppa,* the booklet explained, symbolizes the new home that
the couple will create together. When Jason reached the *chuppa,* his best
man helped him into his white *kittel.* Phoebe's two best friends, Cindy
Chan and Shanti Chervu, both of them mathematicians, were now
floating down the aisle in their ivory bridesmaids' dresses. Now Debby,
smiling warmly, followed by Jason's three-year-old cousin, Gabriella,
the flower girl, forgetting to scatter her petals.

And now here was Phoebe, Chloe on her right side, Sasha on her
left, both with candles. Each row silently stood up to honor her as she
walked past them. Jason waited under the *chuppa,* still praying, bending back and forth in the manner of Jewish males in prayer. He was
turned around, his back toward Phoebe as she approached him down
the aisle. Slowly he turned to her, his lips still moving, his eyes on his
bride. Chloe could never have imagined a man's face so ardent, calling

out his love. Phoebe smiled up at him through her veil, her smile warm and confident. It was Jason who was crying, his lips still moving in prayer and his eyes overflowing.

Phoebe circled round Jason seven times, a number, explained the pamphlet, that alludes to many things, including the number of times in the Torah where it is written ". . . and when a man takes a wife." Two blessings over wine were made, one praising God for creating the vine, the other praising Him for giving us the holiness of marriage. Phoebe's veil was lifted so that she could sip from the silver cup. Jason placed the ring on Phoebe's finger, saying in Hebrew, "Behold you are consecrated to me with this ring in accordance with the laws of Moses and Israel." The *ketuba* was read aloud in Aramaic, and then seven "honored guests" (according to the pamphlet) were called up, one by one, each to recite one of the seven blessings. And then Jason stamped on the glass that symbolizes the destruction of Jerusalem, always remembered in even the happiest of moments.

And with that the little klezmer band burst into song, men dancing before the couple, both of them now smiling broadly. The musicians and the dancing men accompanied the bride and groom down the hall, guests at the Sheraton Meadowlands stopping to smile at the lively procession. A little group of Japanese tourists immediately whipped out their cameras to take pictures. (One could imagine them showing these pictures of what American weddings look like to their friends back in Japan.)

The musicians and dancers led the couple to a room of seclusion, in order, the booklet explained, for them to spend a few moments alone to begin their new relationship as husband and wife. Here, too, it was explained, the bride and groom, who had been fasting in keeping with the solemnity of the day, would break their fast.

Meanwhile, the rest of the guests filed into yet another room of the Sheraton, where the festive meal was to be eaten.

Beatrice had agonized over the caterer, the menu, and all her friends agreed she had outdone herself. Salmon for a first course.

Men and women were seated together at the same tables, but the dancing was separate for men and women, a trail of potted palms going down the middle of the room to serve as a partition.

What dancing this was! Chloe felt herself being swept up into the high spirits that soared around her, everyone wishing her *mazel tov, mazel tov.*

Chloe never spoke easily to strangers, and she didn't speak very much now. Still, she felt strangely united to all these people, who seemed to wish her shining child all the joy and happiness that Chloe herself wished her. And for this Chloe was full of the gratitude that only the deeply shy can feel.

Chloe had thought the dancing spirited before. But now, as Phoebe and Jason made their entrance, the room erupted into so much joy that Chloe could feel the floor of the Sheraton Meadowlands heaving beneath her feet. The men carried off Jason, and the women carried off Phoebe, and the dancing took off with a wild life of its own.

Sasha didn't dance. She stayed near the periphery of the room, archly surveying, keeping up a silent running commentary on what she had taken to calling the "reshtetlization of America." She searched her daughter's face for any signs of irony but found none. Chloe, that most ironical of all creatures, was melting faster even than her makeup.

Phoebe was escorted over to the men's side of the room, where both she and Jason were seated on chairs and then lifted high overhead and held aloft, each taking a corner of a white napkin between them, laughing into each other's eyes. Chloe, her hands clasped in front of her, streamed and streamed.

And then, bringing the newlyweds down to *terra firma* again, the men had burst into the Hebrew song that tells of the woman of valor, the very song that Sasha's father, Nachum, used to sing every Friday night to Leiba.

> Who can find a woman of valor?
> Her worth is far greater than that of pearls. . . .

"So," Sasha addressed Maurice, as she had been addressing him these many years . . .

Strength and splendor are her clothing,
And, smilingly, she awaits her last day. . . .

"So, what do you think of such a wedding for our granddaughter?"

Many daughters have attained valor

"It seems you were right and Jascha was wrong . . ."

But you surpassed them all!

". . . when he said that in a few generations we would all forget who were the sandal-wearers . . ."

Favor is deceptive, and beauty is vain. . . .
A God-fearing woman, she should be praised.

". . . and that's because what Jascha, precious soul, hadn't yet learned . . ."

Give her the fruit of her hand
And let her deeds go forth

". . . is that there's such a thing . . ."

To praise her át the gates!

". . . as mazel!"

Chloe and Phoebe were dancing together now in the midst of the women, these two shy souls, embraced by the crowd of well-wishers, so that they felt no self-consciousness as they hugged one another and danced out their joy in the midst of the clapping, celebrating women.

It saddened her, it angered her, that nobody here could appreciate the enormity of the irony that Sasha alone perceived. Sasha didn't feel like talking to anyone here. Only to Maurice. Only he could understand, as it had been from the very beginning. From that moment in the back room of the Pripetshok, when she had confided the secret of Fraydel to him, until this moment at their granddaughter's wedding—he had always been the repository of Sasha's story, as she had been his, and nobody else would ever be able to understand.

Our daughter and our granddaughter, both of them so educated, one a professor at Columbia, the other a professor at Princeton: where is their cynicism? Tell me, beloved, *where is their cynicism?* She alone would stay here sitting, keeping the seat of the scoffers warm.

Suddenly a stranger's hand took hold of Sasha's and yanked her to her feet. Who the hell was she—maybe one of Beatrice's friends? A short little lady, she barely reached to Sasha's shoulder, yet she had the iron grip of a gladiator. She glanced up at wondering Sasha and gave her such a queer smile, so drolly knowing, that Sasha stared back, flabbergasted. Who the hell *was* she?

The makeup lay on her sharp features as thick as greasepaint, and in her yellow eyes—such a color!—was the wild mirth of pure amusement. She looked like Alan Dershowitz in drag—with exactly his hairdo, only hennaed bright red. Maybe she had even read his bestseller, such a chutzpa she had! And also such a grip! Whoever she was, she wouldn't let Sasha go, and she was pulling her by the hand across the dance floor of the Sheraton Meadowlands, so that Sasha was forced to follow behind her, no questions asked.

The whole roomful of people was dancing, not a soul remained seated or still, and the floor was heaving beneath them. The next course of Beatrice's carefully planned menu, a soup of some sort, sat on the tables getting cold, and nobody, not even Beatrice, could care less.

The stranger gave Sasha a healthy shove into the center of the dancing, where Phoebe and Chloe joyfully took hold of her, the three of them laughing into one another's faces like three young schoolgirls, while all around them the women moved like circles spreading in water.

And Sasha and Chloe and Phoebe were all dancing together, their arms linked around one another's waists and their feet barely touching the billowing floor, as they swirled in the circles drawn within circles within circles.

And so it goes on, it goes on. Always unpredictable, rarely exactly what we had feared, almost never exactly what we had hoped. Chance is always bringing forth our productions, the true impresario nonpareil, despite our grand illusions. It's chance behind those tragedies that are beyond all telling, but also behind the happy endings, too. Randomness favors neither the one nor the other, so they happen, both of them, and we're found unprepared, left gasping in disbelief that things could have turned out so. This is what Sasha knows, what she has always argued deep in her heart with her Maurice and his Spinoza. If the world were really made up of logic and nothing but logic, beloved, then where would be the theater?

By the way, Sasha had been right when she had warned, there under the blooming apple tree in Phoebe's backyard, that Phoebe's baby already had a mind of its own. But Beatrice had also been right, that it would be a boy. They're neither of them women with whom to trifle.

Mayer Kantor, named after his great-grandfather Maurice, was born within twenty-four hours of Sasha's pronouncement. Chloe had heeded her mother's apodictic summons and had gotten herself down to New Jersey in time to greet her grandson's arrival into this world.

The *bris* of little Mayer will be—"God willing," his parents have requested that I add—next Thursday morning, at seven o'clock A.M., in Congregation Z'chor Et Ha-emeth in Lipton, New Jersey. You are all, each and every one of you, invited. Beatrice has taken over all the arrangements, so it's sure to be an event that will be well worth the trip—even to such a place as Lipton.

And may we all only meet at happy occasions, the face pressed up outside the window kindly disposed toward the fragile life that lies within.